By Laura Lippman

LAURA LIPPMAN

The Sugar House

A TESS MONAGHAN NOVEL

HARPER

An Imprint of HarperCollinsPublishers

HARPER

An Imprint of HarperCollins*Publishers*
10 East 53rd Street
New York, New York 10022-5299

Copyright © 2000 by Laura Lippman
ISBN 978-0-06-207079-1

First Harper premium printing: March 2012
First Avon Books mass market printing: August 2001
First William Morrow hardcover printing: September 2000

Visit Harper paperbacks on the World Wide Web at
www.harpercollins.com

10 9 8 7 6 5 4 3 2 1

This book is for three women who changed my life:
Michele Slung, by asking a single question
Joan Jacobson, by asking for another page
and Melody Simmons, by daring me to dream a dream.

ACKNOWLEDGMENTS

First and foremost: love and undying gratitude to John Roll, who makes everything possible. For those who believe nothing good ever came of the Maryland General Assembly, all I can say is that I met my husband on the floor of the Senate, and have never regretted it.

My colleagues at the *Baltimore Sun* continue to help me get things right in spite of myself. Mike James and Kate Shatzkin of the *Sun* wrote the articles that inspired this book. I am indebted to William F. Zorzi Jr. and Tom Waldron, who have long been my patient guides to the Maryland political scene. Tom Stuckey of the Associated Press and Rick Tapscott of the *Washington Post* also contributed to this book, although they may not realize it. Thanks, too, to the editors—Eileen Canzian and Robert Benjamin, in particular—who gave me a front-row seat on the 1998 governor's race. Joe Mathews shared his South Baltimore expertise. Peter Hermann, as always, was a cherished technical adviser.

Susie Rose arranged my first shooting lesson; any errors are the result of an inattentive pupil. I'd never have met Susie if it weren't for Sherry Dougherty and Sandee Mahr, so a toast to the Misses Chardonnay, Merlot, and Cabernet.

A factual note: Maryland has only forty-seven senate districts. There has never been a senator from the forty-ninth district in Maryland. There has, however, been a governor who held an AK-47 on a smirking reporter. Of course, he's no longer governor. He's now the state's comptroller.

A Baltimorean is not merely John Doe, an isolated individual of *Homo sapiens,* exactly like every other John Doe. He is John Doe of a certain place—of Baltimore, of a definite home in Baltimore. It was not by accident that all the peoples of the Western world, very early in their history, began distinguishing their best men by adding of this or that place to their names.

—H. L. Mencken, *Evening Sun,* February 16, 1925

Never get caught with a dead girl or a live boy.

—A political maxim of unknown origin

The Sugar House

PROLOGUE

H enry looked at the tape recorder on the table in front of him. Voice-activated, the cop said. You talk, the wheels turn. He coughed, clearing his throat, and sure enough, the wheels lurched, then stopped.

My name is Henry Dembrow, he began. But they knew his name, it wasn't the one they wanted. They kept asking him about the girl, and he didn't have a name for her, not a fragment, not even a fake one. Why wouldn't they believe him? *My name is Henry Dembrow*. He knew he was talking because he could see the tape recorder's red light, but he couldn't hear his voice, couldn't tell if it was inside his head or out. He could hear other things—the wheezey breath of the one cop, like an old dog sleeping, the other cop's shiny loafer going tap, tap, tap. Tap, tap, tap. He had small feet, that cop. But Henry couldn't hear his own voice. It was as if he had a bad cold, his voice seemed to be coming from so far away. *You talk, the wheels turn. You talk, the wheels turn.*

The cop sitting across from him read the date

into the recorder, November 17. He could hear him okay. "Henry, I want you to confirm for the tape that this is your statement, that you haven't been coerced in any way."

What? A song played in his head. *I'm just sittin' here watching the wheels go round and round.* Only those weren't the real words, exactly. No, they hadn't made him say anything, because he'd been saying what they wanted to hear from the moment the patrol car had found him on Fort Avenue last night. Before then, even.

"I also want you to state for the tape that you were read your rights, and you understand them."

Uh-huh.

"Could you please say yes or no, Henry?"

Yes or no, Henry. The cop didn't smile. Okay, yeah, he knew what he was doing.

The wheels had stopped turning. Watch the wheels, Henry. Watch the wheels. You talk, they turn. Talk, turn. Talk-turn, talkturn, talkturn.

"Henry?"

They were nice, these guys. The patrol cops had been sons of bitches, yelling in his face, all jacked up. Macho, macho men. These homicide detectives talked in soft voices, couldn't be sweeter. Good cop, good cop.

"Henry?"

His mouth was dry. He had asked for a Coke, not a Pepsi. Was that the kind of thing you complained about here? He guessed not, but he couldn't drink Pepsi, he just couldn't, wouldn't even use a Pepsi can to get high. Ruthie had always made fun of him, said he was a sap to think things were dif-

ferent. She swore she'd put a blindfold on him someday, like a taste test at the mall. But he could tell,
and it did matter. Not only the difference between
Coke and Pepsi, but Wise potato chips and Utz,
Little Debbie's and Hostess. Duron and the Hech-
inger store brand of spray paint. He could tell.

The cop who had been hanging on the edges of
the room, pretending like he didn't care what was
going on at the table, piped up. He was a little guy,
pretty as a girl, except for the acne scars.

"What happened yesterday, Henry?"

Yesterday. Not even twenty-four hours ago—it
was morning now, he was pretty sure, although
there were no windows to the outside here, no light.
But he could feel the morning. In Locust Point,
Ruthie would be getting up about now, putting on
the coffee.

Yesterday—another song was starting in his head.
He had gotten up at seven. Ruthie didn't let him
sleep in. She said he had to keep regular hours, like
he was working. Read the want ads, write down
what he was going to accomplish that day, one-two-
three. Which made Ruthie sound like a hard-ass,
but she was pretty nice. Just yesterday, she had made
him cinnamon toast for breakfast, using one of those
old McCormick shakers, the yellow ones with the
cinnamon and sugar mixed in, in the shape of a
little bear, like they had when he was a kid. Back
when McCormick was still downtown, and the
whole harbor smelled of cinnamon when the wind
cut right.

Ruthie was going to the parish, a meeting about
the Sour Beef dinner. The crafts table, that was it.

One woman had made forty crocheted Kleenex box covers. Forty! And every one crooked. He and Ruthie had laughed about that. He hoped she would remember how they laughed, bank it for a while. One day, they would laugh again, but for now, he had to break her heart.

He turned on the television after she left. Spent some quality time with the people who came in pairs—Don and Marty, Katie and Matt, Kathie Lee and Regis. Once, they had a local show like that. *People Are Talking*. Oprah Winfrey, with an afro as big as a satellite dish. The white guy had an afro, too, come to think of it. Hey, can a white guy have an afro?

The fat cop wasn't biting. "Yesterday morning, Henry."

But this is part of the story. Because he had started thinking about how Oprah had belonged to Baltimore once, how Baltimore used to have everything it needed, right here. Not just Baltimore, but Locust Point. The neighborhood was a world complete. His dad had walked to work. Went out the door to Domino's, was there in five minutes. Said living in Locust Point was like living on an island. *Warter all around, warter all around*, he had said in his thick Bawlmer accent. Henry was fourteen before he ever went north of Pratt Street. On his own, that is, not riding in the family car, or on a bus for a school trip. Walters Art Museum, those big vases, the shot tower. And they said he was killing his brain cells, but look at everything he could remember. The National Aquarium, eighth grade, he had grabbed Helen Jukowski's hat and thrown it in the harbor because she had the prettiest hair he had ever seen. Not much of a face—no chin—but white-gold hair, streaming down her back, long and straight when all the other girls were getting those tight perms.

On the television, they were singing a song. An old song, it sounded like an old song, but it had a line about cocaine in there. Funny—you don't think about cocaine being around in the olden days. Kathie Lee made a face, like she didn't like having to sing that one word, but she couldn't think of another one to put there, although lots of things rhymed. Spain, rain. Windowpane, Great Dane. Ridin' that train.

Cocaine. Now that was a drug. It really fucked you up. The stuff he did, it was legal, how bad could it be? Nothing legal ever killed you all at once, that was for sure. Sometimes the *Beacon-Light* had stories about how some bad heroin came to town, people keeling over right and left. You never heard of anyone dying from a single cigarette, or a beer. Or a huff. You had to do it a lot, and he didn't do it that much.

Hardly any at all, honest.

"When did you leave the house?"

Must have been ten or so. It had been nice for November. Mild. He grabbed his denim jacket instead of his down coat. See, that's why he had the rubber hose in his pocket. Not because he was planning anything. It was just there, from the last time he had worn the jacket, which shows how long it had been since he had siphoned anything, weeks and weeks. If it had been colder, if he had taken the other coat, if he had gotten that hit of gasoline he was going for . . . but he didn't. Don't tell me what might have been, Ruthie always said.

He walked up to Latrobe Park after the guy at the gas station chased him off. Were the wheels turning? He really couldn't tell what was inside his head and what was outside anymore. Maybe he never could. His words felt like sand in his mouth, like he'd taken a tumble in a wave at Ocean City, swallowed half the beach. But he wasn't going to drink that fucking Pepsi, no way.

"Henry?"

He went to Latrobe Park, and that's where he saw her.

The fat cop sat up straighter in his chair, the pretty one unfolded his arms.

She had looked like a kid, at first. Maybe it was because she was on a swing. Or maybe because her legs had no shape, no shape at all. And her hair was stuffed into one of those knitted caps, like some goddamn Rastafarian, although the pieces that straggled out were straight and fine, dark brown. There was something about her face that made you want to look at it. Not sexy, not sexy at all, more like a flower in a vase. He hadn't expected that.

She had been cool to him at first, scared beneath the cool, but he had expected that. He turned it on, not boy-girl style, but brotherly. She said she was hungry—said it like it surprised her, like he should care—and he had his opening. A little bottle of glue from the store, he told her, nothing more. A little bottle of glue, and she could use what was left over to buy what she wanted. They'd have themselves a party back at his house.

You have a house, she asked. Yeah, he had a house.

With a phone? Of course we got a phone.

Okay, she said.

She bought the weirdest stuff, he couldn't help noticing. Cool Whip, a big package of M&M's, a bag of Fig Newtons. He took her to the house, to the little scrap of backyard. He told her about his dad, and Domino's, how it was called the Sugar House once. She said yeah, yeah, she knew all that.

The glue didn't do much for him—he needed the real thing, industrial, maybe some spray paint, but he'd get that later. She turned her back on him, mixed the M&M's into her Cool Whip with her finger, then dragged the cookies through it, like it was dip. Then she stopped, laughing a little.

What's so funny, he had asked.

It's not that good, she said. It's just not that good. No shit.

I want an apple, she said. Or some orange juice. Real food. You got any real food? And she had tried to go up the steps to the house, which he couldn't let her do. No, no, no, she couldn't go in the house, not Ruthie's house, he couldn't let it happen in the house.

She had turned back at the noise, at the sound of something scraping. He tried not to think about what he had seen in her eyes at that moment. She started to scream; but he had already placed his hand over her mouth. She jerked away, she tried to run, and that's when she fell. The backyard, it's all concrete, and she hit it hard going down. She was dead, or going to be. An accident.

"Then why did you tie your hose around her neck?" That was the pretty boy. But Henry honestly can't remember.

Funny, the one thing he remembers is how sour her breath was, beneath all the sweet she had eaten. It was as if she were dead all along, inside, as if she had never been alive at all.

1

Sour Beef day dawned clear and mild in Balti-more.

Other cities have their spaghetti dinners and pot-luck at the local parish, bull roasts and barbecues, bake sales and fish fries. Baltimore had all those things, too, and more. But in the waning, decadent days of autumn, there came a time when sour beef was the only thing to eat, and Locust Point was the only place to eat it.

"I'm going to ask for an extra dumpling," Tess told her boyfriend, Crow, as his Volvo edged for-ward through the neighborhood's narrow streets. The unseasonably warm day had sharpened her appetite, but then a cold one would have done the same thing. Just about everything goosed Tess Monaghan's appetite. Good weather, bad weather. Good news, bad news. Love affairs, breakups. Peace, war. Day and night. She had eaten when she was depressed; happy now, she ate more. Then she worked out, so she could eat again.

But the primary reason she ate was because she was hungry, a feeling she never took for granted.

"You deserve an extra dumpling," Crow said. "You deserve whatever your heart desires. What do you want for Christmas, anyway?"

"Nothing, I keep telling you, absolutely nothing. I have everything I want." She squeezed his knee. "Although if I could have anything, it would be one of those neon signs you see at beauty supply stores, the ones that say 'Human Hair.'"

Crow started to slide the car into a mirage of a space, only to realize the gap was really an alleyway. He sighed philosophically. "Locust Point feels like it's at the end of the world."

"Just the end of Baltimore."

"Isn't that the same thing?" He was teasing her, in a way that only he could. There was no bitter under Crow's sweet, no meanness lurking in his narrow face. When they had first known each other, that almost-pretty face had been lost under a head full of purple dreads. Shorn now, and back to his natural black, Crow was a guileless little beacon, beaming his feelings out into the world. She liked that in a man.

Unless the man was her father, standing on the church steps, frowning at his watch. Her Uncle Spike was next to him, chewing placidly on a cigar. Uncle Spike didn't take time so seriously.

"Great, we're late, and we'll never find a parking space this close. Look, even the fire truck is illegally parked."

"Just for carry-out," said Crow, who couldn't shake his bad habit of thinking the best of everyone.

"See, there the firefighters are now, with a stack of plastic containers. What does sour beef taste like, anyway?"

"Like sauerbraten, I guess. Not that I've ever had sauerbraten."

"I thought sour beef *was* sauerbraten."

"Yes, but—well, Baltimore, Crow." Funny how much could be explained with just those four words. Yes, but, well, Baltimore. "If we don't get in soon, there'll be a line. The dinner's late this year, because of a fire in the kitchen. Usually it's before Thanksgiving."

"Why don't I let you out here, and then come in when I find a place to park? Just save me a seat—and make sure it's next to you."

Tess leaned across the gearshift for a quick kiss. Crow grabbed her and gave her the sort of deep, passionate, open-mouth probe suitable to sending a loved one behind prison walls, or into the French Foreign Legion. Since they had reunited this fall, he was living in the moment with characteristic fervor. Tess found it overwhelming, exhausting, and altogether glorious.

Although the glory faded a little when she surfaced for air and found her father's blue eyes focused on them in a hard, unapproving stare. Tess disentangled herself, slipped out of the car, and crossed the street, wishing she didn't blush so easily. It was the one thing she had in common with her father, one of those red-all-over redheads.

"You went all the way to Texas to get *him*?" Patrick Monaghan asked, not for the first time.

"She brings 'em back alive," Uncle Spike said

around the butt-end of his cigar. His bald head gleamed in the weak winter sun, and his liver spots seemed to have multiplied since Tess last saw him, making his resemblance to a springer spaniel all the more pronounced. "Her and Frank Buck. They bring 'em back alive. He's a good kid, Pat—"

"*Kid* being the operative word," her father said.

"Just six years younger, Dad," said Tess, determined not to let anything mar this annual ritual. "If the sexes were reversed, you wouldn't think about it twice."

But the word *sexes* was a mistake, even in a neutral context. Her father winced at the associations it raised.

"Has he had any luck finding a job?" Uncle Spike asked.

"The state's hiring," her father put in. "Your Uncle Donald says he could find something for him at the Department of Transportation. He's got a lot of pull now, since he was posted to the comptroller's office."

Tess laughed. "Crow as a state employee? I can't quite picture that. Don't worry, he'll find something. He's part time at Aunt Kitty's bookstore through Christmas, playing a few gigs around town. But that's more for his own pleasure than the money."

"An out-of-work musician," her father mused. "Yeah, that's what I envisioned the day you were born, honey. It's what every father wants for his little girl, you know. Does he have a criminal record, too? That would just make my day."

Tess considered and rejected several replies. "Let's get inside, before the line gets too long."

A volunteer, resplendent in a green and red double-knit pants suit, took their money and pointed them to four places at a long cafeteria table in the farthest corner of the parish hall. Tess inhaled—deeply, happily, nostalgically. Food was only part of the draw here. Sour Beef Day was a *scene*, and the Monaghan-Weinstein clans had always been in the thick of it. Politicians paid their respects, in memory of the power Uncle Donald, her mother's brother, had once wielded behind the scenes. Shadier types shook Spike's hand, whispering things better not overheard.

And everyone, it seemed, had a kind word for her dad. He had worked this territory thirty years ago, when he was just starting out at the liquor board, and he was still much beloved.

Today, as they squeezed their way through the narrow aisles, Tess found herself on the receiving end of the occasional back clap and elbow squeeze. "I seen about you in the *Star*," one old man cackled. This didn't quite track. Did he mean he remembered her bylines from the *Star* before it folded three years ago, or was he referring to the profile the *Beacon-Light* had finally deigned to run? In her opinion, it had been a snarky piece, full of stupid private-eye puns. Still, it was ultimately less embarrassing than her ranking on the local city magazine's list of "hot" singles. Tess suspected her father of rigging that bit of false advertising. She loved her hometown, but it was too damned easy to be a celebrity here.

"You look better in person," another man said, his back slap landing a little low of the mark. "You're really just a girl, ain'cha? A girl in a pigtail, not that much different than when you was riding your tricycle around the Stonewall Democratic Club."

Her father glanced back over his shoulder, smiling, and suddenly it didn't matter how she was known, or where she was patted. Tess felt like royalty, a legacy from two families—maybe three, given that Spike's relationship to the Monaghans and Weinsteins had never been settled to anyone's satisfaction. She was proud to be descended from this long line of b'hoys and muldoons, the political foot soldiers who had made the city work. Well, who had once made the local Democratic clubs and city elections work. What followed was out of their hands.

They were taking their seats when Crow arrived, breathing hard from his run through the neighborhood. Normally given to exuberant, bear-hug greetings, he restrained himself and offered his hand, first to Spike, then to Patrick. Her father looked uncomfortable at even this brief contact.

"I had no idea this was such a huge thing," Crow said. "I had to park at Fort McHenry, practically."

"No South Baltimore politician with half a brain would dare miss it," Patrick said. "State Senator Dahlgren's already here, working the crowd. He's over there talking to Senator Delia, paying his respects."

"Which is funny," Spike said. "'Cause Locust Point don't lie in the first congressional district, and that's the prize Kenny Dahlgren has his eyes on these days, even if he does have zero name recognition. He ain't a smart fellow, is he?"

Her father shook his head. "No, he's just scared because the last election was so close. It reminded him he needs to do the basic stuff, not take anything for granted."

"Sure," Spike said, laying his cigar next to his plate, a treat for later. "I guess it's just coincidence he's in the newspaper every day now, spearheading that investigation into his poor sap of a colleague who had the bad luck to be the first one caught in the new ethics law."

Tess turned toward the front of the hall and saw a man with the bland good looks that politics favored. Senator Kenneth Dahlgren, another lawyer in the so-called citizens legislature of Maryland, which was ninety percent lawyers, with the occasional beautician, farmer, and schoolteacher to keep it honest. He looked earnest and humorless, the kind of dullard to be avoided at any cost.

"No name recognition?" Tess said. "Try no face recognition. That's the most forgettable man I've ever seen."

Now the young man at his elbow, following so closely he might be a bodyguard, was more intriguing, one of the most beautiful men Tess had ever seen. One of the most beautiful *people*, period. Indian, his coloring begged for a Whitman sampler of bad metaphors—caramel skin, chocolate eyes, a mouth red and ripe as a cherry center. Tess had to remember to close her own mouth as she stared. The man didn't project a sexual aura, so much as he brought to mind a host of exquisite objects that made one dizzy with longing. Ode to an Indian urn, she thought. Baby, you can sit on my mantel anytime. If

Crow ever vacated the premises, she amended in her mind. A recent convert to monogamy, Tess had the convert's typical zeal for her new religion.

Yet no one else seemed to notice him. Beauty for beauty's sake was not a prized commodity in South Baltimore. The sour beef diners tried to push past the young man and toward the senator, children swamping the mall Santa. Gimme, gimme, gimme. Only their lists were full of road projects and state grants, zoning variances and jobs for otherwise unemployable relatives.

And not a single one was claiming to have been a particularly good boy or girl.

"I can't believe he's our best hope to win the first," Spike muttered. "All politics is loco."

"Local," Crow corrected, even though he knew Spike had mis-spoken on purpose. "I'm pretty sure Tip O'Neill said all politics is local."

But the mere sight of Dahlgren had made Spike grumpy. "It's one thing to be ambitious, and my hat's off to anyone who can get Meyer Hammersmith to sign on as his campaign chairman. Meyer's a rainmaker, and a class act. But Dahlgren don't play the game. He cares only about himself. He's jumping 'cause he knows his seat is going to be carved up in redistricting. If he had worked with his colleagues to begin with, they wouldn't be so gleeful about screwing him after the Census."

"A Democratic congressman will do more for the state than anyone in the General Assembly." Tess sensed her father was disagreeing just for the fun of getting Spike worked up.

"Do more *to* the state," Spike said. "Maryland, my Maryland. The despot's heel is on the shore, for sure." In his Baltimore accent, the state song became "Merlin, my Merlin" and the word *despot* sounded more like a place to catch a train.

The waitress took their orders, sour beef all around, and everyone wanted an extra dumpling, although Tess debated with herself back and forth. Diet averse, she believed one should always eat what one wanted, but knowing what one wanted—ah, that was another question altogether.

No longer able to contain herself, she leaned forward: "Who's the pretty boy with Dahlgren?"

"Adam Moss, his chief of staff," her father said. "Came down from Massachusetts, I think. Has a rep for being very bright, very quick. People underestimated him at first, him being so young and all. But I hear he's good. Good enough that someone tried to start a rumor he was queer, hoping it would tarnish Dahlgren."

"C'mon," Crow said, eyes bright. He loved anything that smacked of inside information. "Being gay doesn't matter anymore. Look at Barney Frank."

Patrick gave Crow a smile so patronizing Tess wanted to kick him under the table. "*You* look at Barney Frank. Things haven't changed as much as you think. People started gossiping about Moss because they wanted to create trouble for Dahlgren. But it didn't work. Dahlgren's married to his high school sweetheart, had twin daughters a year ago."

"A week before Election Day," Spike said. "Had

his wife induced and held a press conference at the hospital."

"Why are you so hard on Dahlgren?" Patrick asked Spike.

"Why are you so soft? He forced out Senator Ditter, the guy who got you appointed to the liquor board, in one of the ugliest, dirtiest primaries I ever seen. Ditter was a good guy. These new inspectors that Dahlgren appointed, they're such sticklers they take all the fun out of running a tavern. It's enough to make a man think about gettin' out of the business."

"Ditter did himself in, with that kickback scandal, and almost brought down all of us with him." Patrick spoke slowly, as if the memory still caused him some pain. Tess remembered when they had come for Ditter, how helpless her father had been to help his old patron. "Dahlgren could have pushed for a total housecleaning of my office, forced us all to resign just to make a show of how he was starting fresh. But he let those of us who were already there prove ourselves. That's class."

The moment was tense, and it was a godsend when plates started appearing before them. They had given their food orders to a short, wizened woman with cropped gray hair and bifocals on a beaded chain. The woman who returned with their food was considerably younger—and friendlier, at least to the men.

"An *extra* extra dumpling for you, hon," she said to Pat. She was around forty, with the kind of compact, curvy body that aged well, as long as the waist stayed slim. Hers had. In a tight green sweater and matching eye shadow, she was a classic Baltimore hon, knockout variety.

"Thanks, Ruthie. You already know Spike. This is my daughter, Tess."

"And Crow," Tess prompted. "Crow Ransome, my *boyfriend*."

"And Crow," her father echoed weakly.

Ruthie inspected Tess. "This the one?"

"My onliest one."

"She looks awfully young."

"She's thirty."

"Well, honey, that is young."

"She's wise beyond her years, though. And a hard worker, too."

What was her father doing, trying to sell a horse? Tess had an uneasy feeling Ruthie was about to pry open her mouth and start counting teeth.

Instead, the waitress frowned and said: "Well, I'm pretty busy here."

"Sure. I just wanted you to meet. We'll talk later, all of us. Maybe go to one of the old places around here."

"Not around here," Ruthie said shortly. "I like to get out of Locust Point sometimes."

"Frigo's then. For old time's sake."

"Frigo's?" Ruthie took a minute to think. "Why not? It will bring back some memories, won't it?"

She edged away, hips swaying in such an exaggerated fashion that they bounced off men's shoulders as she moved between the tables.

"What was that about, Dad?"

"Nothing much."

"Dad." Tess crammed thirty years of hard-earned petulance into that one whine of a syllable. "What are you and 'Ruthie' going to discuss at Frigo's?"

"You'll be there, too," her father assured her. "It's not as if we're plotting behind your back."

"*Dad.*"

Her father pressed his fork through one of his dumplings and took a large mouthful that apparently required much careful chewing before he could speak again. "She needs a private investigator. I recommended you."

"I don't need the work," Tess said reflexively, almost truthfully. Between her last case, which had paid far more than she ever dreamed, and the recent sale of some family property, she was flush by her standards. Five figures in her bank account, and that wasn't counting the zeroes to the right of the decimal point.

"It's an interesting case," her father said. "I've never heard of anything quite like it."

"Tell me in twenty-five words or less."

"Tonight. Frigo's. That's two words. Look, you'll like Ruthie. She's good people. We go back."

"How far back?" Tess asked.

"She was a barmaid around here, then at Frigo's, while she was going to community college for a bookkeeping degree. Didn't she even work for you for a while there, Spike?"

"Yeah, just for a little while, before she went to Frigo's. Fifteen years ago? Something like that."

"Thirteen years ago," her father corrected.

"How *precise* your memory is," Tess said. "If Ruthie

is such a dear friend, how come I've never heard of her before?"

"Maybe he's taking ginkgo biloba," Crow suggested. "Although it's my theory that memory isn't really affected by age. You just have so much more to remember, the longer you live. And, unlike a computer, you can't run a program to tidy up everything in there."

Now that he was the beneficiary of Crow's aimless chatter, Patrick seemed to find him absolutely charming. "You know much about computers? I hear that's a good field to get into. Lots of money. Start a little company and then—boom—you're a rich man."

"It's not for me," Crow said. "I need more interaction with people. I was thinking of going to Baltimore Culinary College, but I feel as if I've been in school forever. Don't worry about me, Pat. I'm finding my way."

He smiled sunnily at Pat, who tried to smile back. Such a slacker mentality must be pretty alien to her father, Tess thought. At Crow's age, Patrick Monaghan had been a husband and a father, working in the job he held to this day. If he were ever unhappy or unfulfilled in his work—well, he had never assumed there was an alternative.

Tess's eyes tracked Ruthie as she worked the parish hall. She had the moves of a former barmaid—she could dip and weave with the heavy trays, pivot at a moment's notice, without ever spilling a drop of gravy. She also could turn her "customer face" on and off at will. At one point, she ended up in the senator's path, and the two orbited one another, fake smiles in place. The only difference was that Ruthie dropped her smile once their little dance was done, while Dahlgren's never slipped.

"So did you and Ruthie decide on a time for 'our' meeting?" Tess asked.

"After I get off work, about six-thirty? You like Frigo's, they have good mozzarella sticks." Her father knew her so well. Well enough to know she'd be hungry in five hours, no matter how many dumplings she had. Well enough to know that her curiousity alone would pull her to Frigo's, with or without good mozzarella sticks.

"That would work," Crow said. "We're going to drive up to Hampden to see the miracle on Thirty-fourth Street. You know, the one block that goes crazy with Christmas lights? Then we're meeting Whitney for dinner. But our reservation isn't until eight-thirty."

Spike looked up from his food. "Whitney? You mean the scary one?"

"No, you know Whitney. She was my college roommate, the one who just got back from Japan," Tess said.

"Like I said," Spike said around a mouthful of food. "The scary one."

The senator was homing in on their corner of the parish hall. "Monaghan," he said, clapping Patrick on the back. He was good, Tess decided, he had the politician's hale and hearty moves down perfectly. Then again, if he were really good, she wouldn't have noticed it was an act.

"Senator Dahlgren," Patrick said, beaming at the

recognition. "And Adam, Adam Moss, isn't it? I've heard a lot about you."

Up close, Adam Moss's dark eyes were heavy-lidded and secretive, while his cherry-red mouth made Tess finally understand what it meant to have Cupid bow lips. He was poised, too. He didn't play the usual game of pretending horror at the idea that others had been talking about him. In fact, he didn't even bother to reply. His face was impassive, as if it were a given of his existence that people talked about him. They probably did, Tess thought, when you looked like that. What had Kierkegaard written about actresses? They knew they were on everyone's lips, even when they wiped their mouths with their handkerchiefs. She bet Adam Moss was coming up on a lot of local handerkerchiefs.

Dahlgren shook hands all around, making eye contact, pretending fervent interest in the person at the other end of the arm, at least for the three seconds that the hand clasp lasted.

"Nice to finally meet your family, Pat," the senator said. "Family's very important."

"Thank you, Senator." Tess disliked seeing her father so puppy eager for the good opinion of a backbencher like Dahlgren. Oh well, anyone who had a job had to brownnose now and then. She did it, too, and hated herself in the morning—until she made her bank deposit. "Any chance you're going to be making an official announcement soon about your status? I hear you've been raising money hand over fist since Meyer Hammersmith signed on as finance chairman."

"Well, Meyer's not on board officially," Dahlgren said, his fixed smile never wavering. "As for my future plans—I like to say discretion is the better part of valor."

"Shakespeare," Crow said. "*Henry the Fourth, Part One.*"

"Really?" Dahlgren said. "I mean—of course."

"It's not like you don't have plenty of things to keep you busy in Baltimore and Annapolis. Like, these houses that keep gettin' tore down because they screw up the demolition permits." Spike's low grumble seemed to startle the senator, as if a family pet had begun speaking. "Or maybe this could be the year the senate scholarship program finally gets defunded. I guess you'll support that change, you being Mr. Ethics and all."

Dahlgren's smile was beginning to look a little strained. "I don't know about you, but I'm not hearing a lot of complaints about senators helping kids go to college."

"I think it's the fact that the aid package seems tied to the parents' political patronage that has people upset," Spike said, his tone as pleasant, and insincere, as Dahlgren's.

Adam Moss leaned forward and whispered something into his boss's ear, his voice so low that even an expert eavesdropper such as Tess was at a loss to catch a word. Dahlgren listened intently, his head cocked in the manner of the RCA dog. Nipper and his master's voice, but which was which in this relationship?

"Adam reminds me the ethics committee is meeting in Annapolis in less than thirty minutes and I am the chair, after all," Dahlgren said. "Even by legislative standards, I'm running late."

"You gonna bounce him?" Spike asked.

"Bounce him?"

"Senator Hertel. You know—the poor dumb sap who didn't get his hand out of the cookie jar fast enough when you all decided to clamp the lid down. That's his crime, innit? Not being a crook, 'cause you're all crooks, just being dumb enough to get caught. Kinda like musical chairs. The cheese stands alone."

"Farmer in the Dell," Crow said under his breath.

"My committee meets privately, but I can assure you we are taking the accusations against our colleague very seriously," Dahlgren said. The answer didn't quite match up to Spike's question. It was probably the rehearsed sound bite the senator used for television interviews, where there was little risk of follow-up. "We need to work swiftly, so we can settle this matter before the General Assembly convenes in January. But we are not acting hastily."

"If there's anything worse than a lynch mob, it's a lynch mob that takes its time," Spike observed.

Adam Moss was already leading Dahlgren away from them, his arm a rudder in the small of the senator's back. Angrily, Patrick pointed his fork, half a dumpling on the end, at Spike.

"I can't believe you needled him about senate scholarships," he said. "Who do you think you are, that shit-for-brains who writes editorials for the *Blight?*"

"I got no problems with senate scholarships," Spike said. "It's nice, old-fashioned, out-in-the-open patronage. Tess even got a little one, didn't she? But I do like yanking Dahlgren's chain. First Ditter, now Hertel."

Crow said: "Did anyone else notice how good-looking he was?"

"The senator?" her father asked.

"No, the guy with him. Didn't you think he was good-looking?"

Spike looked confused by the question, while Patrick appeared horrified. Tess squeezed Crow's knee beneath the table, and he squeezed back. It was nice to be in synch. She felt she had to defend him, get back at her father for the way he had treated him today.

"About Frigo's tonight—" she began.

"You can't back out," her father said. "I promised."

"No, I'll be there. But *you* won't. My business dealings are confidential. You may have acted as matchmaker, but that doesn't entitle you to sit in on the wedding night."

Her choice of metaphor was exact. She wanted him to wince this time, and wince he did. "I already know what she's going to tell you. So how can it be confidential?"

"My business, my rules. You want to shop around for another private detective to help your old friend, feel free."

"She's not an old friend, exactly," Pat said. "But, okay—your business, your rules."

He returned to his food, leaving Tess to wonder just what Ruthie was to her father, if she wasn't an old friend, exactly.

2

Thank God for bars." Ruthie Dembrow leaned back in a booth at Frigo's and, after a quick, guilty glance around the old neighborhood tavern, lit a cigarette. "Smoking is beginning to feel like a criminal act, you know? And when I come here, I always feel like I should be working, even though it's been years."

"Come the day, you might not even be able to smoke in bars," Tess said. "I hear Montgomery County wants to ban it *everywhere*."

"Well, that's D.C.," Ruthie said, in a tone that suggested a place thousands of miles away, instead of forty-five minutes down the Interstate.

"Smoking isn't my vice of choice, but I can't imagine bars without cigarettes." Tess liked going home with smoke in her hair and clothes, waking up to the smell the next morning. It reminded her that she had had a good time the night before.

"Henry used to give me such a hard time about my Kools." Ruthie's lips twitched. "Said it was going to kill me one day. I guess the joke's on him."

"Henry?"

"My brother." Her lower lip continued to tremble, until she finally sucked it beneath her top teeth and bit down hard. She had plump, cushiony lips beneath the coat of coral lipstick she had more or less chewed off. On a richer woman, Tess might have suspected silicon injections. But Baltimore hons started lower when they resorted to plastic surgery.

"My brother was named Henry Dembrow," Ruthie clarified, in case Tess couldn't put that together. Her dad must have done quite a sales job on her abilities.

The conversation stalled, as it had stalled several times in the ten mintues they had been sitting in the bar. Ruthie Dembrow didn't seem to have a clue how to begin her tale of woe, which made her unusual in Tess's experience. Sure, she had known would-be clients who hemmed and hawed at first, primarily because they disliked telling a stranger about intimate problems. She also was used to people who couldn't tell a story for anything, who thought the beginning went about as far back as Genesis, and that every tangential thought, every narrative cul de sac, must be explored en route.

But even the worst of the lot—the stammerers, the blushers, the liars, *especially* the liars—had an opening line or two. They had rehearsed them, standing in front of bathroom mirrors, or talking under their breaths as they drove. They were Hamlet, this was their soliloquy, the first and last time they might hold an audience in their hands.

Not Ruthie, though. Tess was going to have to pull it out of her.

"Why do you need a private detective?"

"Last year . . . well, almost thirteen months ago." She took a long swallow on her Miller Lite. Her hands were shaking. "I'm sorry."

"Take your time."

"It's like this, Tess." Her named sounded strange, coming from those plump, coral-flecked lips, although Tess couldn't have said why. "My brother Henry killed a girl last year. It was an accident—they were sniffing glue in my backyard. He panicked when she tried to get into our house. He thought she was going to try and take some stuff, I guess. Anyway, she fell, cracking her head open on the pavement. But he admitted it, he took responsibility for what he did. Right from the very beginning, he didn't try to make any excuses."

She paused, green eyes wide and solemn, as if waiting for Tess to acknowledge the remarkable moral fiber of her brother, this veritable modern-day George Washington. I cannot tell a lie, I cracked her head open while fighting over some airplane glue.

"Uh-huh," Tess said, nodding and smiling. As long as you nodded and smiled, she had learned, it didn't matter what you were saying.

"He went to trial, got ten years, and was sent to Hagerstown this past summer. It wasn't the worst thing that could have happened."

"No, not at all." It was, for example, better than having your brains oozing out of your head on some concrete patio in Locust Point.

"It was his last chance to clean up, you see. Prison, I mean. They have a Narcotics Anonymous group there. It was his chance to get clean for once. I hope you don't think I sound cold, but in some ways it was the happiest day in my life when I saw Henry go off to Hagerstown. Nothing else had worked. No matter what I did, he always went back to huffing."

"I hear that literally destroys brain cells," Tess offered, then felt fatuous. Ruthie was probably an unwilling expert on the topic.

"It's a stupid high," Ruthie said, inhaling fiercely on her cigarette. "Look, I'm no angel. I like to drink. If I have a gentleman friend, I drink with him. If I'm alone, I might drink a beer or two. When I was working two jobs and going to community college, I took speed to get through exams. But sniffing glue and spray paint, sneaking up on gas pumps—I can't imagine anything dumber. I kicked Henry out three times in the last two years."

Tess dropped the smile, which now seemed inappropriate, but continued to nod.

"I also took him back three times. He was my baby brother, I practically raised him after our mother died."

"Was there a big age difference?"

"Eighteen years. He was a change-of-life baby. Mother died of lung cancer before he was two." Ruthie sucked on her cigarette as if to taunt whatever gods she believed in. "She was forty-seven. Dad made it to fifty-five before he went. Brain tumor."

In another city, or another neighborhood, perhaps this double dose of tragedy would have been shocking. But cancer was one area where Maryland stayed competitive, year in and year out, thanks to families like the Dembrows. Bad habits, bad diets, bad workplaces.

Tess realized Ruthie had spoken of her brother in the past tense.

"Henry didn't make it, did he?"

Ruthie shook her head. "He was stabbed to death his first month in Hagerstown. His first month. There was a fight, and the guards all went running to one part, Henry was left where he was, nobody around. But when it was over, Henry was the one who was dead. I thought Hagerstown was going to save him, but it ended up being the death of him."

Fairly classic prison shanking scenario, but Tess didn't think this assessment would comfort Ruthie Dembrow. It was a sad story, too, and one Ruthie carried with not a little guilt. Maybe her eyes, and her mouth and her hair had not always been so hard.

Still, Tess couldn't see where a private investigator came into play. She wondered if Ruthie was going to try and sue the state, claim the guards were negligent in her brother's death. If so, she wanted no part of it. Tess was probably Ruthie's last resort, the only person left after being turned down by every ambulance chaser in the city. There was just no money to be made suing state government. They were careful to write the laws so their mistakes carried no penalties. A guy who had served ten years for a robbery he hadn't committed, who had lost most of his twenties to the state prison system, had gotten $250,000, parceled out over six years.

The credit card commercials said some things were priceless, but Maryland's Board of Public Works had come up with a pretty exact figure for a man's youth.

But that man had been innocent at least. Henry Dembrow had killed a woman. Tess didn't believe in the death penalty, but she didn't lose too much sleep over fate getting the job done.

"I'm not a lawyer, Ruthie. I'm an investigator."

"I know that."

"So what do you want from me?" She knew she sounded impatient and not a little crass, but she was to meet Crow for dinner in less than forty-five minutes.

"I want to know why my brother was killed."

"Ask the prison officials."

"They say he was in the wrong place at the wrong time."

"Not very satisfying, but the truth seldom is. Why would they lie?"

"I don't think they're lying. I think they don't care." Ruthie leaned toward Tess. "But isn't it awfully coincidental, my brother getting killed after he killed someone?"

Tess managed, with great effort, not to sigh or shrug. "I'm surprised it doesn't happen more often. Killers serve time alongside other killers. I've even heard that some of these guys are not successfully rehabilitated by the system."

"You know, you remind me of your dad."

"Really?" Tess almost never heard this. Although her hair had glints of red in it, and she freckled during the summer, her mother's dark good looks and strong features had crowded most of the Monaghan influence out of her face.

"Yeah, you both think you're funny, but you're not."

"My dad thinks he's funny?" Tess wasn't trying to be a smart-ass, it just slipped out. She had never noticed Patrick had much of a sense of humor. Then again, maybe this was his idea of a joke. "Look, you said I was going to be intrigued by what you had to tell me. So far, I'm not exactly on the edge of my seat."

"Maybe it's time to strap yourself in. Ever heard of a Jane Doe killing?"

Tess finished off her beer and looked for the waitress, hoping to signal for the check. "Sure. They find a body, they can't identify it at first, maybe not ever. Jane Doe, John Doe. Happens all the time."

"My brother was convicted for killing a Jane Doe. How often does that happen?"

"It can't."

"It does. It did."

Ruthie smiled triumphantly, aware she had Tess's full attention. Her mind raced, trying to fit the pieces together. "How could that be? If they know who killed her, they have to know who she was. No victim, no murder."

"Oh, there was a victim. They had a body. They just didn't have a name. No ID, and her fingerprints didn't match up, either. Not in all the country."

"Missing person?"

"They ran down some leads, but it never came to anything. When the trial was over, she was history. If anyone's mourning her, they're doing it privately."

Ruthie leaned forward. "I think they're getting their revenge privately, too. Henry was killed because of who he killed. What other explanation is there?"

Tess leaned back against the cracked leatherette of the booth, still trying to fathom how anyone could swim through all the identity nets of the modern age, untouched, unknown, untraceable. No fingerprints meant no criminal record. It also meant she hadn't worked for certain government agencies, or applied to be in the Big Brother/Big Sister program. The lack of a missing persons report indicated no one cared when Jane Doe didn't come home one night.

"If someone cared enough to kill Henry," Tess said slowly, "why didn't the person come forward and claim her body? Why would someone let her continue to be known as Jane Doe?"

Ruthie had an answer at the ready. "There are people who don't much care for police, or official channels for things. They're the same kind of people who might kill a man in prison, you know what I mean?"

She knew. "But you're not asking me to find them, right? Because if such people exist, I don't want to know them."

"All I want is a name, an ID. I'll take it from there."

A Christmas carol boomed from Frigo's jukebox, so tinny and speeded up that Tess needed a moment to place the familiar tune. "What Child Is This?" Very appropriate. She was still thinking about Ruthie's theory, trying to find all the flaws.

Like a bridesmaid's dress made by a neighborhood woman who tippled, it didn't hang quite right.

"Ruthie, is this your way of making amends, some sort of Christmas mission? If I find the girl's name, are you going to track down her family, give them a chance to reclaim her bones and lie beneath her own marker, in her hometown cemetery?"

Ruthie's green eyes were even greener above her tight turtleneck, the same one she had worn at the Sour Beef dinner, to such great effect. "I don't care what happens to that glue-sniffing skank in the next life, or the life after that. I want to know who my brother killed because I know he died for a reason. I'll start with a name, if you can find one."

"And if I can't?"

"Merry Christmas, you still get your fee. Pat explained that part to me."

Tess sensed this toughness was an act, but she couldn't figure out whether it was for her benefit, or Ruthie's. "Look, I understand. You want a reason for your brother's death. You want it to matter. Has it occurred to you that Jane Doe has family out there somewhere, family with even more questions than you have?"

"Fuck them. Fuck *her*. She shouldn't have tried to get into my house. Then Henry wouldn't have pushed her, and none of this would have happened. Okay, maybe Henry isn't dead directly because of her. But the two things are connected. I want to know who she was, how she came to meet my brother that day, why she was in a neighborhood where she didn't belong. That's all."

No, Tess thought, you want someone to blame,

someone other than yourself. She hadn't been able to save her brother, so what? They would have been okay if Jane Doe's family had been able to save her. It was a head-on collision, and all Ruthie wanted was the comfort of knowing her brother wasn't the one who crossed the center line.

"I'll see what I can do," she said.

"You're a good kid, Tesser."

If her name had sounded odd enough in Ruthie's mouth, her family nickname seemed a sacrilege.

3

"Holidays in Baltimore don't end," Crow observed. "They merely succumb."

Tess glanced approvingly at him, forgetting for a moment the snarl of traffic that had them stuck on a ramp to the Jones Falls Expressway. She didn't have a clue what he meant, but it held the promise of being diverting. For Crow, Baltimore was a second language—one he spoke exceedingly well, but with odd formalisms that gave the native new insights.

"Keep going," she encouraged him.

"Well, it's very good at dressing up for holidays, isn't it, enthusiastic about the build-up. Look at all of us, in a traffic jam because we want to see the lights on Thirty-fourth Street in Hampden. But the city's not much good at the moment itself. As soon as one set of decorations goes up, I always have the feeling that people can't wait to tear them down and start preparing for the next one."

"Yes," Tess said, even as she edged the Toyota onto the ramp's not-quite shoulder and put it in reverse, rolling backward toward Madison Street. He had given voice, as he often did, to something she had long felt but never been able to express. Crow held a mirror up to her life. Only it wasn't her own reflection she noticed so much as the beaming, happy face above the frame, a face that promised to love what she loved—and to love her as well. "They tore down the cornucopia and Pilgrim cutouts before the sun set on Thanksgiving, and now they're already itching to retangle the lights they just put up, to unwrap the doors they've made look like Christmas boxes and cover them with red foil and Cupids for Valentine's Day."

Horns sounded angrily as she squeezed down the narrow channel and into the intersection. Tess assumed the other drivers were just angry they hadn't thought of the idea first, or because their cars were too wide. Served them right for driving SUVs.

"And once the Cupids go up, they'll already be thinking about shamrocks, green foil and Saint Patrick's Day."

"As one of our local literary lights likes to say, welcome to the church of the next right thing," Tess said, thinking of a short-story writer who had given a reading at her Aunt Kitty's store just a few nights back, an exuberant man with the unlikely name of Ralph Pickle. He had filled Women and Children First with his ex-girlfriends, ex-fiancées and ex-wives, who bought multiple copies of his book. Kitty had encouraged him to write more—and date more.

Tess was now in the middle of Madison Street, where she braked sharply, jerked her steering wheel to the right, then headed up the Fallsway, which ran between the JFX and the prison.

"Like a hostess, who puts out guest towels, then paces in the hallway, worried someone might actually use them," Crow continued.

But Tess, glancing at the prison wall that ran the length of the block, was thinking about Henry Dembrow now. She still couldn't imagine a scenario in which someone would allow a loved one's body to go unclaimed, yet went to the trouble of exacting revenge against her killer. Ruthie was grasping at straws. Well, as long as she was willing to pay her usual hourly fee, Tess was more than happy to indulge Ruthie in this particular game of pickup sticks. Besides, her father had said he owed Ruthie a favor, and her father considered favors a kind of currency, more important than money. She was really indulging him.

She took the Preston Street overpass above the clogged highway, then headed north, feeling smug. So smug that she shot past her turn at 29th Street, losing any advantage she had gained.

"Damn, now I'll have to double back."

"It's eight-fifteen," Crow said. "We're supposed to meet Whitney in fifteen minutes." He sounded worried. Whitney scared Crow a little. Whitney scared almost everyone, except Tess.

"She's always late."

"She's always late, except when we're late, and then she gives us unmitigated shit."

"Let me try one more approach into Hampden, this time from the north." Tess had a peculiar vanity about her ability to find shortcuts and new routes through her hometown. They had set out to see the lights in Hampden, and she would not be denied.

They were in Baltimore's richest precincts now, Guilford and Roland Park, where the homes were decadently large and the tax bills were a kind of status symbol. Look, the houses seem to proclaim, we're paying $12,000 a year in property taxes and we still send our kids to private schools! These rambling mansions filled Tess with loathing—and yearning. One stone house had stood empty for years, neglected and haunted looking, until an exasperated neighbor purchased it to protect his property values. She could never forget that story, never stop marveling at the idea that some people bought houses the way she bought sweaters at The Gap.

The truth was, she often thought long and hard about that second sweater.

"What's up there?" Crow said, pointing to a side street after she turned onto Cold Spring Lane.

"More rich people, I suppose."

"No, these houses look much smaller. Turn up there, Tess. I've never noticed this neighborhood before."

"But the lights—"

"They'll be there for the rest of the month. We're here, right now. Besides, you promised you were going to be more spontaneous, remember?"

She remembered no such promise. But it did seem unlikely they would make it to 34th Street with enough time left to take in the full spectacle, so she headed up the dark road. A few modest strings of Christmas lights illuminated the hodgepodge of

houses. There were semi-shabby shingle-sided affairs, old farmhouses and duplexes. Semi-detatched
as they were known in Baltimore. Tess always
thought this would make a good term for relationships as well. Not hers, though. She and Crow were
semi-attached—together, joined at the hip, and other
body parts as well. She had lost him once, through
carelessness and stupidity. She couldn't quite say to
him, forever and ever, but she could and did for-
swear stupidity.

"There's a meadow back there, and a park. You'd
hardly know you're in Baltimore proper at all,"
Crow said. Tess didn't point out they could still hear
the traffic on Cold Spring. "What is this place?"

"Evergreen." She wasn't sure how she knew the
name, but she was confident of it from the moment
she said it. "These duplexes—this is where the
people who built the big houses in Roland Park
lived during the construction."

"Designed by Frederick Law Olmsted," Crow
said solemnly. Facts were serious, sacred things to
Crow, but then—he had never been a reporter. "Roland Park had the first shopping center in the United
States."

"I know, I read the historic marker outside the
old Baskin Robbins, too."

"Let's bring Esskay up to run in that meadow,"
Crow said. "When spring comes. We could bring a
picnic, explore the woods over there."

"It's not even winter yet, and you're talking about
spring. Don't get so far ahead of yourself. That's
what *you* promised, remember? One day at a time."

"Do you think," Crow said with the smallest of sighs, "that the AA motto is really appropriate for a relationship?"

She turned into a narrow lane, thinking it was an alley, but houses hugged the hillside here. Most were large, the legacy of Baltimore's Catholic roots. Tess had grown up among people who had five children, eight, ten, even thirteen. Now her friends who had three children seemed vaguely apologetic.

But there were some small cottages here, too, tucked among the rambling old Victorians. It reminded her of the Black Forest, not that she had ever seen the Black Forest. But she had been raised on Grimms', the real Grimms', where Cinderella's stepsisters mutilated their feet to get into that glass slipper, and a father cut off his daughter's hands and breasts out of pure spite.

The words *Black Forest* made her think of cake, which made her realize how hungry she was. Time for dinner.

Whitney Talbot had already been seated at their table in the Ambassador, a once fusty restaurant that had found a new, improbable second life as a lushly appointed Indian restaurant. Her face was turned away from the door, but Tess knew her by the long, sharp bones poking through her winter white pantsuit, the arrogant lift of her head. Really, Tess thought, all she needed was a pith helmet to complete the illusion that she was on the veranda of a grand old Calcutta hotel, snapping her fingers impatiently for another gin rickey.

"Don't tell me," Whitney said in the clear, ringing tones of a Baltimore valley girl. "You were dressed and ready to go, then took one look at each other and ripped one another's clothes off, carried away by the passion of your rediscovered love."

"Not at all," Tess muttered, blushing, in part because Whitney's voice carried so well and in part because she was not far wrong.

"Hi, Whitney," Crow said, taking the seat farthest from her. "How's the job hunt?"

"I'm not on a 'job hunt,'" she corrected, lifting her chin higher still. "I'm trying to decide what I want to do with my life. My future vocation is just one element of my quest, and probably the easiest to solve. The *Beacon-Light* has already offered me my old position, but I don't want to write editorials anymore. I seem to have run out of opinions."

Tess almost snorted water through her nose. "That'll be the day. But I am surprised they wanted you back, given the way you left." Whitney had quit the paper under a cloud, although the only thing she had ever done wrong was save Tess's life. It turned out there had been an office pool, and one of the clerks made $200 for having Whitney as the "one most likely to go postal." Terribly unfair and not at all accurate, but what could one do?

"New management," Whitney said airily. "The five top editors aren't even sure who Spiro Agnew was, and his past is much more accessible than mine."

"Didn't they keep your personnel file?"

"Shredded. My mother's lawyer made a call."

Tess looked fondly at her old friend. It's a rare person who can get away with the sentence, "My mother's lawyer made a call."

"Well, *I'm* on a job hunt," Crow said cheerfully. "Shockingly, a degree from the Maryland Institute, College of Art is not a hot commodity on the market. So Tess is the only one of us who's gainfully employed."

"Gainfully might be stretching it, but I do have some work. Interesting work at that."

"Details?" Whitney pressed.

"Confidential, dearest. You know that."

"Of course. Why else would I care? Besides, maybe this is what I was meant to do with my life. We can be Starsky and Hutch. It goes without saying that I'll be the tall blond one."

"Wasn't he the wife beater?" Tess asked. "Which would be forgivable, since he got counseling, but he also sang that awful, awful pop song. The one where he rhymed 'reminiscing' with 'kissing.' Hutch was really much sexier."

"Does this scenario make me Huggy Bear?" Crow wondered. Ah, Nick at Nite and TV Land, Tess thought, our true universal language.

"Can't you tell me anything?" Whitney asked.

"I can tell you it's a Jane Doe case. I'm trying to identify a dead girl, a homicide victim. Hey, why is it Jane Doe? Or John Doe? How did that usage enter the language?"

"It's from common law," Crow said. "John Doe was the plaintiff and Richard Roe was the defendant."

Whitney was not put off the scent so easily. "No, really, why couldn't I be your partner?"

So many answers occurred to Tess that it was hard to pick just one. "Because I work alone. Because I can't afford you. Because you would go cross-eyed with boredom the first time you had to do surveillance, or sort through receipts found in a Dumpster dive. Besides, what use are you now that you no longer have access to the *Beacon-Light*'s resources? I have to pay Dorie Starnes for the kind of stuff you used to give me for free."

"Oh well, it was just a passing fancy. I think what I really want is my own talk show, one of those NPR ones, all erudite and earnest," Whitney said. "You know, one of the really boring ones, where the guest is always some State Department undersecretary no one has ever heard of."

"How does one go about getting a talk show?" Crow asked.

Whitney waved her hand in the air. "I haven't the vaguest idea. But how hard can it be?"

A waiter was unloading a trayful of appetizers at the table—meat and vegetable samosas, nan, a round of Kingfisher beer. Apparently Whitney hadn't waited for them to order the first course. Tess wondered if she had allowed them their choice of entrées. The maddening thing was, Whitney often did know better than Tess what Tess really wanted, or needed. If she had saved her life once, in the literal fashion, she had saved it a hundred times over in other ways. Tess was never bored when Whitney was around.

"I think," Tess said, "you should get an advice column, one where people write to you about their most heart-felt problems and you respond by telling them the proper timetable for wearing white shoes, and why it's gauche to get the Caesar salad at Eddie's already mixed, instead of with the dressing packaged on the side."

"I'll add it to the list, dearest. Right after ballet dancer and just before fireman." Whitney's voice sharpened. "Oh stop it, you two, just stop it."

Beneath the white tablecloth, Crow's hand returned guiltily to his own lap.

4

It was a busy Monday morning at the morgue on Penn Street, the corridors overflowing with the weekend catch from throughout Maryland. Nothing like the combination of hunting season and Christmas cheer to up the number of bodies who needed their passports stamped before they could continue on their journey. Tess, trying to act nonchalant in the extreme, waited among the gridlocked gurneys for the assistant medical examiner who had autopsied Jane Doe a little more than a year ago.

She had been here before, the first time as a rookie night cops reporter, learning the ropes. An older reporter tried to test her mettle, but it had been Tess's good fortune to arrive on a day when death, if not exactly on holiday, was definitely slacking. Only one body was out in plain view, an overweight young man who had died of a heart attack while interviewing for a job at JCPenney's.

In the eight years since then, Tess had seen many more bodies—unexpected bodies, fresher bodies, riper bodies, in less contained circumstances. But a girl never forgets her first corpse. He had been blue, the pale blue used in raspberry-flavored Ice Pops. Tess had felt, well, mortified on his behalf. Whatever his life plans, they hadn't included being a blue, naked prop in the ritual hazing of some cub reporter. He had looked unreal, and Tess found it hard to imagine he had ever been flesh-colored, much less alive.

She had been only twenty-two.

"Miss Monaghan?" Dr. Olive Horvath, the assistant M.E., motioned for her to follow her into a small conference room. Harried, bristling with impatience before Tess had spoken a single word, she made it clear that Tess was at the bottom of the list of things she had to do today, and she was eager to draw a line through her.

"Here," she said, brandishing a folder.

"Where?"

"Here."

Tess had expected an attendant to lead her to a drawer somewhere and slide out the preserved remains of Henry Dembrow's victim. She had steeled herself for this, in fact. But Jane Doe's body was long gone. No room at the inn, not with the city homicide rate still in the top five nationwide.

"Buried in a pauper's grave down at Crownsville," Dr. Horvath explained. Pink-cheeked, with sky-blue eyes and thick, honey-colored hair, she was not so much pretty as in vivid good health, which was jarring in this setting. "We have her DNA, prints, and blood work on file, but we don't have the room for that kind of storage, not for a closed case. It's standard practice with the Jane and John Does, or anyone whose body isn't claimed."

"Do you know that name has an origin?" Tess asked, thinking to delight the woman with her scrap of knowledge. "John Doe, I mean. My boyfriend explained—"

"Nope, never really thought about it." It was clear that the living, and their customs, held little interest for Dr. Horvath. "Look, do you want a copy of my report? It's fifty cents a page."

Tess was familiar with this racket: City, state and federal agencies charged ten times the going rate for photocopies, if only to keep the nuisance factor down. Normally, she wouldn't have thought twice about taking this out of her expenses, but Ruthie Dembrow's finances were limited. As was her father's patience, if he found out she was feather-bedding a client he had referred to her.

"Is there a break room, where I could read it and take notes? I'll let you hold my driver's license for collateral."

"No need for that," Dr. Horvath said. "I'll find a spot for you, and you can drop the report off at the front desk when you're done. Tell them if you need any copies, and they'll help you out. I've got work to do." She led Tess to a small room with a coffeemaker and an old-fashioned vending machine that looked as if it hadn't been used for years. Tess wasn't sure if they even made Zagnut bars anymore.

"Our old smoking lounge," the assistant medical examiner said, her voice wistful. "Now we have to go stand in front of the building, like addicts on some drug corner."

"You smoke?"

"When you spend your day looking at healthy young men, with pristine organs and beautiful arteries—young men who just happen to have bullets in their brains—you become a little more fatalistic, I guess. Death has its own timetable."

Her eyes lingered briefly on Tess as if she could see through her, as if she could gauge every slice of pepperoni pizza devoured, every drink consumed, every joint smoked. Tess felt like the transparency in the old *World Book Encyclopedia*, the one she had studied to master the rudiments of male anatomy. She couldn't help wondering how her arteries would rate with Dr. Horvath.

Suddenly, a Zagnut bar seemed like a very good idea.

The autopsy report was slow going for someone whose last science class had been the required chemistry lab for Western High School sophomores. Where the science was clear, the English was murky. The bureaucrat's motto: Why say it once, if you could say it three times, in three increasingly clunkier sentences? Tess read carefully, taking notes as she went, backtracking over and over again. At the end of the hour, she had only a page of notes.

Jane Doe, estimated age 15–25. Caucasian. Cause of death: head injury, consistent with a fall. Length of rubber tubing tied at neck post-mortem. 5–7, 118 pounds. Brown hair, blue eyes. Black tattoo, on left ankle a straight line, two inches long, appears to be

quite recent, still some blood and scabbing around it.
Enamel on teeth badly decayed. Fingerprints taken,
no matches found. Has never given birth. No scars.

A photograph was stapled inside the file. Tess avoided it for as long as she could, but she finally confronted Jane Doe's death mask. Death by a massive head injury, combined with living on the streets, didn't bring out the best in a person. Jane Doe's eyes were closed, her face bruised, at once lumpy and hollow. The tip of her tongue protruded from the corner of her mouth, her farewell to the world that had treated her so badly. The rubber tubing around her neck, fashioned into a bow, was particularly obscene somehow, an ugly posthumous joke. Henry must have lingered over the body, Tess thought, needing to defile it for some reason. Why?

Still, the vestiges of a pretty face remained. Jane Doe had a sensual mouth; a straight, neat nose; and the loveliest brows, thick and natural looking. Working-class Baltimore women tended to overpluck and tweeze, laboring over their eyebrows the way some worked their tiny row-house gardens. Ruthie Dembrow, for one, had that overarched, perpetually surprised look. She'd be better off if she misplaced her tweezers for a few months. Not Jane Doe.

Tess handed the report back to the front desk clerk. "I'd like one page copied, if I could. Well, not a page, really—but this photo. Could you do that?"

"It won't come out very well," the clerk warned her.

"I know," Tess said, pushing two quarters toward her. "But I want it anyway."

Funny, the Polaroid photo reproduced almost too well. Jane Doe's face was so pale, her features so dark, the rubber tubing at her neck darker still. Tess folded the paper into fourths and hid it between the pages of her datebook.

After the medical examiner's office, Tess stopped at the police department to pick up the transcript of Henry Dembrow's confession. No fifty cents a copy here, not as long as Homicide Detective Martin Tull was on the force.

"You want to go over this with me?" he asked, and Tess knew *he* wanted to go over it with her. Tull did favors in exchange for full disclosure. It wasn't that he didn't trust her, quite the opposite. Tull had learned the hard way not to ignore Tess's instincts.

"We can walk over to that place on Guilford," he said, his girl-pretty features wistful. "The one with Peet's Coffee and all those bars."

"Bars?"

"You know, the salad bar, the soup bar, the sandwich bar, the cookie bar, the juice bar . . ."

Tess made a face. The morgue hadn't dented her appetite, but she had other ideas for lunch. "I'd rather falafel."

"You mean you'd rather have a falafel, don't you?"

"No, I use falafel as a verb. Let's go to Cypriana, I'll falafel, then we can have coffee, after. My sandwich card is filled up, and I'm entitled to a free one."

"Falafel, it is. Hey, can you gyro, too? Or souvlaki?"

"Don't be silly," Tess said. "Obviously, those don't work as verbs at all."

Cypriana's was housed in the old lobby of one of Baltimore's many defunct newspapers, the *American*. Tess had worked down the block at the old *Star*, now an Inner Harbor parking lot. She wondered if the city's sole surviving paper, the *Beacon-Light*, might one day fold, too, if its lobby would become a series of small shops, or an avant-garde art gallery. A world without newspapers seemed increasingly possible to her—and perhaps not that tragic. She had survived the transition. Others would as well.

She ordered the "ultimate," chicken, falafel, and feta cheese wrapped in a pita, drenched in a sauce whose ingredients were zealously protected. Garlic, however, was clearly part of the mix. Tull opted for a small salad, dry. They found a table next to one of the large windows overlooking Guilford. Tull cast a longing glance across the street, where his Peet's coffee waited for him. The homicide detective was one of those odd people who didn't care about food, who considered it nothing more than fuel. He probably wouldn't bother to eat at all, but his stomach needed some lining for the ten-plus cups of coffee he drank every day.

"So, Henry Dembrow," he began.

"Henry Dembrow's victim," Tess amended. "His sister thinks her brother was killed in prison for a reason."

"Which lies in the identity of Jane Doe." Tull chewed on a forkful of greens. "She's wrong, of course."

"Agreed, but I can't see how it would hurt anyone, trying to find out who the girl was."

"No, it's a good exercise for you, in fact. The question is, how do you, without access to all the tools and databases we have at the department—"

"Without *official* access," Tess said, smiling at him. Unattached, she had never allowed herself to flirt with Tull. Now that she was back with Crow, it seemed perfectly safe to flutter her lashes a little. Tull was fine-boned, an inch or two shorter than she was, with even, perfect features thrown into sharp relief by his acne scars. It was those little scars that made him so attractive, not that Tull ever seemed to notice. "I was married once," he liked to say, in a tone suggesting it was a childhood communicable disease, like measles or chicken pox. Once you had it, you had it.

"Without access," he repeated now, in a firm tone. "So, what can you do that we didn't do?"

"Not give up."

"Don't be rude, Tess."

"I'm not, but it's true, isn't it? With Henry's confession in hand, it had to be less urgent to identify Jane Doe than it was to close your other cases. You're supposed to catch the killers, not identify their victims."

"You'd be surprised how a case like this eats at a detective. I was the secondary. The primary on the case, David Canty, took it very much to heart. He did everything possible, even planted a few stories in the *Blight*, hoping to stir up some leads."

Tess couldn't help smiling at this. Newspaper reporters liked to think they used people. They hated to acknowledge how they were used and manipulated. But it was a two-way street, this avenue paved with rationalizations about the public's right to know and the public good.

"I noticed she had a tattoo, a fresh one, a line at the ankle—" Tess began.

"We checked," Tull said. "I personally called every goddamn tattoo parlor in the city and the county, to see if anyone remembered a girl like her coming in just before she was killed. No one did. Although if she had a tattoo, she was at least eighteen, or had a fake ID. It's not legal to tattoo a minor."

"Could have been a do-it-yourself job."

Tull shook his head. "Too professional looking."

"I assume you tried to match her with missing persons reports, too?"

"Yeah. That's the worst. Families coming in, looking at a dead body to see if it's their dead body. They're relieved when it's not, but they're also frustrated, because it means all they can do is go home and wait."

Tess's sandwich was long gone, but Tull was still picking at his salad. From here, she could see the corner of Baltimore Street, *the* Block—the Tick-Tock club, the sad little sex shops and peep shows. Once, all runaway girls had ended up here. Now there was so much competition.

"Someone, somewhere must miss her," Tess said. "Every death has to alter the world in some way, don't you think?"

Tull gave her a fond smile, the kind Tess hated. "Most people get tougher, the more death they see. But you, you're still all squishy and sentimental. Next thing I know, you'll be telling me you've found religion, and you'll start lugging your little piano down to the Block, playing for the passersby. Sister Tess Monaghan, in her black orthopedic shoes, running her own mission of mercy."

The image made Tess laugh. She knew those women; she had tossed coins in their cups on Friday afternoon, glad someone wanted to save a few souls. "If I find religion, I'll have to embrace the Muslim faith so both parents can be furious with me."

Tull surprised her by leaning forward and wiping a piece of feta from her cheek. His touch was a father's touch—well-meaning, but too gentle to get the job done. Mothers knew how hard to rub a stained cheek. "You know, if you plan on any more human contact today, you might consider a breath mint."

Tess took over, cleaning her own cheek. "I think I'm just going to go back to my office, read these files, and canoodle with Esskay, whose breath is always much worse than mine."

"And someone pays you for this? Man, I want a gig like that someday. You need a partner?"

"Everyone wants to be my partner these days." Tess thought about Whitney's similarly facetious offer just the other night. At least, she hoped it was facetious. "Why is that? Does my life really look so cushy from where you sit?"

"Actually, it looks . . . happy. You look happy, ever since you got back from Texas. And back with Crow."

"I guess I am," Tess said, then looked around nervously. Too late—there wasn't even a splinter of wood to knock in this room of formica tables and plastic chairs. She rapped her knuckles on her forehead, figuring it was hard enough to count.

5

Tess supposed there were worse things than finding one's erstwhile boss at the breakfast table almost every day, wearing his robe and eating bran flakes, but she had yet to think of any.

Oh yes, there was one—knowing that said erstwhile boss was sleeping with one's aunt.

"Hello, Tess," Tyner Gray greeted her the next morning, his smile so smug that it could make the Chesire Cat disappear from shame. "We didn't hear you come in last night, but then—we were busy."

"Roll a little closer to the table," she said, nudging his wheelchair with her hip. "I need to get into the refrigerator."

"I thought you ate at Jimmy's most mornings," he said, even as he complied. The kitchen was large, or so it had seemed before Tyner came along. "Is it true that you got one of the new waitresses fired for putting cream cheese on both your bagels, or is that just more Fells Point apocrypha?"

Tess leaned into the refrigerator, checking out her options. "In the off season, when we're not rowing, I like to come downstairs and have breakfast with Kitty and her man of the moment. Some of them even cook. The one before you made Belgian waffles."

"Well, if I were you, I'd become resigned to toasting my own bagels this winter," he said. "Kitty's talking about installing an elevator so we can use her rooms on the second floor." Since taking up with Tyner, Kitty had limited herself to the cramped rooms behind the store.

"Don't count on it. Kitty has been in the boyfriend-of-the-month club for as long as I've lived here." Tess sniffed the half-and-half. Kitty drank her coffee black, so the cream she kept for guests and her tenant-niece sometimes went bad. "Why do you think she'd change her ways for you?"

"Because I'm so good," Tyner said. The waxy container of half-and-half slipped through Tess's hands, but she caught it before it hit the floor.

"*Gross.* If the cream wasn't sour to begin with, then that remark definitely would have curdled it."

"Crow said he was going to pick some up while he was out walking Esskay," Tyner said complacently, turning a page of the newspaper. "Rumor has it that your apartment has a kitchen, but you can't prove it by me."

"Are you two sniping at each other again?" Kitty's voice was sleepy as she padded into the kitchen, tying the sash of her peach robe. Fifteen years older than Tess, she looked much better in the mornings, with her fair skin and tousled red hair. But it was her sweet, open disposition that bound men to her. "They come for the curls," Crow once said, "but they stay for the temperament. Kitty's like a hearth where every man wants to warm himself."

"Then why isn't Tyner burnt to a crisp by now?" Tess had lamented.

It wasn't that she disliked the irascible older man. He was a good rowing coach and a decent lawyer, who threw her work and represented all her clients for a small fee, so she could claim privilege if the police ever hassled her. But Tyner in love was unbearable. He beamed. He smiled. He gazed adoringly. Some mornings, it was all Tess could do not to toss her waffles on the *Beacon-Light*'s local section, which happened to be the only part of the paper that Tyner didn't commandeer.

"You can't expect our relationship to change just because you two are boyfriend and girlfriend now," Tess told her aunt. "This is how Tyner and I always talked to each other. You just used to take my side, remember? You're a traitor to your gender and your blood."

But Kitty wasn't listening. She leaned over Tyner's shoulder, pretending interest in the newspaper he was reading, letting a hand rest on his shoulder. Tyner picked it up and kissed her palm.

"You know," Tess said, aware no one was listening, "Jimmy's is looking better and better. Tell Crow to meet me there."

It was almost ten before she set out for Locust Point. Funny—she saw the neighborhood every day, from across the water, rowed her Alden along its ragged shore, yet all she really knew of Locust Point was Fort McHenry and the Domino Sugars sign, which she could see from the makeshift terrace outside her bedroom. She tried to remember to look at it every night, just before bed. So much had changed in Baltimore, it was reassuring to go to sleep with that static neon vision blazing red in her mind's eye. As a child, she thought God might be lurking behind the sign, because if she were God, that was where she would make her heaven. Atop a neon sign overlooking Baltimore, guarding a mountain of sugar.

On a map, Locust Point looked cramped and narrow. Yet once Tess crossed Key Highway, there was a feeling of expansiveness, as if the sky were deeper here, the city miles away. She had heard rumors of yuppies, drawn by inexpensive rowhouses with water views, but there was little evidence of such an invasion. Even with the big employers disappearing—Procter & Gamble, the shipping jobs—the neighborhood was strikingly unchanged. One could imagine Locust Point inside a plastic globe, synthetic snow sifting down, no one ever getting in.

And no one ever getting out. It seemed an unlikely place for anyone to die as a stranger, yet Jane Doe had done just that.

Tess parked her car on Hull Street, a few doors down from the Dembrow rowhouse. She was going to walk where Henry walked, or at least where Henry had said he walked the morning of Jane Doe's death. She was even starting out at the same time, so the light would be more or less the same. Of course, December was not November, but it was close enough. Even the weather was the way it had been thirteen months ago, sunny and unseasonably mild. Henry had gone out the back door, so she walked to the alley and touched the gate, almost as if beginning a game, and started on her way.

She was not Tess Monaghan, she kept telling herself. She was Henry Dembrow, a twenty-one-year-old huffer aching for a high, seeing the world through itching, watering eyes that evaluated everything for its potential utility toward this goal. Such eyes would look for the glint of coins on the sidewalks, or untended purses in cars. Would he notice copper downspouts, too, or iron balustrades? No, Henry wasn't enterprising enough to gather metal to sell, to make the trip to the salvage places that asked no questions of the men with shopping carts. He wanted things easy.

He had remembered stopping at the corner gas station, so Tess stopped there, stepping into the warmth of the inevitable mini-market. The manager had chased Henry Dembrow from here the day of the killing, according to the police report, but hadn't noticed any girl. Tess grabbed a handful of mini Goldenberg Peanut Chews from a box next to the cash register. To each his own high.

"Manager around?" she asked the young man at the cash register, whose coloring and dark hair suggested he was Middle Eastern. His badge, however, identified him as "Brad."

"I'm the manager," he said, in a Baltimore accent so heavy and thick that he must be a native, or someone who had immigrated in the cradle. Tess wondered if his parents ever second-guessed their sacrifices, coming halfway around the world so their son might have the opportunity of speaking a pitch-perfect Bawlmarese.

She raced through what she thought of as the hard part—her identity, what she was doing, how she knew to ask for him. In her experience, it was those first sixty seconds, from the moment she flashed her P.I. license to the end of her pitch, that she was most likely to earn someone's cooperation. Older people were the easiest, if only because they were so often bored out of their minds that they welcomed any distraction. Men were curt, but they usually found the time, as long as she did the little-me, big-eye, big-chest thing. Women were more skeptical, because women spent their lives listening to bullshit.

Foreigners, those who had known less free societies, were the most leery. They didn't believe anyone could speak openly, about anything. Throw in the words *police business* and they closed down completely.

Brad-the-assimilated was cooperative, he just didn't know anything.

"I remember Henry, sure. I ran him off from the pumps at least once a month. But I didn't see him with any girl that day. Or any day, for that matter. Girls liked him, he was shy, kinda good-looking. Henry didn't care. He was interested in only one thing, getting high."

"Maybe she came in on her own." Tess showed him the sketch police had used a year before, probably shown to Brad at some point. It wasn't great, but it was preferable to the corpse photo. "Forget about Henry. Did you ever see her?"

Brad shook his head. "Not that I noticed. Sorry."

"I saw her."

The voice, very high and sweet, came from the rear of the store, where there was a magazine stand. Tess glanced toward the sound and found herself staring at the cover of a fashion magazine, one promising failproof tips for thicker hair, thinner thighs and better orgasms. The magazine lowered, and the gaunt, painted, pouting model fell like a mask to reveal a pretty, moon-faced teenager. She looked young not to be in school. All the eyeliner in the world—and it appeared this girl had used all the eyeliner in the world—couldn't age this baby face.

"Don't fib, Sukey," the manager scolded her. "This woman is doing serious work. She doesn't need to hear your stories."

"It's not a story," the girl insisted, cheeks flushing. "I did see her. Not with Henry, but in Latrobe Park, earlier that week. She had a fuzzy coat, with a fur collar. She was waiting for someone. Someone was supposed to meet her, but the person never came."

The detail about the coat was dead-on. It also was on the posters the police had distributed, so Tess wasn't too impressed.

"Why didn't you tell the police this a year ago, when they were trying to identify her?"

Sukey rolled her eyes. "Because I didn't know her name, which was the point, right? You asked if anyone *saw* her, and I did. I even talked to her a couple of times."

"You talked to her, but she didn't tell you her name."

"We're talking, and we haven't exchanged names, have we?"

"Sukey."

She tossed her head. "You only know my name 'cause Brad used it."

"Tess Monaghan." She held out her hand.

Sukey put down the magazine and came out from behind the aisle of canned goods that had hidden her body from Tess's view. She was plump, even by South Baltimore standards, so her age was hard to ascertain. Packed into jeans, a tee-shirt, and a Starter jacket, she was full of jiggling curves. Early adolescence, Tess thought. Or a steady diet of Mounds bars.

"Sukey Brewer." She took Tess's hand tentatively, shaking more at the fingertips than at the palms. "Are you really a private detective?"

"It's not something you lie about," Tess said. "Unless you're really twisted. How come you're not in school, Sukey Brewer? You don't look old enough to be a dropout."

"Field trip day. My class went to the Smithsonian. My mom forgot to fill out the permission slip on time, so I'm hanging out here. I'm sure as shit not going to go to school if no one else is there."

"She's a good kid," Brad volunteered. "She helps me out here, sometimes, doing inventory. I told her she can have a real job here when she turns sixteen next year, and has a work permit. But don't believe a damn thing she says."

"That's not fair, Brad," Sukey said. "Most of my stories are true. I just don't get all the details right, sometimes. Like the newspaper, you know?"

"Tell the lady about the bank robbery you saw on your way over here this morning, even though there's no bank between here and your house."

"You weren't listening. It was an armored truck, one of those red-and-black ones," Sukey said. "Money was flying through the air, and people were grabbing it, then running away. It was wild."

"Wild," Brad repeated dryly, giving the word its Baltimore pronunciation: Wahhhhld.

Tess was not interested in that day's robberies, real or imagined. "So, a year ago, you noticed this girl in the park. A girl in a fuzzy coat with a fur collar. What time was this?"

"About two or three."

"She was dead by then."

"The day before, I mean. I saw her the day before."

"Why weren't you in school that day?"

"Half day, teachers' conference. I had a book I wanted to read—I read a lot."

Brad nodded. "She does, she reads a lot. Which is why her head is so filled with nonsense."

"I like to read on the swings. If there are mothers there, with the little kids, it's . . ." Her voice trailed off. Tess, taking in Sukey's round figure and guileless face, could imagine why she might want to be in sight of someone's mother. She wished she knew a way to tell the girl that everyone's adolescence was horrible, that no one was spared. But people had tried to tell her the same thing fifteen years ago, and she hadn't believed them.

"You said you talked."

"We did, kinda. I mean, I said 'Nice day,' and

she said she'd seen better. I showed her the book I was reading and she said it looked pretty good."

Sukey looked at Tess expectantly, as if hoping for praise. Tess tried to smile and nod, although the girl hadn't told her anything helpful.

"Was that all you said? Did you see her leave?"

"I left first. My mom calls at three-thirty, I'm supposed to be home by then. But the girl—this was funny, I remember it almost word for word—she said: 'Tell me what you think you'll be when you grow up.' And I said, 'I dunno. I'll probably just work at the Sugar House after I graduate from Southern. Get married, have some babies.'"

A modest goal, but at least she was trying to do it in the right order. So many local girls omitted the getting married part.

"And she must not be from here, 'cause she said 'The Sugar House? What's that?' So I told her about Domino's and she smiled, in a kind of weird way and said: 'That's funny, because I worked at a place with a name almost like Domino's, and it could have been called the Sugar House. Then again, maybe the Sugar House is where I lived before, although I always thought of it as the Gingerbread House. You know, Hansel and Gretel, the witch in the oven. Other people said it was a cake, but I never saw that. It was the Gingerbread House, and I never could get that witch in the oven. In the end, every place you go is the Sugar House.' She asked me if I knew what she meant, and I said, yeah, I did." Sukey looked mystified. "Actually, I thought she might be a little crazy."

Brad rolled his eyes. "All lies, I'm betting. When

Sukey tells a story in so much detail, it's always lies. Why do you make things up, Sukey? What book did you get that from?"

Sukey's eyes seemed on the verge of tearing up, but this was a girl with plenty of experience at stemming her own tears. She took a deep breath, opened her eyes very wide, and the film of tears receded. "I'm telling the truth this time. I do sometimes, you know. She said more stuff, too, stuff I wasn't supposed to tell. She said she was a runaway. She had lived in a big mansion and gone to boarding schools. She said her father was the richest man in the world, and he was going to miss her like crazy."

Even Tess could tell this part of the story wasn't true. But she held up a hand before Brad started to berate Sukey again. "If I learn one new thing about a case, I'm doing well. You saw the woman I'm trying to identify, the two of you spoke. As far as I'm concerned, I owe you. Could I buy you that magazine you were reading, or one of the paperbacks in the rack? My way of saying thank you."

Sukey sucked on her plump lower lip. "Can I have both?"

Brad looked ready to scold the girl again, but Tess's laugh kept him from saying anything.

"Why not?"

Sukey picked out a *Teen People* and a thriller, something that was all Swiss numbered accounts and globetrotting psychopaths, with a lovely but lethal lady in pursuit. The cover showed a woman's shapely legs, cut off at mid-thigh, a 9mm dangling by her lace garter belt.

"This is sort of what your job is like, right?" Sukey asked, studying the cover.

"Sort of," Tess said. "Although I tend to cover myself below the waist when I'm working."

She didn't have the heart to tell Sukey what her job was really like, how boring it could be, how routine. Tess was going to spend the rest of her day poring over phone books and CD-Rom telephone directories, looking for places with names like Domino's, which should be called the Sugar House, unless it was the Gingerbread House, or a cake. It was her willingness to share details like this that had put Tess on the "do-not-call" list for every city school's Career Day. She also didn't see any point in mentioning that she was going to check to see if there had been an armored car robbery in Locust Point this morning.

The truth was, she couldn't imagine any assignment more dangerous than being a teenage girl, at large in the land with an overripe body and a face full of yearning. Bring on the globetrotting psychopaths. They couldn't be anywhere near as terrifying as adolescent boys.

6

Some people panic at December's darkness, despairing to see the sun go down before they leave work. But Tess had always found comfort in the shorter days. The winter months gave her permission to relax. It was pleasant, cozy even, to sit in her office and feel the shadows encroach around her and her computer screen. On this particular afternoon, the ebbing light was at least a sign of progress. The sun came up, the sun went down, and the only thing she knew was what she already knew: Jane Doe had a conversation with Sukey on the swings at Latrobe Park.

Unless she didn't. Sukey wasn't a liar, Tess realized. She wasn't mean, she wanted nothing from her stories, except a little attention. The robbery tale even had a germ of truth in it. The desk sergeant at the Southern Precinct confirmed a bakery truck had hit a light pole in the neighborhood, and some kids had carried away cakes and pies before police arrived. Sukey had changed the bakery truck to an armored car, the sweets to money, thinking, in her innocence, to make the story better. Yet the truth was so much more entertaining. Tess had even phoned in the item to her *Beacon-Light* friend, Feeney, made an early Christmas present of this slam-dunk brite. No, Sukey was a fantasist, trying to make something out of the dreary reality of the life around her. Then why couldn't she imagine a life for herself that would take her down Fort Avenue and out of Locust Point? Why was she cutting school and thinking her own future was limited to a job at the Sugar House?

A knock sounded on the door, slightly tentative. From the outside, the office probably looked dark. "Come in, it's open," Tess called out, turning on the desk lamp and feeling as if she had been caught doing something. What, she wasn't sure.

Her father's red head poked around the door, the way he had poked it into her bedroom all those years—unsure of his welcome, a little nervous about entering what he considered a feminine precinct.

"I can't believe you don't keep this locked," he said. "You should have a buzzer system, throw the deadbolt the minute you come in."

She usually did, but being scolded by her father made her feel contrary.

"I don't worry too much. After all, I have this fine watch dog—" the greyhound, Esskay, unrolled stiffly from the sofa, did her salaam stretch, and presented herself to Patrick for the obligatory tribute she demanded from everyone who crossed the threshold.

"And a gun in my desk drawer."

If Tess were in therapy, a psychiatrist probably

could have spent many, many hours on the immense pleasure she took in brandishing her .38 Smith & Wesson at her father just then. But, really, the gesture said more about her relationship with her gun than it did about her relationship with her father. When she first opened the office, she had kept it in the wall safe. She had been literally gun shy, afraid of her own weapon. She soon found there was no percentage in having a permit to carry if she didn't keep the gun close at hand. The fact of gun ownership didn't intimidate anyone, she needed the weapon nearby.

Besides, she had fallen a little in love with her Smith & Wesson. It felt good in her hand and it was much more reliable than other tools of her trade— the cell phone, the computer, her instincts.

"Put that away," her father said. "It's not a toy."

"No, but it looks like one, which is probably why kids are always picking them up. What brings you here?" she asked. It occurred to her that this was only his second visit to the office, the first being the "grand opening" where her mother had tried not to weep and Patrick had recommended burglar bars for all the windows.

"I was in the neighborhood," he said, and she let the lie pass. She knew—and he knew that she knew— the East Side had never been his territory.

He glanced around her office, which she thought looked best in evening's dim light. The walls, which probably had layers of lead paint beneath the eggshell white Tess had slapped on last summer, didn't look as rough, the floors weren't as noticeably wavy. "I keep hoping you'll do well enough so you could afford a nice little office in one of those strip centers out York Road, or toward Ellicott City."

"I could swing that, if I wanted to," Tess said, her tone a little curt. Maybe she should have brandished her bank book at her father, instead of her gun. "But some of my clients couldn't. I need to be near a bus line, or the Metro, limited as that is. Not everyone owns a car, you know."

"But that's not the kind of clientele you want," her father said. "You want to be in a place where suburban ladies feel comfortable pulling up in their mini-vans."

"The suburban ladies like this location just fine. It gives them a thrill, as if they were coming into the city to score crack. They already feel degraded, hiring a private detective, so they might as well get the full slumming experience. I think they're disappointed that I don't have my name on the door in gilt letters, and a secretary named Velma out front."

"Still, if you want to impress someone—"

"I can always meet them at the bar at the Brass Elephant, or the coffee bar in the Bibelot bookstore in Canton. But I don't much care for clients I have to impress." She had clawed some wisps of hair loose while working on the computer, now she pushed them back behind her ears. "Don't worry about me, Dad. I'm doing fine."

"I know you are." Patrick took the seat opposite her desk. She could tell he didn't like being on that side of the desk, sitting across from his daughter. Esskay hooked her nose in his armpit, trying to lift his hand toward her head. Esskay believed all human hands existed to rub her, just as all sofas were invented for her to sleep on.

"If you know my business is going well, why did you send Ruthie Dembrow to me with a loser case that I have about a one-in-a-million chance of solving?"

"I told you, I didn't do it for you, I did it for Ruthie," he said slowly. "I think Ruthie's crazy, you want to know the truth. What happened with her kid brother tore her up. Maybe she should be spending her money on a therapist, or going to some spa. I told her that, she said this is her cure, finding out what happened."

"How do you know Ruthie?"

"I told you. She was a cocktail waitress in Locust Point years ago. Even worked for your Uncle Spike for a summer."

"I don't remember her."

"There's no reason you would. It was around the time you went off to college."

Tess wanted to ask her father a few more questions about Ruthie. But she wasn't sure she was ready for the answers.

"It's late, for you to be out. Mom will be holding supper, wondering where you are."

"Not tonight. She's in a book club."

"She's in a book club?" Tess had not heard about this development, and she subscribed to a strict double standard with her parents: She told them nothing, no matter how important, they must tell her everything, no matter how insignificant. Her father looked forlorn, and his drop-by suddenly seemed less sinister. He just didn't want to go back to the dark house in Ten Hills and eat whatever Judith had left him in her color-coordinated Rubbermaid containers.

"You want to grab a bite?"

"Just us?" he asked, and she realized it was never just them, there was always Uncle Donald or Uncle Spike or Judith.

"Why not?"

They sat in silence, mulling their own answers to that question. Finding none, they ended up at the Austin Grill, part of the renovated American Can Company complex, one of the many unlikely success stories in the once-working-class neighborhood of Canton.

Tess wanted to go Salvadoran—her taste buds had been somewhat transformed by her recent trip to Texas. But the Austin Grill was about as far as her father could go, culinarily.

He studied the menu as if it were in Sanskrit. "It all looks very . . . exotic."

"Have the fajitas," she said. "It's just meat in some bread, think of it that way. I'm going to have migas. Oh, and two Shiner Bocks on draft, please."

Her father frowned. "You're driving."

"You're driving farther. It's one beer, Dad. Get a grip."

He looked around the restaurant, surveying it with a practiced eye. Like an architect who couldn't help seeing the details that went into a building, Pat was never truly off-duty when he was in a bar. His gaze was drawn not to the sponge-painted red walls and industrial pipes running through the ceiling, but to the patrons in the high booths, the bartender behind the counter.

"Ten years ago—heck, five years ago—I would have taken odds they'd never get this old place developed. Wish I'd bought me some real estate in Canton. Never did have an instinct for making money. If you had told me people would want to live in these little old rowhouses, just because they can see water—" he shook his head. "But what do I know? Other than the fact that if I was on duty, I'd be writing this guy up for serving underage drinkers."

Tess looked at the crowd, which was chic, by Baltimore standards. Almost everyone was wearing black, although there were a few patches of bright, preppy colors bursting through, the usual pinks and greens.

"They don't look like college kids to me," she said.

"That's because they've put a lot of effort into not looking like college kids. Too much effort. The drinks give them away. The boys go cheap and the girls go sweet. See that table over there. The guys all have Budweisers, the girls have—what is that, anyway? Strawberry margaritas."

"Swirlies, as the menu would have it."

"Yeah, well I bet a lot of them will be going swirlie before the night is over. But it's not my problem, not my territory." He took a chip from the basket, held it tentatively toward the salsa, then decided to eat it plain. "Oh, like an Utz corn chip," he said. "Where's the boyfriend tonight?"

The boyfriend. As if saying the name was too painful.

"I'm not sure. We have a new policy. If we want to see each other, we have to ask at least twelve hours in advance, make a real date. No—" she stopped, blushing, realizing she had almost used the term "booty call" in front of her father. *Dear Mom. I'm sorry I gave Dad that fatal heart attack at the Austin Grill. Apparently, he didn't know his thirty-year-old daughter was having sex.*

Her father was blushing an even deeper red. It must be awful, in some ways, for a man to have daughters. Fathers knew how men think.

Several silent swallows of Shiner Bock later, her father thought of something to say.

"So now you know how a liquor board inspector looks at a bar. What does the private detective see?"

Tess looked around. "The couple in the corner? One of them, maybe both of them, is stepping out on someone. My guess is he's married—he has a ring, and he's older than she, by a good bit. He's eating, but she's not. In fact, she looks as if she's been living on fumes for a while. Her eyes are fixed on his face, while he's looking at his enchilada."

"Maybe she's in love and he's not."

"That wouldn't cancel out my thesis."

"What's the point of cheating on your wife if it's not for love?"

Tess couldn't decide if she found this sentiment reassuring or unnerving, coming from her father.

"None, I guess," she said, although she didn't believe it. In fact, it was her contention that most people who cheated, men and women, were concerned with anything but love. She had slept with another woman's man out of childish self-pity. Of course, that was before her conversion to monogamy.

"You never told me how your work for Ruthie is going, anyway."

From adultery to Ruthie. Tess didn't even want to contemplate that connection in her father's mind.

"It's not. I had one little lead, but it hasn't gone anywhere. A kid down in Locust Point—a girl who may or may not be a pathological liar—told me she talked to the girl and she said she had worked at a place with a name like Domino's, a place that might as well be called the Sugar House. I spent the afternoon calling every Domino pizza takeout in the city, along with sundry plumbing supply companies, candy shops, taverns, and anything in the Yellow Pages that began DOM. No one remembers a girl who dropped out of sight a year ago, but then, who would?"

"You worked the phone book?"

"What else is there?"

"Well, if it's a city bar, it might be Domino's on the application, just a blank storefront on the street, and no phone listing at all. You ever see those weird little places, the ones that look like someone's house except for a neon Bar sign in the window? They have names, but they're not written down anywhere. Except on the applications. Or they might have one name on the sign, another on the application. Sugar House—Domino's. It's a long shot, but if you want to come in and look at the files, they're public information."

"But if it's not a bar . . ."

"Then you've lost about twenty minutes out of your life. And it's all on the clock, right? You're getting paid, what do you care?"

The fajitas arrived. They always reminded Tess of a magic act, the way smoke poured from the hot skillet as the meat sizzled. Once the waiter was gone, Patrick looked helplessly at the little dishes arrayed in front of him, the basket of flour tortillas.

"How do I do this, anyway?" he asked Tess.

"You must be the last person in America to eat a fajita," Tess said, showing him how to assemble the skirt steak, *pico de gallo*, and guacamole in a tortilla, feeling a surge of affection. She had a sudden image of sitting opposite her father in some nursing home, pouring his Sanka and cutting his meat. It was unbearably sad to think of him that way. She was glad her father was still young, that those days were far away. She liked the relative irresponsibility of being a daughter.

"Yeah, I may never have eaten a fajita—" Patrick hit the *j* hard, "but there's plenty of other things I've done."

She decided not to ask for details. Maybe she didn't want to know everything about her parents after all.

7

Her father's idea of checking the bar files was as good as any she had, which was to say not very. Certainly, it didn't seem particularly urgent when Tess rose the next morning, not as urgent as her desire for a specific kind of rush, a rush found only in one place. She hurried Esskay through their morning walk, then headed to a small, perfectly kept rowhouse not even 500 feet from where she lived.

"I need a Laylah fix," she told Jackie Weir when she answered the lacquered goldenrod door on Shakespeare Street. "Has she eaten breakfast yet? May I take her to Jimmy's with me?"

"She's *not* eaten breakfast, but that's not my fault," Jackie said drily. "The kitchen is knee-deep in Cheerios and bananas. Please take her with you. Keep her for a little while, why don't you? You can bring her back when she has a college degree."

"Right," Tess said. She'd hate to see what happened to anyone who dared to get between Jackie Weir and her toddler daughter, Laylah. She followed

Jackie into the kitchen, noting with great glee the disorder that Laylah brought to what otherwise would be a too orderly house. She had wrought the same transformation on her just-so mother, softening the grim perfection that had been her trademark. If anything, Jackie was more beautiful these days, lipstick forgotten as often as not, her clothes decorated with juice stains and smashed banana bits.

"What brought on today's sudden urging?" Jackie asked, wiping down Laylah's face and then lifting her from her booster seat. They were both still in their night clothes—a pale pink sleep suit for Laylah, a red cashmere robe over what appeared to be silk pajamas for Jackie. "Did the biological clock go off in the middle of the night? Did Crow try that 'I-want-to-have-a-baby-with-you' crap that some men think is so sexy?"

"Please—I don't have generic baby needs. I have Laylah needs, pure and simple. Morning, sweetie."

"Sssser. Sssser." Laylah held out her arms to Tess and chugged her feet, as if she could run through the air. Tess thought she might be able to. She looked like more of a person as she grew, but she still had her Puckish features, her endless delight at the world around her. People who didn't know better were always commenting on the resemblance between mother and daughter. Their skin was the same color, a velvety dark brown that was richer, lusher than the prosaic comparisons it inspired. But Jackie's features brought to mind Nefertiti, while Tess never looked at Laylah without thinking of an African-American Harpo in full googly mode.

And never failed to feel better for it.

"What does Laylah want for Christmas?" She asked her question sotto voce, as if Laylah might know what was going on.

"*Nothing,*" Jackie said, her voice sharp, her smile fond. "Between your mother and you, this girl is already spoiled rotten. It won't be long before she's presenting me with a careful list of her material needs, with links to Internet toy sites, and a cc of her e-mail to Santa. Let's enjoy this part while it lasts."

Laylah pulled at Tess's braid with warm, sticky palms. She liked to pull on Esskay's tail, too, but the dog wasn't as easygoing.

"Whatever you say, Mom. What do *you* want for Christmas, by the way? You're terrifying to shop for, your taste is so good."

"I'd like a four-year plan that will put Baltimore schools on track before I have to start paying $10,000 a year for Laylah to go to private school, or give her a crash course in Catholicism so she can attend the parish school. I'd also like a boyfriend who's not a spoiled momma's boy, and peace on earth, goodwill to men. But I'll settle for a scarf with some green in it, to go with my new suit. You?"

"Same, except for the green scarf. I could use some earrings that make me look like a grown-up."

"Can't be done, child," Jackie said. "Much as it pains me to say it, some things are beyond the power of accessorizing."

They smiled at each other over Laylah's curly head. Tess and Jackie were relatively new friends, and the relationship had almost the same tang as two lovers might have at this six-month mark. To make it more complicated, they had met through Tess's business, only to find out they had more in common than Tess had ever dreamed. They were still courting each other, with Tess being the one who had to pursue a little harder. Jackie had a natural reserve, she kept most people at arm's length. She was not unlike Whitney that way. Right now, for example, Tess would have liked to make some physical contact, to squeeze Jackie's arm or give her a hug. But it was unthinkable. So she kissed the top of Laylah's head, hoping Jackie knew the kiss was for her as well.

"I'll drop her off before I go to work," Tess said. "What times does the babysitter get here?"

"Nine," Jackie said, holding out her hand and letting Laylah grab it. "Try to keep her hat and mittens on, even if it is only two blocks from here to Jimmy's. It's raw this morning."

"Okay, mommy."

"Mommy," Laylah said suddenly, as if it were a wildly original thought, a concept of her own invention. "Mommy, mommy, mommy, mommy."

And Tess knew whatever she got Jackie for Christmas, it could never match the gifts that Laylah gave her every day.

Take Your Daughter to Work Day was still twenty years in the future the last time Tess had visited the sad little downtown midrise that housed the liquor board inspectors. It hadn't changed at all, which was mildly disheartening. Perhaps it was simply too ugly to tamper with. Employee's daughter or no, she followed the procedure required of all visitors, calling from the lobby and waiting for an escort upstairs.

"Your father's out, but he told us what you wanted," said the secretary, Marley, who greeted her. A new face to Tess, but she acted as if they were old friends. If this had been her mother's office, Tess would have worried that her life was the office soap opera, a tale told in exhaustive detail over every lunch hour and coffee break, until everyone felt as if he or she knew her. But her father wasn't as inclined to babble about his life.

"I have to say, from what Pat says you're looking at, it sounds like kind of a wild goose chase."

"You're telling me," Tess muttered. How many bars did Baltimore have anyway? Given the size of the files before her, it appeared there was one tavern for every one hundred citizens.

A man in a boxy leather jacket walked through the office, head down as if distracted by his own thoughts. Still, he managed to give Tess the quick once-over some men automatically throw toward any remotely female form. Tess had even seen them do it at mannequins in department stores.

This man blushed when he got to the face. "Tess," he said. "Little Tess. How long has it been?"

She recognized the man as one of her father's longtime colleagues. Not a friend—her father always said he wanted to be respected, not liked. But he thought well of this guy, she remembered that much, if only because he was one of the few old-timers left, and this gave them a bond. She groped for the name. George Foreman, Georgie Porgie, Gene—Gene Fulton.

"It's been quite some time if you still think of me as 'little' Tess. I hit five-nine in the eighth grade." She didn't use his name, because she couldn't decide if he was still Mr. Fulton to her, or now an equal named Gene.

He apparently suffered no such confusion, given the way his heavy-lidded eyes continued to track up and down, up and down. Big Tess was fair game in a way that Little Tess had never been.

"When you going to settle down and give your old man some grandbabies?" Gene asked, as if he couldn't sleep nights for wondering if Pat Monaghan was ever going to dandle a baby on his knee. Tess knew he was fishing, trying to find out where she was on the dating-engaged-married-divorcing continuum.

"Between us"—Tess leaned forward, a finger on her lips, knowing her words would get back to Pat before the day was out—"sooner than he might think."

"You engaged then?" That was Marley. Tess had suddenly dropped off Gene Fulton's radar. Some men live to poach. Others figure it's too much trouble. Fulton was a lazy bastard, bless his heart.

"Practically," she said. "I wouldn't be surprised if there was a jeweler's box beneath my tree this Christmas."

Which was the truth, because she was sure Jackie would, in fact, find the perfect pair of earrings.

"Huh," Fulton said. "Well, don't be a stranger. I've got my beeper, Marley, anyone needs me."

Tess was left with the files. The temptation was

to plunge in, but she had learned to be systematic in such things. One by one, bird by bird, she'd go through each report, looking for the syllable *Dom*, the word *sugar* or an owner's name that correlated. On a computer, she could have done this in seconds, but Tess preferred paper files. She was no Luddite, but she knew the trade-offs in using computers. A search could be too targeted, too easy. On the Internet, plugged into a search engine, one traded serendipity for straight-up dippiness, for page after page of worthless hits, while the thing one wanted might be tantalizingly out of reach, a single keystroke off. Getting lost had always been part of the journey for her.

Within an hour, she had three viable candidates—Hummers Café, whose owner was listed as Harold Sugarman; Bo's Tavern, which had started life as Dom's Tavern; and Domenick's, owned by Lawrence Purdy. Although the last seemed the most promising, it had the skimpiest file of the three, with none of the usual neighborhood complaints about noise and after-hours operation.

"Why's the file so thin? Others are inches thick."

Marley had a smug, knowing look. "They're either very well-behaved, or"—she glanced around, saw no one, decided to lower her voice anyway—"very connected."

"I thought the bribery and fraud trial against the old boss and Billy Madonna would have slowed down any such activity."

"You can chase a few bears away from a honey pot, but as long as it's there, the bears are going to keep coming back. A lot of bar owners are willing to pay for special favors. An inspector would have to be almost *inhumane* to be tempted."

The secretary's little malaprop might have afforded Tess some pleasure, if it weren't for the implication. "You're not saying my dad—"

"Pat Monaghan? Oh no, Tess, I didn't mean anything like that. Honest as the day is long. But he's one of the old guys, been here almost thirty years now. He made a career here. It's the ones who come and go who are trouble."

Tess checked her watch. "Ten-thirty. I guess it's too early to start visiting bars."

"Not necessarily. Under law, you can open as early as six A.M."

"You know, I've never actually needed to know the legal time to *start*." The thought was oddly cheering. Obviously, she wasn't anywhere near as decadent as she sometimes feared.

Hummer's Café, out on Arabia Avenue, was closed and the dusty windows indicated it had been a long time since anyone had worked in the small frame house. Tess had slightly better luck at Bo's, once known as Dom's, which appeared to have taken its original name from the Latin *dominatus*—to rule, to exert control, to charge people ridiculous amounts of money for drinks, simply because they were served by men and women in rubber suits.

Yet Bo's, which happened to be in one of East Baltimore's old synagogues, seemed strangely tepid to Tess, sort of the TGIFridays version of an S-M club. Of course, it was only noon when she arrived there, not exactly the hour at which such clubs thrive, and she did not have much experience in these matters. Like most well-brought-up women of her generation, Tess had practiced her masochism privately, within the confines of relationships.

But she was pretty sure that S-and-M shouldn't be so . . . clean, so desultory, so absent of shock value. Baltimore just didn't do debauchery well, but it kept trying.

The manager was not happy to have a private investigator on the premises, but he eventually stopped running his long, twitchy fingers through his dyed blond hair and got down to cases.

"I've been here two years," said the man, who had identified himself only as Hurst. "Not Horst," he had made a point of saying, "Hurst." He was extremely tall, perhaps six-foot-six, rail-thin, and tricked out with so many nervous mannerisms that he seemed to be one gigantic tic of a man. "The turnover is constant, but no different from any other bar or restaurant in the city. In fact, I think we keep our people a bit longer. Our customers tip terrifically, which really doesn't make sense. If you were going to stiff someone, wouldn't it be in a place where you were supposed to be, um, in command?"

"Would you have noticed if a girl just disappeared one day and never came back?"

"It happens. It happens all the time. It's not the kind of job where people give two weeks notice and ask for references, you know what I mean? Do you have a photo?"

Tess didn't want to show him the photo of Jane

Doe's corpse. It wasn't only that it seemed less than helpful—she couldn't imagine anyone making an ID from the battered, bulging face. But the photo seemed pornographic to her, degrading.

She showed him the police sketch instead, although she doubted it was a good likeness. The drawing was a little flat, but it had the particulars—the shape of the face, the high cheekbones, the large eyes beneath the winged brows, the archer's bow of a mouth, with its plump lower lip.

"Pretty," Hurst said. "But it doesn't ring any bells."

Tess noticed his pupils were pinpricks set in amber, that his hands kept returning to his lank blond locks. A man with his own problems. Bo's clientele probably came for the speed and stayed for the decor. She wondered how long Hurst had been helping himself to the house wares.

"I never knew this place existed before I checked the liquor licenses this morning, but I know there are bars that try to draw as little scrutiny as possible, for their clientele's sake. Does Bo's have a nickname? A kind of code name used by the people who come here, or work here?"

Hurst looked mystified. "Why would a place named Bo's need something like that? We have tourists wander in who think we're a crab house as it is." He giggled. "And I guess we are, sometimes. Not everyone is as clean as he should be, you know."

"Does anyone ever call this the Sugar House?"

"I should hope not." He made a face. "That reminds me of that hideous song. Besides, whatever this place is, it isn't sweet."

Tess looked around. It was so perfect for her

purposes—an S-and-M bar that trafficked in crystal meth, which had once been called Dom's. But if Bo's wasn't sweet, neither did it seem particularly threatening.

"Who comes here?" she asked Hurst. "I'm not asking for names, I'm just curious. Is there really a demand for this kind of place in Baltimore?"

His bony shoulders popped up and down in what might have been a shrug on a person moving at normal speeds. "Kids come for the music and . . . side benefits. But we get a lot of fat, middle-aged guys from Linthicum. Go figure."

Tess felt like saying: "Well, I'm tracking down a lead that came from a pathological liar. Go figure." But it was only noon. She might as well check out the last place on her list, Domenick's in Southwest Baltimore. Her mind was already skipping ahead to lunch, trying to remember if there was a decent place left to eat in Sowebo since Mencken's Cultured Pearl shut down.

Southwest Baltimore was an object lesson in what can happen when a neighborhood's ballyhooed renaissance falls short of the mark. Dingy and defeated, it reminded Tess of someone who jumps from one rooftop to the next, only to dangle by his fingernails from the downspout. Most of the restaurants that had cropped up in the neighborhood's hour of hope had moved on, as had their bohemian clientele, artists attracted by the low rents. Hampden, up north, was the happening neighborhood now. No more Mencken's Cultured Pearl, or Telltale Hearth, or Gypsy Café. At one point, the city had even put H. L. Mencken's house on the block. Officials backed off, claiming it was a misunderstanding, but Tess never doubted they would have sold the place if they could have. The sad fact was that the biggest tourist site in the area was "The Corner," an open-air drug market immortalized in a book by the same name. Politicians held press conferences there and the city routinely swept it clean, as if it were the only place in Baltimore to buy crack cocaine. When Hollywood came to town to film *The Corner*, the real corner wasn't even good enough. The caravan of movie trailers—and, more important, the trail of money left in their wake— had ended up in East Baltimore.

But even in the most depressed areas, people need a place to throw back a drink or two. Domenick's, housed in an end-of-group rowhouse, provided a clean, quiet place to do just that. The sign out front said only Bar, as if it were a generic place to drink. Inside, it proved to be just that. A place for regulars, this was clear to Tess when every pair of eyes in the quiet bar fixed on her. It was one o'clock, a little early to begin drinking, but not so early as to be ashamed of it. Besides, these were men and women whose days started earlier than most, if they started at all.

She took a seat at the bar and asked for a beer.

"What kind?" asked the bartender. He was a thin man in his middle forties, with a stoop and a very bad toupee. Hard to imagine telling your troubles to him.

Tess recognized the question for the test that it was.

"Not Natty Boh," she said, "not after they left town. And I guess I can't have a Carling Black Label either. What do you have on tap?"

"Michelob."

"Michelob's fine."

"Not light beer, you understand. Just Michelob."

"I never opt for the 'light' version of anything," Tess said. "Do you serve any food?"

He tossed her a stained paper menu, which featured the usual bar delicacies and a few local specialties. Tess, who had been skimping on vegetables of late, soothed her conscience with an order of green pepper rings dipped in powdered sugar. Then she sat back and studied her surroundings, trying not to be obvious, given that the other customers continued to steal looks at her.

It was a plain, no-nonsense bar. One television set, tuned to ESPN and muted. The lower part of the walls was paneled, while the upper portion was covered with gold-flecked mirrors, which may have been intended to make the bar seem wider than it was, but the mirrors were now so smeary with age that they had a funhouse quality. A minimum of neon signage, a cigarette machine, two video poker machines, with the usual disclaimers about being for recreation only. Right. The booths along the wall were filled, mostly with men. One woman, maybe in her sixties, with dark hair and a doughy face creased by a lifetime of Luckies. No one was speaking, and no one else was eating. The only sounds were the bells and whistles of an old-fashioned pinball machine, over which two stringy young blond men were practically davening.

Perhaps no one ever ate here, for the young waitress who brought out her green pepper rings was clearly overwhelmed by the task. She held the tray out in front of her, arms locked, eyes almost crossed in concentration. She traversed the short distance from the kitchen door to Tess's barstool as if walking across ice. No wonder—she wore ridiculous shoes for a waitress, lace-up platforms with four-inch heels. Tess had waited tables off and on during college, and she knew you had to sacrifice style for comfort. This girl would learn.

"Green pepper rings?" she asked in a sweet, high voice. Well, it was clear why she was hired. She was extraordinarily pretty in a fresh, wholesome way that made Tess feel craggy, old, and tough as leather. Pink cheeks, shiny brown hair, big blue eyes, and an almost comically perfect figure, an hourglass perched on long, coltish legs.

"Just put 'em down, Terry," the bartender said, obviously unimpressed with her skills.

She placed the plate in front of Tess with a hard clatter, so the pepper rings jumped, and she did, too. Then she scurried back into the kitchen.

"You the owner?" Tess asked the bartender, fairly sure of the answer.

"Manager."

"How long you worked here?"

"Off and on since it opened."

She pulled her wallet from the knapsack she carried in place of a purse—a wallet thick with bills, she let the bartender's eyes take that in—and showed him her license, then the sketch. Even before she could explain what she wanted, he was shaking his head. "No one I ever knew."

"What about the other folks here?"

He held up the sketch. "Anyone know her?"

A few customers squinted at the sketch, but no one got up to take a closer look.

"Sorry."

"Is the owner around?" she asked.

"The owner?"

"Lawrence Purdy. I checked your file at the city liquor board."

"Why would you do that?"

"Because this girl, the one I'm looking for, told someone she worked at a place with a name like Domino's. When I checked the files, I found Domenick's and thought that might be it."

"Well, it wasn't."

"Anyway, Lawrence Purdy—"

"He's not real active. Bought the place as an investment, I run it. Never shows his face around here. He probably couldn't pick me out of a lineup."

"Interesting figure of speech," Tess said. "You ever been in a lineup?"

The bartender's eyes met hers, and he grinned. "Nope."

Her fingers were caked with powdered sugar. She wiped them off on the paper napkin as best she could, then counted out several bills for the check that the bartender had left by her plate. Five dollars total. Not bad for such a nutritionally complete lunch.

As she stood to leave, the waitress skittered out

of the kitchen and began clearing her place. She almost made it back to the swinging kitchen door before she dropped the plate on the worn linoleum floor, where it shattered into dozens of white shards.

"Your tip will just about cover that," the bartender told the girl, and the patrons in the bar laughed, with the exception of the guys at the pinball machine, who didn't seem to notice anything but their game. The girl flushed, but she did not look particularly embarrassed, or cowed. More puzzled than anything else, Tess thought. It was as if she had awakened from a dream and found herself in this musty little tavern, wearing an apron and waiting tables, but she couldn't quite believe it. She had the look of a girl who was waiting for her life to begin.

Tess wasn't going to be the one to break it to her that it already had.

8

Tess wanted to go in search of Lawrence Purdy, Domenick's owner, that very afternoon, but she had a long-standing date to go Christmas shopping with Whitney.

"I've done most of my shopping," Tess had objected, when Whitney demanded her company. "I did it early so I wouldn't have to go into a mall this time of year."

"But I need moral support," Whitney had said. "Besides, you can use the time to browse, figure out what you want for Christmas. Crow told me he's asked you a dozen times what you want, and you always say nothing."

"I tell my parents the same thing," Tess said. "Can I help it if I'm the girl who has everything?"

She really was having trouble coming up with a list of anything she needed, much less wanted. Having lived close to the bone for a few years—although not quite as close as she now remembered those times—Tess had broken herself of the habit of desiring things. Besides, knowing you could afford what you wanted made these items less urgent. The problem was, she was scared to invest her money; she kept everything in her checking account, so her bank balance was now almost embarrassingly large. Even Whitney was impressed; she whistled when she saw the balance on the ATM slip. Whitney being the sort of friend who would look, unself-conciously, at a friend's ATM slip, if it were left out in public view. Tess caught her reading it when she came back from the bathroom.

"Sorry," Whitney said, but she didn't sound particularly contrite. "Old habits die hard. Reading upside down is one of my talents, I like to keep my hand in."

Tess sighed and dropped into her chair. The greyhound, fast asleep on the sofa, mimicked the sound exactly.

"Esskay sounds just like you," Whitney said. "So put upon."

"I don't know why. *Her* friends respect her privacy."

"Bad day at the office, dear?"

"Futile one. I didn't have much to begin with. Now I seem to have less. The Sugar House. I thought it seemed too good to be true, and it was."

Even while Tess was speaking, Whitney continued to snoop, her restless hands poking at various items on the desk. She examined a framed photograph of Crow and Esskay, opened the lid of the old blue Planter's Peanut jar that Tess used for receipts, looked skeptically at a skeleton in a rowboat, a piece of Mexican folk art that had arrived just yesterday from San Antonio, an early Christmas gift.

When Whitney reached for the Dembrow file, Tess stopped her.

"Confidential."

"But surely that doesn't extend to *me*."

"Especially you. I've never known anyone who liked to trade in privileged information the way you do. You'll be out on the Christmas cocktail party circuit, entertaining your mother's friends with the sordid details about my Jane Doe."

"I should be able to read the autopsy," Whitney wheedled. "It's a public document, and I'm a tax-payer."

"It's not the official autopsy, it's my summary of the autopsy. No one is entitled to it except me, and my client." But Tess extracted her typed notes from the folder, placing the rest of the file in her desk drawer, and locking it. Whitney was like a toddler. When she wanted a lollipop, you diverted her with a carrot, and she eventually forgot the lollipop had ever existed.

Once she had permission to look at the report, she quickly lost interest, skimming the page, making a face where the information was particularly graphic, stopping at another point to nod, then moving on. Then her green eyes narrowed, and jumped back to whatever had caught her quicksilver attention the first time.

"You say her teeth were rotted."

Tess knew where Whitney was going, she had been there herself. "Yes, I asked the assistant medical examiner about that. But you can't make an ID through dental records unless you know which dental records to check. It's not as if there's some computer database and you can plug in the description of the molars and it will kick the match back to you in twenty seconds. Although I suppose it could happen one day. Online teeth identification, DNA testing—"

"That's not my point," Whitney said impatiently, jabbing her finger at the line. "The report said the back teeth are eroded, the enamel gone. You know what that means."

Tess did, or she did now that Whitney had reminded her. How embarrassing to have missed this detail. It was as if an alcoholic had looked at an autopsy in which someone's liver was clearly diseased, and been too deep in denial to make the connection.

"Eating disorder," she said, smacking her own cheek, punishment for her own tunnel vision. "Bulimia. A habit of long-standing, if her teeth were showing signs of decay."

"And?"

"And, what? So she had an eating disorder. What am I going to do with that information? It's an interesting detail, but it's not going to help me identify her."

"It narrows the range of possibilities. Now you know she was from a middle- or upper-middle-class family."

"That's a stereotype, Whitney. All classes, all races, experience eating disorders. Even some men have been diagnosed with bulimia and anorexia."

"Yes, and every now and then some Eastern Europe pituitary case finds a job in the NBA. There's a difference between stereotypes, based on bigotry, and generalizations, which are extracted from the fact that some groups do dominate in certain areas. Well-to-do white girls rule in the world of eating disorders."

"Really? Then how come little working-class *moi* flirted with bulimia in high school, while you never had a problem?"

"Oh, you were more of a social climber than you'll ever admit. Going to Washington College, trying out for crew. I used to worry you'd go whole hog, marry some guy named Chip who wore plaid pants and loafers with no socks. Besides, who said I got off scot-free? I had my own brush with it, back in college."

Tess shook her head, annoyed that her friend's competitive spirit never seemed to rest. "I don't think so, Whitney. I was your roommate, remember? You couldn't have hidden it from me. I can spot compulsive overeaters in the grocery store, just by the way they load their carts."

"Not at Washington College, at Yale." Whitney had transferred after their sophomore year, correctly deducing that, in a world gone label mad, a brand-name college was essential. Back then, her ambitions had been aimed, laserlike, at the *New York Times* and a foreign assignment. "I missed an entire semester. Didn't you ever wonder why I graduated six months after you did?"

"I assumed you lost some credits in the transfer."

"What I lost was my breakfast, lunch, and dinner every day for almost three months. I had to be hospitalized for electrolyte imbalance."

Tess's mind wanted to reject this information. Whitney had never had a weight problem. Then again, eating disorders weren't about weight. They were about everything *but* weight. The scale's daily verdict was simply a way to measure one's entire self, and you always came up wanting. It was just a number, they kept telling you. But this was a world where numbers mattered more than anything, a place of ceaseless top 10 lists, top 100 lists, the *Forbes* 500 and the *Fortune* whatever. Homeless men knew how high the Dow closed yesterday, and everyone wanted to be number one. All Tess had wanted was to weigh 120 pounds.

Twelve years ago, after waking up in the hospital, her stomach pumped of the Ipecac she had used to purge, she had made a deal with her body: *Tell me what you want, really want, and I'll give it to you. A brownie when you want a brownie, a piece of fruit when you want a piece of fruit.* It wasn't always easy to hear her body over the roar of the other voices in her head, the ones that swore a bowl of raw cookie dough would solve all her ills, but she could usually zero in on the right signal. She hadn't weighed herself for ten years, and she closed her eyes when she climbed on a doctor's scale.

"How did it happen to you, Whitney?"

"Rowing was a lot more competitive at Yale. My only shot was the women's lightweight four. But I'm tall as you, and leaner. I didn't have much fat to lose. But I tried. God knows I tried." Whitney's thin mouth curled at the memory. "Only problem was that, once I got my weight down, I kept passing out. Hard to win a race when a rower loses consciousness."

Tess had a guilty desire to know more. She and

Whitney had traveled in the same dark country, they spoke a language only a few knew. It was so tempting to delve into the details—*laxatives or self-induced vomiting? What was the biggest binge you ever went on? Did you ever wrap yourself in plastic while doing sit-ups? Run seven miles after eating a half gallon of chocolate chip ice cream?*

Tempting, but probably not healthy.

"Okay, say you're right. Jane Doe had an eating disorder, and she took it a lot further than we ever did. Which, you think, means she's not some street kid, but a nice little middle-class girl. So why hasn't her family come forward? Why isn't there a missing persons report on file?"

"I can't do all your work for you, Tesser. Maybe they don't care. Maybe they don't know she's gone. Maybe both. The autopsy said she could be in her twenties. There are people who are estranged from their parents, you know."

"Really? How does one manage that?"

Whitney stood up and stretched, gave her friend a knowing smile. "As if you could survive without your parents. You'd die if you didn't have them meddling in your life. Speaking of parents—I have a very precise list from my mother, telling me the exact brand of suede gloves I am to give my father for Christmas this year, and where to find the linen handkerchiefs for Marmee—"

"God, I'd forgotten you call your grandmother Marmee. How Louisa May Alcott. Is she as much of a sanctimonious prig as the real Marmee, making you give away your Christmas gifts to the less fortunate?"

"—and, of course, Mother has ordered my Christmas cards for me, from Down's Stationers, and given me a list of people I might have overlooked for my gift list. In fact, she's put everyone on the list but herself, claiming she doesn't want anything. What she really means is there's not a thing I could give her she wouldn't return, so why bother? I think I'll find something especially hideous, something monogrammed that can't be exchanged."

"How do we reward ourselves at the end of this ordeal?" Tess asked. She disliked shopping under most circumstances; the mere thought of a mall in high season made her feel claustrophobic. There would be crowds and Christmas music and, she knew with a sudden and certain dread, robotic figures standing in mounds of white cotton, waggling their heads to and fro.

"We could head back to Belvedere Square, go to Café Zen or Al Pacino's."

"Pizza would be perfect. Maybe I'll even be virtuous and get one of their low-fat pizzas, the kind they make with soy cheese, or whatever it's called."

"You start eating shit like that, and I'll disown you as a friend." Whitney's face was uncharacteristically grave. "You shouldn't joke about our old bad habits. Do you know how lucky we are that we're relatively normal, that we didn't do lasting damage to ourselves?"

"Relatively lucky, relatively normal, relatively happy, and driven mad by our relatives."

Like a dog with a bone, Tess worried the little bit she had, growling over it, turning it around in her mouth, trying to make it new. Jane Doe had said she worked at a place with a name like Domino's. Tess had found three such places, but the girl wasn't connected to any of them. Still, it was all she had. That, and Whitney's insight, which told Tess more about herself than it did about the dead girl. How could she have missed the eroded back teeth? One couldn't say she was in denial, exactly, more a state of amnesia. Had she forgotten how sick she had been? Was that a sign of health?

She was driving out Frederick Road, near her parents' house, to the address given in the liquor board file for Lawrence Purdy, owner of Domenick's. True, the bartender had said Purdy was an absentee owner, sitting at home and collecting checks, but he might know something about his own operation.

He lived modestly, this Lawrence Purdy, in a plain brick rowhouse on West Gate, near Tess's former middle school. The house was neat, but the porch steps creaked ominously beneath her feet and the trim needed painting.

A small, white-haired woman answered the door. That is, she opened the door, the chain still on, and peered at Tess through the locked storm door.

"Yes?"

"Is Lawrence Purdy here, ma'am?"

"I am *Mrs.* Lawrence Purdy, yes."

Distinction noted. "Is your husband home, ma'am?"

"My husband has been dead for almost a year." She said this proudly, as some other women might announce their husbands' lodge affiliations, or military service.

To Tess, whose family was intertwined with bureaucracies at every level of government, it was not surprising that a bar license could be out of date. "So you now own the bar on Hollins Street, in your husband's place?"

"Mr. Purdy never owned a bar. He didn't even take spirits."

They had conducted this entire conversation through the storm door. And, although the December day was bright and sunny, the wind was kicking up, blowing right through Tess's all-weather coat. "Do you think we could continue this conversation inside, ma'am?" She had her billfold at the ready, and she flipped it open to her ID, anticipating Mrs. Purdy's next question. "I'm a private investigator. I'm looking for a young woman who I think might have some connection to the bar. Your husband's name was on the license as the owner."

Mrs. Lawrence Purdy shut the main door—didn't slam it, just shut it. At first, Tess thought their conversation must be over, but then she heard a scrabbling sound on the other side of the door and realized that the woman was fumbling at the chain, her hands slowed and stiffened by age. At last, the door opened, and Tess watched as Mrs. Purdy worked the latch on the storm door.

"It was not like Mr. Purdy to have secrets from me," the woman said at last, as she led Tess into the dim living room. The house was dark, even for a rowhouse that was not an end-of-group. It was dark even for an older woman's house, with heavy draperies over pull-down shades. A slight dent showed where Mrs. Purdy had been sitting in an easy chair when

Tess had knocked, but not what she had been doing. There was no book or newspaper nearby, no bag of knitting or sewing kit. Tess passed her hand over the old-fashioned television set. Cold to the touch.

Mrs. Purdy misinterpreted the gesture. "I don't see as well as I used to," she said. "Dust builds up."

She resumed her spot in the dent, while Tess sat carefully on the edge of an old-fashioned chair with a needlepoint seat. It looked fragile, barely equal to the task of supporting a real human's weight.

"It's possible," Tess said, "that the bar belonged to another Lawrence Purdy. Or that your husband owned it at one point, then sold it before he died."

"Was there money?"

"Money?"

"From the sale. If there was a sale, wouldn't there be money?"

"I was just . . . hypothesizing. I don't know what's true. I only know his name was listed on a license."

"Oh." The story no longer seemed of much interest to the woman. She was nicely dressed, Tess noticed, for sitting quietly in her own home, doing nothing. She had on a knit pant-suit, a style which Baltimore women of a certain generation still favored. And why not? The old-fashioned polyester was durable, washable, and the colors stayed bright. Very bright, in the case of Mrs. Lawrence Purdy, tropical orange, with a striped jersey beneath the boxy jacket. The fact is, someone could buy this outfit at one of the city's retro stores and, with the addition of the right shoes, look incredibly stylish. Not Tess, because she wasn't built to wear clothes that required irony. But someone thin, someone like

Whitney, could pull it off. The thought of Whitney running around in bright orange double knit made Tess's lips twitch.

"Something funny?" Mrs. Purdy asked.

"No. I admit I'm puzzled, though. You say your husband died a year ago."

"Of cancer." This, too, was said with pride, as if it were a singular achievement. "Before he went on disability, he worked for the state."

"In what capacity?"

The question confused Mrs. Purdy. "I don't know if he had a capacity," she said. "He just had a job."

"And, to your knowledge, he never owned a bar on Hollins?"

Mrs. Purdy shook her head. "He was sick a long time before he died. Longer than the doctors thought. I took care of him here at home, me and a nursing service that our health insurance paid for. It was hard."

Mrs. Purdy had a classic Baltimore accent, a slippery sound of such distinction that it had defeated some of the world's finest actors. "Hard" was "hahrd" in her prim mouth, while "home" was "hoooooohme." Tess tried not to smile.

"Is this his signature?" She handed Mrs. Purdy a copy of the license application.

"Yeah, but who's this?" Her stubby finger pointed at another name on the paperwork. Arnold Vasso.

"Just his lawyer."

"Not our lawyer. Our lawyer is Sonny Cohen. Mr. Purdy always said you had to have a Jew for a lawyer."

Theresa Esther Weinstein Monaghan could not

let that go by. "What about for your doctor and accountant?"

"Oh, well, with these medical plans today, who gets to pick your own doctor? Anyway, I don't know this guy. Never heard of him."

But Tess had, she realized. The name, Arnold Vasso, had slid past her because the lawyer hadn't seemed important. Such documents always had lawyers' signatures, but they were just hired guns. Tunnel vision again. But this lawyer was better known as one of the state's top lobbyists. It made no sense for him to be involved in such a low-rent transaction. Arnold Vasso was so out and out sleazy he had achieved a kind of purity: He did everything for a payoff. Not money necessarily, he got that from the clients who paid him $400 an hour to represent them in Annapolis, where he was one of the top earners. Still, Arnold Vasso never scratched someone's back without getting his own scratched twice.

"Did your husband ever mention Vasso?"

"I told you, I never heard of him. But I guess no one ever tells anyone everything."

"Let's hope not," Tess said absently. In her mind, she was already en route to Annapolis, where Arnold Vasso could be found any time the General Assembly was in session. Even a closed committee meeting, convened for no reason other than to railroad one of its own, would draw Vasso.

After all, vultures don't discriminate when it comes to carrion.

9

Cannibalism was considered a private affair in the state capitol, so the joint committee on ethics was allowed to meet behind closed doors. Reporters, with few other legislative stories to chase this time of year, lined the hall outside the hearing room, waiting for breaks in the action so they could try to gauge the progress of the hearings. Tess took her place next to them along the wall, wondering if Vasso had come and gone already. She could check out his office, in one of the pricey, refurbished town houses near State Circle, but everyone knew that Vasso was never in his office. A good lobbyist never was. The reporters, most of them strangers to her, looked at her curiously, trying to figure out why a civilian would be camping here. She recognized only one, Tom Stuckey, the slight Associated Press reporter who had been in Annapolis longer than any of the elected officials. Well into his fourth decade in the job, he was the closest thing the State House had to an institutional memory, yet he remained remarkably sane.

But she couldn't tell the *Beacon-Light* reporter from the *Washington Tribune* reporter, a sad state of affairs indeed. Tall, rangy men in their thirties, they both wore navy sports jackets, khaki pants, white shirts, and moderately interesting ties. On the other side of the hall, the television reporters were similarly indistinguishable, whether male or female—glossy of hair, vacant of eye.

"Hertel's only problem," one of the newspaper reporters was saying, "is that he's a white guy. They kicked out Larry Young, so they have to expel a white guy to make it all nice and even. Especially since Young was acquitted of the criminal charges."

"They already did that," the other print reporter objected. "Gerry Curran, remember? They were already even-steven. This isn't about affirmative action, this is about Dahlgren wanting to be a glory hog, trying to build up his name recognition for the congressional run."

"He's not going to run for the first," the other scoffed. "He likes sure things too much."

The two continued to argue, but it was a languid, no-stakes debate, its only purpose to pass the time. Tess smiled, remembering when a State House job had been her fervent ambition, back in her reporter days. Her bosses at the *Star* had worried her family was too connected to state politics. "It's not that you'd be too nice. You'd go the other way, to prove you weren't cutting anyone any slack," the state editor had told her. "Besides, you're young. You have all the time in the world." The *Star* folded less than a year later, making the whole discussion moot.

The truth was, she wouldn't have been much

good, although not for the reasons the editor had cited. Political coverage required schmoozing, a skill Tess lacked. Few females could do it. The senators and delegates feared, quite rightly, that women didn't play by the rules, that they wouldn't protect them from their own verbal slips. Once, Whitney had been at a hearing on proposed legislation intended to ensure financial support for battered women. A senator from the upper shore had asked, in his drawling country-boy accent: "Under this bill, could a boy go out on a Saturday night, pick up a gal, have sex with her, pop her in the eye, and then have to pay her support and give up his house? Doesn't seem fair, does it?"

The male reporters covering the story had let the comment go, but Whitney had written an editorial about it. The resulting fall-out had forced the chastened senator to work with the advocates to write a better bill, so it should have been a win-win scenario. But Whitney later told Tess that the senator was, on one level, right: The bill didn't distinguish between violence in ongoing relationships and one-night stands gone bad. His question had been insensitive, but his eye for the law unerring. Whitney had won a little skirmish, only to lose an important ally.

The double doors of the hearing room opened and the cluster of reporters perked up. The only person to emerge, however, was Adam Moss, the pretty-boy aide to Senator Dahlgren. The television reporters didn't appear to know who he was—after all, he wasn't in the face book of senators and delegates. But the print reporters trailed him down the hall, cajoling him in soft voices. Tess saw no reason not to tag along. It was a public building, she was the public.

"You'll have to ask the senator," Moss was saying, his lovely mouth curved in a slight yet superior smile. "I'm not at liberty to speak for the record. The senator will tell you when he thinks the committee will vote."

"Then what?"

"You remember the drill, how it worked with Senator Young. Although I think Senator Hertel, if recommended for expulsion, will see the wisdom in resigning, rather than forcing the General Assembly to kick him out."

"You're saying Hertel has agreed to resign?" Tess admired the reporters' technique. They kept their pads in their back pockets, as if this were still a casual conversation, but the tenor of the conversation had changed. The game was afoot.

"There's the senator," Moss said, pointing back to the double doors, through which a steady stream of people now poured. The television reporters had clustered around Dahlgren, lobbying frantically for the live shots they needed to do at noon. "Ask him, once the television reporters are through. Or ask Hertel."

A short, round man scurried by them, his head down. He looked pale and utterly confused, like a prize hog who had just been taken on a tour of the abattoir.

The print reporters loped down the hallway after him, leaving Tess and Moss alone.

"You're not a reporter," he said.

"I was."

He stared her down and she was the one who finally broke the gaze, if only because it was unnerving, gazing into that perfect face. Adam Moss's confidence was unseemly in one so young. Looking at him, Tess found herself thinking inexplicably of the Vermeer exhibit that had come to Washington a few years back. Adam Moss had the same golden light in his face.

"Do you find the legislative process so interesting, then?" he asked Tess.

"No," she responded truthfully. "I came here looking for Arnold Vasso."

"Are private detectives going to hire him to protect their interests next session? To ensure that people's private lives remain as open as possible, so they can do their dirty little jobs?"

She did not recall her job had been mentioned when they met at the Sour Beef dinner.

"Vasso's name cropped up in a file connected to my case. It's a long shot, but he may be able to help me. If I can find him."

Moss checked his watch. "Try Piccolo Roma, over on Main Street. Vasso has a standing reservation. And he's going to be eating alone today, because his lunch date is standing him up."

"Would that be you, or Senator Dahlgren?"

"You ask too many questions. You should learn how to take what is given to you, and leave gracefully."

"Sorry, I don't have your boarding school manners."

"But you could acquire them," Adam Moss said. "Anyone could, with just a little effort."

Arnold Vasso's regular table was in the window at Piccolo Roma, off to the side—visually prominent, but out of eavesdropping range.

"Mr. Vasso?" she asked, as if she wasn't sure it was him. The fact of a question in her voice would stop him, she figured. Arnie Vasso wanted it both ways, wanted to work behind the scenes and still be well-known as a fixer. He had an enviable kind of fame, she supposed. Unknown to the public at large, but a star within this tiny galaxy.

"Guilty," he said, his smile automatic, his hand shooting out and shaking hers, even though she had not offered it.

"I'm a private investigator in Baltimore. I'm trying to identify a girl who might be connected to a bar on Hollins Street—"

"I never touched her!" He threw his hands up in the air in mock innocence, still smiling.

"I guess that would be funny," Tess said, "if she weren't actually dead."

Vasso had the decency to look embarrassed. "I'm sorry, when you said identify, it didn't occur to me . . . I didn't think you meant . . ."

Tess waited, letting him twist and stammer a little longer.

"The bartender at Domenick's said he didn't recognize her from the sketch I have. I went to see the owner, only to find out he's been dead for almost a year. The widow never knew he had a bar.

And, although you were his lawyer at the license hearing, she never heard of you either."

Vasso looked around. A reflexive gesture for him. His eyes were probably always sliding from side to side, making sure no one more important had come into the immediate vicinity. Tess saw a bald man bent over a piece of paper several tables away, doodling on the back of a receipt with an old-fashioned fountain pen, but the restaurant was otherwise empty.

"Let me buy you lunch."

"This really won't take very long," Tess said.

"Better yet. Then we can talk about more interesting things. Look, I don't like to eat alone. Since the rules changed, and I'm not allowed to treat our public officials unless they declare it on their ethics forms, it's harder for me to find someone to keep me company. Please, have a seat." He gave her a shrewd look. "It doesn't hurt anyone to be seen with Arnold Vasso."

They were definitely being seen, and not just by the lunchtime crowd on Main Street, a mix of tourists and government workers. Tess had the feeling that the waiters were speculating on Vasso's business with a woman who clearly was not one of his monied clients. Given the mix of people that Annapolis attracted, it was an informal town, so her jeans and turtleneck sweater were not out of place here. Still, she felt odd, sitting across from Vasso in his expensive blue suit. Expensive, but tight.

"That guy over there?" Vasso asked out of the corner of his mouth.

"Yes," Tess said, glancing back at the bald man, who continued to doodle with small, tightly controlled strokes, as if he were working on an elaborate design.

"Meyer Hammersmith. You know him?"

"Know of him."

"I can't believe he's working for Kenny Dahlgren. Hammersmith's a classic limousine liberal, while Dahlgren's the kind of Democrat who'd be at home in the far right wing of the Republican party. Politics makes—"

"Strange bedfellows?" Tess offered.

"No. I was going to say politics makes me hungry. What are you having?"

They ordered, and Vasso seemed almost amused at the amount of food Tess required. In fact, now that she was sitting across from him, Vasso seemed amused by everything Tess said and did.

"Are you really a private investigator?" he asked.

"Yes. I got my license by apprenticing with a former policeman." A former policeman who did nothing more than lend his name, Keyes, to her business and take a small commission at month's end.

"Gun and badge and everything?"

"Not a badge," she corrected. "A license. But a gun. A thirty-eight Smith and Wesson."

"Do you have it with you right now?"

"Are you crazy?"

"Just curious. I don't think I've ever met one of you before. Except in divorce cases, you know. The usual surveillance thing. I hired one for my second divorce. I've been divorced four times. Now ask me how many times I've been married."

Tess was feeling agreeable. "How many times have you been married?"

"Three!" He smacked the edge of the table, pleased with himself. When Tess didn't laugh, he added helpfully. "It's a joke. My last marriage was so bad, I always say I divorced her twice, just to make sure."

"But that's not the one where you used the private detective."

"No, that one wasn't about cheating. It was just about hating each other's guts."

A fragment of a story came back to Tess, something about Vasso breaking into an ex-wife's house and leaving behind a large hog in gastric distress. By the time his wife returned late that evening, the carpeting throughout the first floor of the home was ruined. He had avoided criminal charges, though. His wife had ended up selling the house, at a loss, so Vasso was out a good chunk of the equity. But that hadn't been the point for him. Winning had been the point and, according to his internal scoreboard, Vasso had done just that.

Vasso was now looking intently at Tess's hands, which embarrassed her. Even facedown on the white tablecloth, so her rowers' calluses were hidden, they were not her best feature. As short as she kept her nails, they always looked a little ragged. She put them in her lap, beneath the tablecloth.

"You're not married," he said. "See? I could be a detective, too."

"Maybe I just don't wear a ring."

"Women always wear their wedding bands."

"Maybe the fifteen-karat diamond is loose in the setting and I dropped it off at a jewelry store to have it repaired."

"I don't see you with a big diamond." Vasso studied her. "Because I don't see you keeping company with the kind of men who can afford big diamonds. But you could, if you wanted to. In fact, maybe you'd be interested in meeting some of my clients during the session. Some of the ones who come in from out of town, don't know anybody in the area. I give a little party in January, you should drop by."

Was Vasso trying to pimp her? Tess decided not to think about it. "So, Lawrence Purdy, owner of Domenick's. Ring a bell?"

"Not really. I probably did it as a favor, you know. Stepped in, helped out a friend."

"Who?"

"I have a lot of friends. I have a lot of friends because I don't tell their business to just anyone who drops by. Lawmakers have to make disclosures, I don't. But it wasn't a big deal. A guy needed a license to run a bar, that's all. I went before the commission with him."

"So why doesn't his wife know about this, or you?"

"Look, liquor laws are crazy—"

"I know, my father is a city liquor board inspector."

Vasso gave her a hard look. "So you know. Law says you have to live in Baltimore City if you want to own a bar in Baltimore City. Is that fair? Is it even constitutional? Or maybe you had a little youthful indiscretion, ended up with a rap sheet. Law says you can't own a bar in that case, either. So there are owners, and there are owners of record. I'm sure the gentleman whose name appeared on the license was the owner of record."

"But he's dead."

"I guess the city liquor board doesn't stay on top of its paperwork. But you can ask your daddy all about that." Vasso squinted at her again. "Patrick Monaghan, right? Tight with Senator Ditter? Related somehow to old Donald Weinstein, as I recall."

"My mother's brother."

Vasso smiled knowingly. "He was good, your uncle. You know, with that kind of pedigree, I'd think you'd be down here. I could see you as a lawyer on one of the committees."

"That would require going to law school."

"Then you could be a lobbyist. Although I suppose you'd be one of the do-gooder kinds. Not much money in that, but with the right wardrobe, you could do all right."

"Sure, as long as I let the committee chairman grab my knee under the table." One of the state's most powerful delegates had done just that and lost the judgeship he so coveted, only to be re-elected to the General Assembly. "Do you think that's what the early Marylanders were thinking when they chose 'Womanly Words, Manly Deeds' as the state motto?"

"Here's the thing." Vasso had a piece of lettuce half in, half out his mouth, but he didn't seem to notice. "If some senator wanted to grab my dick before he voted for one of my bills, I'd say 'Help yourself.'"

"Here's the thing" Tess parroted back. "How often does that really happen?"

Vasso slurped in the leaf he had left dangling on his lip.

"I'm just saying women have some advantages, if

they want to tap into them. Some do. Believe me, some do."

"How am I going to find out who really owns that bar on Hollins Street?" Tess wasn't even sure why it seemed so important. The discrepancy in the bar's ownership didn't make it any more likely that Jane Doe had worked there. But it was a lie, and other people's lies made her crazy.

"Ask your daddy." The simple phrase sounded ugly, insinuating. "Not that he knows anything. But he should know enough to tell you to drop it."

Tess looked at Vasso, who was bent over his plate, dredging a large piece of foccacia through olive oil. From this angle, she could see the tanned bald spot at the crown of his head, see the way his neck oozed from his collar in tight little rolls. For the first time in her life, she knew how to use "oleaginous" in a sentence.

"I'm not really hungry," she announced.

"But you've got all this food coming."

"I'm sure you'll find a way to write it off. Or find some senator who's willing to eat my leftovers. Hey, maybe you'll get lucky and he'll grope you under the table."

Vasso's mask of bonhomie slipped just a little then. Without his fake smile in place, he looked shrewd and not a little scary.

"Maybe you don't want to be my friend, but you don't want to be my enemy, either. I'm a hired hand, I work for those who pay me and stay on the good side of those who can help me bring home the goodies for my clients. Someone asks me to go to a liquor board hearing, help a guy out, it's no skin off my butt. And it's not exactly a conspiracy, you know what I mean? If you were one of those little Columbia J-School grads that the *Blight* sends down here from time to time, I'd understand why you had such a big stick up your ass—"

"Your butt, my butt, could you work your way toward a different kind of imagery?"

"Hey, I gave you polite already. All I'm saying is your uncle worked for one of the biggest crooks that ever came through Annapolis, and that includes Spiro T. Agnew and Marvin Mandel. Your dad was appointed by Senator Ditter, who wasn't exactly racking up high scores on Common Cause's list of good legislators. So who are you to get all huffy and holier-than-thou about how business is done down here? Let me put it for you this way: It's none of your fucking business. I don't know from any dead girls, but I know you're going to be one sorry little girl if you don't leave some stuff alone. Just let it be. Now let's have some antipasto, talk about the weather, and why the Ravens suck."

"I'm sorry, I just don't have any appetite."

Vasso laughed, and grabbed another piece of bread from the basket. "See, it's all personal with you. I guess I was wrong. Even with the right clothes, you'd never make it down here."

Tess got up to leave, bumping the table with her hip so that a glass of ice water toppled into Vasso's lap.

"You stupid—"

"An accident," she said, and it was, except in the Freudian sense. "Don't take everything so *personally*."

10

Highways were too conducive to thinking, and Tess didn't want to be alone with her own thoughts. She bypassed 97, smooth and new, and took Route 2, the old Governor Ritchie Highway. It was a relief to concentrate on the stop-and-go traffic and potholes, rather than reflect on her almost-dinner with Arnie.

The thing was, he was right: She did take things too personally, and now she had made an enemy for no good reason. Even sleazeballs had their uses. Especially sleazeballs. Her mother's voice scolded inside her head, recounting the virtues of honey versus vinegar, vis-à-vis fly catching. Then Ritchie Highway rewarded her with its endless snarls and wretched drivers, and Tess managed to crawl outside of her own head and stay there for most of the way back to Baltimore.

Her brain kicked in again as she crossed the Patapsco on the Hanover Street Bridge. By force of habit, she glanced west first, toward the boat house. No one on the water at this time of day, this time of year. Then her eyes tracked east, toward the Key Bridge, Fort McHenry, and Locust Point.

Locust Point. What if Sukey had been lying about everything? Or not lying exactly, but so desperate to please that she had made up the little shred of conversation with Jane Doe, just to have something to say, just to please another grown-up. Tess decided to detour through Locust Point and question the girl again, ever so gently. She couldn't get back the time she had already dribbled away, but she could stop throwing good effort after bad. Why did she even care who owned Domenick's? The bar's screwed-up license didn't have anything to do with Jane Doe. Once again, she had mistaken momentum for progress.

So, find Sukey, put it down. The only problem was, Tess couldn't remember the girl's last name, or where she lived, and she didn't want to wander the streets of Locust Point, asking if anyone knew a round-cheeked girl named Sukey, given to fantastic tales.

The mini-mart at the gas station seemed a logical place to start.

"Try Latrobe Park," advised Brad the convenience store manager. "She got a new book out of the rack today, said she was going to read."

"A little raw to read outside, isn't it?"

"She always says to me she doesn't like to be inside unless she has to." Brad tapped his forehead. "She's odd, that girl. She'll tell you blue is orange, and not know the difference herself. She can't help it. When she's saying it, she believes it."

"Yeah, that's what I'm worried about."

Tess left her car and walked to the park. Locust Point was a strange mix of residential and industrial. It seemed amazing that people would have chosen to live cheek by jowl with marine terminals and manufacturing plants, but this had been the norm for Baltimore's lower-middle-class families after World War II. If there were still good jobs here, it might still be the norm. Today's kids, faced with so few opportunities, left these neighborhoods readily enough, but the older folks stayed on and on. Down at Wagner's Point, where the neighborhood was little more than a toxic dump, people had fought leaving even when the city announced a buyout.

It was home, they said. How can you put a price on my home?

Tess found the swings, but Sukey was nowhere in sight. She sat in one, imagining she could channel Jane Doe, that the young woman had left some trace of her identity on this rectangular piece of wood. The autopsy said she could be anywhere from her late teens to her early twenties, but Tess knew, just knew, she was on the younger edge of that range. Maybe seventeen, eighteen tops.

She dragged her toes in the groove beneath the seat, much too long-legged to make it go. And much too old, not that such a consideration would have stopped her. She remembered the wondrous discovery that a swing would move, would soar ever higher, through the simple pumping action of one's own legs. Her earliest physics lesson. Actually, her only physics lesson. At seventeen, informed that she was not required to take any more science classes under state law, Tess had decided she knew enough about light and particles and inertia.

At seventeen, she thought she knew enough about everything.

Seventeen. Junior year. She had a boyfriend, she was on the honor roll and the track team, and she could make calories disappear by sticking her finger down her throat. She ate whatever she wanted and never gained weight, thanks to her magic finger. Poor Billy Baker. She couldn't have been fun to kiss, given her hobby, but he never complained. They had met in his parents' basement rec room after school, stealing shots from the wet bar, messing around, solving a few algebra problems in their downtime. Latchkey kids. Funny to think about all the dire predictions people had made about such arrangements.

Funny to think how many of them had come true. And yet here she was, relatively unwarped, and Billy was a lawyer last she heard. Corporate, on a partner track with a staid firm, but with a little do-gooder vein, which he indulged through the board of some nonprofit. The thing was, every generation had done such things, but parents once had the good taste not to confront their children so directly. The more the behavior was dragged out into the open, the worse things seem to be. If Tess's parents, God forbid, had sat down with her and tried to have a Meaningful Chat about contraception and alcohol and marijuana—and how using the second two tended to compromise one's ability to focus on the first—she would have felt obligated to find other ways to rebel.

A string of popping sounds and a girl's high, thin wail jolted Tess out of Billy Baker's basement. Once, she might have mistaken the strangely hollow sound for gunfire, but Tess knew the kind of noises guns made. Yet the girl's cry was clearly a distressed one, almost involuntary. The sequence repeated itself—pop-pop-pop, the thin, keening wail.

Tess jumped to her feet, but the source of the noise was hard to track in the open park, where sound bounced erratically, competing with the chatter of seagulls and the traffic along Fort Avenue. Tess began to walk swiftly in what she hoped was the right direction. She climbed a small rise, so she was now looking toward the Patapsco River's Middle Branch. The day was cold, but bright, and the water appeared darker and bluer than it normally did, with diamond-bright froth on the breakers. Three boys ran into her line of vision, tossing something. She heard the pops again, saw long thin lines of smoke rising above their heads. Firecrackers.

Another scream, and there was Sukey, well ahead of the three boys, but steadily losing ground, perhaps because she was running with her hands clutched to her head, a paperback book pressed against one ear.

"Jesus, drop the book, Sukey," Tess muttered to herself, even as she found her own legs sprinting across the park. "You can always get another goddamn book."

She was running on an angle, trying to intersect the boys before they reached Sukey. She wished she had her gun, then damned the wish as irresponsible and callow. Waving one's gun in public was not effective problem solving. Besides, any one of these boys might have a gun, or another weapon.

The bottom line was, she had nothing.

Except her mouth. A stray piece of poetry flickered through her brain—*All I have is a voice*—and she found a banshee cry rising in her throat. If it startled her, it flabbergasted them. The boys stopped, taking in this strange apparition, this Amazon of the Patapsco, this Valkyrie, running toward them and screaming.

"What the fuck?" one asked, while the others merely gaped, open-mouthed, providing an excellent view of South Baltimore dentistry, or the lack thereof.

Now just a few feet from the boys, Tess slipped her backpack from her shoulder and began swinging it by the strap, screaming all the while and continuing to run straight toward them. She thought, to the extent that she was thinking at all: *They're going to stop in their tracks from sheer shock, and then run away, or they're going to attack me instead of Sukey, and she can run for help.*

Instead, they began screaming and laughing, pointing their fingers at her and chanting, presumably the same chant they had been using to torment Sukey.

"Fat pig, fat pig, fat pig, fat pig."

The words hurt, nonsensical as they were, or would have hurt if she hadn't been almost blind in her rage and fear. How could anyone tell children that only sticks and stones caused pain? Tess felt as if she were thirteen again, running from the neighbor boy, Hector Sperandeo. He had done far more harm with his taunts than with the lacrosse ball he slammed repeatedly into the small of her back. But she wasn't running away this time. These boys were thin and gawky, South Baltimore rednecks so malnourished from their junk food diets that they probably had rickets or scurvy. She could take them.

She saw the tallest boy pull another firecracker from the pocket of his denim jacket and light it with a Bic, holding it aloft with a snarky grin. Twirling her knapsack like a bolo, she swung it forward and landed it in his midsection, knocking him to the ground, the burning firecracker still clutched in his hand.

"Let it go, Noonie, let it go," one of the others screamed as the stunned boy tried to get his breath. "You'll lose a finger, the way Joey Piazza did."

The boy uncurled his fingers and the firecracker rolled away, but only a few inches. One of the other boys then kicked it with his foot, just before the fuse burned out. Set off in the grass, it seemed so innocuous. Pop-pop-pop, a small puff of smoke. Tess watched to make sure it didn't ignite the dry grass.

Noonie clambered to his feet, still breathing heavily. All three looked at Tess uncertainly. Logic must have told them she was no threat—she was alone, and a female at that, armed with nothing more than a knapsack.

Then again, what kind of adult acted this way? They smelled something crazy on her. They backed away, sneers in place, but just barely.

"Fat pig has a dyke friend," said the one she had knocked down. Noonie, the group's alpha male.

"Dyke," the others echoed. "Ugly dyke."

They turned and ran, Noonie calling back over his shoulder. "Too bad for you. You have to be a boy to get the fat pig to drop her pants. Not that any boy wants her."

Tess didn't bother to reply. The adrenaline was beginning to ebb from her body; she needed to concentrate so her legs wouldn't shake too visibly. When they were out of view, she turned and walked over to Sukey. Good thing she hadn't needed the girl to run for help. She was rooted to the spot, silent tears coursing down her bright red cheeks, her latest paperback novel held so tightly in one hand that it had started to bow.

"What was that about?" Tess asked, then realized what a stupid question it was. What was it ever about? It was about being an adolescent, about needing to make someone else as miserable as you were.

"They do it all the time," Sukey said, her voice casual and grown-up, as if she were trying to deny the tears on her face. "They steal firecrackers from the rail yard, throw them in people's yards and back porches. They don't like me because I won't . . . go with them. We're in the same class, and I do better 'n them. That's all."

Tess knew it wasn't close to all, but she let it go. "Let me walk you home."

"I don't need a babysitter." Sukey's usually sweet voice was fierce.

"Well I do. Walk me to my car?"

Those were terms Sukey could accept. They began walking. Tess noticed the girl was studying her in a sidelong glance, trying to match her stride for stride, although her legs were so much shorter.

"Were you scared?" Sukey asked, as they waited to cross Fort Avenue.

"Petrified. But I was angry, too. So angry I didn't have time to think. I shouldn't have hit the one boy, Noonie, but I couldn't think of anything else. It would serve me right if there was a cop on my doorstep tonight, ready to take me in for assault."

"It was self-defense," Sukey said. "And everyone knows Noonie is an asshole."

"Strangely, being an asshole is not considered a mitigating circumstance. Besides, it's not up to the cops to sort out whether something is self-defense. That's why it's a better idea not to resort to violence. Luckily"—Tess grinned—"they didn't get my name. What are they going to do, go to the district and swear out a complaint on Tall Dyke with Braid?"

Sukey laughed. A little shakily, but she laughed.

"Are you a dyke? I mean—a lesbian?"

"No. You know, someone calling you a name doesn't make you that name."

Sukey's voice was about as low as it could be and still be audible. "I'm fat. They say I'm a fat pig, and they're right."

It was a test, and Tess wasn't sure she could pass it. What did Sukey want her to say?

"Here's a break in the traffic. Let's run for it."

They scampered across the lanes. A pickup honked, some Baltimore grit boy, grinning stupidly at them.

"Wanna get high?" he called from his window.

"Not with you," Tess said, then regretted her flippancy. But if she had gone into some zero-tolerance swoon, Sukey would have fingered her for a hypocrite.

On the other side of the street, Sukey said: "See, he asked you, not me. Because I'm fat."

"He didn't ask *me*. He asked some girl he saw flouncing across the street. He asked an ass, he asked a pair of breasts. Not me, Sukey. My parts. When you're a female between the ages of fifteen and fifty, life is a chop shop and you're a Toyota Corolla."

Sukey would not be comforted. "Maybe they start with your parts and work up to seeing a whole you. It has to begin somewhere, somehow. But with me, all they see is a blob."

"You're not a blob."

"Aren't you going to tell me I have a pretty face, too?"

Tess stopped walking. She wanted to touch Sukey, to pat her arm or take her hand, but she sensed the girl would recoil at any physical contact, no matter how small.

"Do you brush your teeth every day?"

"Huh?"

"I asked if you brush your teeth every day."

"Of course I do, after every meal."

"Then you've looked in a mirror and you know you have a pretty face. I don't have to tell you that. No one can tell you that. Oh, they can tell you, but they can't make you believe it. And Sukey—"

She had the girl's full attention now.

"You should know this. Whatever you weigh,

whatever you look like, there are boys who are going to tell you that you're pretty. That you're beautiful, that they love you, that there's no one like you. And at the moment they say it, they mean it. Boys will say anything to get what they want. It's the moment after they have it that you have to worry about."

Sukey tossed her hair. "Boys. I don't need to go with *boys*. Lots of older guys ask me out."

This, Tess suspected, was not one of her lies. Or if it was, it wouldn't be for long.

"Yeah, I know about those men. Guys in their twenties who come around girls your age, who seem so mature and cool. They've got cars and spending money. They followed me home from school, too. But the thing about a twenty-five-year-old who goes after a fifteen-year-old is that he's already been turned down by a whole decade of women, you know what I mean? He just keeps moving down the ladder until he hits someone young enough and"—she had started to say "dumb enough" but stopped herself—"and naive enough to buy it."

Sukey looked unconvinced. Tess understood. As frightening as it was to have an older man call to you from his car, it was exciting, too, and pleasurable. Sukey wasn't ready to give up that tiny bit of fizz in her life, the consolation prize for the boys who threw firecrackers and called her names.

"What if it's true love?"

"What if?" Tess wanted to tell her it was almost never true love, but Sukey's books told her something different. It wasn't just paperback writers who believed in love, either. The guys themselves thought it was love, at least for a minute. Strange love, perverted love, twisted love, but always love. She decided to change the subject.

"You know, I was at the swings for a reason, Sukey. I was looking for you, thinking about Jane Doe. Are you sure she said what she said, about how she had been at a place that sounded like Domino's, and lived in the Sugar House?"

"It wasn't the swings."

Great, the story was already changing.

"You said—"

"We ended up at the swings. But I met her up at Fort McHenry, on a bench overlooking the water. A bench where I go to read. She said she was supposed to meet someone there. She said it was the only place in Baltimore they both knew, where she felt safe, because you can see so far in all directions, and no one can sneak up on you."

Tess tried not to show her exasperation. "Why didn't you tell me this before?"

"You made me nervous, you didn't give me time to tell it from beginning to end, and Brad was there, doubting every word I said. We walked down to the swings together. That's when she told me the stuff about the Sugar House, and a place like Domino's, only not the same. Don't you believe me?"

"Of course I believe you." *I believe you believe what you say, which makes you even harder to fathom.* "But I haven't been able to find any place quite like that. Not a place that knows Jane Doe. What did she look like?"

Maybe it hadn't even been Jane Doe, just another woman wandering through at the same time, and Sukey's imperfect memory had dressed her in Jane Doe's wardrobe.

Sukey thought about this. "She looked like a painting."

"A painting? Any particular one?"

"No, I mean—even though she was dirty and her hair was tucked up in this hat, you just wanted to look at her. For a moment, I thought she might be somebody famous, because she didn't look like anyone you see on the street, you know what I mean? It was like Julia Roberts, or some big movie star, but different. I just wanted to . . . look at her." Sukey blushed. "I mean, I'm not queer, I don't like girls, but she . . . I'd never seen anybody like her."

"So you walked down to the swings—"

"SUKEY BREWER." A woman's voice, shrill and frantic, cut through them like a hard wind. Tess saw Sukey at age forty, short and round beneath a towering brunette beehive, bustling toward them.

The older Sukey grabbed the girl by the elbow and swung her around. "I have been looking *everywhere* for you. I told you to come straight home this afternoon, because I needed you to watch your baby brother while I go shopping. You were supposed to be home an hour ago, not hanging out in the park, telling stories to whoever will listen."

The woman dragged Sukey away, with hardly a glance in Tess's direction. Red-faced Sukey stared at the pavement, mortified, not even bothering to say goodbye.

Then again, for an adolescent, the mere revelation

that one actually had parents, had emerged from another person's flesh, was enough to cause acute embarrassment.

Tess walked back to her car and wondered where Sukey had been going with her new version of the "I met Jane Doe" story. Then she wondered why she cared. As surely as Fort Avenue dead-ended at Fort McHenry, she had come to her own dead end. Nothing to do but turn the car around and go home.

11

Three hours later, Tess was still in a funk, a bleak, mean mood, as bad a mood as she could imagine. She went to the boxing gym in her neighborhood, where she used the weights and exercise equipment, but not even a good sweat could boil this defeated feeling out of her. Slumped at her desk, still in her workout clothes, she had an inspiration and began dialing Whitney's various numbers. The cell phone answered.

"What's up?" Whitney knew it was her, she had Caller ID, which Tess kept meaning to get her number blocked for. She considered telecommunications the modern-day arms race, and she believed in constant one-upmanship.

"Any chance of shooting tonight?"

"Absolutely." Whitney's certainty about everything was always refreshing. "My parents' place?"

"Well, we could go to my folks' place, but if you set up a target on a tenth of an acre in Ten Hills, the neighbors tend to get all squirrelly."

"Okay, meet me in an hour," Whitney said.

"The sun will be down by then."

"No problem. We'll just shoot from the glow of the headlamps. Night training, you know."

Whitney's family lived in the valley. Which valley, Tess had never been sure—Worthington or Greenspring, she got them confused. The more pressing question was valley of *what*. It wasn't as if there were mountain ranges in this part of Maryland, just rolling hills. But that's how it was known, this mix of huge old houses and farmland beyond the Baltimore Beltway. *The* Valley.

It was colder in the Valley, and darker and starrier. What's the difference between the rich and the rest of us? They have more money, and they have more stars in their night sky. Tess had known Whitney for more than a decade, but she had never gotten over feeling like a trespasser when she turned up the long drive to the Talbots' stone farmhouse, a place so simple and well preserved that even the most cloddish social climber could see it outranked the nearby mansions. And that was before one factored in the 50 acres of prime Baltimore County real estate, just screaming out to be turned into 100, maybe 150 "executive" homes. When Whitney wanted to torment her mother, she claimed she would do just that with her inheritance.

Whitney was full of shit. She loved her childhood home so much she wouldn't move out, preferring to live in a small guest house rather than find her own place in the city. She had sworn, upon returning from Japan, that she was looking for a condo or a rowhouse, but she was proving to be more particular than Goldilocks.

"I don't know why it's so hard," Whitney said a little plaintively. "All I want is an old place—but with the kitchen and systems updated, of course. A water view. And a neighborhood where there are things to do, but I don't want to worry about parking and congestion."

"How many real estate brokers have you gone through so far?" Tess asked her.

"Three. Four. No, just three," she said, pulling on a pair of boots in what she called the "great room" of the four-room guest house. Her mother had decorated it as if it were a hunting lodge, which suited Whitney. "The last one didn't call back when I left a message about a place I saw in Federal Hill. I think my photograph may be circulating through all the offices. Who cares? No one buys a house in December, anyway. It can wait until spring."

"What about your privacy?"

"Oh, they never come up here. If anything, I'm the one who's barging in on them all the time, borrowing things, stealing food."

"But they can see your house from their breakfast table. If you brought someone home—"

"Brought someone home? Tess, you know I'm a sexual camel. I can go *years* in-between. I had sex in Japan. I'm not due for a while."

"You had sex in Japan?" This was new. "You didn't tell me."

"It's not like it was the first time, I told you all about that." So she had, in detail so clinical and detatched that it would have put an eighteen-year-old Tess off men forever, if she hadn't ventured into the territory first. "And it wasn't love. Just the usual, ohmigod, I'm ten thousand miles from home, there go the last of my inhibitions kind of thing. The need for distance only seems to increase. First it was college, on the Eastern Shore. Then New Haven, or New York on the weekends. Now Japan. I may have to move to New Zealand to have any sex life at all."

"Was he Japanese?"

"One was."

"*One?*"

"There was an Englishman, too." She grabbed her fair hair and crammed it under a battered tweed hat, the kind that older, preppy men wore. "It was fun." She said this as if it was a rather sudden revelation. "I may even try it again sometime."

They drove in Whitney's new Suburban to a cleared field at the property's edge, where Whitney had already set up two cardboard torsos. With the car running, she left the headlamps on, so they were in a small circle of light.

"It's colder than I thought," Tess complained. "My hands are blocks of ice."

"Don't you dare wear gloves," Whitney decreed. "Gloves are for sissies."

Tess loaded the Smith & Wesson, then fired off her six rounds. She always lost count, and had to click at least once on the empty chamber to be sure the gun was empty. She hadn't practiced for a while, and her sighting was off. It was disgraceful, really, how easy it was for someone in Maryland to buy and keep a gun, with no proof of one's ability to use it.

"You're pulling to the right," Whitney observed. "My turn."

Whitney, whose first gun had been a hunting rifle, preferred a Berretta for target practice, a semiautomatic with a magazine. The first time Tess had seen a magazine, she had said: "Oh, like a Pez dispenser." Because she always had trouble loading Pez dispensers—the candy tended to snap out of the plastic column and spray all over the room—she had decided she was better off with the Smith & Wesson.

Whitney was faster than Tess, much more expert, and her shots were neatly clustered at the center of the torso.

"Want to try mine?" she asked.

Tess shook her head. "I've tried it. Between the recoil and the casings flying out the side, it makes me a nervous wreck."

She took aim again with her .38. Not as good as Whitney, but better.

"Now try it from leather," Whitney instructed.

"Oh really—"

"Come on. Cops have to do it. Why not you? You think everyone who takes a shot at you is going to send you an engraved invitation first, so you know to have your gun handy? I've got a holster in the Suburban, let's try it."

Tess was clumsy at this. The local gun ranges didn't allow members to draw from leather, so she had almost no experience.

"My turn," Whitney sang out, as if they were playing jacks.

The night was cold and still, sharp with the final, decadent smells of autumn. Tess had thought she couldn't last long in such cold. But her concentration made her forget everything, except the gun in her hand and the target ahead of her. There was room for nothing else in her head. Not for Ruthie, not for Jane Doe. Not for Sukey, not for bars whose licenses listed dead owners. Not for smarmy Arnie Vasso. There was only the night and her gun.

Before she knew it, two hours had passed.

"You know what? I think this is better than yoga. I never feel so relaxed and smoothed out as I do after shooting."

"I think it's better than sex," Whitney said. But she was grinning in the glow of her headlamps, mocking her own cool Wasp couth.

Back at the house, they cleaned their guns, washed their hands, built a fire in the stone fireplace, and fixed mugs of tea with brandy. Food was more problematic. Whitney's cupboards held only a very old package of Carr's water biscuits. The refrigerator was slightly better—a jar of olives and a bottle of vermouth. The freezer had a bottle of gin, a bottle of vodka, and a frozen dinner so encrusted with ice that Tess could make out only a few letters on the label.

"Spinach," Tess guessed. "Or maybe spanakopita. Whitney, what do you live on, anyway? My place isn't that well-stocked, either, but I'm a few steps from about a dozen restaurants, not to mention Kitty's kitchen. You can't even get a pizza delivered out here."

"I eat up there," she said, indicating her parents' house with her chin, not at all embarrassed. "Or I get carryout from Eddie's. Or Graul's, or Sutton Place. I've been living off Eddie's Caesar salad. And salmon cakes."

"Salmon cakes?" Tess had a vision of the prepared food at Eddie's, arrayed beneath the glass counter, the people lined up two to three deep. There was fried chicken and tenderloin and pasta and London broil and turkey meat loaf and whipped potatoes. There were sesame noodles and barbecue ribs and pork chops and couscous and red pepper hummus. "Why would anyone eat salmon cakes?"

"They're very good with saltines."

"How did someone with such bad taste in food ever develop an eating disorder?"

"It's not really about the food, as you well know. Which reminds me—I've been doing some thinking about your problem."

"My problem." Because Tess was lying on the floor, her mug of tea balanced on her stomach, she couldn't lift her head to look at Whitney. "What problem?"

"Your bulimic Jane Doe, remember? Did it occur to you that if she was far enough along to have significant tooth damage, she might have received treatment somewhere?"

"Sure." Actually, it hadn't. "But every hospital and psychiatric clinic in the country treats eating disorders now. It doesn't exactly narrow the search."

"True. But not every eating disorder clinic is known as the Sugar House."

Tess removed her mug from her belly and sat up. "What are you talking about?"

"The Sugar House. Didn't Jane Doe say that's where she'd been?"

"How do you know that?"

"You mentioned that part to me. Besides, as I told you, I can read upside down. And you were in the bathroom quite a while that evening."

Whitney preened, pleased with herself. She had removed the ridiculous tweed hat, but she still had on her ancient corduroys and a thick sweater with a border of flowers across the top. Flushed and fair, she could have been hugging a tree in one of those sorority girl composite photos.

"There's a clinic called the Sugar House?"

"Actually, its alumnae tend to call it the Wedding Cake for some reason. But a Wedding Cake could be a Sugar House as well, right? It's a small treatment facility on the Eastern Shore, very exclusive. The rates run $2,000 a day, and some girls stay there for up to a year."

Tess did the math in her head, if adding three zeros to 365 and doubling the figure can be described as doing math. "That's impossible. No one has $730,000 a year."

"Oh, some people do," Whitney assured her. "And I guess there are still some health plans out there that pay for such things, although I don't know any. It's for rich girls."

"Jane Doe wasn't a rich girl."

"So you keep insisting. But do you have a better lead?"

She didn't. But she also didn't want to encourage Whitney to think of herself as Tess's partner in this endeavor.

"How did you find this place, anyway?"

"I went through the licensing division of Health and Mental Hygiene and asked for a list of every residential treatment center that handled eating disorders. I noticed the one in Easton because it was near my parents' place on the shore, and because it had such an odd name. Persephone's Place. They were very secretive when I called, wouldn't give out any information and said they took referrals from only a few select doctors. I asked for the doctors' names, and the woman on the phone said it didn't matter, they were full for the foreseeable future. According to the licensing information, they can take up to twenty patients. That's almost $15 million a year, if the beds are staying full."

Tess would have whistled at that figure, if she could whistle. "They should call it the *Green* House. But if the woman on the phone is so uncooperative, how did you find out it's known as the Sugar House?"

"Talked to the competition, of course. You can't make the kind of money Persephone's Place is making without making other folks jealous. I found a slightly seedier place in Annapolis—it charges only $1,000 a day—and the director there was happy to tell me that Persephone's Place was overpriced, overhyped, and poorly named."

"Poorly named?"

"Would you name an eating disorder clinic after a girl who has to spend half the year in hell, just because she sucked on a few pomegranate seeds? The clinic may know how to treat eating disorders, but it sure doesn't know its Greek mythology."

"And you think our Jane Doe—" Tess winced; she didn't want to get into the habit of using "our" and "we" when discussing her work with Whitney. "You think Jane Doe, wandering through Latrobe Park, is really some little rich girl who bolted from the Sugar House?"

"I think it's something to check out," Whitney said. "I'm free tomorrow. Want to drive over to the shore together? We can spend the night at my folks' place, maybe even drive up to Chestertown, play at being returning alumnae."

"I promised to spend the day with Crow. He wants to see the Christmas garden at the Wise Avenue firehouse."

"Oh." Whitney frowned into her glass. "Well, we can do both can't we? Go to the stupid Christmas garden, and then head for the shore and find Persephone's Place. All three of us? I like him, you know. I feel badly I ever twitted you about him. He's the perfect postmodern boyfriend. Just try to keep the public displays of affection to a minimum."

Whitney's tone was light, as if the words she had spoken were of no consequence. But Tess knew her well enough to recognize an important concession. She liked Crow, she approved of him. And once Whitney liked someone, it was forever.

But all Tess said was: "You're very understanding, for a camel."

"Humph." Whitney got up and went to a butler's bar in a corner of the room, where she kept a collection of silver martini shakers and every kind of glass imaginable. Martini glasses; old-fashioned glasses; champagne flutes; wineglasses, white and red; gold-rimmed shot glasses. Tess had a feeling she was going to be spending the night on Whitney's sofa. It was either there or Baltimore County's northwest precinct, on DWI charges.

Whitney selected the largest shaker and two martini glasses. "I wonder," she said, heading for the kitchen, "if camels feel vaguely superior to those who need water all the time."

12

Twenty-four hours later, Tess and Whitney sat at the end of a winding, two-lane road that dead-ended at a locked gate. There was no sign identifying the property and a thick grove of pines hid whatever lay between them and the bay. But there was no doubt in Tess's mind that this must be Persephone's Place.

"The chain-link fence seems to run the length of the property," Whitney said. She was riding shotgun, as she had all day, while Crow and Esskay waited for them back at the Talbots' summerhouse. "And there's razor wire along the top, so it's not just for show."

"Is the fence for keeping people out, or keeping people in?"

"Both, I'd imagine."

They sat in the idling car, studying the fence. It had been a long day, longer than they had anticipated when they had crossed the Bay Bridge a little after lunchtime. Time had seemed elastic—they had browsed through the local stores, stopped at a bar in Easton for a Wild Goose ale, along with some french fries and onion rings. Tess loved the Eastern Shore in the off season—the bleached marsh grasses, the pale sky that yellowed at the edges, like an old photograph. She had liked showing everything to Crow, who was, as usual, enchanted. It had been easy to lose sight of why they were here at all.

But she had forgotten how short December days were, and they were suddenly two hours away from darkness when they began making inquiries about Persephone's Place, whose mailing address didn't show up on any of the maps of the shore counties. Tess had assumed it was the kind of open secret that locals would know, just the way they knew how to point one toward the various millionaires' mansions along the bay and its inlets.

But they were too clearly outsiders, and the Eastern Shore was not a place that embraced outsiders. It saw itself as separate from the rest of the state and still smarted from the time a sitting governor had referred to it as a shithouse. Four years at Washington College, on Tess's part, and a summerhouse that had been in her family for three generations, on Whitney's side of the ledger, didn't make them locals or earn anyone's trust.

The bartender, the hunters who lined the bar— they all looked through Tess when she tried to broach the topic. The hospital staff in Easton told Crow it would be a breach of confidentiality to discuss the clinic, which at least confirmed it was out there, somewhere. Finally, Whitney had thought of going to drugstores—not the quaint, old-fashioned family operations that could still be found in places like

Easton and Chestertown, but the new twenty-four-hour CVS and Rite Aids that had opened in strip malls along Route 50.

"You can't run a medical facility for rich bulimics without crossing paths with an all-night drugstore," Whitney had reasoned. "I'll go in first and scope it out. If there's a young woman behind the counter, we'll send Crow in. A man—you take it, Tess."

"Who died and made you führer?" Tess asked.

"I can't help it if I have natural leadership abilities," Whitney replied. She sauntered into the drugstore, returning a few minutes later with a copy of *Harper's* magazine and a twenty-ounce Mountain Dew. "The pharmacist on duty is a girl. Take it away, Crow."

"What do I say?" he asked. Asked Whitney, Tess noticed, not her.

"Tell her you need medical advice. You found an empty Ipecac bottle in your girlfriend's car, and you want to know if you should be worried. No—your sister's car, so she thinks you're in play. Let that lead to a general discussion of eating disorders and treatment. Tell her you've heard about this Persephone Place—"

"No—" Tess kneeled in the driver's seat so she could turn and face Crow. "Specific names make people a little more suspicious. Grope for the name, or get it wrong. She should feel she's leading the conversation."

Crow leaned forward and kissed her. "I find this enormously exciting. It's like our first date, when we broke into that lawyer's office together."

"That wasn't exactly a date," Tess felt compelled

to say, but Crow was already out of the car. Esskay, usually so unflappable, made a strange, high-pitched sound at the back of her throat. She was probably asking Crow to bring her back a candy bar, or a beef jerky strip. It had started to drizzle, and they watched him run across the parking lot, his step so light and carefree that he appeared to be skipping.

"Is it just me, or does he find everything enormously exciting?" Whitney asked at last.

"Pretty much everything," Tess conceded, trying not to sound smug. The way she brushed her teeth, the way she stretched in the morning. The way she read the newspaper, the way she scrubbed the sink. This, too, would pass, so why not enjoy it?

Crow being Crow, he stayed in the store for almost forty-five minutes and returned not only with the clinic's location, but a detailed biography of the young pharmacist, which he delivered in her patois and accent. "She has three kids, not a one of 'em over six years old, and her husband got laid off twice in the past two years, and he sure does hate to be stuck at home with them. But she sure as hell doesn't make as much money as you might think, and the hours are all erratic—"

"Fascinating," Whitney snapped. "Did she know about the clinic?"

"Oh sure, she told me that right away." He unfolded a piece of paper. "She even drew us a map. You were right, they've had some middle-of-the-night calls. Although she said it's primarily Sundays, when most of the other places are closed. The pharmacy doesn't deliver, but she'll drop stuff off at the end of her shift, for extra money."

The clinic proved to be considerably south of where they were, on the other side of the Talbot house in Oxford. They left Crow there to baby-sit Esskay—Tess didn't want to think what the dog might do, alone with Mrs. Talbot's family heirlooms—and found the unnamed, unmarked road just after sunset.

Now it was dark, Eastern Shore dark, the kind of complete night that never came to Baltimore. They could smell the bay, but couldn't see it. The only sound was Tess's Toyota, rough and asthmatic sounding, sending puffs of white-gray smoke into the night air. She wondered how far the sound traveled, how far it had to travel before it alerted someone to their location at the gate.

"What are you waiting for?" Whitney asked. "Don't you think you can talk your way in? You have a perfectly reasonable request—you're a private eye, you want to know if Jane Doe might have spent any time here."

"They made this place awfully hard to find," Tess said. "Besides, they probably treat famous people. Their antennae will go up if I say I'm a private investigator."

"You've got to try something," Whitney said, "Nothing ventured—"

No one killed. But no, she wasn't being fair to herself. No one had ever gotten killed because she asked a few questions. Well, almost no one.

They pulled the car up so they were even with a call box. Tess pushed the button marked Talk.

"Hello."

"Yes?" a voice replied quickly, almost too quickly, suggesting the possibility the car was already on a video monitor somewhere. Tess couldn't see a camera, but she kept her head inside the car just in case.

"Yes?" The voice repeated, now impatient. It was a woman's voice, and Tess had a feeling the clipped, mechanical tone was not the intercom's distortion.

"I'm a private investigator from Baltimore, working on a missing persons case." Better not to mention the dead part, at least not yet. "It's possible she once stayed here."

"Our client list is confidential," the voice told her. "We can't confirm or deny who stays here. It's a medical facility."

Time for the dead part. "This particular client is beyond caring about such things. She was murdered in Baltimore a year ago."

There was a series of clicks, as if a button was being depressed over and over again, while the voice mulled its response. "Murdered in Baltimore? One of our girls? I think not."

The voice made it sound as if Baltimore was simply too declassé a site in which to be murdered. Palm Beach, perhaps. San Francisco, certainly. Acapulco—*claro que si*. Baltimore, never.

"Still, I'd like to show you an artist's sketch, see if anyone can identify her."

"A sketch? Don't you have a name?"

"The name is what I'm trying to find. The girl was never identified. I thought I told you that."

Again, a series of clicks. "But the name is the very thing we could never give. I hope you understand."

"I *don't* understand. This girl is dead, she has no privacy or confidentiality left to protect. But I have a client who is very keen to identify her."

"Really? Who's your client?"

"Confidential," Tess said. She almost wished a video camera were trained on her, so it could see the gleam of her teeth as she smiled.

The voice was not amused. "One of our security guards is coming to the front gate. It's your choice to leave now, or make his acquaintance. Although you are on the other side of the fence, you're still trespassing. In fact, the final quarter mile of this road belongs to us. There's a sign advising you that you're entering private property—a large sign, with bright red letters on a white background, visible even at night. You were trespassing once you drove past it."

Tess saw a pair of headlamps approaching through the trees. She hesitated for a moment, then backed the Toyota onto the road and turned around. She went as slowly as she could, as if to say: I'm going because I want to, not because you're making me.

They were on the public portion of the road when Whitney finally spoke. It was only then that Tess realized how uncharacteristically quiet she had been.

"A private road. So that's why we couldn't find it on a map."

"One mystery solved at least."

They rode in silence until they found the highway back to Oxford. Then Whitney said: "Turn the radio on and see if we can find a forecast for tomorrow. We'll need to check the weather."

"Why, for God's sake?"

"Because a good sailor always checks the weather."

"I hardly think I want to spend a December afternoon sailing on the bay, all things considered. Let's just go back to Baltimore, or spend the day in Chestertown, like you said. I'll figure another way to make a run at Persephone's Place. I can always claim I'm an investigator for the Department of Health and Mental Hygiene."

"I wasn't thinking of taking the sailboat out. We'll use the motor boat, the old Boston Whaler my father keeps. One if by land and two if by sea, old buddy, and it's two lanterns aloft in the belfry arch tonight."

"What the hell are you talking about?"

"D-Day at P's Place. You're going to storm the beach tomorrow, and there's not a damn thing they can do about it."

13

The sun was barely up when Tess and Whitney left the Talbots' dock the next morning. They were in the Boston Whaler, a motorboat that Whitney's father had inexplicably christened the *Homswoggle II*. Or maybe there was an explanation, but Tess had decided a long time ago it wasn't worth pursuing. The Talbots specialized in detailed and obscure stories.

"I'm reasonably sure how to get there," Whitney said, frowning at the nautical chart in her lap, as they moved slowly away from the dock.

"Only reasonably sure?" Tess repeated, waving in what she hoped was a reassuring way to Crow and Esskay as they disappeared from view. "I'm not happy about staying behind," he had told her this morning, burrowed beneath the quilt on Mr. and Mrs. Talbot's bed. "Someone has to watch Esskay," Tess had countered. "Besides, you have your own part to play here, if everything goes as planned."

This now seemed like a very large "if."

Whitney was frowning at the great expanse of

water before them. Above, seen from the twin spans of the Bay Bridge, the Chesapeake wasn't quite so formidable. "I've figured out where we were last night and if I'm right, it backs to this inlet."

"And if you're wrong?"

"Then we abort. Besides, we won't do anything until we're close enough to see the place. You know the cover story."

"About that cover story—" Tess looked down at the gray water churning beneath them. She and Whitney had been out in this boat many times before, making fun of the mansions that the nouveau riche built along the bay's shores. But that had been on sultry July and August days. She could almost smell those days—the sun, the water, the breeze, the suntan lotion—on the life jacket she had donned.

There was no sun today, and the wind felt like tiny knives pricking at her face and neck.

"The life jacket. It's really just for show, right?"

"More or less. I'm going to try to get you close enough to wade in, but you never know. You're a strong swimmer, right?"

"Pretty strong. But they have to have a doctor on the premises, right? And he'll be bound by medical ethics to check me out for hypothermia."

"I hope so," Whitney said. "Then again, it would give us some leverage, wouldn't it? A licensed treatment center without a doctor on call. I'm sure that's not legal."

Tess didn't say anything, but she thought leverage was pretty inconsequential, once you were dead. She glanced at the sky. Overcast, yet Whitney swore there was no chance of rain. She wondered what would happen if she proposed switching places. But she could never find her way back to the Talbots', and she wasn't confident she could handle the boat alone, even under the best conditions.

Almost forty-five minutes had passed before Whitney steered the boat into a narrow channel, cut the motor, and let it drift. "Does this look like the place we saw last night?"

"We didn't see anything but chain link and razor wire last night," Tess said, squinting at the large white house sitting back from the shoreline. "But, yes, it could be the place."

It was a rambling white Victorian, with pink trim. Someone's old summerhouse, enlarged over the years in a random fashion. It clearly was no longer a vacation home. Persephone's Place, if this was it, had an antiseptic look, a marked indifference to its surroundings that bordered on hostility. There was no dock, for example, and the glassed-in porch at the rear of the house was small, curtains drawn against the winter light, as if no one there ever dared to watch a sunset. The grounds were bare and open, with the bald, raw look more common to a spanking-new development. Yet the tall, spindly pine trees at the property's edge had to be decades old. Even as it shut the rest of the world out, Tess realized, Persephone's Place denied privacy to its residents. There was no place to hide here, no spot where one would be out of view.

"It does look like a wedding cake," Whitney said. "Even the trim, all gingerbread and curlicues and rosettes. You feel you should be able to break off a piece and eat it. Just looking at it makes me vaguely nauseous, as if I'd been on a little binge."

"Hansel and Gretel," Tess said, remembering a scrap of Sukey's conversation with Jane Doe. "The Sugar House."

They were very close now, the boat passing under a tree whose branches bent so close to the water that they had to bow their heads. At the last minute, Whitney reached up and grabbed the branch, keeping the boat from drifting any closer to the fringe of sand and gravel that passed for a beach.

"Here," she said. "This is as close as I go. Remember I have to putt-putt out very slowly, so make sure I'm out of the inlet before you draw attention to yourself."

"Do I have to get all the way wet?" Tess asked. "Maybe if I just could climb out here, and walk along the shore—"

"All the way wet," Whitney said firmly. "You have to give the impression that you could keel over at any moment. It's the only thing that's going to keep them from sending you straight to the sheriff's office for trespassing. I hope."

Tess sighed and kneeled on the starboard side of the boat. She tried to remember the jump she had learned as a lifeguard at Hunting Hills Swim Club years ago, with legs spread open, so the head didn't submerge. At least, that had been the theory. She couldn't recall if anyone had ever done it successfully.

"Go," Whitney hissed. Did she actually lean over and push her? Tess had no memory of jumping, just a sensation of cold unlike anything she had ever known. Gasping for breath, dog-paddling because of the cumbersome life jacket, she made her way for shore. Behind her, she heard the *Hornswoggle II* pulling away, but she didn't look back. There was no going back. She'd rather crawl to shore than climb back into the boat and skim across the bay in her sodden clothes. She had dressed in thin layers, unwilling to sacrifice her suede jacket to this enterprise. In fact, she had raided Mr. Talbot's closet, availing herself of the soft, old fishing clothes he had amassed over years of coming to the shore. But they were shockingly heavy when wet, and her feet and hands already felt as if they were encased in concrete.

By the time Tess stumbled to the shore, she did not need particularly advanced acting skills to convey the fact that she was wet, chilled, and very glad to be alive.

Too bad there was no one there to appreciate her arrival. For it was not yet 7:30, according to her watch, and the Sugar House was quiet. She crawled slowly up the hill, finally pulling herself to her feet, and staggered toward the house.

It was only then that she noticed a girl looking at her from a small casement window on the third floor.

"Sister Anne, Sister Anne," Tess breathed, thinking of the Bluebeard legend. "What do you see? What *did* you see?"

She studied the girl's face, oddly dark and mottled, but that was probably a shadow from the lace curtain she had pushed aside. Her expression was

curiously impassive, as if there were nothing unusual about a soaking wet woman weaving up the
sloped lawn. Had she seen the boat enter the inlet,
watched Whitney push her from the boat? When
she caught Tess looking up at her, she quickly ducked
out of sight.

Or perhaps she had left the window because of
the two men in white uniforms rushing across the
lawn toward Tess.

"What are you doing here?" one man asked her.
"This is private property."

"I—capsized," Tess gasped, her teeth chattering
helpfully.

"Where's your boat?" the other asked.

"Sank. G-g-g-gone," she said, waving a hand toward the bay, trusting Whitney was long gone now,
not even a speck on the horizon. "All gone. Lucky
to be alive."

Now a woman came running across the lawn.
Tall, with a dancer's posture, she managed to look
elegant even in a chenille bathrobe and duck boots,
her auburn hair flat from sleep.

"Is it—" she looked at Tess. "How did she come
to be here?"

Tess remembered that clipped, mechanical voice
from the night before. Funny, it sounded even less
human in person.

"Boating accident," one of Tess's attendants said
helpfully. Although they had grabbed her roughly
at first, they were being gentle now, holding her
firmly as if they believed her legs might go out from
under her at any moment. Her limbs shook convulsively, Method acting at its finest.

Yet the woman evinced no sympathy for her.

"I suppose I'll have to find her some dry clothes," she said.

"Don't you think you should have Dr. Blount look at her as well?"

The woman sighed, overwhelmed by the imposition of this uninvited guest, with all her needs. "That, too," she said.

The two men helped Tess across the lawn, speaking over her head as if she were unconscious, or deaf.

"Funny, isn't it?" said the one on her left. "I mean, she's so heavy."

That hurt a little, and Tess wanted to explain her clothes had taken on quite a lot of water. But she decided someone who had just been rescued from the sea would not have the energy to object to such a personal comment.

"You mean because she's wet?" the other asked, puzzled.

"No, because she's *normal*. I'm so used to those little bits of bone and flesh we have around here."

"They're not all skinny." The two apparently were inveterate arguers, determined to disagree whenever possible. "Besides, she's a lot older."

"Some of the girls here look old."

"But they're not."

"Yeah, but—"

There was a short flight of steps at the side of the house, which led to a small porch. The two men, bickering all the while, expertly flipped Tess into a horizontal position, grabbed her at the armpits and knees, and carried her into the house. The woman waited impatiently inside.

"Take her into one of the examining rooms," she said. "I don't want the girls to see her. You know how any deviation from the routine upsets everything around here. Besides, I don't want them to think . . ." her voice trailed off as she led Tess's carriers through a narrow hallway. They turned and bumped her head, hard, on the molding along the wall.

"Oops, sorry," one said.

"Watch what you're doing."

"You know," she said, feeling very stupid. "I *can* walk."

No one seemed to hear her.

The examining room was not the kind of cold, clinical doctor's office to which Tess was accustomed. In fact, it seemed to strive for a kind of accidental air, as if the paper-covered table and cart of gleaming instruments had been introduced on a whim into what was otherwise a small sitting room. The walls were painted a warm cream color and heavy linen curtains hung in the one window. The doctor's chair was a wingback, the desk an old secretary. The patient's chair was a Victorian lady's chair, with a needlepoint back.

"I'll bring you dry clothes," the woman said. "I'd offer to wash yours, but I don't want to keep you here too long."

Don't want you to be here too long, Tess amended in her head.

No more than five minutes passed, but Tess found

she couldn't stop shivering, and she wondered if she might have put herself at serious risk. Finally, the woman returned with a Henley shirt, sweat pants, and clean white socks. She made no move to leave and Tess, feeling uncharacteristically modest, found herself stripping beneath the woman's gaze. Her flesh was gray-blue at the extremities, and everything continued to wobble.

"I'm sorry, I didn't mean to watch you," the woman said. "Force of habit."

This only served to make Tess feel considerably more nervous and exposed.

"I mean—" the woman had the grace to look mildly embarrassed. "I mean, I'm so used to checking the girls here."

"Of course." If Persephone's Place treated girls with eating disorders, the staff probably would watch them as closely as possible, looking for signs of weight loss.

"Of course?"

Tess remembered just in time that she was a stranded boater who had no idea where she was.

"I'm sorry, I'm so cold, I don't know what I'm saying."

Once she was dressed, the woman gave her a blanket to wrap around her legs. She then pulled out a blood pressure cuff and a thermometer, one of the horrible new ones that barely fit beneath the tongue. Tess hated having her blood pressure taken—she always felt as if her arm were going to explode—but she couldn't object with the thermometer in her mouth. The woman wrote down her findings, then leaned against the closed door.

"Now," she said, "where are you staying? I can have someone on staff take you there."

Tess, Crow, and Whitney had planned for this contingency. Good thing, as Tess's brain wasn't working well enough to improvise. "I'm visiting friends down near Oxford. I can call them and get directions—" she leaped to her feet, as if planning to find a phone. Then she quickly glanced around the room, checking the position of all sharp objects and hard corners, and faked what she thought was quite a realistic little faint. She had experienced the real thing just once, and had only a vague memory of what it had been like. Still, she thought she did it rather well.

Pulling the cart down with her was not part of the original plan, but it helped to sell it.

"Christ," the woman said impatiently, and fled from the room. Tess kept her eyes shut and counted to one hundred, then two hundred. Someone had come into the room and was watching her. She waited to feel hands at the pulse points on her wrists or neck, but nothing happened. She counted to three hundred. She could feel the heat of another body coming close to her, peering at her. She opened her eyes, expecting to see the Dr. Blount the woman had mentioned.

Instead, the face looming above hers was an odd little monkey-girl, a gaunt mask of flesh with fine hair covering the jawline.

"Jesus Christ," she said, crawling backward, crablike, from the apparition. *I'm supposed to be at a clinic*, she thought, *not on the fucking island of Dr. Moreau.*

But now she saw the figure in front of her was a

girl, a stick figure lost inside a billowing white night-gown. The girl from the window. Sister Anne, Sister Anne, what did you see?

"Lanugo," the girl said.

"I'm Tess."

The girl smiled at her, a smile so old and world-weary that some ancient relative must have left it to her in a will.

"Lanugo is why I have hair on my face. When you get thin enough, your body starts to grow hair, to keep you warm. You ought to see my back and arms." She sounded enormously proud of herself. "My name is Sarah Whit-taker."

"Hi, Sarah," Tess said. She was still lying on the floor.

"People have tried to get out of here before," Sarah said, "but no one has ever worked so hard to get in."

Shit, she had seen everything from her window. She could rat Tess out in a minute.

"I capsized," Tess said tentatively, waiting to see if Sarah was going to contradict her. Footsteps were coming toward them, several pairs.

"Okay," Sarah said, seating herself in the doctor's chair and picking up a stethoscope from the mess of instruments on the floor, placing it on her own bony chest. "You capsized."

The woman and the two orderlies came back through the door, accompanied by a man this time.

"Sarah—this room is off limits," the woman said, taking her by the wrist and leading her away. The doctor leaned over Tess and she caught his breath, a sour blast that he had tried to coat with some peppermint flavor. The orderlies were going through the pockets of her damp clothes, but there was nothing to be found. Crow had remembered that detail.

"You're fine," the doctor said, although he had done no more than take her pulse and peer into her eyes. His voice was much too loud, given how close he was to her. "Just fine. Now why don't you tell us where you need to be, and we'll get you there."

"I don't know my way around the shore that well. Could I call my boyfriend, and you could give him directions to come get me here? We're staying at his parents' house." This lie not only gave her more time at Persephone's Place, it also established that she would be missed if she didn't come home. Another one of Crow's ideas, and Tess was suddenly glad for it. She did not feel safe here. "While I'm waiting, I could have a cup of coffee or tea, maybe warm up a little."

The doctor grumbled, but handed her the phone from the wall, and let Tess punch in the numbers. Crow picked up at the other end, his voice almost bursting with excitement, now that his turn had arrived. Tess passed the receiver to the doctor for directions.

"You're over near Oxford?" the doctor asked. "Well, it shouldn't take you too long."

Shouldn't, but would. Crow wasn't going to be in any hurry to get to Persephone's Place. He was going to get lost, he was going to take wrong turns. He had it all mapped out. The woman led Tess to an empty dining room. After a few minutes, she brought her a cup of coffee.

"Do you have milk?" Tess asked. The woman looked blank. "For my coffee? Half-and-half would be better still."

"Of course. Do you . . . do you want something to eat as well?"

"Please. Toast, an English muffin, a bagel. Anything bready to help my stomach settle down from all the bay water I swallowed."

The two orderlies came into the dining room. They seemed proprietary of her somehow, like boys who had found a stray dog and were trying to convince their parents to allow them to keep it as a pet.

"Is this your home?" she asked.

The question made them smile and shake their heads, but they didn't say anything.

"Then what is this place? A bed-and-breakfast?"

"Something like that." It was the woman who answered, returning with a china cream pitcher and toasted raisin bread. Tess could tell just by looking in the pitcher that it was skim milk, not even two percent, much less half-and-half. Yet the butter appeared to be real butter. "More of a school. We offer individually developed curricula for young women who can't thrive in more traditional settings, for various reasons."

"How many students do you have? Or should I say patients?"

"Clients." She was well-rehearsed. "Just twelve right now."

"The girl I saw, when I regained consciousness— the one who said her name was Sarah—she told me she had something called lanugo. What's that?"

The woman gave Tess her version of a warm, fond smile. She still wore her robe, but she had bedroom slippers on now and had found a chance to comb her hair back into a smooth knot. "You must have been hallucinating. Our girls sleep in on Sunday mornings. Would you like more coffee? Carl, Wally—aren't you on duty?"

The orderlies, looking sheepish, left the dining room, as did the woman. Tess, left alone, wondered what to do next. She was clearly in the right place, but how did she segue to Jane Doe, without blowing her cover?

This was something she, Whitney, and Crow had not planned out in advance. They had focused their energies on getting her in, and keeping her there for as long as possible. Now inside, it was up to Tess to figure out how to get people to talk to her.

"Hey, where are my clothes?" she called out. No answer. Good, that was license to get them on her own. She walked back to the examining room, where she found her sodden clothes in a plastic bag, but little else. The room had been put back in order, the instruments taken away. Back in the hallway, she kept going in the other direction. A door was ajar, and she glanced inside, noting a bank of computers, almost gleaming with newness, their monitors blank. She kept walking until she came to the kitchen, a cold place full of metal appliances and surfaces, sterile as an operating room. There was a rear stairway here and she began to climb it, as quietly as possible. She peeked into the second floor, which looked like a fairly nice hotel hallway, with pale blue carpeting and matching floral wall-paper. Remembering Sarah's face at the casement window, she kept going. The third floor was a converted attic, with sloping eaves and only two doors along its hallway. The bay would be to her left, Tess judged, and she knocked softly on that door, then opened it.

Sarah Whittaker, seated in a black Boston rocker, still in her white, high-necked gown, could have been an illustration from some nineteenth-century children's book. Except for the hair on her face, of course.

"Where am I?" Tess asked her.

"Persephone's Place."

"Does it have another name?"

"I call it hell on earth, but I've heard other people call it lots of things."

"The Wedding Cake, the Gingerbread House?"

"Yes."

"The Sugar House?"

Her features puckered. Hers was such a small face, so shrunken and gaunt, her expressions were tiny, too. "That's a new one. But I like it. The Sugar House."

"Is it a school, as the woman told me, or a clinic?"

"Both." Sarah hugged herself, not as if she were cold, but as if she were enjoying a private joke at someone's expense. "And you've got everyone *discombobulated*. You've disrupted the schedule. Breakfast is at eight on Sundays, but they can't bring us out of our rooms until you're gone. They could bring us trays, but that's antithetical to the treatment. We have to learn to eat like normal people, which means letting other people watch. The compulsives, especially. We have two of those right now. Bulimia. How *tacky*. You'd never catch me sticking my finger down my throat."

"You're anorexic."

The girl wasn't impressed by Tess's insight. "That's easy enough to see, isn't it?"

"How long have you been here?"

"Three months."

"I'm looking for a girl who might have been here over a year ago. Has anyone been here that long?"

"Doubtful. Three months is the average, in fact." Sarah got out of the rocking chair and walked over to the window where she had been keeping vigil when Tess first saw her. "I'm considered quite pathological. Much worse than my cousin. She came home *cured*." She permitted herself a tiny giggle. "Like bacon."

"When was this?"

"Last summer."

Which could be right, if Jane Doe was here in the months just before she died. A long shot, but it was all she had, all she was going to get.

"And your cousin's name is—"

"Devon, Devon Whittaker."

"Where's your cousin now?"

Before she could answer, the auburn-haired housemother yanked open the door.

"This is not a public area, miss." Her mechanical voice buzzed with anger. "I'm sorry, but you must not wander around the premises. It's upsetting to our girls. Please come back downstairs until your friend arrives."

"Miss Hollinger—" Miss Hollinger. The name was for Tess's benefit, and she dutifully filed it away. Sarah kept her face toward the window, but her voice was sweet and plaintive. "It's almost Christmas. Do you think I'll be allowed to go home? The family is going to Guadeloupe soon, as we do every year. All the cousins, I mean, even Devon. She made the honor roll at Penn, did I tell you that? Everyone's so proud of her."

"Well, that depends on you, doesn't it, Sarah? If you make the right choices, the kind of choices Devon made last year, you'll have a lovely Christmas."

Sarah did not turn around, did not acknowledge in any way the help she had given Tess, just stood in her window, looking across the bay. The light shown through her white gown, and Tess could see the dark hair along her arms and back. Lanugo. Sister Anne and Bluebeard, all rolled into one. She hoped this frail child would make the right choices, the ones that would allow her to leave this place in a stronger, sturdier body.

But she feared spring might never come for this particular Persephone.

14

Only Whitney professed to be surprised when Tess began developing the symptoms of a raging head cold within hours of her impromptu bay swim.

"Getting your head wet in cold weather doesn't cause colds," Whitney proclaimed the next morning. Proclaimed, it should be noted, over the phone, intent on keeping herself at a safe distance from whatever germ Tess carried. "That's the oldest of old wives' tales."

"Yes, but a wet head, wet feet, and wet internal organs when the temperature is in the forties—don't you think that could make one the teensiest bit ill?" Tess was irritated, and frustrated. How could her body let her down when she was so close to finding Jane Doe?

"All in your head," Whitney insisted.

"Of course it's in my head. It's a *head* cold."

"Get lots of rest," Whitney said, as if this were a revolutionary piece of advice. "And eat a lot. Feed a cold, starve a fever."

"I'm pretty sure it's the exact opposite."

"Okay, then do *that*."

As it happened, Tess did neither. She ate as she always ate—heartily, happily—while discovering that technology made it almost too easy to work from one's sickbed. Crow, who was temping in Kitty's store for the holiday rush, left her Monday morning with a mug of cocoa and her laptop. By 10:30 A.M., she had exhausted the garden-variety directories in trying to track down a current phone number for Devon Whittaker. She had several numbers for other Philadelphia Whittakers, but she was too stuffed up to bluff her way through phone calls to people who might or might not be relatives. They'd think they were getting obscene phone calls from Donald Duck.

Tess then searched the online archives of the Philadelphia papers, looking for the name Whittaker. The surname was there, it was all over the place, in the benign, bland bits that made up the society pages, but she couldn't find it attached to Devon. By lunchtime—a scorched but well-intentioned grilled cheese from Kitty—she conceded defeat and made a snuffly call for help to Dorie Starnes, one of the robber barons of the Information Highway. There was no freight that Dorie couldn't highjack, but she charged dearly for her black-market goods, especially if speed was required.

A restless Tess had progressed from bed to sofa when Dorie arrived the next day. Her cold was now mostly in her chest, leaving her with a wet, slushy cough and a wonderfully husky, Lauren Bacall voice.

"I wish I could lie around on the sofa when I was sick," Dorie said.

"You can," Tess rasped. "You're the one who works for a corporation, the one with paid sick leave and medical. I'm self-employed, and pay for my own health insurance."

"I run my own business, too."

"From your office at the *Beacon-Light*."

Dorie shrugged. She reminded Tess of a robin, with her round, full torso and ruffled, cowlicky hair. "They get what they pay for."

Esskay wandered out of the bedroom and began circling excitedly at the sight of a guest. Dorie, who wasn't much taller than she was wide, held her ground, putting out a tentative hand. "Nice doggie," she said, fingers tapping the top of Esskay's skull the way someone else might dribble a basketball. Luckily, Esskay wasn't fussy about human contact, as long as she got some. She returned contentedly to bed. It had disrupted Esskay's routine, having Tess at home during the day. When left alone in the apartment, Esskay was used to moving freely from bed to sofa and back again, and now here was Tess taking up her space, throwing little bits of tissue around.

"Ready?" Dorie asked. Tess was one of the few customers that Dorie didn't exact payment from before she spoke. Suspicious of computers, hostile toward paper, she worked from her own memory, which she claimed was impeccable. "Devon Whittaker is a student at Penn—"

"I knew that. I told you that."

Dorie didn't acknowledge Tess had spoken. "—but

she lives off campus, in an apartment. She's nineteen years old and her phone number is unlisted."

"But you got it."

"I couldn't charge these prices if I didn't." She recited it, wincing slightly when Tess wrote it down.

Tess didn't ask how Dorie had gotten the number. Don't ask–don't tell was the cornerstore of their working relationship. She suspected Dorie used the *Beacon-Light*'s commercial side to run credit checks on people, which was definitely illegal. Besides, even if Dorie's methods were within the law, Tess wasn't sure she wanted to know all her secrets. She liked Dorie's magic act aura.

"Finding this girl was actually much simpler than most of the stuff you bring my way," Dorie said. "But then, she's only nineteen. It's hard to leave too many electronic footprints at that age. How many addresses can you have?"

Something in Dorie's voice tripped Tess's paranoia switch. "Have you ever run my vitals through your programs?"

"You're not much of a challenge. Baltimore is full of people who know your business, and how to find you."

"That's not a no," Tess pointed out.

"It's not a yes, either."

"What's my middle name?"

Dorie struggled for a moment, torn between her natural inclination toward secrecy and wanting to show off.

"Esther," she said. "But anyone could know that."

"Last address?"

"One-oh-six West University Parkway."

"Weight on my driver's license?"

"A lie. A flat-out lie."

What could Tess say? It was.

The next morning, her head clear, her voice still pleasingly husky, Tess took the train to Philadelphia. She had not called Devon Whittaker first. She almost never called first. No one wanted to hear a stranger's voice on the phone. Strangers never brought you good news. And the phone was so easy to slam down, to avoid, to screen through an answering machine or Caller ID. Doors were bigger, harder to shut, and most had only a fisheye to give you a distorted view of the visitor on the other side. As long as Tess wasn't holding a copy of *The Watchtower*, she was pretty sure she could gain entrance to anyone's home.

Crow dropped her off at Baltimore's Penn Station, embracing her as if they were to be parted for weeks, or even months. He was romantic, in the best sense of the word, and she was beginning to accept that his love for her was not a passing phase.

"Do good," he told her. "Be safe."

"It's just Philadelphia. You know what Philadelphia is? It's Baltimore, only bigger."

"Call me as soon as you know if you found her. I feel as if I have a stake in this, too." He kissed her again. They were drawing a small crowd.

She suspected he was inspired, in part, by the old-fashioned train station. It was small, with only six gates. But the ceilings soared to wonderfully wasteful heights, and high-back wooden benches lined the walls. Tess much preferred it to Washington's Union

Station, which had been turned into a mall, with glossy restaurants and movie theaters. Here, it was possible to imagine Ingrid Bergman slithering by in a trenchcoat, spies exchanging briefcases, lovers meeting surreptitiously.

The tiles on the tote board swirled and clacked, the "All aboard" sounded. Tess settled into a window seat on the east side of the train, because this provided the best views. She was the only person she knew who considered the trip scenic. But then, Tess had always been intrigued by the rear view of things, which she found truer, full of unexpected glimpses into people's real lives. She was fascinated by what people did when they thought no one was watching. Not sex per se—she had no interest in spying on people in bed, unless someone was paying her to do it. Even then, she held her nose. No, she liked to watch people hanging laundry and scratching themselves, having desultory arguments with children and spouses. Everyone wore masks these days, and they seldom slipped. The extreme was the reality-based television shows, where people created meta versions of themselves by trying to act in a way they thought was natural.

The train was already crossing the Susquehanna River. Wilmington and Philadelphia were only minutes beyond. Tess hunkered down with a map, trying to figure out if Devon's apartment was near the train station, or if she would have to take a cab.

She had a photo of her, from last year's Penn freshman face book. Again, she hadn't questioned Dorie's methods, had just paid up. It wasn't the best reproduction, a printout from a scanned photo. Devon Whittaker appeared pretty, in a dull, flat way, but also looked much older than the average college freshman.

It was past eleven when Tess found Devon's apartment building. She tried the buzzer in the foyer, but no one answered. She was in luck, there was an open square across the street, with a bench that afforded an unobstructed view of the building's front door. It was cold for outdoor surveillance and she was downwind of a cheesesteak vendor, which made her ravenous. The long, gentle fall had lulled her into complacency; she hadn't dressed warmly enough. She could get a cup of coffee, but that would present another problem common to surveillance: the bathroom issue. Tess was on mailing lists for catalogs offering all sorts of interesting solutions to this problem, but many of them were anatomically unsuitable for her. She subscribed to mind over matter. So far, it was working.

Mind over matter was still working for her, barely, when Devon Whittaker walked right by her less than two hours later. She even stopped in front of Tess, inhaled the steam blowing from the cheesesteak cart, then made a face as if she found it noxious. Tess caught up with her just outside the door to her apartment house.

"Devon Whittaker?" Nothing like a person's name to get his or her attention.

"Yes?" She responded as anyone would, with the usual mix of suspicion and puzzlement. Who would have your name except a process server or the

Publishers Clearinghouse Prize Patrol? Her key was out, she was ready to slide past Tess and into the apartment.

"I'm Tess Monaghan. I have a message for you from Sarah, your cousin."

This interested her even more than her own name. "Is she okay? Has anything happened to her?"

"Could we talk inside? I'm chilled to the bone."

Devon fumbled with the door, which had a balky lock, and walked up one flight to an apartment overlooking the park where Tess had been keeping her vigil. It was not a typical college girl's apartment, furnished with cast-offs and the landlord's things. Nor was it a pampered darling's lair. The living room was clean and simple, with the kind of basic IKEA pieces one expected from young newlyweds. A dining area had been set up at the far end, and the kitchen was just beyond, separated by a counter. There were three closed doors off the hallway.

"Nice place," Tess said. "Do you have a roommate?"

"No—I mean, yes, I do live with someone. You said you had news of Sarah. Is she okay?"

"As okay as anyone there, I guess. I don't know what she looked like when she went in."

Devon had bypassed the living room and seated herself at the dining room table, as if she wanted something large and substantial between her and the world. "She was on the verge of going into a coma."

"I guess she's better, then."

"What did she want to tell me?"

"Actually—" how Tess hated that word, how she disliked the part of her job where she admitted to the half-truths already told, the deceptions and manipulations already employed. "She simply told me where to find you. I needed to talk to someone who was at Persephone's a year ago, because there's a possibility that a girl who's now missing was there at the same time. Sarah told me you were there then."

"She's missing, but you don't know where she was to begin with?"

"It's complicated," Tess said. She pulled the artist's rendering of Jane Doe from her knapsack. Devon studied it intently, frowning.

"This face is a little too round," she said at last, "and her hair was much fuller, very thick and dark. But it could be Gwen Schiller."

Gwen Schiller. Tess tested the name, and it felt right. *Gwen Schiller*. She took the sketch back from Devon, looked at it. Gwen Schiller, Gwen Schiller, Gwen Schiller.

"I suppose her father hired you?" Devon asked. "About time."

"No. Until you told me her name, I didn't know who she was. Who's her father?"

"Dick Schiller, of course."

Tess needed a second, maybe two. "Dick Schiller, the guy who invented the e-mail software that Microsoft bought out? He's practically a billionaire."

"On paper," Devon said, as if her family's mere millions were in something else, like gold bullion. Or blue blood. "But if Dick Schiller didn't hire you, who did?"

Her killer's sister. But it wasn't time to say that, not just yet. "You and Gwen knew each other at Persephone's Place?"

"We overlapped there by several weeks last year, yes." Devon had a natural wariness about her, she never seemed to relax.

"Who left first?"

"I did. I was discharged just before Labor Day, so I could start classes up here."

"When did Gwen"—the name was still a wonderful novelty in her mouth—"leave the clinic?"

Unconsciously, Devon combed her blond hair toward her face, as if to cover it. She bore a superficial resemblance to Whitney, with her thin body and pale hair. But where everything about Whitney was sharp and bright, this girl seemed soft and dull.

"They didn't tell you?"

"They wouldn't tell me anything. I met Sarah . . . by accident." True enough. "She sent me to you."

Devon stood up abruptly, paced toward the kitchen and back, almost as if she were lost. "The thing is, you just have to make it to your eighteenth birthday. I kept telling Gwen that. Four months. Four months, and she'd have been able to check herself out, no matter what her dad and stepmother said."

"How's that?"

"When you're eighteen, and you've been involuntarily committed—and almost everyone at Persephone's is there involuntarily—you can petition the court, argue you're healthy enough to leave, no longer a threat to yourself. The people at the clinic let you go if you even threaten to do it, as long as you can get up and walk around. They don't like to go into court, and they have a waiting list, so the beds never go empty. Gwen was going to be eighteen on January thirty-first. But she couldn't wait, so she bolted."

"Ran away."

"Yes, a few weeks after I left. Persephone's kept it quiet, I guess. It wouldn't do much for their reputation if it were known that the daughter of one of their richest, best-known clients had run away. Where is Gwen now, faking amnesia in some hospital, hoping her father will interrupt his round-the-world honeymoon and pay some attention to her?"

Tess walked over to the window, which overlooked the park where she had sat staring at the cheesesteak vendor and his stand. She had a name; Jane Doe would become Gwen Schiller within hours of her return to Baltimore. Her remains could be exhumed from the pauper's grave in Crownsville, her case could be truly closed. But knowing who she was only made it more unfathomable that she could have gone unidentified for so long.

"Devon, I'm sorry to be the one to tell you this, but Gwen Schiller is dead. She was murdered in Baltimore last November sixteenth, probably not long after she ran away from Persephone's. The man who killed her confessed to the crime, but she didn't have any identification on her."

"Gwen's dead?" Devon's reactions seemed a beat off. As thin as her face was, emotions took a long time reaching it. "You said last month, though?"

"No, November sixteenth a year ago."

"It couldn't be . . . it can't." Devon began pacing again, as if lost in her own apartment. "Gwen was so strong, so defiant. She was going to get well out of spite. She could take care of herself. She's the last person I'd imagine dying."

The implication was that there were so many other girls Devon could imagine dying.

"What else can you tell me about her?"

"Gwen?" Devon hesitated. "The first word you think of is beautiful. That sketch doesn't capture it. Even sick, she was beautiful. Strong-willed, too. We all were, but she was the toughest by far. She didn't like what money had done to her family. And it didn't help that her mother was dead, and her dad had this trophy wife who hated her guts."

"An evil stepmother." Tess was remembering that it was a stepmother who left Hansel and Gretel in the woods, where they stumbled on their own version of the Sugar House. *Some girls call it the cake, but to me, it's the gingerbread house, and I just can't get that witch in the oven,* Gwen had told Sukey.

"Are there other girls who might remember her, who she might have tried to contact once she ran away?"

"Not really. Faye Maffley was there that year, and nowhere close to going home when I left. She was still telling doctors she had rearranged her DNA by spending two hours a day on the Nordic-Track. Patrice Lewison was at the other end of the range, she's probably been out almost as long as I have. But it's not boarding school. You don't go there to make friends. You go there to get out."

"By getting better."

"Or worse. If you get sick enough, if you get so thin your health is compromised, they'll take you out by helicopter to one of the Baltimore hospitals. Didn't you see the helicopter landing pad when you were there?"

No, Tess had missed that.

A key scraped the lock, and the door opened. A tall, broad-shouldered woman who looked vaguely Scandinavian crossed the threshold. She carried a bag of groceries in her sturdy arms.

"Devon—you have a friend?" It was a cautious question, deferential, asked in slightly stilted English.

"A friend of a friend," Devon replied swiftly. Tess didn't mind letting this woman know who she was, but she realized secrecy was a natural impulse for Devon. There was a furtiveness about the girl, an inevitable byproduct of eating disorders.

"Is she staying for lunch?"

"No," Devon said firmly.

"I just came to ask Devon if she knew where I could find an old friend. She helped me out quite a bit."

"I see." The woman went into the kitchen and began putting away the groceries. "What do you wish for lunch today, Devon?"

Devon put her fingers to her mouth, began chewing on her nails. "I ate on campus," she began.

"Devon." The woman's voice was sharp, but friendly, as if this were all a great joke, a daily ritual.

"Soup?" Devon spoke as if this were a quiz and she might provide the right answer. "With crackers."

"A soup with things in it, I think," her room-mate said. "Not tomato or broth, but chicken with noodles or beef with vegetables."

"Okay." She sighed. "Okay. Let me walk Miss Monaghan to the door, and I'll come back and eat my soup."

She accompanied Tess not just to the front door, but to the apartment's entrance, and out to the side-walk. "I'm sorry about Gwen. I really am. I probably should have cried or something, but nothing in my body works right anymore, not even my emotions. I'm too shocked to cry."

"You didn't know her that well," Tess offered.

"No, but—I can't believe she's been dead so long, and I didn't know it. That the world didn't know it. You'd think it would be national news, Dick Schiller's daughter being killed. You sure it was November sixteenth last year?"

"Positive," Tess said.

"It seems like such a long time ago. Hilde up-stairs, that woman you just met, she moved in with me a year ago. She's another one of my conditions, you see. My parents didn't want me to live on cam-pus because college girls get so weird about food. But they didn't trust me to be on my own. So they pay that Valkyrie to live with me, watch my food intake. Nineteen, with a governess. It's quite a way to live, isn't it?"

She sniffed the breeze, which carried the smell of frying onions and greasy meat and cheese. A wonder-ful smell in Tess's opinion, but Devon recoiled a little bit, as if the aroma alone might enter her body somehow, sneak a calorie or two into her system.

"Devon, are you . . . better?"

"That's a relative term, isn't it? But yes, I'm better."

"Are you well?"

She smiled, shook her head. "No, I've pretty much destroyed myself. I'll never have children, I've shortened my lifespan, my organs are all fucked up. When I wake up in the morning, I can barely find my pulse. Sometimes, I think I'm dead. Then again, I all but died several times before I went to Persephone's."

"Did Persephone's help you?"

"Maybe. I don't know. I was in a lot of places, five in all. My cousin Sarah will beat that record before long. I liked some more than others, but they were pretty much all the same. A little therapy, a little medication, all kinds of behavior modification. None of it worked for me. At some point, I decided to get well. I happened to be at Persephone's when that happened. Sometimes, I think the intersection of desire and treatment can't be faked, or orchestrated. It's a decision. You decide to live. Then you spend the rest of your life second-guessing that decision."

There was a rapping on the window above. They looked up to see Devon's "governess" waving happily, motioning for Devon to come in.

"Lunchtime," Devon said. "Soup with things in it. Oh boy."

Tess stopped at the cheesesteak cart before trying to find a taxi back to the train station. It was as good a version of the famed local dish as any other, she supposed. Famed local dishes were usually overrated, more about nostalgia and stereotype than real taste. The thing was, after spending even a short time with Devon Whittaker, eating was too fraught with significance. She couldn't stop thinking about food, about the process. How odd it was to sink her teeth into something and tear away, ripping flesh, chewing it into ever-smaller pieces. One reason Tess had never smoked cigarettes was because the action seemed essentially ludicrous. Suddenly, eating seemed no less ridiculous. Halfway through the sandwich, she tossed it in the trash.

In the cab on the way to the train station, she looked at the sketch she had shown Devon. Gwen Schiller. It was a good name for her, old-fashioned in a way, capturing some timeless quality in that face. Gwen Schiller. When she had been Jane Doe, it had made sense for her to die in someone's cemented-over backyard in Locust Point. She had been a street kid, a huffer, someone who would never be missed. But Gwen Schiller, no matter how much she professed to loathe her father and step-mother, shouldn't have been able to go missing for so long. Someone should have noticed she was gone.

Someone should have cared.

15

Within a day, dental records obtained from a Silver Spring orthodontist made it official. The Dead Girl Formerly Known as Jane Doe was Gwen Schiller. Martin Tull was impressed, and generous enough not to hide it.

"I can't believe how much you did with so little," he kept saying to Tess. They were sitting in a sub shop near police headquarters. Tess was never really comfortable inside the stale air and unrepentantly macho culture of the city police department. Cops made her nervous. She couldn't help thinking they knew her every misdeed—every red light run, every mile over the speed limit.

"I started with a lucky break and Whitney turned it into something concrete. She was the one who picked up on the significance of the decayed back teeth."

"Beginner's luck. You were the one who parlayed it into establishing the girl's identity. How did you track down the friend?"

"I think this is one of those things that falls under our don't ask–don't tell policy."

"Misdemeanor or felony?"

Tess was toying with a turkey sub, her usual—lettuce, tomato, extra hots, no mayo. So virtuous it practically qualified as health food. She didn't have much of an appetite as of late.

"I'm not sure I broke any laws per se. But you'd still feel obligated to lecture me, so let's leave it alone. How are her parents doing?"

"About how you'd expect. We had to call her father to ask for the name of their daughter's dentist. He can't help knowing what that means. The thing that gets me is the father insists there's a missing person report, but I sure never saw one. I think I'd remember a billionaire's daughter from Potomac. Talk about a red ball."

"A paper billionaire," Tess said, remembering Devon Whittaker's dismissive tone. "You'll tell them face to face, right? Not over the phone?"

"Yeah." Tull pinched the flesh between his thumb and forefinger, which meant he had a headache. "I'd like you to be there."

"No way. My ghoul days are over, I don't have to confront grieving next of kin anymore."

"Yeah, it sucks. But it's a cinch they'll ask me something I don't know, Tess, and I'll look stupid. We already look stupid. And when the father finds out his daughter's killer is dead, his rage isn't going to have any place to go. He's going to blame the police."

"Not Baltimore PD," Tess said. "Montgomery County, or some Eastern Shore county, maybe even the State Police, wherever he filed the report. All she did was die in Baltimore."

This failed to cheer Tull. He switched hands, pinching the flesh on the right one as he trained his brown, sorrowful eyes on Tess. They had met over a corpse, and it had occurred to Tess more than once that if someone had to show up on your doorstep with news that was going to destroy your world, Martin Tull was the man for the job.

But just because someone was good at something didn't mean he liked it. Besides, he wasn't asking her to do it in his stead, merely to watch, back him up. It wasn't much of a favor, given all the favors he had done her.

She reached for his hand to shake it.

"Thanks, Tess," he said, then pulled his hand back and resumed his headache cure.

"You know," she said, "if you didn't drink so much coffee, aspirin wouldn't hit your stomach so hard, and you wouldn't have to rely on pinching your pressure points to get rid of these headaches."

"If I stopped drinking coffee, the withdrawal headaches would be so bad that no amount of aspirin could touch it. My one vice, Tess. Isn't everyone entitled to at least one?"

"I couldn't be friends with someone who didn't have at least one vice."

Tull's pager went off. She offered her cell phone, but he waved it off as if it were a bribe and went to the pay phone on the wall. His voice rose so quickly, in anger and surprise, that she could hear it across the room.

"What? *What?* Where did you hear that? No, no comment. No comment means no comment. Later. You'll be glad you waited, I promise. No. No." He hung up. "Shit."

"What was that about?"

"Herman Peters, the police reporter at the *Blight*, is already sniffing around. Someone told him we have an ID on Jane Doe, and he wants to go with it. No name, just the fact we ID'd her. I tried to tell him it will be a better story if he'll wait until I notify next of kin, but he's not buying it. I sure wish I knew who leaked it."

"Could be your own communications department, trying to grab a little good press." *And shaft me in the process.* If there was going to be a story, Tess should be part of it. She had earned a little free publicity.

Then she thought of Gwen Schiller, dead forever, and felt a twinge of guilt.

"Naw, those guys don't know anything unless they're told. Could be the medical examiner, could be the orthodontist for all we know. Anyway, you ready to take a little ride in my deluxe city vehicle? The sooner we get this done, the less I have to worry about her parents reading it in the paper, or seeing it on television."

"Where are we going?"

"I told you, I set up a meeting with the Schillers, all the way down in Potomac."

"I thought they were coming up here."

"These are rich folks. We go to them."

* * *

Tess thought of Potomac as an old money enclave, full of Kennedys and horsey types. There was even a saddlery shop at the main business intersection, which locals, predictably, referred to as the village.

But new money had taken up residence here, fortunes so vast that they couldn't be housed in the older mansions, with their laughably small bathrooms and lack of central air conditioning. Some of these were large and garish, the epitome of nouveau riche. But the most expensive of the new homes had been designed to look old. The Schillers lived in one of these.

The father was younger than Tess had expected, barely in his forties, with a boyish face and an asymmetrical white patch in his dark hair that made him look as if he had been slapped with a paintbrush. The stepmother was older than Tess expected, in her late thirties. Given what Devon had said, Tess had expected a trophy wife, but Patsy Schiller was more like a prize given out at a boardwalk shooting gallery. Blond and blue-eyed, she wore a pink suit and white blouse that were too ugly not to be expensive. Unfortunately Patsy's figure, all breast from collarbone to waist, wasn't quite right for the lines of couture clothing.

"Nice house," Tull said, as the couple welcomed them inside. The foyer was the size of the average Baltimore billiard hall.

"We haven't finished decorating," Patsy said. She had the supercilious air sometimes mistaken for a grand manner. Tess knew instinctively how she had come to be Mrs. Schiller, saw the transformation as clearly as a trailer in a movie theater. She must have been Dick Schiller's secretary or administrative assistant, indispensable and sweetly officious. She had brought him homemade cookies on occasion, brushed up against him while handing him his phone messages.

And widower Dick Schiller, who made Bill Gates look as if he had a really good haircut, probably couldn't figure out what to do with those breasts except marry them.

"We finished decorating, once," he was saying now, his voice glum and weary. He understood this polite chatter could last only so long, that Tull didn't want to break the bad news while they were standing in the foyer. "Then we started over, when we returned from our trip."

"I thought it would cheer you up, getting rid of all that furniture Gwen's mother had picked out," Patsy said, patting his arm. "Besides, our decorator said those old things would never have worked in this house."

Gwen's mother, Tess noted. Not a name, not "your first wife," which would have emphasized her connection to Dick. Just Gwen's mother. Tull caught her eye, noting the same verbal tic.

They sat in the living room. For all the Schillers' money, it looked like one of the high-end display rooms at Ethan Allen to Tess. The furniture was oversized, and so shiny it appeared to be coated with oil. But maybe there were subtleties in the surroundings that were lost on a little prole like her.

Now that they were seated, Tull spoke swiftly, giving the news the way a skillful doctor would administer a shot to a frightened child.

"We asked you for Gwen's dental records because new information indicated your daughter might be the victim of a homicide, a victim we could never identify. I'm sorry to tell you the dental records establish she was, in fact, our unidentified victim."

"Homicide?" her father said. Patsy furrowed her brow. Her surprise was genuine, but she didn't have any other emotion to put behind it. "Murdered, my daughter was murdered?"

"Yes, sir," Tull agreed, not bothering to make the kind of distinctions that judges did. Murder was a legal term. Henry Dembrow had been found guilty of manslaughter. "She was killed by a man who found her living on the street in Locust Point, and promised to help her out. This would have been about six weeks after she left the clinic."

"Will you ever catch the person who did it?"

It was a logical question, one Tess and Tull had expected.

"We know who killed your daughter," the detective said. "We arrested him, he confessed. But he couldn't tell us anything about his victim, not even her name. We sent him to prison this year."

Where he died, Tess thought. But she knew why Tull didn't tell that part, not just yet. He wanted to give Dick Schiller the fleeting comfort of having an enemy.

"Who is this man?"

"Just a stupid punk kid. A huffer."

"Huffer?" Dick Schiller echoed.

"A glue sniffer, someone who inhales paint and gasoline fumes."

"People do that? On a regular basis?" Schiller looked amazed, but Patsy was nodding, almost unconsciously. Oh yeah, Tess thought, definitely a secretary who married the boss. She could almost pick out the zip code in Prince George's County, one of the little working-class enclaves where the girls dream big, inspired by local heroine Kathie Lee Gifford. You can take the girl out of Bowie, but you can't take the Bowie out of the girl.

"Yeah, I'm afraid they do."

"I don't know Locust Point," Patsy put in. "Is it near Canton? We have some friends who live in the Anchorage. They have the prettiest view."

"Other side of the water, ma'am."

Dick Schiller, to his credit, did not wish to discuss Baltimore real estate. "The man who killed my Gwen, how long will he be in prison?"

Tess liked him for the use of the possessive.

"He's dead," Tull said. "He was stabbed to death."

The room was silent, a silence that not even Patsy was foolish enough to fill. In less than five minutes, Dick Schiller had found out his daughter was dead, his daughter had been murdered, his daughter's killer had been caught, her killer was dead. Most people complain justice is slow, but it had moved much too swiftly for Dick Schiller.

"Was Gwen using drugs, too?"

"*No.*"

The question had been Patsy's; the emphatic denial came from Tess. She couldn't help feeling fiercely protective of Gwen.

"I was just asking," the stepmother said. "After all, she had . . . other issues."

Tess studied the second Mrs. Schiller. She was so curvy, so pink and white, the colors of her outfit repeated in her fair, ripe flesh and carefully made-up face. She reminded Tess of the old-fashioned refrigerator cookie still found in some Baltimore bakeries, a round disc with pink swirls running through the vanilla dough.

It was a kind of cookie that looked better than it tasted.

"Mr. Schiller, how did Gwen's mother die?"

"Ovarian cancer," he said. "She went very fast. At least, that was her doctor's frame of reference. It may have been fast in medical terms, but it was agonizingly slow for us."

"Was she very thin, toward the end?"

"Yes." He looked at Tess curiously, trying to figure out where she was going. "Yes, quite thin."

Tess didn't push it. It was just a hunch, an inexcusable, pseudo-psychiatric leap of faith. But it didn't surprise her that a teenage girl who had seen her mother waste away, then watched her father bring home this strawberry sundae of a woman, had a complicated relationship with food.

"Do you have a photo of Gwen? In all the time I was looking for her, I've never known what she truly looked like. All I had was an artist's sketch." And a photocopy of a Polaroid of a corpse.

Schiller gave Tull a questioning look, as if he had already forgotten why she was here. "Tess is a private investigator. She's the one who identified your daughter after the police department had given up.

We wouldn't be here today if it weren't for her efforts."

He left the room and returned with a framed studio portrait, the eight-by-ten from a standard school package, with blue skies in the background. It was an old photo. Gwen had braces, the gawkiness of a middle schooler. The part in her hair was crooked, as was her smile, and her eyes were halfclosed.

She was also one of the most beautiful girls Tess had ever seen. Like a painting, Sukey had said, or someone famous. Tess understood now. Gwen's hair was glossy, as Devon had noted, her eyes dark and bright, her features perfect and yet not. Tess could stare at this photograph all day, dissect it a thousand ways, and never be able to explain why Gwen Schiller was so arresting. The dark hair, the fair skin, the lush red mouth. She could pass for Snow White.

And everyone knows what Snow White's stepmother did when she found out she had competition in the fairest-of-the-land department. Tess would have bet all Schiller's paper billions that Patsy had been the one who pushed for Gwen to be hospitalized, while she and her husband went on their extended honeymoon.

"She was lovely," Tess said, handing the photograph back.

"She is, isn't she?" Schiller said, still not ready to speak of his daughter in the past tense. "Her mother and I never knew how we produced such a specimen. Andrea was pretty, but in a more earthbound way. And me—well, you see what I bring to the table, genetically. I used to tease Andrea, ask her if she had been having sex with a swan behind my back."

"A swan?" Patsy looked mystified. "That's sick."

"It's how Helen of Troy of was conceived," Tess said. "Zeus disguised himself as a swan and impregnated a woman named Leda."

"Oh, yeah. Helen of Troy. The one with the face that launched a thousand ships, and the Trojan Horse, and all that."

Tess thought it was as concise a summary of Homer as she had ever heard. Maybe Dick Schiller could make his next billion by starting an Internet company that sold Patsy's interactive Cliff Notes over the Web.

Schiller was staring off into space. He hadn't cried, not yet. Days might go by before he did. But Tess suspected that once he allowed himself to grieve for his daughter, he might never stop. A dead wife, a dead daughter. Patsy would be a comfort to him, Tess had to give her her due. Whatever her limitations, Patsy Schiller wasn't the kind of woman who died young. She was pragmatic, she looked both ways before crossing streets, or marrying billionaires. She would take good care of her husband, if only because it served her own strong instinct for self-preservation.

"You know, I'm in the information business," Dick Schiller said at last. "I can't help thinking how ironic it is that my daughter could go unidentified for nine months, just because a missing persons report was filed in one jurisdiction and she died in another."

"We're not exactly at the cutting edge of technology—" Tull began, but Tess interrupted him.

"What do you mean, nine months? Gwen was missing for more than a year."

"Gwen walked out of the clinic on her birthday, January thirty-first. I think I know my own daughter's birthday. She had turned eighteen, and they couldn't hold her legally against her will. The clinic staff tried to notify us before she left, but we were en route to—I'm not sure where we were in January. Chile?"

"Wherever we were right before Brazil," Patsy said, adding for Tull and Tess's edification: "We were in Rio for Carnival."

"Gwen didn't check herself out, that's the point," Tess said. "She ran away in October of the previous year, well before her birthday. Devon Whittaker told me she heard about the escape from someone else who was still at the clinic."

"Impossible," Dick Schiller said. "We continued to receive e-mail from her through January. Not much, I grant you—she was very angry at me for putting her in Persephone's—but she stayed in touch."

"Through e-mail," Tess said.

"Right."

"And you knew she was the one writing the e-mail because . . ."

Schiller put his head in his hands. "Because it came from her e-mail address at the clinic. How stupid can I be to think that means anything? Anyone who had her laptop could have used it to send me those notes. No wonder they sounded so stiff and impersonal. But Jesus Christ, why would the school wait so long to report her missing?"

"Because they didn't want to appear negligent," Tess said, working it out for herself as she spoke. "Gwen ran away, probably to punish you for putting her there. Maybe she thought you'd go crazy, offer a huge reward, or at least come home from your honeymoon. But the clinic decided to risk not notifying you, to stall until her eighteenth birthday. Then, at least, they could say she left legally, instead of having to admit she had run away. I imagine Persephone's long waiting list might have been somewhat diminished if the news had gotten out about her escape."

"All this subterfuge, to disguise the fact that a girl had run away?" Dick Schiller shook his head. "It seems excessive."

It did, Tess thought. The clinic was hiding something else, something bigger. But what?

"Where is this place?" Tull asked her, his mind following the same trail.

"On the Eastern Shore, near Easton," Patsy said. "It's quite nice. I thought Gwen would be happier in some place that didn't look so much like a hospital."

Maybe, Tess thought. *Or maybe you thought you'd be happier if she were tucked away in some place far away from Potomac, even while you were trotting around the globe.*

"We need to get out there," Tess said. "We need to get there with a warrant before Herman Peters extracts Gwen's name from someone, which will give the clinic a heads-up that we know she was dead three months before she was reported missing."

Tull stood up. "We could drive straight there, radio the state police and county officials to meet us there. If Herman is pushing too hard, the department might make the information public, and it will be all over WBAL and the television stations. They've got no reason to hold it back. They knew I was meeting with Gwen's next of kin this afternoon. But it would still take us two hours to get over there."

"Three hours, once you factor in afternoon traffic on the Capital Beltway," Schiller said. "However, my company has a helicopter on call. My old company, I should say, but I think they'd let me use it under such extraordinary circumstances. Would that help?"

"Sure." It was Tess who answered, not Tull. He gave her a look as if to say, *Why do you think you're coming along for the ride?* She knew, in the end, he would let her go with him. It was only fair, after she had accompanied him here, and Tull was always fair. She couldn't wait to step out of a helicopter on the clinic's grounds, to let them see who had brought the police to their door. One if by land, two if by sea, three if by air.

It was their fault. They should have let her in the first time she asked.

16

Tess did a pretty good job keeping her stomach south of her throat until the helicopter was about halfway across the Chesapeake Bay. She clenched her fists, trying to hide them from Tull. There was more swaying than she would have expected, a rocking motion not unlike being at the top of a Ferris wheel, although this was side to side, instead of back and forth. It seemed to take forever to cross the wide expanse of water and head south, toward the protected cove where Persephone's Place waited.

Waited unwittingly, Tess hoped, because otherwise this whole exercise was pointless.

"You're sure there's a place for me to land?" This was the pilot, a stone-faced man who gave the impression that he considered this particular assignment no different from ferrying corporate executives around the Mid-Atlantic region.

"There's supposed to be," Tess shouted back.

"Don't see it yet. We may have to improvise."

"Everyone's in place on the ground," Tull put in.

"The state police have blocked off the road leading to the school, and the Department of Natural Resources police are at the cove's edge. All they need is the go-ahead from us. You ready, Tess?"

He was grinning at her, obviously attuned to the second, third and fourth thoughts that had dogged Tess since she had talked her way into this helicopter. She was grateful now that she had only picked at her lunchtime sub. Eaten, it seemed, about a million years ago, back in a place called Baltimore, when the matter of Gwen Schiller's death was still tragic, but not particularly sinister or mysterious.

Tess nodded, and the helicopter began its vertical descent, its propellers whipping the branches of the trees at the property line. Tess wondered if Sarah Whittaker was watching this scene unfold from her casement window on the third floor. They were on the ground blessedly quick. Ducking their heads beneath the blades, Tull and Tess ran toward the white-and-pink house. He had lent her a shoulder holster, so she looked quasi-professional, the bulge of her gun visible beneath her suede jacket. Sirens sounded in the distance, and the state police rolled up the drive, even as the DNR police massed on the shore behind them.

Once free of the helicopter, Tess began enjoying herself immensely. Girls were pouring from the house—one, three, five, eight, a dozen in all, all quite thin and frail looking. She thought she glimpsed Sarah's furred face among the girls, but they looked startlingly alike. Behind them came the orderlies who had tended to Tess after her shipwreck, and behind them even more staff, all new to her. Finally, she saw the auburn-haired woman and the doctor.

"Capsize again?" This was the woman, Miss Hollinger, her mechanical voice as crackly as dry ice today, steam coming out of her mouth in the cool air, a coat thrown around her shoulders. The doctor was not so cool; he moved toward them, then started back toward the house, only to find state police blocking his way.

"Baltimore City police," Tull said, showing his badge. "Homicide."

"Homicide?" The woman's puzzlement was sincere. "No one has ever died here."

So you're not surprised to find the police swarming over the lawn, but you are surprised to find out it's related to a homicide. Interesting, Tess thought.

"One of your patients, Gwen Schiller, was killed after leaving the school."

Miss Hollinger hugged her elbows, but said nothing. She was trying to keep her face empty, but Tess thought she saw an excited glimmer in the pale blue eyes.

"She was killed November sixteenth."

Tess was right. The woman had to fight to keep from smiling. "I'm sorry to hear that. She was a lovely girl. But I don't see how it concerns the clinic. Gwen checked herself out in January, when she turned eighteen."

"Oh, I'm sorry, I didn't make myself clear," Tull said, with deadly politeness. "Gwen Schiller died on November sixteenth of last year. Almost three months *before* you told her father she was missing. Do you bring a lot of people back from the dead here? Because if you do, I'd sure like to get in on the ground floor if you ever have a stock offering."

"I don't think I have anything I want to say to you," Miss Hollinger said with an admirable, if infuriating, dignity. In her silk print dress and burgundy heels, head held high, she could have passed for one of the patients' mothers. "Not until my lawyer arrives."

Sarah Whittaker came down the porch stairs, her insubstantial frame lost inside a sweatshirt and leggings. She tugged at Tess's sleeve to get her attention, then jumped back, as if fearful Tess might try to return her touch.

"How will you arrive next time? On horseback?"

"I don't think there will be a next time, Sarah."

The girl looked up at Tess. Her eyes were dull, like a dying animal, her skin chalky and dry. She could have been a dandelion gone to seed: One puff and she'd disintegrate, carried away by the wind. "They'll have to send us home now, won't they? I'll get to go home for Christmas after all, go to Guadeloupe with the family."

"I suppose so," said Tess, who had no idea what would happen.

"Well, I'm not going to wear a bathing suit," Sarah said. "No way. I'm positively gross."

"Oh Sarah—" Tess assumed she was worried about the hair on her face and back, her pallor.

"I mean my thighs," Sarah said, holding one forward, smacking the leg to make the nonexistent flesh jiggle. "They're *huge*."

* * *

Given the number of people involved, Tull and the other law officers decided to keep everyone at Persephone's for questioning, rather than try to bring them into the state police barracks, or the Baltimore police department. The girls were of little help—none of them had been here the previous fall, when Gwen had run away—and the auburn-haired Miss Hollinger, who Tess thought of as Big Nurse, was coolly silent.

But the sour-breathed Dr. Blount was not as composed when Tull got him alone in the clinic dining room. The two sat across from each other, while Tess hugged the wall behind Tull. She wasn't supposed to be there, but Tull wasn't up for the scene that would result if he tried to have her removed.

"I should have a lawyer," Dr. Blount proposed tentatively. It sounded like a question, and Tull treated it as such. The doctor had been Miranda'd, of course, recited the rights that most schoolchildren knew better than the Pledge of Allegiance thanks to television. But Tull, like most seasoned homicide detectives, believed there was some play in the clause about the right to counsel. Until the doctor emphatically and definitively held out for a lawyer, Tull was going to pick at him.

"You really want a lawyer? Because if you want one, you can have one." Tull turned back to address Tess. "It's funny, isn't it, how the guilty guys always want a lawyer?"

"I'm not guilty of anything."

"Oh." Tull looked confused. "But didn't you say you wanted a lawyer?"

"Well—I can have one if I want one, right?"

Tull sighed, hunkered forward, as if dealing with a sweet but very stupid child. The doctor had a little boy's face, ruddy and fat-cheeked. "Look, you can pick up the phone right now and ask for a lawyer. But then I'm done talking to you, because he's not going to let you say anything. So we can't make a deal, can't sort anything out. I mean, there are levels of illegal activity here, it probably wasn't even your idea. But—you want a lawyer, call a lawyer. I don't have a problem with charging everyone with the same thing, figuring it all out later. My only problem is where to lock you up for the night, here or in the city." Tull pretended to think. "I guess I gotta take you back to city jail."

"What kind of charges are we talking about, exactly?"

"Filing a false report—"

"We didn't do that." Dr. Blount's voice held a note of shrewdness, but it only served to make him more pathetic. "The family did."

"Based on information you gave them," Tess said, unable to contain herself. "By the way, did you continue to bill them? I think that constitutes fraud. If an insurance company is involved, I feel sorry for you. I'd rather owe the meanest loan shark in East Baltimore than have an insurance company after me."

Tull gave Tess a warning glance over his shoulder. But she wasn't sure he had worked out the fraud angle. It had only occurred to her when she had seen the clinic's patients arrayed on the front porch, and begun calculating how much money each one brought in at $2,000 a day.

"Who is she, anyway?" the doctor asked.

"Trainee," Tull said. "An overeager trainee, but with a good point. I'm sure the files the state police are going through will show if Gwen Schiller's family was billed after the date she walked away."

"It was never our intent to defraud anyone," Dr. Blount said. "We do good work here, important work. It didn't seem fair to let a couple of people jeopardize it."

"A couple?" Tull asked.

He hesitated. "Are you sure I don't need a lawyer?"

"There's a difference, you know, between keeping quiet while someone does something you know is wrong, and doing it yourself."

Yeah, a difference of five-to-ten years. Tess was finding a perverse enjoyment in the scene. So far, the only interrogations she had been privileged to watch had put her on the doctor's side of the table. Tull had a rep as an interrogator, and now Tess knew why. He was like a cat persuading a bird to take a nap between his front paws. Tull's face even had a certain catlike cast, with his high cheekbones and glittering brown eyes.

"It was Sheila's idea," the doctor said.

"Sheila?"

"Sheila Hollinger. The redheaded woman. She's the director here. I'm in charge of the medical division, but she's the administrator. She keeps the beds full, and the waiting list long, so we don't have to worry about meeting our monthly bills. I know it sounds like a lot, what we charge, but this is an expensive operation. When Gwen started kicking up a fuss, she could have really hurt us."

"Kicking up a fuss," Tull's voice was at once knowing and inviting, creating a silence for the doctor to fill.

"She said one of the staff members raped her," Dr. Blount said, as if remembering a minor annoyance. "A teacher, who oversaw the girls' lesson plans. We confronted him immediately and he admitted the incident, only he said it was consensual. We fired him. What else could we do? It's not as if we were negligent. We do a background check on everyone who works here. It was an isolated incident."

"An isolated incident." Tess didn't realize she had spoken aloud until Tull glanced at her.

"He said, she said," the doctor said helpfully.

Tess pressed her palms against the cream-colored wall. It was cool to the touch, smooth as ice cream. Everything was so pretty here, so perfect. Everything except the patients themselves, who had destroyed their bodies, their complexions, their teeth, even their organs. Yet Gwen Schiller's beauty could not be snuffed out; she had still been beautiful when Sukey saw her. She had a bloom that nothing could strip from her—not her own habits, not the streets, not this clinic.

"But Gwen said she was raped. She didn't describe it as 'consensual.'" Tess loved Tull for pressing this point home.

"Yes, that was her story. But she would have said anything to leave here, to force her father to come get her. She was very fixated on getting his attention, on disrupting his new marriage any way she could. I am a psychiatrist, I understood the dynamics of the situation very clearly."

Tull let this pass. "What was the time frame? When did Gwen arrive, and when did she make the complaint?"

"She arrived in late August and hadn't been here two weeks when she went to Sheila with her story." The doctor pulled himself up, a little self-righteously, puffing out his chest and his shoulders. "The staff member was dismissed by the end of the day, I can tell you that much."

Tull nodded, as if admiring the doctor's decisiveness. "So Gwen tells you she was raped, and you fire the guy. Did you have her examined, or ask if she wanted to file a criminal complaint?"

"She didn't say anything until several days after the incident." That word again. Tess wanted to tell the doctor a fender bender was an incident, rape was a crime. "And, as I said, there was no way of knowing what really happened."

"Didn't you find it coincidental that she ran away a few weeks later?"

The doctor's narrow shoulders sagged, but his pity was only for himself. "We thought she would contact her father immediately, and that would be that. Then, a few weeks after she disappeared, her father wrote to her via the school's e-mail account and we realized he didn't know she was gone. It was our computer system. It was easy enough to change Gwen's password and send her father e-mail. We had kept her disappearance from the other girls, so we didn't have to worry he might hear from anyone else. We didn't see the harm in letting her father think she was still here, as long as we continued to look for her. Her eighteenth birthday came and went, and we never found her, so we told her father she had checked herself out, which really wasn't that far from the truth. As for the billing—we didn't know what else to do. But of course, we'll give the money back, every penny of it. We never meant to deceive anyone."

Dr. Blount looked at them beseechingly. Criminals were always so sure of their right to empathy. Tull turned to Tess, disgust sharp in his face, even as his expression warned her to control herself. He need not have worried. She was still standing by the wall, her palms pressing against it hard enough to leave grimy marks, or so she hoped.

Her only fear was that if she lost contact with the wall, her hands would wrap themselves around the doctor's throat and never let go.

17

―――――――――

"I need you."

The voice was Crow's, coming to Tess through the fog of sleep. For once they were in his apartment, because they had drunk too much at dinner, and Crow's small nest had the virtue of being within stumbling distance of the Brewer's Art.

Half-awake, Tess rolled into him. Dream and reality merged, enriching the other. They often came together this way and she liked the illicit, phantom quality of these meetings. Not even Crow's fumbling in his nightstand drawer disturbed the mood.

"I need you," he repeated.

"I need you, too," she assured him. At other times of the day or night, they were more apt to say "I love you," possibly "I want you." Or, in imitation of a song that Crow particularly liked: "Baby, take it all off." But in the middle of the night, it was always: I need you.

The only problem was that Crow's midnight raids tended to wake Tess up, while he slept more soundly than ever. She lay in his arms, feeling last night's alcohol buzz shift into this morning's hangover. Martinis, followed by many glasses of red wine, and a memorable dinner, not that she could remember a bite of it. Veal? Lamb? Something tender and young and decadent. They had been celebrating, but Tess was no longer sure why.

The events of the past two days ran through her mind like a slide show. There was Tull, presiding over a press conference at the state police headquarters, explaining how she had identified Gwen Schiller, and how the clinic had deceived Gwen's parents. He held back the information about the sexual assault—even in death, Gwen deserved her privacy. It would get out, eventually, as state agencies moved to close down Persephone's and strip the clinic of its license. But Tull was determined the information wouldn't come from him.

Next slide. Tess saw Herman Peters, the boy-wonder police reporter who looked so deceptively innocent, scribbling away in his notebook with an excitement that bordered on the sexual. She saw the gleam in his eye when she began telling how she had faked the capsize, remembering to give Whitney full credit for the idea and the execution. Some reporters had laughed, and she hadn't liked that part. *A girl is dead,* she had wanted to say. *A beautiful girl is dead, and she shouldn't be, and the only thing I've done is make it possible for her father to take her remains from a pauper's grave at Crownsville.* Tess saw herself, angry and flushed. She mentioned going to Philadelphia, although she didn't name Devon. Tess's mother called the next morning and asked why she couldn't have put on some lipstick, if she was going to be all over the news, maybe comb her hair. Her father said she looked great, but could she smooth things out with Ruthie, who wasn't too happy to learn about the break in the case at the same moment the rest of Baltimore did. "Sorry, Dad, we were running against the clock," Tess said, but she saw his point.

A booth in Frigo's Bar. Ruthie Dembrow's mouth was a grim, straight line, no lipstick to brighten it. Tess had done what she had asked her to do, yet she had not found what Ruthie wanted. There was no connection between Henry and Gwen. The people who knew the secret of Gwen's identity had no idea she was dead, so how could they have sought revenge against Henry?

"But this hospital, this clinic," Ruthie had said, her overarched brows drawn down in a frown, her eyes locked on Tess's. "If they knew it was her, wouldn't they want it to be secret, so they didn't end up in all this trouble?"

"You mean, did the people at the clinic have Henry killed, in case it turned out he did know who his victim was? I honestly don't think so, Ruthie."

"It doesn't feel right to me," Ruthie insisted. "He was talking about a new trial, an appeal. Did I tell you that? He said there were mitigating circumstances."

Didn't they all, Tess thought. She thought again about the rubber tube, how Henry had stopped to play a joke on Gwen's corpse. Ruthie didn't know her brother as well as she thought she did. Even with the cops, he had played the stoned huffer for all it was worth. "I know he didn't mean to kill her, Ruthie. But he did."

She thought her voice was gentle. Ruthie was beyond being comforted.

"You think you're better than me, don't you? You can't imagine anyone in your family getting into trouble like this."

In fact, she couldn't, but she wanted to be conciliatory. "You forget my Uncle Donald worked for a senator who was convicted of mail fraud, and we make it a point not to inquire too closely about Uncle Spike's business dealings. My family's not so clean."

"You can say that again." Ruthie looked at the check on the table. Tess had refunded part of the retainer, which she thought generous—in truth, she had earned every last cent. But she felt guilty that the case, which had brought her glory, had done nothing for Ruthie's grief, provided her no closure. "So you're done now."

The implication being that Ruthie would never be done, that for her, this would never be over.

"Look, you did a good thing, Ruthie. I know you don't have any feelings for Gwen Schiller, but there's a father who knows where his daughter is, who can begin to grieve for her, and it's because of you. It's a good thing, even if it's not the answer you wanted. Even if it's not an answer at all. Sometimes, there is no 'why' to things."

"Henry was so scared of going to prison," Ruthie said. "He thought if things dragged on long enough, he might be able to serve his whole time in city jail.

Just his luck, he had to be the one guy in Baltimore to get a speedy trial."

The city courts were famously clogged and had gone through an embarrassing period in which case after case was thrown out because of unconstitutional delays or lost evidence. Tess had heard of other men awaiting trial who preferred the city jail to the state prison system. But the finer points of incarceration escaped her.

"He confessed," she reminded Ruthie.

"Who doesn't when they get a hold of you? In the end, when he saw he was going to go to Hagerstown, he tried to take it back, but the judge wouldn't hear of it. He had a crappy lawyer, the guy shoulda done something. You get what you pay for, or so I thought."

"I gotta go," Tess told Ruthie. It was past eight, Crow was waiting for her at the Brewer's Art.

"Yeah, I guess you do," Ruthie said. "It's funny about your family, how things always work out for the Monaghans."

Tess stopped. "What do you mean by that?"

Ruthie tapped a cigarette out of her pack, whacking the pack with great force.

"Nothing, nothing at all. Thank your father for me. He owed me a favor, and you were it. You did your job. I guess if I don't like the way it turned out, I got no one to blame but myself. And my stupid brother."

Eight hours ago, Tess had been inclined to agree. Now, awake in the dark, she found herself thinking about Henry's death. Life was built on coincidences, but this one did have a stink to it. Sure, people died in prison, given the nature of their roomies, but it happened far less often than it did in the world at large. In Henry's case, a fight had broken out in a different part of the cell block, yet he was the one who had been killed. It had the earmarks of a hit, a planned execution.

Ruthie had come to Tess thinking there was an Old Testament logic to her brother's death, an eye for an eye. Someone who knew Gwen, but didn't want to own up to her identity for whatever reason, had sought to avenge her death.

But what if Henry was killed to end a trail, to silence someone who knew more than he was telling? What had happened to Gwen in the weeks she was missing? What kind of life had she led on the streets of Baltimore?

The place where I was it had a name like Domino's, but I guess you could call it the Sugar House, too, she had told Sukey. That wasn't Persephone's.

Tess dressed quickly in the dark, left a note for Crow on his bedstand, and walked-ran through the deserted streets to the parking garage where she had left the Toyota. The world was dark at four A.M., although not as dark as it might have been, given the Christmas lights everywhere. She drove to her office, taking care to lock the door behind her, and pulled her file on Henry Dembrow.

She read his confession again, the transcript from the tape that police had made. It was different, somehow, knowing Jane Doe's name and background. Small details took on a new poignancy.

I told her about Locust Point, my dad, how Domino's

used to be called the Sugar House. Yeah, yeah, I know that, she said.

That matched Sukey's story. Everyone said Sukey was a liar, but so far Tess had caught her in nothing but truths, at least when it came to Gwen.

She scanned through the other papers Tull had given her—the charging documents, the official notices that went back and forth throughout the trial. She had paid only cursory attention to these before. Henry Dembrow's trip through the legal system hadn't been about identifying his victim.

But there was a memo, noting that Henry Dembrow was changing representation in the case. Henry had apparently dropped the public defender, someone named Hank Mooney, and switched to a private attorney. Common enough. Baltimore's P.D.s were good, but a lot of criminals made the mistake of thinking you had to pay for value. Never mind that one of the city's most celebrated criminal defense attorneys had watched as a mentally retarded client went off to serve a life sentence, for a crime it was later proved he didn't commit. "You get what you pay for, or so I thought," Ruthie had complained. Henry went to prison on the private attorney's watch, not the P.D.'s.

A private attorney named—Tess flipped through the papers—Arnold Vasso.

Arnie Vasso, power lobbyist. Arnie "I don't practice law, I perfect it" Vasso. Arnie Vasso who had no rep as a criminal attorney, but sometimes did favors for friends, as he had told Tess over their Piccolo Roma lunch. Arnie Vasso, who had engineered the bogus license for a bar called Domenick's, had represented Henry Dembrow, who had killed a girl who said she once worked at a place that sounded like Domino's.

The world was full of coincidences. Where would *Reader's Digest* and movies-of-the-week be without them? But in Arnie Vasso's world, nothing happened by accident.

Tess checked the "It's Time for a Haircut" clock that hung on her wall, an artifact from a Woodlawn barbershop where her mother had taken her for buzz cuts. Hence today's long braid. Tess sometimes wondered if everyone's life was lived in reaction to those first ten or fifteen years, when one had no control. The clock said 4:30 A.M., much too early to call anyone.

She didn't need to call anyway. She knew how the conversation would go.

She'd ask Ruthie if she had hired Arnie Vasso.

Ruthie would say no, Vasso had phoned her up and offered to take the case pro bono, as a favor to a pal at the Stonewall Democratic Club. Something like that.

Tess would ask Ruthie if a good night's sleep had changed her mind, if Ruthie still believed Henry's death was connected to Gwen's death.

Ruthie would say yes, she would always believe this, she didn't care about all the reasons Tess had piled up, the neat little sandbags of logic intended to hold back her intuition. She knew the two things were related, she would go to her grave believing it.

And that's when Tess would say: Me too.

18

The public defender who had been assigned to Henry Dembrow's case was a large man. Not fat, but huge, tall, and broad-shouldered, with a frame so big he appeared to have been made from leftover dinosaur bones.

"Hank Mooney," he said, standing up when she entered the Hasty Tasty, a diner favored by courthouse types. His knee bumped the table, and his coffee sloshed from cup to saucer. "Shit."

His voice was mild, as if he were used to such accidents, as if his size put him on a constant collision course with life.

"Hey, that's why they have saucers. Tess Monaghan."

"Nice to meet you." His handshake was gentle, restrained. "I've heard a lot about you."

"From—"

"Feeney, mainly."

"Then most of what you know is true, and what isn't true is at least interesting." Kevin Feeney, the *Blight's* courthouse reporter, was an old friend, his devotion to her exceeded only by his devotion to making stories about her more colorful. At least he didn't put his fiction in the newspaper, unlike some reporters Tess had known.

She asked for coffee and a pair of bagels, having skipped breakfast that morning. She had wanted to avoid meeting Tyner in Kitty's kitchen. He wouldn't approve of what she was doing. She wasn't sure she approved, so she didn't want to subject herself to anyone else's doubts. But she needed Hank Mooney's help if she was going to confront Arnie Vasso with anything other than her hunches.

"I don't have much time," Hank said, turning a tree-stump-sized wrist to look at his watch. "Another day, another docket."

He was smiling, though, energy brimming out of him in much the same way his coffee had run out of his cup. Tess had thought a public defender would be more beaten down, struggling under a staggering caseload, wrestling with the realization that the only thing that really separated him from a criminal attorney was the salary. But Hank Mooney looked as if he couldn't wait for his workday to begin.

"Do you remember Henry Dembrow?"

"He'd be a hard one to forget, even if the case hadn't been in the news lately."

"Because of the Jane Doe angle."

"Yeah. And because she was a white woman murdered in Locust Point. Most of the people murdered in Baltimore are young black men, killed on the East or West sides. Jane Doe—"

"Gwen Schiller." Having restored the girl's name, Tess was determined to make others remember it.

"She was unusual in every way. I shudder to think how the case would have been handled if they had known who she was at the time. Her father probably would have been breathing down the state's attorney's neck, screaming death penalty."

Tess wasn't sure if Dick Schiller was capable of screaming for anything. Any rage he could feel now was directed at the clinic. Gwen had been alive for six weeks after running away. Forty-two days, forty-two lost opportunities to change her destiny.

"I understand you moved to have his confession thrown out, on the grounds he was denied counsel."

"It was worth a try. I was hoping he might be so high when they interrogated him that he was incapable of informed consent. Did you listen to the tape?"

"I read the transcript."

"He sounds a little spaced out on the tape, but he's not confused. If anything, I had the impression he thought he was being really crafty."

"Crafty?"

Their food arrived. Mooney's breakfast was surprisingly small, a glass of grapefruit juice and a toasted English muffin, which he ate dry. Tess had expected a Paul Bunyan–esque stack of hotcakes, maybe a Western omelet the size of her head. Mooney bit into his English muffin with a sound like someone's spine cracking, scattering crumbs down his front.

"Yeah, I know—the kid was a hardcore huffer.

Yet Henry thought of himself as real smart, an operator. It was like he had some scheme he didn't want to tell me. Then he got his own attorney, and it wasn't my problem anymore. Hasta la vista, baby."

"Arnie Vasso."

"Really? I guess I must have known that at some point, but with my caseload, I don't have the luxury of worrying about former clients. Funny choice. Vasso doesn't know shit about criminal law."

"He knows enough to keep himself out of jail, unlike some other Annapolis lobbyists."

Mooney liked that. He laughed so hard he almost spilled coffee down his shirt front. "Point taken. Look, all I'm saying is that with my caseload, I don't ask a lot of questions if a client says he's got the money to hire a private attorney."

"Did Henry ever mention a bar called Domenick's?"

He shook his head vigorously side to side, like a dog shaking himself dry. Hank Mooney was really quite appealing, in his big-boned, shambling kind of way. Tess tried to think of female friends who might appreciate his charms. Jackie was too fastidious—she'd have bailed at the crumbs. And Whitney was secretly as much of a snob as her mother. The only reason she'd ever date a public defender was to torture Mrs. Talbot. Kitty's taste was famously inclusive, but Kitty was lost to her for now.

"Bars weren't Henry's scene. He was essentially a very solitary guy. No friends, no interests. I always thought huffing appealed to him because it's a real antisocial high. You don't need a buddy, you don't have to go to a shooting gallery, or leave the neighborhood to score. He didn't really care about anyone. Except his sister. He adored her, he kept telling me he was going to make everything up to her some day. Shit." Another glance at his watch. Luckily, he remembered to put down his juice glass before he flipped his wrist. "I'm going to be late." He waved frantically at the waitress, sideswiping a water glass, which Tess caught just before it tipped.

"You go. I'll get this."

"You sure? I don't feel like I helped you much."

"Hey, you're a public servant. You help the tax-payers every day."

Mooney smiled a little ruefully. "Yeah, I help you a lot. I try to win freedom for the guys who strip your cars, break into your houses. I get acquittals for the guys who are shooting each other over the drug trade in West and East Baltimore. I'm an Eagle Scout."

"You ever kept an innocent person from going to prison?"

"An innocent person? I'm not sure there is such a thing. But, yeah, I've had clients who didn't do what the prosecutors said they did, and I've gotten them off."

Tess smiled. "Then I think you're entitled to at least one free English muffin now and then."

Tess found Arnie Vasso in the gallery above the Senate floor, watching with great delight as the Maryland Senate tried one of its own. Senator Hertel, as it turned out, had decided not to go quietly. He was forcing his colleagues to cast him out. The proceedings had excited the seasonally deprived media far more than they did the public. The press seats on the Senate floor were full, and cameras lined both sides of the chamber.

But in the gallery, Vasso was one of only a few diehard political junkies drawn to the spectacle. He sat in the back row, arms folded across his chest, eyes bright with a strange hunger, as if he were watching some kind of blood sport.

"Why are you wasting your time here?" Tess asked him.

"It's history," he said curtly, not even turning his head toward her.

"More of a tradition, if you ask me. It's the third time it's happened in the last three years."

He glanced at her, but his attention quickly returned to the floor. Senator Ken Dahlgren, the quasi-prosecutor here, was making a speech about his committee's findings, and how they had reached the recommendation for Senator Hertel's expulsion. Somehow he managed to reference the Founding Fathers, Abraham Lincoln, and something about how the Maryland State House was the oldest legislative building in continuous use. Tess thought he looked a little waxy and unreal, like Dan Quayle caught in the headlights. But hers was evidently a minority opinion.

"He's good," another spectator whispered.

"The next congressman from the first district," someone agreed. Vasso cocked an eyebrow, but said nothing. He obviously considered himself above such low-level political speculation.

"I need to speak to you," Tess said.

"When they break."

"It's about Henry Dembrow."

Vasso took his eyes from the Senate floor, but only for a moment. "When they break."

"I need to speak to you now."

"Your needs don't interest me much. You want my time, get elected to something."

"It's about Henry Dembrow."

"You're repeating yourself."

"It's about Henry Dembrow and a place called Domenick's and the strange coincidence that the same Annapolis lobbyist stepped in and dusted off his barely used shingle when they needed help."

Had her voice risen? She could swear Dahlgren had glared up at the gallery, lost a step in his carefully planned speech, then resumed again. Vasso's hand closed over her wrist and he all but dragged her into the hallway, as if he had been the urgent one all along.

Once in the corridor, she took her arm back.

"You're proving to be a real pain in the ass," Vasso said. "I'm sorry, I guess that wasn't very PC of me."

He was trying to act jocular now, as if this were some joke between the two of them. People were passsing through the hall, mainly secretary types from the offices on this floor, but Vasso was being careful not to draw too much attention to himself, or to her.

"The girl that Henry Dembrow killed was identified recently."

"So I heard. Nice bit of publicity for you. Lots of potential. Don't fritter it away, looking for connections that don't exist, or weighing yourself down with losers. Yes, I represented Henry Dembrow. As I told you, I do favors for people."

"Who was that a favor for?"

"I believe I also told you there's no point in doing favors if I'm indiscreet. Baltimore is a small town, everyone's only one or two people apart here. I tried to help a kid in a jam. I helped a bar get its liquor license. No connection."

"*You're* the connection."

Adamancy was all she had going for her. Vasso glanced over her head, back at the doors to the Senate chamber.

"You're spinning your wheels," he said.

"Is it true that Henry Dembrow was going to file for a new trial, based on inadequate counsel?"

"He wouldn't be the first man to wake up in prison and start thinking about ways to get out, and pointing fingers." His voice had lost a little of its rat-a-tat slickness. "Henry watched too much television, he kept saying it was his understanding that I'd be able to get him out on a technicality because I was so 'connected.' I told him the only technicality I could find was that he didn't want her to die, but if you shove a woman standing at the top of a flight of concrete steps, that's intent as far as the law's concerned. He made it personal, tried to threaten me, and I told him I'd do anything to protect my reputation. He backed off."

"Actually, I made that part up."

Vasso looked at her blankly.

"The part about Henry asking for a new trial. But thanks for confirming that he was considering it. And that you would do quote-anything-unquote to protect your reputation."

Vasso brushed the lapels of his suit, as if he had been in a fistfight, and yanked the sleeves down over his wrists. Hand-tailored suits didn't do as much for a man if he kept gaining weight after the fitting.

"Can I give you some advice?" he asked Tess. "Take a branch off the family tree. Your father understands how things work, when to push, and when to walk away. Your father knows all about favors. Someone wants me to step in, do a little pro bono for some bozo, I'm fine with that. I didn't do it for Henry, you get me, or his bitch of a sister. The real owner of Domenick's doesn't want his name on the license. Maybe it's because he doesn't live in the city. Maybe it's because he has a criminal record. These are just hypotheticals, I hope you understand. But bar owners all over the city find ways of getting around the regs. I helped one out. That doesn't make me the fucking missing link."

"Henry Dembrow died for a reason. Maybe Gwen Schiller did, too."

"Everyone dies for a reason. Everyone dies for the *same* reason—their heart stops."

"Then you'll never die, because you've got no heart to stop."

Vasso smiled. Everything was a game to him, Tess saw, and the score was kept in dollars and cents. He didn't believe in anything—Democrat or Republican, pro-life or pro-choice, right or wrong. Pay him, he was yours. If the American Cancer Society threw more money at him than the cigarette industry, he'd carry their water, fight for their bills. He could lobby for any side of any issue, as long as he was paid to do it. What some people called a devil's advocate.

"It slows you down," he said, "caring too much. You've got a case tied up neat as a Christmas package. Henry Dembrow confessed to killing that girl. You found out who she was, and now everyone thinks you're a fucking genius. A fucking genius with a nice rack. You should be out getting corporate accounts, not wasting time on looking for explanations that don't exist. But I'll tell you this much: I don't know anything. I make it a point not to know anything I don't need to know. Which is what makes me so smart."

He walked back into the Senate gallery. Tess caught a burst of oratory as the door swung open. Words, words, words, words, words. Everyone was so full of words down here.

Tied up neat as a Christmas package. She wished Vasso had used a different image. Now she was reminded of Gwen, in the crime scene photo, that piece of rubber tubing tied in a bow at her neck.

Like someone's present, Tess realized.

Tied to someone's past.

19

Your father knows all about favors.

Tess started to call Pat from her cell phone, then thought better of it. Vasso was full of shit, throwing out her father's name with the same instinct that caused some street kid to insult your mother. Vasso was an old chauvinist who thought Tess's daddy could boss her around. There were favors, and there were favors. The liquor board had a less-than-illustrious history, but her father had never taken a dime from anyone, never bent the rules for anyone. Well, maybe for Spike, here or there. But that was different. That was family.

She felt as if her car were heading up 97 on its own. The Toyota seemed full of purpose, as if it always knew where it was going, while she felt lost and confused. Vasso's words were like a slow-working poison moving toward her brain.

Your father knows all about favors.

The Toyota headed up Martin Luther King, but hung a left instead of a right, heading into the

Hollins Market area. Winter light wasn't kind to the neighborhood. She had to park several blocks away from Domenick's, but she found a space on a small alley street. When she walked in, it was as if no one had moved in the days since she had first visited. Same bartender, same two young blond guys playing pinball, same old men in the booths, same lone woman in the corner.

"I need the owner," she told the bartender.

"Not here," he said.

"Gwen Schiller worked here," she announced to the room at large. No response. "Gwen Schiller, the girl who was killed by Henry Dembrow in Locust Point last year. Before she died, she told someone she worked here."

The only sound in the room was a pinball, rolling down the length of the table and past flippers, flippers that were not engaged. She had everyone's attention.

The woman in the corner lowered her newspaper and spoke. "People say lots of things. That don't make them true."

"You the owner?"

"I run the place."

"What's your name?"

"My name is for my friends. You going to be my friend?" Tess didn't say anything. "I'm Nicola De-Santi. My husband was Domenick DeSanti."

"So you're the real owner?"

"I run the place," Nicola DeSanti repeated, and Tess wondered how she was defining "place." The bar, the neighborhood, the precinct, the ward, Southwest Baltimore?

"How do you know Arnie Vasso?"

"We move," Nicola yawned, "in the same circles." Tess couldn't imagine her moving at all. Her dark hair had almost no gray in it, her flat brown eyes were shrewd.

"What about Henry Dembrow?"

"Never knew no Henry," she said, and went back to her paper. The two blonds sauntered out of the bar, as if responding to some signal Tess had missed. They made a point of getting too close, of brushing by her, and she caught their scent, body odor with an overlay of something pharmaceutical. The pinball machine gave off one last ring. Game over. Show over.

"Gwen worked here, though."

"Never knew no Gwen."

"She might have used a different name."

"Might of." Nicola DeSanti's voice was mild, even agreeable. So why did she frighten her so much?

"Would you at least look at a photograph of her, just to put my mind at ease?"

"No," Nicola DeSanti said.

The waitress who had brought Tess her green pepper rings on her first visit came out of the kitchen then. She was wearing an ivory dress, semi-formal, and not quite right for any occasion. The dress looked as if it couldn't decide whether it was intended for a cocktail party or a first communion. Some female instinct told Tess that a man had picked out the dress, a man who didn't know too much about clothes.

"What do you think?" Her question seemed to be for the room in general.

"I think," Nicola DeSanti said, "that you should go back in the kitchen and wait for your ride."

It was only then that the waitress registered Tess's presence. She nodded, flustered, and backed out of the room. She seemed nervous in the dress, as if worried about keeping it clean. A legitimate concern in dusty Domenick's, but wouldn't the kitchen have more hazards?

"Gwen worked here," Tess said. Not a question this time.

"I don't think so," Nicola said.

"How can you know, if you won't even look at her photograph? How can you be so sure, unless you do know Gwen already?"

"Her picture was in the paper."

This wasn't a cross-examination, there was no jury to which Tess could appeal, or point out the inconsistency in the woman's conversation. She wondered if the waitress might have known Gwen, but she was so clearly new—Tess remembered how overwhelmed she had seemed, just carrying a tray, how she had dropped everything with a crash—that she couldn't have been working here a year ago.

She left the bar. No one said goodbye. Instead of walking back to her car, she went around the block and headed down the alley behind Domenick's. There was a large green Dumpster there, and she crouched behind it, watching the back of the bar. Something was wrong, something was missing. It was the smell of food. Granted, no one was in Domenick's eating just now, but taverns always smelled of the fried foods they served. And her hiding place, the Dumpster, should have been a stew of ripe, rotting smells. She glanced inside—bottles, cans, broken-down cases. Go figure, the owners of Domenick's didn't recycle. Still, whatever brought people to Domenick's wasn't the food. She had probably been the first person to eat there in ages.

She wedged herself behind the Dumpster, lying flat on the ground, and continued to watch the back door. She didn't know what she expected to see, but her gut told her that if a girl in an ivory dress disappeared, she eventually had to reappear. Fifteen minutes passed—a short time, yet much longer when one was lying on a cold, rough patch of cement. A car pulled up in the alley. From her place on the pavement, all Tess could see were tires, a strip of shiny maroon paint on some kind of sedan. Gray trousered legs went from the car to the back door, disappearing inside. Soon the same legs appeared, accompanied by a pair of girl's calves. Tess couldn't help noticing that the girl's legs were stubby and thick-ankled.

"I thought they were going to pick me up," the girl was saying.

"Here? No, not here. I told you. You're going to Harbor Court for tea."

"Iced tea in winter? That's all I get? Jesus, I thought this guy had money."

"Hot tea, with little sandwiches. You'll like it. Just don't eat too many. This is a look-see, remember. You might not get it."

"And it's a good thing to get?"

"Honey, it's the best gig in town. If you get it. Most don't. For every ten that go, maybe one gets picked."

They climbed into the man's car. Tess was able to catch sight of the license plate, the make of the car. A Mercury Marquis, fairly new. She waited until it turned out of the alley and then stood up, unkinking her knees, brushing herself off. She wondered if she could pass muster at the Harbor Court's high tea. She'd have to. She walked slowly through the alley, and the five blocks back to her car. Running, rushing, attracted attention, and it didn't gain that much time in the end. She'd make it to Harbor Court before tea was over.

Or so she thought, until she rounded the corner and saw the blond duo from Domenick's, sitting on the trunk of her car.

20

W here you been?" asked one, hailing her as if they were old friends.

"Yeah, where you been?" echoed the other. "We've been waiting for you. You been talking to Gee-gee all this time?"

"Gee-gee?"

"It's what we call my grandmother," the first one said, scowling, daring her to make something of it.

My grandmother, not our, she noted. Then they weren't brothers, although they could have passed. Could have passed for twins, in fact. Two Baltimore punks with the unhealthy pinkish pallor that always reminded her of the inside of a white rabbit's ears. In the dim light of the bar, they had looked stringy and small. Now she saw they were taller than she was by several inches, with taut neck cords and sinewy forearms.

"I was walking around the neighborhood. I decided while I was here, I'd take a tour of Mencken's house." She was counting on them not knowing it was closed, because she was counting on them not knowing who Mencken was.

"The Mexican restaurant?" the other one asked. "That's long-gone."

"Not Mencken's Cultured Pearl, the writer's house. The Mexican restaurant was named for him."

"Bullshit," the first one said. "Ain't no writer famous enough to have his house be a museum, much less a Mexican restaurant."

"Not many," Tess agreed.

"Yeah, where is this place?"

"Over on Hollins, across from the park. I'll show you, if you want to walk up there with me." She was screwed if they took her up on her offer. The Mencken House had been closed since the City Life Museum had gone belly-up and parceled out its holdings.

Then again, she might be able to outrun them in the park. Maybe.

"I hate fucking museums," the second one said, leaning back against the rear windshield, his hands behind his neck, as if to catch a little sun. "When we was in school, they were always dragging us to those fuckin' places. They'd take us to the B&O, right here in our fuckin' neighborhood. Like I give a shit about trains. I liked the FBI, though. That was cool."

The taller one got up and walked around the car, leaning against the Toyota's driver-side door. Tess would have to push him away to get her key in the lock. That's what he wanted, she realized with a sinking feeling. He wanted her to make the first move, and then he would make the second.

"You like Domenick's?" he asked. "You keep coming around."

"I've been to friendlier places."

"Well, it's a neighborhood joint, and this isn't your neighborhood, is it?"

The one sitting on her trunk sat up and began to bounce, so her car moved beneath him, jouncing on its worn shocks. Tess took out her keys and tried to reach around the other one in order to open her door. He grabbed her wrist, hard. What was it with men and her wrists today?

"Don't," she said.

"What?"

She wished she knew. "Tell your friend to stop rocking my car."

"He's not my friend, he's my nephew."

"That's a fact," the other one said, still bouncing with an almost autistic rhythm. Close up, she could see their eyes were bloodshot, their pupils dilated. Mean and high, a great combination.

"I got a sister sixteen years older 'n me. She and my mom had us the same weekend. We're closer than some brothers I know. Gee-gee is my grandma, his great-grandma. She calls us Pete and Repete. Pretty cool, huh?"

"It's practically 'The Brady Bunch,' right here in Sowebo."

He squeezed her wrist harder, bringing her hand up to his face as if it were a small animal he had caught by the scruff of the neck. Tess tried to figure out if she could use the keys clutched in her fist to scratch him, or gouge his eyes. But that would address only half her problem.

238 | LAURA LIPPMAN

Repete got off her car, came and stood behind her. She was now pressed between these two not-quite-men, no-longer-boys. They could have been anywhere between seventeen and twenty-two. Tess hoped they were on the older side. The younger they were, the more dangerous they would be. Their clothes were slightly rank, as if they had been worn a few days running. But their skin gave off a sweet, sticky smell, suggesting a teenager's diet. Mountain Dew, rubbery sweet tubes of strawberry licorice, pink Hostess snowballs.

"He's older, by a day," the nephew, Repete, said in her ear. "But I'm bigger."

He ground his crotch into her backside. Not much happening there, not as much as he seemed to think. Tess tried to tell herself they wouldn't dare to do anything, not here. It was light out, she was on a busy street, cars were going by. All she had to do was scream, run into the traffic, find a way to grab her cell phone from her knapsack and punch in 911.

She saw a woman walking her dog and their eyes met. Tess let the woman see her fear, tried to put the shared history of their gender into that one look. She said nothing, yet it was the loudest plea she had ever made in her life.

The woman crossed to the other side of the street and turned her back to her.

"I don't think you should come back here," Pete said.

Her mouth was dry. "I agree."

"If you come back here, you're ours. You know what I mean?" He pressed a thumbnail into the side of her throat. "Gee-gee said we could."

The nephew held her by the hipbones and the uncle humped her leg the way a dog might. Tess felt something at her back, something much too hard to be part of anyone's anatomy. A knife.

The uncle released her hand, and the two stepped away from her so quickly she almost fell. She wished her hand wasn't shaking as she unlocked her door, but her fear made them happy, so perhaps it wasn't a bad thing.

Uncle Pete blocked her car door with his body, placed his grubby hand on the side of her neck, as if to caress her. "I usually let him do the girls," he said, jerking his head toward Repete. "He likes it better. But I'm willing to make an exception in your case."

Tess nodded, past caring. Pete stepped back and she turned the key, but nothing happened. She didn't have her foot on the clutch. She tried again, the car started and she began to drive, mindlessly following the one-way streets, until she realized she was on Frederick Road, headed away from the city, toward her parents' house in Ten Hills. She turned around, but lost her way, caught by the neighborhood's triangles and diagonals. Funny, she knew Southwest Baltimore well, or thought she did. She got her bearings by pointing her car toward the ballpark and the purple accents of Ravens Stadium. *Harbor Court*, she reminded herself, *I have to go to Harbor Court.* Her legs were shaking so hard that she had trouble with the play on her clutch, and the car kept stalling out.

Once downtown, she pulled into the first parking garage she saw, although she was several blocks shy of the hotel. She ran across Pratt Street and through Harborplace, where children waited in line at Santa's candy cane house. The child on Santa's lap was crying, of course. The child on Santa's lap always cried. Only the nonbelievers got through the meeting with any nonchalance, using the tradition to manipulate parents toward the right purchases. Santa Claus and clowns—why couldn't adults remember their own terror at these suspicious characters, why did they allow these red-nosed men to thrust their faces at children, who grew up and repeated the mistake? Repeated all the same mistakes, straight down the line, generation after generation.

Tess was shaking so hard now that she had to sit down, if only for a minute. She'd still make Harbor Court, she told herself. Tea was not a rushed affair, they'd still be there. She sat on a bench facing the water, hugged her knees, and began sobbing so recklessly and unself-consciously that the children in Santa's line turned to watch with something akin to admiration.

21

Her face was still red and blotchy when Tess banged through the front doors of Women and Children First almost an hour later, but she could blame the December wind if anyone noticed. Luckily, the store was thronged with customers, so Kitty and Crow could barely afford to call out a greeting, much less indulge in a prolonged interrogation about how she had spent her day.

But observant Crow did say, even as he worked the cash register with his deceptively laid-back efficiency: "You okay? Your eyes look kind of swollen, and your face is puffy."

"Really? Must be something in the Chinese carryout I had for lunch. Is Tyner coming for dinner tonight?" Her question was for Kitty, who was ringing up a set of out-of-print Oz books. Not the truly rare ones, just the white cover editions of the 1960s. But Kitty had found out that self-referential boomers would pay astronomical prices to reclaim the artifacts of their childhoods, even if the books weren't rare by strict collectible standards. Her only problem was staying ahead of eBay and other online auction sites, which were cannibalizing so much of the children's books market.

"He's already here," Kitty said, nodding toward the rear of the store. "We're so swamped he volunteered to assemble gift packages."

"Tyner is putting together your Christmas gift baskets? This I gotta see." Tess pushed through the swinging doors, into the small storeroom that separated Kitty's living quarters from her business.

Tyner was seated at the round oak table in the kitchen's center, mangling sheets of red and green cellophane in his hands. A stack of empty wicker baskets sat next to his wheelchair, while the table held the piles of books and tchotchkes Kitty used for her largely Charm City–centric themes. Tess recognized the basket in front of Tyner as a "sampler" of Kitty's favorite living fiction writers—Anne Tyler, Stephen Dixon, Ralph Pickle, Dan Ellenham, Sue Roland—as well as a small box of Konstant Kandy peanut brittle and a snow globe with an Inner Harbor scene inside. The paperbacks had been tied together with gold string, and arrayed in shredded green-and-red confetti. Theoretically, all Tyner had to do was bring the cellophane to a point at the top, tying it off with a gold ribbon, then place the finished basket in one of the preassembled cardboard boxes, surrounded by bubble wrap.

But the cellophane was too slippery for him, slithering to the floor. In the process of reclaiming it, Tyner rolled back and forth, leaving a few tire tracks. All in all, he looked about as helpless as Tess had ever seen him.

She loved it.

"Let me," she said at last, taking the basket from him.

"Damn cellophane," he said. "How can anyone work with this stuff?"

"You're welcome. Why would you offer to do something for which you're so ill-equipped?"

"It wasn't my idea exactly," Tyner said. "I wanted to work out front, but Kitty said she needed me here."

"Tactful of her. She probably just thought it was bad business to send the customers rushing out of the store in tears. You never did master the concept that the customer is always right. Unless *you're* the customer, of course."

Tess consulted the list in front of Tyner. The next order was for a "Crabtown Special"—a set of H. L. Mencken's *Days* books, a tin of Old Bay seasoning and two crab mallets. Tess's hands fell naturally into the rhythm of assembling the items. Last Christmas season, she had still been filling in at the store, even as she began working toward getting her private investigator's license. In hindsight, it seemed a most desirable job. The hours were regular; Kitty had made sure her staff had medical benefits.

Besides, no one ever backed bookstore clerks against their cars, threatening to rape them if they showed their faces in a neighborhood again. And sleazy lobbyists didn't play the dozens with you, insulting your father just for the hell of it.

Tyner watched intently as Tess assembled the next three or four baskets, then started on the next, a Birdland special, which was built around the histories of the Orioles and the Ravens. He was never going to be as fast as Tess, and his ribbons left much to be desired, but he was catching on. They worked in a companionable silence, making steady progress.

"Something you want to talk about?" he asked after a while.

"Is it that obvious?"

"It is to me."

She told him of the day's events, hoping she wouldn't become emotional. She hated betraying any weakness in front of Tyner. Funny, the conversation with Vasso troubled her more in the retelling than the encounter with Pete and Repete. At least they hadn't been so damn oblique, or dragged her family into it.

"You get the license plate on the car you saw in the alley?"

Tess nodded. "But it's blocked. The MVA lets citizens safeguard their information now. As a licensed PI, I think I can still get it, but it means a trip to Glen Burnie tomorrow."

"Did you go to Harbor Court Hotel?"

"Of course. I didn't see the girl, though, and all I know of the man with her is that he wore gray trousers and drove a maroon car. She was probably in a private room."

"A prostitution ring."

That was the nice thing about Tyner. His mind worked quickly, and he always saw where she was going, even if he didn't necessarily agree it was the right direction.

"What else? I've never heard of Nicola DeSanti,

but Baltimore has so many low-level criminal bosses that no one can know all of them. The bar is clearly a front for something. I'm betting her husband's name isn't on the license because he was a convicted felon. When she took over, she saw no reason to bring the paperwork up to date."

"You going to ask Tull to run a background check on her or the late Mr. DeSanti?"

Tess shook her head. "No. I thought about it. I even considered filing charges against those two guys. But I don't think the police department is going to be as inclined to help me out when I'm trying to pry open a case they consider closed twice over."

"Tesser—" Kitty's influence had softened Tyner, made him a little nicer. He was not as quick to tell Tess that she was wrong, or thinking poorly. He resorted to tact. This should have been an improvement, but it was more like having a Band-Aid lifted very slowly.

"Just say it, Tyner. No Zig Ziglar homilies, please."

"You could be right. Gwen Schiller may have worked at this bar. She may even have been a prostitute there. But do you really think they'd kill her for that?"

"Maybe there was something else. Maybe she saw something, or heard something. They could be running numbers through there, or drugs."

"So Nicola DeSanti hires Henry Dembrow, an addled spray paint addict, to kill her? Pretty farfetched."

So it was. Tess was going on her gut, and what did her gut know about anything? Pete and Repete weren't likely to take a shine to any stranger who showed up at Domenick's. They hadn't threatened her because she had asked about Gwen, but because she came back, asking questions.

She tied a ribbon on the last basket, a Decadence Deluxe: John Waters's essays, *Tender Is the Night*, which Fitzgerald had worked on while Zelda had been in and out of the local mental hospitals, a box of Rheb's chocolate, and a bottle of Boordy, a Maryland wine.

"Sometimes," Tyner said, "things really are what they appear to be. A stupid kid knocks down a girl, she cracks open her head. He runs. She dies. End of story."

"Sometimes," Tess said, agreeing, yet not. She was staring at the bow on the package. Why had Henry marked Gwen's body, as if to send a message to someone? "And sometimes you just have to go back to the beginning, and start all over again."

"Back to Locust Point?"

"No." Funny, she had been speaking just to be speaking more or less. But Tyner's question made her focus, made her see where the beginning was. "Back to the liquor board. That's where I found the discrepancy in the license, where I found Arnie Vasso's name in the file."

It also happened to be where her father worked. Her father, who knew all about favors.

She found him at his desk the next morning, doing whatever he did at his desk. Funny how little she knew about his work. Liquor board inspector had always sounded so self-evident. Had she ever asked her father a question about his job beyond, "How was your day?" She didn't think so.

Nor had she registered how impersonal his office was, for a man who had been in the same job, the same cubicle, for thirty years. The only touches he had added were three photographs. One of him with Senator Ditter at the annual Crisfield Bull Roast; a startlingly sexy photograph of her mother, when she was still Judith Weinstein; and an old photo of Tess, circa junior high. Taken during her plumpest period, it showed a girl with a face as round and shiny as a full moon, hair in two thick plaits. All she needed was a horned helmet and she'd have been Ring Cycle–ready.

"I really wish you'd get rid of that," she said, as she had said every time she visited the office since it had appeared on his desk.

"It's cute," her father protested, truly perplexed. "You look so healthy."

Presexual, he meant. Climbing trees instead of boys.

But she was still his little girl, even at five-nine and God knows how many pounds. Mindful of this, she edited carefully as she told him about the parts of her investigation that had touched on Domenick's.

He was worried, even after hearing the PG version.

"Nicola DeSanti," he said, shaking his head. "Jesus, Tess, she's bad news."

"I picked up that much."

"Why are you still poking around, anyway? You

did what Ruthie asked. Don't get caught up in her sickness about Henry. It's normal for family to want to think the best of family, but you don't have to fall in." He shook his head again. "Ruthie. She always was a pit bull when it came to her little brother."

"Daddy." He was usually Dad to her, sometimes Pop. He hadn't been "Daddy" for twenty-five years. "Did you ever work that territory?"

"No." It took him a second to get the intent behind the question, then he was wounded. "*No.* Jesus, Tess. You think I'd be mixed up with something like that? Thanks a lot. In fact, the territory belongs to one of the new guys, straightest arrow in the office. One of Dahlgren's hand-picked boys. Eric Collins. He doesn't even *drink.*"

"It's not drinking we're talking about."

"Look, I saw him this morning when I came in. Let me see if he's still out there; you can talk to him yourself about Domenick's."

Her father's office was a place entirely without distractions, not even a view. There was a window, but her father left it covered by heavy, old-fashioned Venetian blinds. Tess tried separating the blinds so she could peek through, but the window was so dirty that it might as well have been opaque.

"Here's Eric," her father said. "What do you want to ask him?"

The man was young, and earnest looking, with freckles and a cowlick. He wore gray trousers, Tess noticed, but then, so did her father. So did a lot of men in Baltimore.

"Have you picked up on anything at Domenick's?"

she asked him. "Any complaints, any hints that they're doing something other than serving beer?"

He shook his head. "It's one of the few places over there no one ever complains about. They close on time, they don't make noise, they don't serve underage kids."

"What about the girls?"

"What girls? I've seen a barmaid here and there, but it's not like they've got B-girls at the counter, trying to hustle guys for dollar drafts, or dancing on the tables. You've been there, you've seen it. It's a neighborhood joint. Yeah, Nicola DeSanti may be running her rackets through it, but that's not my problem, you know? I can't even catch her paying off on video poker. And she's death on drugs, I can tell you that much. She's old-fashioned that way."

"What about the fact that a dead man is listed as the owner?"

The young inspector rolled his eyes. "So, I haul them in, and next thing you know it'll be her daughter or her cousin. Everyone knows how that works."

A straight arrow, and not stupid, but uninterested in converting the rest of the world.

"Sorry, Tess," her father said. "You're not going to find any answers here. You may have to accept there are no answers, not to the questions you're asking."

She left, feeling dejected. It had seemed so promising. Gene Fulton fell into step beside her as she walked down the stairs to the street.

"Looking good, Tess," he said. "I saw you on the television the other night."

She was surprised to find him so determinedly chummy. She thought the bit about her imminent engagement would have killed his fleeting interest. Maybe she could show him the photo of herself in her father's office. That should dampen any man's ardor.

"Well, you know what they say, Mr. Fulton." She deliberately avoided using his first name. "The camera adds ten pounds. But it's good for business."

"Guess you don't get to take much time off, being self-employed and all. You working through the end of the year, or you going to give yourself a little holiday, hit the party circuit?"

Oh please, not an invitation. She was not up to the tact required to deflect an unwanted date.

"I thought I was going to be working, but now I'm not so sure. My dad says I've got a dog by the tail, and he just might be right."

"Well—" they were down at the street now, and Gene had his keys out, twirling them in his fingers. "Give yourself a break. Take it easy. You're young, you should be having fun."

She braced herself, but there was no followup. He simply waved and crossed South Street to his car, parked illegally in a loading zone. A ticket was on the windshield, but it didn't seem to bother him. Why should it? It was probably a point of honor with him that he could get his tickets fixed. Lord knows no one in Tess's family had ever paid a parking ticket. Fulton took the white sheet from the windshield, crumpled it and threw it in the trash. Tess watched the maroon Mercury pull away from the curb and head down South Street.

Maroon. She remembered a car just that color. Granted, she had only seen the bottom six inches of fender, but it had been maroon. She darted across the street and found Fulton's ticket, crumpled, but at least on top of the trash heap.

She knew before she checked that the license plate would match the one she had glimpsed yesterday in the alley behind Domenick's, that she wasn't going to have to drive to the MVA in Glen Burnie after all.

She started back into her father's office, brandishing the ticket and her notebook. But before she could call upstairs from the lobby, she stopped and retreated to her own car. Loyalty had long ago replaced Roman Catholicism as her father's religion. Confronted with this scrap of information, he'd make excuses for Gene. Worse, he'd probably ask Gene about it, which would tell the folks at Domenick's more than she wanted them to know just yet.

She folded the ticket and put it in her pocket, trying to decide where she should go next. So far, there was one person who had been consistently truthful in talking to her about Gwen Schiller, the only person who had been helpful to her in any way.

Wouldn't you know, it was the one person everyone said was a pathological liar?

22

She found Sukey in Latrobe Park, reading the latest issue of *Teen People*.

"Do you think I could ever look like this?" she asked Tess, pointing to a photo of the latest teen sensation, female variety, a toothpick girl with absurdly large breasts on her bony chest. She reminded Tess of the drawing of the boa constrictor in *The Little Prince*, the one that showed the snake with a pig halfway through its digestive system. Put this girl on her back, and she was more or less the same shape.

"No," Tess said. "Because no one actually looks like that, not even her. Jesus, those can't be real."

"Oh they are," Sukey assured her. "She says right here that she's never had plastic surgery."

"Sukey, do you always tell the truth?"

The girl looked down at her feet, hurt. "Most of the time."

"Which is what everyone does. So why would you assume she's telling the truth?"

This seemed to cheer Sukey up. "Hey, can you keep a secret?"

"Sure."

"I have a boyfriend."

Uh-oh. "Why does it have to be a secret?"

"Don't worry, he's not one of those old guys you warned me about. I mean, he's older 'n me, he can drive and all. His name is Paul." Sukey paused. "He's not a boyfriend-boyfriend. He has a girl. But he likes to talk to me, when she's being a bitch."

"Sukey—" Tess didn't know what to say without sounding as if she were forever contradicting herself. True, she had told Sukey to avoid the boys who wanted girls for their parts. But the talkers could be dangerous, too, in another way. They usually came so much later in one's life. She had known one in her twenties, a man who dropped by to "talk" late at night, after his fiancée had gone to sleep.

"Go on," Sukey said.

"What?"

"Tell me he's using me. Tell me he's using me to make his girlfriend jealous, that he'll always go running back to her. That's what my mother says."

If Mrs. Brewer had been briefed, then Tess was off the hook, freed of feeling she had to be *in loco parentis.*

"He does sound a little, well, confused, but I didn't come here to talk about our love lives." Sukey beamed at the implication she and Tess were equals, two girlfriends with the same set of problems. "I'm here because we never finished our conversation the other day, the one about the girl I was looking for, Gwen Schiller."

"I figured you didn't need me anymore, once you knew who she was."

There was a sad, lonely note in Sukey's voice. It wasn't reproachful, but it was a reminder to Tess that there were infinite ways in which to use people.

"I never would have found her without you. I said your name on television, didn't you hear?"

"Just my first name," the girl said sulkily.

"As if everyone in Locust Point didn't know who Sukey Brewer was. Besides, I thought your mom might not like it, if I used your full name. She certainly wasn't happy the day she found us talking," Tess said. "She interrupted us, remember? I thought maybe there was something else you were going to tell me, something more about Gwen."

"She didn't look like a Gwen," Sukey said thoughtfully. "She should have had a more flowery name, like Heather, Or Shania."

"Sukey, have you told me everything you know about Gwen?"

For a girl known as a liar, Sukey wasn't much good at hiding her emotions when she was interrogated directly. She made things up, but only for fun, Tess realized. Give her a piece of paper, and she'd just be another novelist.

But for now, she squirmed, refusing to make eye contact.

"Sukey?"

"She needed to make a call. She asked if she could come to my house, but I couldn't let her. My mom would kill me if I let someone in. But I told her there was another way to make her call—" she stopped.

"What, Sukey?"

"You can't tell this part. I'd be banned."

"I won't tell."

She rolled her magazine into a tight log, pressed it against her mouth, muttering into it as if it were a bullhorn. But she ended up muffling her words, not amplifying them.

"I can't hear a thing you're saying, Sukey."

"She didn't have any money, and I sure didn't have any. But she really needed to make this call. So I swiped a phone card. Off the counter, at the mini-mart. From Brad, which made me feel awful, but she needed it so bad. It was only a five-dollar one, and it was a rip-off, the way it counted the minutes. One call, just to leave a message, and it was almost used up. She used it at a pay phone. She made a call, and she said someone would be here to get her in a few hours. She was sure of it. She said she'd have to wait in the park, because Fort McHenry closes at sunset. She said she was going to be okay."

Sukey was close to tears. Tess looked away, letting her use whatever tricks she had mastered to keep them from coming. Why was it so important not to cry when you were a child? She couldn't remember the logic, but she knew the feeling, knew Sukey would feel she had lost face if Tess saw her tears.

"It's not your fault, Sukey. You tried to help her. In fact, you might be one of the few people who ever tried to help Gwen Schiller. There are a lot of people who should feel guilty about what happened to her. You don't happen to be one of them."

"It's so strange," the girl said, sniffling. "Knowing someone who died. I mean, a someone who wasn't a grandmom, or an old person."

"I know," Tess said. Boy did she know. "Let's go to the mini-mart."

"You're not going to make me confess, are you? My mom did that once. She made me go into this store and tell I boosted gum. I couldn't ever go back. I only did it the once."

"Only once?"

"Only once in that store," Sukey confessed.

"I'm not worried about your shoplifting. You should stop stealing, though. You're going to get caught, and there will be consequences."

"I might not get caught." Offered cautiously, as if she were curious to see if Tess would contradict her.

"Maybe not. But you probably will. Everyone gets caught."

"*Everyone?* Then there'd be no unsolved crimes, I guess."

"One way or another, everyone gets caught," Tess amended. "If not in this world, then the next. Now let's walk down to the mini-mart."

At the mini-mart, Sukey bought a fan magazine and a bag of Utz cheese curls, but she found what Tess was doing far more intriguing than the latest news about the pretty-boy band of the moment. Sitting on the curb, her orange-coated fingers dipping in and out of the bag, she watched Tess as if she were a television program, although Tess thought even C-span would balk at airing something this boring. She wrote down the numbers on the three phones outside. Like a lot of the city's pay phones, they were programmed not to take incoming calls, but by calling her own cell phone and using the Caller ID function, she was able to verify each number.

"Is the phone company going to give you a list of the outgoing calls from there on the day before she died?" Sukey asked.

"Not me," Tess said. "But a certain police officer I know will be able to get the numbers. He owes me a favor. I think." Actually, she had lost track on who owed what in the Martin Tull–Tess Monaghan favor exchange. She might have to ask for credit.

"Cool," Sukey said. "You know, I think I want to be a private investigator when I grow up."

"Oh lord, Sukey. Please try to find a real job."

"What's a real job?"

Tess thought about this. "One with paid medical, and a lunchroom with a microwave, maybe even a cafeteria with hot food. Better yet, free long-distance phone calls and co-workers to waste time with. One with United Way drives and employee-of-the-month contests and a company newsletter and endless requests to kick in five dollars here and ten dollars there for Susie in accounting who just had a baby or a wedding or a divorce or a new filling."

She warmed to the subject. "One with a cubicle and a desk that snags your panty hose and endless memos about the right way to dispose of recyclables. And lots and lots of petty intrigue and small-minded politics, all intended to distract you from the fact that you're getting two percent raises from a company that's returning twenty percent to its stockholders. That's a real grown-up's job, Sukey. Not what I do."

Thank God, she thought. *Thank God.*

"So what are you going to do when *you* grow up?" Sukey smiled, pleased with herself at being able to turn that dreaded question on someone else for once.

"I'll worry about that when the day comes."

"Don't be so impatient," Crow said, rubbing the knot that had taken up residence at the base of her neck. "You can't rush the phone company. It's like poking a sleeping dinosaur with a twig."

"I know, I know," Tess said. "But I had hoped to hear from them before the weekend. Waiting is much less tolerable when no one is footing the bill for it."

She took a sip of her eggnog, the sensible kind that was almost all brandy. They were at an open house held every year by one of the old *Star* columnists, who built an elaborate Christmas garden in his basement. In his version of Baltimore, it was still the 1970s, with all the old stores open for business—Read's Drugs, Hutzler's, Hoschild's. He also had learned how to make it appear as if the *Beacon-Light* were on fire.

"The little figures, screaming in the windows?" he told Tess and Crow. "Those are all the editors who refused to hire me when the *Star* folded. The bastards."

"Cool," Crow said.

"Tull says I'll probaby have it first thing Monday morning," Tess said. "It's hard to wait, though."

"I guess it is," Crow commiserated. "Hey, is that supposed to be the governor tied to the train tracks?"

Tess looked closely. "No, it's the senator who blocked the gay rights legislation last session."

Crow wrapped his arms around her from behind, rested his chin on her shoulder. "Now this is my idea of a Christmas tradition. What do you want for Christmas, anyway?"

"A neon sign that says 'Human Hair.' How many times do I have to tell you?"

"Funny, that's exactly what I want."

What I really want, Tess was thinking, is a resolution to this mess before the end of the year. She wanted to look at the log of numbers called from that pay phone on November fifth, and find—find what, exactly? Gene Fulton's home number would work. A call to Domenick's. Then she would feel comfortable telling her father what she knew about his co-worker. He would be outraged, shocked, surprised.

That was what she really wanted for Christmas. She wanted her father to be shocked, truly shocked that there had been gambling in Casablanca.

The list came crawling off her office fax machine the next day. Tull had wanted to bring it by in person— "The numbers are so small, you might not be able to read them from a fax"—but Tess had told him her eyesight was still pretty good.

A day in the life of a city pay phone was more interesting than she would have guessed. There were dozens of outgoing calls, and most were made with some sort of calling card. Tess focused on the local ones first, checking each number against the bound crisscross directory, then using a reverse directory on the Internet if that failed to turn up the number. She ended up calling most of them anyway, just to be sure. It was slow, tedious work, and she found herself wishing that Sukey could see her now. Heigh-ho, the glamorous life.

She concentrated on the local calls, the 410 ones, ignoring the 301s, 202s, 302s, and 215s scattered among the listings. Gene Fulton's number was not among those she checked. Neither was Domenick's. Nor was Eric Collins one of the listings she checked. If there was another name, another number, that Tess thought she might find, she didn't admit it, not even to herself. At any rate, if that number came up, she wouldn't need a directory to identify it.

But so many of the numbers fell outside the listings. She called blind, using different stories to cajole names from the skeptical, harried women who snatched up the phones on the fifth or sixth ring. It was slow going, but by midday, she had hit most of the local numbers on the list.

And she had nothing. Except for a reddened left ear.

She moved on to the 301 numbers, which covered the Washington suburbs and the western part of the state. The Schillers lived in that area code. More nothing. She had not contemplated this much nothingness since she tried taking a philosophy course in her freshman year at Washington College, and discovered it made her head hurt. All these numbers, all these codes, all these calls. How could so much life emanate from three pay phones in Locust Point?

Drug dealers preferred the illegal pay phones around the city, which actually outnumbered the legal ones. The calls made here were probably much more mundane. Car trouble, what was the name of that guy, again, and I'm stopping at the market, do you need anything? All those calls and one of them, just one of them, was Gwen Schiller's call for help.

A call for help.

Damn, she was stupid sometimes. Why would Gwen, alone and scared, reach out to the very people she presumably was running from? Why would she call Gene Fulton, or Domenick's, or anyone in the DeSanti family? Tess had been so intent on finding a link that she had not thought this through properly. Gwen was waiting for someone, someone who had to come to her and find her in a very public, accessible place, Fort McHenry, a place that any out-of-towner could find, a place where no one could sneak up on you. She checked the long distance calls again: There were seven to the D.C. suburbs, four to 202, which was D.C. proper. Two to Delaware, 302. And one to 215, which was Philadelphia.

Philadelphia. Where, as Tess knew, Gwen did have a contact. A contact who said she hadn't heard from her since leaving Persephone's Place.

Tess dialed the number. It rang five times before Devon Whittaker's cool, dry voice assured her that she was so sorry she had missed her call, but please leave a message and she would get right back to you.

Tess wondered if Gwen Schiller had listened to the same message, a little over a year ago.

* * *

It was not a day for trains, to bend her schedule to anyone else's. Tess was in her car within five minutes, stopping only to drop Esskay at Kitty's store.

"Do you think this is what it would be like if we had a baby?" Crow wondered. "You handing it off to me in a Snugli, while you strap on your gun and head out into the world?"

"I'm not strapping on my gun," she said. "I'm just carrying it in my knapsack. And don't talk about babies, okay? One day at a time."

"As long as there's a tomorrow," Crow said, watching Esskay as she climbed into one of the store's easy chairs and made herself at home. Tess was already out the door, her mind racing ahead of her as she sped across Eastern Avenue and then up I-95.

Devon had said she didn't know Gwen that well, but she had known she had left. At the time, she said she had heard it from one of the other girls, but the clinic maintained no one else who was there knew Gwen had escaped. They had kept it quiet.

Besides, why would Gwen call someone who was in? Only someone who was out, and on her own, could help her. Devon was out by then, starting her freshman year at Penn, living off campus. Perhaps Gwen, not knowing about Devon's watchful bodyguard, had expected her to take her in, or at least come to Baltimore to bail her out of whatever trouble she was in. She was waiting for someone, Sukey had told her. The someone never came, so Gwen was still in the park the next day, ready for fate when it arrived in the shape of Henry Dembrow.

It took a solid two hours to make the 100-mile trip to Philadelphia. Tess burned up another 45 minutes in wrong turns before she found her way back to Devon's apartment. She found a space halfway down the street, rang the apartment from the foyer. No answer. She bought a pretzel from a street vendor and took it back to the car. She couldn't remember when she had eaten last.

It was almost dusk when Devon turned down the street. She moved self-consciously—shoulders hunched beneath the weight of her knapsack, eyes on the pavement, her body hidden in the voluminous folds of a man's vintage cashmere coat.

Tess stopped her just outside the apartment building.

"Devon."

She needed a second. Maybe it was the dim light. "The private detective. The one who was looking for Gwen."

"She called you, didn't she? The day before she was killed, she called you."

Devon's eyes returned to the sidewalk, then slid to the right. "I wasn't home. She left a message, but I wasn't home, and I didn't know what time she called. There wasn't anything I could do. Until you came here, I thought she was alive."

"We need to talk about this. Can I come inside?"

Devon nodded, then shook her head. "Hilde's there."

"Are you saying you can't talk about this in front of Hilde? We can go sit in my car if you like."

"No. She'll give us privacy, if I ask."

"Then ask," Tess said. She shouldered her own knapsack, followed Devon into the small vestibule of her building, watched her fumble with the keys at the inside door, which was even balkier than the last time. Tess noticed the veneer around the lock was scratched, which struck her as a seedy note in such a nice building. The stairwell was dark, too, as if the landlord were too cheap to turn on the lights one minute before dusk was complete.

Later, forced to recount the events that followed—and Tess was forced to recount them several times—she remembered feeling as if she had left her body, that she was standing outside herself and what she was seeing. "That's funny," Devon was saying, "the lock doesn't want to—oh, there it goes." Devon flipped a switch, but the stairwell light didn't come on. "Burned out," Devon said matter-of-factly, and began climbing the stairs.

It was then that Tess grabbed her arm and dragged her into the street. She wasn't sure how her gun came to be in her hand, safety off, but she must have opened her knapsack because Devon was holding her cell phone. She heard a voice, her own voice, above the dull roaring in her ears. *Call 911. Call 911.* Even as Devon was trying to make the call, Tess was dragging her across the street, looking for someplace safe, untouchable.

She settled for the Philly cheesesteak cart, stationed behind someone's very nice and very white BMW. Time was out of sequence for Tess. It seemed to her that she threw Devon to the ground before the shots were fired, but that didn't make any sense. The phone bounced from Devon's hand, even as the call was going through. Tess could hear the operator's voice buzzing from the sidewalk, increasingly impatient. "911, may I help you? May I help you? Are you there?" She hoped the 911 operator could hear them, could hear the panicked screams on the street around them.

"Yell out the address," she shouted to Devon. "Scream as loud as you can." A second round of shots, and although Tess did not dare look up, she knew they were coming from Devon's apartment. Luckily, whoever was waiting there had assumed they'd be doing their work at much closer range. They didn't have the guns, or the target skills, for this distance, although Tess heard a few shots ringing into the BMW. The cheesesteak vendor abandoned ship, running down the block. The first wave of sirens started, not too far in the distance. The shots stopped as suddenly as they had begun.

"Is there a back entrance to your building?" Tess asked Devon.

She nodded, looking a little dazed. "And a fire escape. Do you want me to show you?"

"No, I just need to tell the police when they get here. My guess is whoever was in your apartment will leave that way. But we stay here until the cops arrive."

Slowly, Tess was returning to her own body. She became aware of the cold air, the rough sidewalk beneath her cheek, the fact that her left arm was around Devon's narrow waist. People had begun to move in the street again, but no one would come close to them, although a teenage boy kicked Tess's cell phone so it skittered back to her. Maybe it was the gun in Tess's right hand. Maybe it was because no one saw any percentage in cozying up to the targets.

"The cheese and onions are making me sick," Devon said. "The smell, I mean."

"There are worse smells," Tess said.

23

Hilde was dead. The Philadelphia cops, over Tess's objections, made Devon come inside the apartment and identify her keeper's sturdy body. Tess, who knew more about murder scenes than she wanted to, could see that Hilde had been shot as she came through the door, then dragged to the kitchen. The homicide detectives seemed to find this curious, and spent a long time pacing the path of dried blood she had left, looking for pieces of evidence to bag. Why had the body been moved, they kept asking one another, when the answer seemed obvious to Tess. Hilde's killer wanted Devon to be inside the apartment before she knew anything was amiss. A corpse by the front door would have ruined the element of surprise.

She kept her thoughts to herself. Baltimore cops had never been particularly enamored of her ideas, and there she was a taxpayer. Here, she was an out-of-state PI. An out-of-state PI who hadn't bothered to check if her license to carry transferred across the Mason-Dixon line. Oops.

Devon handled herself well. She was tougher than Tess had thought. Oh, she cried, and looked as if she might become sick, yet she seemed remarkably composed. Did she understand she was the intended victim, that Hilde had been nothing but an unexpected obstacle? Probably not, and Tess didn't see any reason to tell her. The realization would come soon enough and, along with it, the electric guilt of surviving when someone close to you is dead. That was the hard part. The secret euphoria you felt at still being alive.

The cops kept Tess and Devon apart as much as possible, taking them to the police station in separate vehicles and sequestering them in different interview rooms. It did not strike Tess that they feared the two women were collaborators, who would conspire to tell one version of events. No, they were from different caste systems. The cops were deferential to Devon—the hometown girl, the Main Line deb, with a Philadelphia lawyer waiting for her at the station, along with her parents. Tess was the scruffy outsider and although they knew she was not to blame for what had happened, they couldn't seem to shake the idea she was a troublemaker. She didn't help matters by refusing to divulge details about the case that had brought her to the City of Brotherly Love.

"Privileged," she said, keeping her voice as polite and cool as possible.

"Privilege is for lawyers, priests, and doctors," one of the homicide cops said.

"I work for one."

"Which one?"

"A lawyer, for Christ's sake. Do you think I had my gun drawn because I was attempting to convert Devon Whittaker to Catholicism?"

The Philadelphia cops enjoyed her sense of humor about as much as the Baltimore cops did. But given that they had one, maybe two less homicides to solve because of Tess, they grudgingly relaxed their hard-ass routine. So she unbent, too, telling them enough to seem almost cooperative.

"I came to see Devon Whittaker because phone logs indicated she had been one of the last people to speak to a woman connected to a case." All true, and straightforward. Trying to explain Gwen Schiller, the Jane Doe murder, Henry Dembrow's sudden demise, and her whole family history wouldn't have shed any more light on the matter.

They seemed somewhat mollified, but they didn't let her go. Left alone with her own thoughts—always a dangerous combination—Tess puzzled over the day's events. Had she been followed? No, she would have noticed a two-hour tail, she was sure of that. From eavesdropping on the cops, she knew Hilde had been dead for a while by the time they entered the apartment. At least, she thought that was what was meant by lividity. Maybe she just couldn't bear to believe that Hilde had been shot even as she sat outside, waiting for Devon to come home from her classes.

Tess had been sitting with her left leg curled beneath her, and it had gone to sleep, all pins and needles. She stood up and stomped Frankenstein-style around the room, not caring if this made for a comic show for the cops on the other side of the one-way glass. She wondered if she was going to have to tell them more before they let her go. She had called Tyner, and he was sending a friend, a local attorney. They had agreed this would be quicker than waiting for him to head up I-95 in his van. Besides, Tyner and Kitty had tickets to the opera that night. *Tosca.*

"I find Puccini the most sensual of all the composers," he had told Tess. "As I told Kitty in bed last night—"

Tess had told Tyner she really didn't need to know where he and Kitty had their conversations, or if they were vertical or horizontal at the time. Really, Tyner was such an adolescent. He wanted the whole world to know that he was in love and, better yet, having sex. To Tess, this fell into the same category as the President's sex life, Bob Dole's Viagra habit, and Larry King's insistence on procreating well into Methuselah-hood. It was beyond too much information, it was instant ipecac.

But she couldn't help noticing that Tyner's friend, when she finally arrived, was a striking woman in her fifties, with dark hair slicked back in what Tess thought of as a Mexican movie star bun. Very Dolores del Río, even if her name was decidedly unexotic: Ellen Cade.

"I work for one of the big boy firms here," she told Tess, offering a soft, cool hand.

"Criminal law?" Tess asked her.

"Constitutional. But I know enough to get by. Besides, it was my impression that you're not going to be charged with a crime. You just want to know how much you have to tell these guys, if you can laim privilege as a contractual employee of an attorney."

"Something like that."

"Let me play devil's advocate: Why not tell them everything?"

Tess thought about this. She was, by nature, a wary person, stingy with what she knew and suspicious of anyone in authority. It didn't help that she wasn't sure what she knew, and if it had any bearing on what had happened today. But a woman had been killed, and Tess was not inclined to solve the crime herself, so perhaps she should cooperate a little.

"I'm investigating . . . I'm not sure what I'm investigating. A girl was murdered in Baltimore a year ago. Her killer died in prison. There are some loose ends around the case, and I'm looking into those for the killer's sister. The dead girl called Devon Whittaker the day before she died—a fact that Devon hid from me when I talked to her earlier this month. I came back today to find out why."

Ellen Cade ran her hands across her head, smoothing her already smooth hair. "The police think Devon was being targeted for a kidnapping. Her family's rich, and quite prominent. She made an attractive target, living off campus, with so few people around her."

"Then why fire at her from the apartment? The gunshots are on the 911 tape and they know from looking at my gun that it wasn't fired today. Why kill Hilde?"

Ellen Cade's shrug was as throwaway elegant as the rest of her. These were not flesh-and-blood

people to her, just names in a theoretical case on
might study in law school. "If you want to go argu
with the police, feel free. But in my opinion, ou
strategy should be all or nothing. You can't te
them just what you feel like telling them. You war
to say what you know is privileged, I'll back you u
on that. If you want to talk to them, I'll stay wit
you, make sure you don't incriminate yourself i
any way."

"What I really need is to speak to Devon."

"When you're a Whittaker, and the potential vic
tim in a crime, the Philadelphia police don't keep
you all night. She was on her way out when I came
in—her parents on one side, the family lawyer o
the other."

"Do you know how I can find them?"

Ellen Cade's eyes were a dark, rich brown, the
color of good milk chocolate, yet devoid of warmth
"I'm not here to broker your dealings with the Whittakers. I'm the go-between for you and the Philadelphia Police Department. The way I see it, you could
be out of here in an hour, or you could stay considerably longer. Which do you choose?"

"Where do the Whittakers live? The Main
Line, right?"

"Short or long?"

Tess sighed. "Short. I have nothing to say to
them. Everything I know is privileged."

"Good girl. I hope you understand I am billing
you for my services. Tyner and I ended on friendly
terms—but not such friendly terms that I give it
away. The way I see it, I gave quite enough while we
were dating."

Great, another factoid about Tyner's sex life. This day kept getting better and better.

Ellen Cade overrated her abilities. Two hours passed before the Philadelphia cops sent Tess off into what was now night. Tess would have liked to crawl into the back of her Toyota and sleep, but that wasn't an option. Instead, she dialed Whitney's house. Not the guest cottage, but the main house.

"Tesser!" Mrs. Talbot's voice was mellow with tiny cracks in it, like good whisky being poured over ice. "We're just sitting down to dinner. But Whitney's at a holiday party held by one of her classmates from Roland Park Country Day."

"That's okay, Mrs. Talbot. I really wanted to talk to you."

"To me?" She sounded at once surprised and flattered.

Tess paused, trying to think of a polite way to ask Mrs. Talbot if she knew the Whittakers of Philadelphia. It would sound as if she assumed all rich, blueblood types knew one another. Which was exactly what she assumed.

"Mrs. Talbot, is your family in the Social Register?"

"Tess, you know I've never cared about such things."

That would be a yes. "Does the Social Register include addresses?"

"Yes, winter and summer. And the yachts, sometimes, if the family uses one." If there was any irony in Mrs. Talbot's voice, Tess missed it. "Why do you ask? Certainly, you know where we live."

"I'm trying to find a home address for the Whit-takers of Philadelphia. They're not in the phone book."

"Which Philadelphia Whittakers? There are several."

"The parents of Devon Whittaker."

"I may have the Philadelphia book around. It's an excellent resource for fund-raising, and you know how many committees I serve on."

Mrs. Talbot put the phone down. Not a minute later, she picked up an extension in another room. "I do have it," she said, a little breathlessly. "Is this part of your work? Am I helping you out? It's rather fun, isn't it?"

Tess had a vision of both Talbot women follow-ing her around, in fetching mother-and-daughter outfits. Starsky and Hutch and the Duchess of Windsor on stakeouts together.

"Rather," she said, trying not to mimic Mrs. Talbot's accent. "If you have the stomach for it." She thought again of Hilde, how her lifeless body had been dragged and bumped across the room, as if she were nothing more than an unwieldy bag of garbage. She remembered the jumbo bag of barbe-cued Fritos the cops had plucked from the dining room table, hoping to find fingerprints on the plastic. Devon Whittaker would not have a bag of Fritos in her pantry, Tess knew, and Hilde probably wouldn't bring such a loaded food into the house. Which meant the killer had sat a few feet from Hilde's body, having a picnic while waiting for Devon to arrive.

She took down the phone number and address

Mrs. Talbot provided, then stopped at a 7-Eleven to buy a map.

It was dark in the suburbs and house numbers were difficult to see. Tess had to get out of her car several times to check the mailboxes at the street's edge. Finally, she found the Whittakers, and headed up the long driveway. She wasn't sure why she felt so cowed—the Whittakers, after all, were just the Philadelphia version of the Talbots, or any number of moneyed, familied Baltimoreans she had known. But this wasn't her territory, she didn't know the connections and history here. If the Whittakers called the cops when she showed up on their doorstep, she could end up back downtown, waiting for Ellen Cade to bail her out a second time.

A man opened a door. Not a butler, judging by his clothes—a tweed jacket over an Oxford cloth shirt, khaki pants—but far from the patrician man of the manor Tess had expected.

"Yes?" Behind tortoiseshell glasses, his eyes were at once vague and nervous. His other features were soft and mushy, more like lumps in gravy than an actual face.

"I'm Tess Monaghan."

"The girl who saved Devon's life?"

"Yes." Left unasked was the question of whether Tess had put Devon's life in jeopardy to begin with.

"Please come in."

She was led into a book-lined study that could have been drawn from the plans for her own dream home—antique Persian rugs, a fireplace, a sofa covered in moss green velvet, the walls lined with books, old books, with worn spines that had known many hands and many readings.

But Devon, sitting in an armchair close to the fire and wrapped in a chenille throw, registered no delight in her surroundings. Despite the throw, and the fire, her body was shaking convulsively. Her face, reflected in the firelight, had a decidedly bluish cast.

"I just feel so bad," she said when she saw Tess.

"About Hilde?"

She nodded. "And Gwen."

Her father stood in the doorway, as if waiting for Devon's permission to enter. Tess wondered if this young woman had always held so much power in her family, or if she had earned her father's deference when she began destroying her body. Maybe that was the reason she had stopped eating in the first place, to gain power.

"You can listen, Daddy. That way I won't have to tell it twice."

The father took a seat at a rolltop desk, out of Devon's sight line. Tess sat on the sofa, facing her. That is, she would have been facing her, if Devon hadn't continued to stare into the flames.

"The first time I came to see you—why didn't you tell me you had heard from Gwen, that she had called you?"

"Are you good at keeping secrets?" Devon asked.

"I like to think I am."

"I'm great at it. Most girls with eating disorders are. I was. So was Gwen. The disease turns you into a sneak, you see. You have to be crafty, to keep people from making you eat, in my case, or making you stop throwing up, in Gwen's case. Even when you told me Gwen was dead, I felt I had to keep her secrets."

"About the rape?"

"And other things."

"What other secrets could Gwen possibly have?"

"The usual. She hated her father"—Devon turned her head toward Mr. Whittaker, but he didn't seem to notice—"for putting her in that place, then going off on his year-long honeymoon with the secretary-slut. That's what she called his new wife. She thought if she ran away, he would have to pay attention to her. It was just a castle in the air at first, a fantasy to talk about at night. But when the teacher raped her, she decided to run away for real."

"How could you know that? You left Persephone's more than a month before Gwen escaped, to enroll at Penn."

Devon pulled the throw more tightly around her. "We stayed in touch. It wasn't allowed, but we did it."

"Not allowed?" Tess asked.

"It was the doctor at the clinic who thought it would be better for you, Devon," Mr. Whittaker said in a soft, shy voice. Tess had almost forgotten he was there. "He said it might retard your progress."

"Dr. Blount." Devon grimaced. "Yes, he was a real prize. You'd pay two thousand dollars a day never to see him again, or smell his rotten breath while he blabbed on and on about all the stupid reasons girls did what they did. As if he knew. As if he knew anything."

"But you're better," Mr. Whittaker said, his voice a plea.

"Sure," Devon said. "I'm better. I'm alive. I've been alive for a whole year longer than Gwen. That doesn't seem fair somehow. I helped her run away, and she ended up dead. Does that mean I killed her?"

"How did you help her?"

"I sent her money, through one of the Mexican women they hired to clean there. She didn't know what she was smuggling in, she just knew she got twenty dollars for every letter she took in. I managed to send Gwen five hundred dollars that way, before she left. You know, she never even thanked me for the money. She was a bit spoiled that way. Gwen was so beautiful that people liked to do things for her, and she grew accustomed to it. When she wanted something from you, she expected to get it right away. She thought you could drop everything and do her bidding."

Tess thought she knew where Devon was heading. "She called you, and asked you to come to Baltimore, didn't she?"

"She left a message on my voice mail, telling me she was waiting for me at a park near Fort McHenry. I didn't find it until evening, when I came home from class. I figured it was too late, by then. The call had come in hours before. Besides, I couldn't figure out a way to shake Hilde. I thought Gwen would call me again the next day. But she didn't."

She tried, Tess thought, thinking of Henry Dembrow's confession. She died trying. *You have a phone,* she asked. *Of course we have a phone.* It was then that Gwen's interest had been piqued, that she had agreed to go to Henry's house with him.

"I still don't understand why you couldn't tell me she called you. It's not your fault she's dead, Devon."

Devon was crying now, tears streaming down her face. "But it is. If I hadn't helped her leave Persephone's Place, she never would have been there, don't you see? All this time, I told myself she couldn't be dead, because Dick Schiller's daughter couldn't die without it being a big deal, right? I told myself that every day for a year, but I never picked up the phone, never tried to call the Schillers' house down in Potomac. Because I knew somehow. I knew something terrible had happened to her."

Sobbing, Devon was a figure of pity, yet her father did not move from his chair, did not try to comfort her. It was as if he was waiting for an invitation. Finally, Tess went over to her and pulled the throw around her shoulders. Devon stiffened at the contact, but she didn't push Tess away.

"You didn't hurt me, by hiding what you knew," Tess told her. "But you almost hurt yourself. Someone else knows Gwen called you. I don't know how, but they do. Someone who wanted to keep you from speaking to me. I'm not sure what Gwen knew, but someone is willing to kill anyone who talked to her in the final days of her life."

"I can't help hiding things," Devon said. Her nose

was running, and her voice was still choked from her tears. "It's what I do. I used to cut my food into tiny little pieces, and push it down into my sock when no one was looking, then throw the socks away after supper. My mother could never understand why I was always running out of tube socks. I told her the dog was stealing them from the hamper."

Mr. Whittaker cleared his throat, but said nothing.

"Whoever tried to kill you thinks Gwen told you something."

"Well, she didn't. The only thing she kept saying on the answering machine was, 'I can't go back, I can't go back.'"

"She meant to Persephone's?"

"I thought so at the time. Although she also said . . ." Devon paused, searching her memory. "She said, 'I can't go back. I can't go with him.'"

"I can't go with *him*?"

"Yes. I thought she meant her father, but it could have been someone else."

Tess shook her head. It was too small a scrap of information to be useful. Besides, it might not mean anything.

"Devon, Mr. Whittaker—" the father hitched his chair slightly forward, but otherwise was silent. "I don't think you should assume Devon is safe, not in the short run. She should be sent some place far away, and I think you should hire a bodyguard for her. If you can afford it."

The last part sounded silly to her ears. There was clearly very little the Whittakers couldn't afford, or wouldn't buy, especially when it came to Devon.

"How long will she have to go away?"

"I wish I could tell you. If Hilde's killer thinks it through, he'll realize Devon has spoken to the Philadelphia police, to me, to her family, and that keeping her silent is no longer a realistic possibility. But I'd go away for Christmas, if it's not too much of an imposition."

"We could," her father said. "We have a house in Guadeloupe."

Of course you do, Tess wanted to say.

"What about school?" Devon asked. "I have finals."

"I'll take care of it," her father assured her. Tess wondered how many times he had made that same promise to his daughter. "You can do them by mail, perhaps. We'll work something out."

"Guadeloupe will be warm at least," Devon said. "I'm cold all the time now. I feel like I'll never get warm again."

"I thought the doctor said your blood pressure would start going up," her father said.

"Doctors," Devon said, cramming more scorn into that one word than Tess would have thought possible.

She stood, ready to leave. "Guadeloupe sounds like a good plan. Don't forget the bodyguard, though. Besides, maybe the Philadelphia cops will surprise us. Maybe it will turn out that this has nothing to do with Gwen at all. Maybe it was a botched kidnapping."

Devon's father seemed to find some comfort in this, but Devon was a harder sell.

"Aren't you in danger, too? They followed you

to my apartment today. They're one step behind you."

"Actually," Tess said, "I'm afraid they're one step ahead of me."

24

It was past midnight when Tess made it home. She had expected little in the way of a welcoming committee—Kitty and Tyner were at the opera, Crow had a gig, and Esskay went to bed pretty early, to prepare for the next day's napping regimen.

But when she tiptoed into Kitty's kitchen to forage for a snack, her stomach less than satisfied by a Roy Rogers pit stop near the state line, her father was sitting at the kitchen table. He had a can of beer open in front of him, and the radio was on—Stan the Fan, or one of those sports talk shows. He had sat like this in their kitchen at home many an evening. If you asked him what he was listening to, or why, he might not have an answer. As a child, Tess had found this odd. But as an adult, she had developed her own fondness for the jumble of voices on talk radio. There was a soothing rhythm in all that chat, a kind of white noise in the locals' nasal accents.

"Mom kick you out?" she asked. Turn your fears

into jokes, and life won't be so inclined to provide the punchline.

"I was waiting for you," her father said. "Kitty left me a key. They're going to be out late—"

"The opera, I know. *Tosca*." She left out the part about how opera affected Tyner. Her father was almost as protective of his only sister as he was of his daughter. The difference being that he wholly approved of Tyner, an older man with a good income, and had yet to approve of anyone Tess had brought home.

"So, what's up?" By turning her back on him and rummaging in the refrigerator, she was able to make the question sound almost casual. *How was your day? Same old, same old. Got shot at, saved a woman's life.*

"You've got to stop what you're doing."

She froze, her hand wrapped around the upper portion of a bottle of Pinot Grigio, her face warm despite the cool air of the refrigerator. For a moment, she thought her father knew of her Philadelphia adventure. But how could he? The *Inquirer* would have a story tomorrow, given the prominence of the Whittaker family, but no one cared about her involvement. She was counting on the cops to misspell her name, counting on the reporter not to track her down, not tonight.

"Stop what?" she asked casually. "Drinking white wine? Hey, I had a hard day. You want another beer?"

"Arnie Vasso called me today. He said you're making a nuisance of yourself. He said you're annoying some people you'd be better off leaving alone."

"I spilled a glass of water in his lap, that's all."

"I'm not talking about Arnie, and you know it. I'm talking about Nicola DeSanti. Whatever you're doing, Tess, drop it. It's not worth it. Not worth your time, and not worth Ruthie's money. Tell your cop friend what you know, and get out of the way."

She poured a glass of wine and sat down across from her father. No use putting the bottle back in the refrigerator. She knew she'd drain it before this night was through, maybe start on another one. "Get out of the way of what, Dad?"

"You did what Ruthie asked. You identified the dead girl. But there's no connection between her and Henry dying, and it's got nothing to do with anyone in my office. That's all there is to it."

Usually, it's the liar who can't make eye contact. But Tess thought it would break her heart to look into her father's steady blue eyes as he piled fiction upon fiction.

"It's not just Gene, is it?"

"I don't know what you mean."

"I mean if Gene Fulton was in this alone, you wouldn't be afraid. You could go to the boss, tell him that he's helping Nicola DeSanti run a prostitution ring out of her bar. Because that's what he's doing, Dad, and you know it. So why can't you turn him in?"

"I'm protecting you."

"Bullshit."

"Tesser!" She almost never used such language in front of her parents. Then again, her father seldom tried to bullshit her. Judith had been the one in charge of parental misinformation, running the gamut from "You'll put your eye out" to "The boys won't respect you if you do that." Patrick had specialized in omission. He sought to protect her from the world by not telling her too much about it.

"Dad—why are you protecting Gene?"

It was his turn to look away. "You know, Gene and I go back a ways. We were never friends, but he's one of the old-timers down there. He got divorced a couple years back, and the judge really soaked him on child support. On top of that, his wife took his kids to Georgia. So he has to pay all this money, and he never gets to see them."

"Which is his justification for taking kickbacks from a small-time criminal. Does he get extra for chauffeuring the girls around, or does he provide that service out of the goodness of his heart?"

"It's legit. It's an escort service."

"Dad, please."

"Look, Tess, it's not like she's selling drugs, or killing people. The girls who work there, they're free to choose what they do, you know? And they're a helluva lot safer than they'd be on the streets, or hooked up with pimps. The old lady screens the customers, has guys take them to and from their appointments."

"Gwen Schiller worked there. She's dead."

"Right. She went out on her own, and got killed by the first trick she turned."

"Is that what Gene Fulton told you? Because it's not true."

"How do *you* know?"

But Tess wasn't telling anyone what she knew, not anymore. For all she knew, everything she had told her father had gotten back to Gene Fulton.

She was trying to remember now if she had told him about the phone logs, or her first trip to Philadelphia.

When her father spoke again, his tone was cajoling. "I'm not saying we're not going to shut them down. I'm just asking you to get out of the way. Talk to your cop friend, the one in Homicide. He'll pass it on to Vice. This doesn't have to concern us."

"And what do I tell Ruthie?"

"That accidents happen. That the past is the past, and we can't do anything about it."

She was holding the glass, but had yet to take a sip. It was cold, she felt the chill of the wine through her fingertips. It was the coldest thing she had ever touched in her life. Colder than snow, colder than the ice that skidded beneath her palms when her father had taught her to skate above the dam at Gwynn's Falls. Falling is part of it, he had told her. You have to fall.

"Daddy—what does Gene have on you?"

The blood that swept across his face made him seem, for a moment, all of one color, the red of his complexion blending into his hairline.

"That's a helluva question to ask your father."

"Yes, it is," she agreed. "But it's on target, isn't it?"

"Ancient history," Patrick said. "Small potatoes."

"Does Ruthie know the story behind these so very ancient, so very small potatoes?"

He nodded. Tess knew the price of asking another question, knew what she was giving up. But she couldn't stop.

"What happened between you and Ruthie?"

An eternity passed in the next five seconds. Her

father studied the top of his beer can. She swallowed some wine, noticing how tart it was, how sharp.

"We met about thirteen, fourteen years ago," her father said. "She was a barmaid in a neighborhood joint, a place that catered to the shift workers in Locust Point. Actually had a seven A.M. happy hour, if you can believe it. But after all, that's when those guys got off and they wanted what anyone wants when he finishes a long day at a hard job. They wanted a beer, they wanted to shoot pool, flirt with a pretty waitress. Play video poker. The usual.

"Ruthie was . . . a stickler. You know, she's kind of churchified, active in her parish. She saw people getting addicted to the machines. Her dad had a problem that way, and it hadn't made life easy on her family. So she decided to turn the owner in. She filed a complaint with me, asked me to keep it anonymous. Problem was, the guy who owned the place was a big contributor to a certain senator. The senator who happened to appoint me. Ditter asked me to look the other way. I did—I mean, it's not like every bar in the city doesn't pay on its video poker—and Ruthie ended up losing her job. Which she blamed me for, and I guess she was right. I got her a job at Spike's, and she got back on her feet, went to school to get her accounting degree."

"And what did you get?"

"What do you mean?"

"I mean, did you stay quiet as a favor to your pal, Senator Ditter, or was there a gratuity built in for you as well?"

Irish temper was a cliché Tess had never actually

experienced. All the temper in her family had come down on the Weinstein side. Her father was a gentle man, hard to anger. So when he rose to his feet, his face now almost purplish red, and began jabbing his finger at her, she was undone by the sheer fact of his rage.

"You want to know what I got, for looking the other way? I didn't get shit. But my daughter, who had decided the University of Maryland wasn't good enough for her, that she had to go to some fancy private school, got a fake scholarship. Ditter set up a little fund, helped to pay your tuition the whole four years. That's what I got. A college education for an ingrate of a daughter who's incapable of ever doing anything just because her old man asks her to."

"I had a senate scholarship," she said. "Sleazy, but legal."

"You got a kickback."

Tess found her mind reaching back, trying to remember the financial aid package her family had pieced together so she could attend Washington College. She had gone after every little pocket of money, no matter how small—grants from the local chapter of the DAR, an essay contest sponsored by the VFW. Her father had told her the state grant was for students who had scored well on the PSAT, but just missed National Merit status. And she had believed him. She believed him because she was eighteen and relatively confident that she was the axis on which the world spun, that she was worthy of all good things that accrued to her.

"You see?" he asked. "You see why you can't say

anything? Gene was tight with Ditter, he knows what happened. He'll take me down with him, if he suspects I had anything to do with this. You gotta stop."

"But it's not fair," she said.

"Jesus Christ, Tess."

"What you did, what Gene is doing—it's not the same. He's taking a bribe from a pimp, and he's going to go on doing it. You bowed to political pressure and were rewarded after the fact."

"Once it's in the newspaper, those are the kind of fine distinctions that will be lost, Tess. The statute of limitations may have run out on what I did, but the morality police can come for you anytime. Gene and I will both be fired, and no one will touch me, because I'll be a snitch. I'll be a fifty-two-year-old man, with no connections and no real skills. No one will hire me."

"Someone—"

"No one, Tess. I can't afford it. I can't afford to lose my job. Don't you get that? So unless you're ready for your mom and me to move in with you, I'm begging you to drop this, before it's too late."

Tess thought of Philadelphia, of Pete and Repete, perched on her car like a couple of buzzards. She knew it was already too late, but she could not bear to tell her father this. Children protect their parents as surely as parents protect their children.

They do it the same way—by lying.

"Okay, Dad," she said. "I won't press the issue. I'll tell Tull what I know, and then I'll let the whole thing drop."

Her father came around the table and hugged

her. They were not a physical family, so it was an awkward, clumsy embrace, but no less sincere for its clumsiness.

"You're a good girl, Tesser," he said. "I'm proud of you."

Tess, her head bumping beneath her father's chin, thought of how long she had waited to hear those words.

And how unfortunate it was that they had to come now, when she was lying through her teeth.

25

In her office the next morning, Tess clicked her way to the *Philadelphia Inquirer*'s Internet site and found the story about Hilde's slaying. It wasn't played on page one, as far as she could tell, and the juiciest details—the gunfire, Tess and Devon taking cover behind the cheesesteak cart—were missing. Nor was there anything about a possible kidnapping. In fact, Devon's name didn't even appear in the story, so the Whittakers must have more pull than Tess realized. According to the *Inquirer*, the woman killed was a "Swedish nutritionist," living here on a visa. The landlord said she had a roommate, but the roommate had not been home at the time of the slaying and was not available for comment.

"Not available for comment." Newspaper-ese for "I fucking couldn't find her, okay?" Tess sat back in her chair, feeling safe. If the police were withholding Devon's role from reporters, then Tess's identity also would remain a secret. There would be no awkward questions to answer from the Philly press, which meant it would be unlikely that the story would trickle down Interstate 95 and show up in the *Blight*. She had escaped being the local angle.

Then she checked her messages.

"Miss Monaghan?" The voice was male and bill-collector polite. "Herman Peters, at the *Beacon-Light*. I had a tip this morning that you might know something about an incident in Philadelphia yesterday. I need to ask you a few questions."

Great. Herman Peters was only the sweetest, gentlest, and most indefatigable son of a bitch at the local paper these days. One of the Philadelphia cops must have been checking her out through Baltimore PD and hit one of Herman's sources, who had then offered this tidbit to him to make him go away.

She gathered up her keys and knapsack, jangling the hook on Esskay's leash, which signaled the dog to roll from the sofa and follow her out. It suddenly seemed like a good day to work at home, where Kitty could keep unwelcome visitors at bay.

But when she stepped out the door to her office, Herman Peters was getting out of a surprisingly clean Honda Accord, talking on a cell phone.

"Yeah, I heard the fire call for Northwest," he was saying, as he walked toward her. He spoke rapidly, so rapidly that it was almost as if he were speaking in a foreign language. "Vacant rowhouse. We don't need to worry about it unless the wind picks up, and it goes to extra alarms. Gotta go— I'm here on an interview."

"That's okay," Tess said sweetly, walking past

him and unlocking her car door. "I'm on my way out, anyway. Why don't we catch up later?"

Herman Peters had brown eyes that Keene would have been proud to paint and bright pink cheeks that brought to mind impossibly wholesome activities, like cross-country skiing. However, Tess knew from her *Blight* friends that he hadn't taken more than one day off in the last two years and outside murder scenes provided the only sunshine and fresh air in his life. Cal Ripken's streak had ended, but Peters hadn't missed a homicide yet. This had led to a saying around town: If a body drops and the Hermannator isn't there to hear it, does it make a sound?

He was a crafty son of a bitch, too. Instead of trying to change Tess's mind, he took a package of Nabs crackers from his pocket and offered one to Esskay. The dog all but dragged Tess back to the man she was trying to avoid.

"So, about Philadelphia—" he said, offering Esskay a second Nabs.

"It's not a city I know very well," Tess said. "I used to go there when I competed in crew races, but I haven't done that for years."

"Then what were you doing there yesterday? Patching the crack in the Liberty Bell?"

"Davy Crockett," Tess sang back to him. "I bet you had a little raccoon cap when you were younger and galloped around the yard on a hobby horse, shooting at imaginary Mexicans."

"Actually, I did have a coonskin cap, when I was a little kid."

"And that would have been, what, three years ago?"

The Nabs were gone, but Peters was now stroking Esskay's muzzle and scratching her behind the ears, and the dog was so rooted to the spot that Tess wasn't sure she could yank her away with both arms. She remembered yet another stray piece of gossip she had heard about Peters: Despite his boyish looks, or perhaps because of them, he was extraordinarily successful with women. He had triple-timed female co-workers at the paper, and then hooked up with some starlet who was making a movie in town.

All this, without ever taking his beeper off.

"I can get the police report from Philadelphia," he told her. "I'll have it faxed to me this afternoon. I'll let them keep back whatever they're keeping back, as long as I can have the part about you. That's all our readers care about."

Tess experienced the kind of disgust and anger only an ex-reporter can feel for the press. Peters had no standing, he couldn't force her to talk about what had happened. Without her account, she doubted he could piece a story together. But he could make her life hell in a dozen different ways. She had to make a deal, had to persuade him to trade what was in the box for what was behind the curtain.

"What happened yesterday is a tiny detail on a much larger canvas. The Philly paper won't scoop you because the Philly cops are holding back the most interesting stuff, in order to protect the life of a possible witness." Slight lie there, but only slight.

"I'm really small potatoes." Her father's leftover phrase. It tasted like soot in her mouth.

"But you're the local angle," he repeated, ever dogged.

"Think big, Herman. If you're patient, I'll give you a head start on the story when it finally comes together." It was an easy promise to make, and it would be an easier one to break if she had to. She didn't owe Peters anything.

"You didn't cut me in on the Gwen Schiller story early. We had the Washington media breathing down our necks on that, because her family lives in Potomac. They had us surrounded."

Ah, so there was the grudge unmasked. Peters was pissed because he had been forced to scrounge for scraps at that feeding frenzy of a press conference, which had come too late in the day to allow the *Blight* to put together the kind of comprehensive package on Schiller that the Washington paper had been able to churn out effortlessly.

"It was the communications officer's idea to schedule the press conference on the television stations' time clock. I'd have much rather given it to you first. You're the only reporter in town whose work has any nuance."

Peters's cheeks bloomed even rosier at this praise and he put his hands in his pockets in aw-shucks mode. Esskay head-butted him, and he resumed petting her.

"Is it a good story?"

"I don't have all the pieces yet. But so far it has sex and death and civic corruption."

His brown eyes glowed the way Esskay's might, contemplating another package of Nabs. "That's a good start."

"But just a start. When I move toward the finish line, I'll call you. Tell me how to get you on that."

Tess gestured toward Peters's belt buckle and he looked down, momentarily confused. Once he realized she was talking about his beeper, he gave her the number, as well as his office, home and cell phone numbers.

"You're on call," she said. "You're the first one I'll contact. I assume you'll do me the same courtesy if you hear of anyone trying to slip my name into the paper for any other reason?"

"It's a deal," he said, shaking her hand.

"Just remember, Peters. Keep thinking big."

"My beeper," he said.

"I didn't hear anything."

"It's the vibrating kind."

"Well, then you must be one of the happiest men in Baltimore, given how many times it goes off in a day."

But Herman Peters was already getting back into his car, off to visit Baltimore's latest ex-citizen.

As soon as he was off the block, Tess retreated into her office and called Martin Tull.

"Thanks for those phone numbers," she said.

"Did it pan out?"

"No, I guess the kid was lying to me. But I still appreciate the help. Who does that, anyway? I mean, is it one person at the phone company, or do they have a whole department?"

"It's not like you can do that on your own, you know. You have to have a legit reason for getting phone logs."

He knew her so well. For a moment, she was tempted to tell him about the prostitution ring at Domenick's, just as her father had asked her to do. But if vice detectives busted the place, she was even less likely to know how Gwen's fate was connected to the bar. No, she would do it her way, but quietly, so her father wasn't on the receiving end of any more calls from Arnie Vasso.

"I know I don't have carte blanche at the phone company. I'm just appreciative. I was going to send a little Christmas remembrance. You can't begrudge me the right to try and make friends, to stay on someone's good side. They did a rush job. I want to say thank you."

"What kind of Christmas remembrance?"

"A Noël buche, something like that."

His voice still reluctant and suspicious, Tull gave her the name and number. Then he asked: "Were you in Philadelphia yesterday?"

"Yeah. Divorce case. It got ugly."

"So it would seem. Philadelphia homicide called down here today, wanted to know if you were legit. Rainer took the call. He said you were okay, for a dope-smoking smart-ass lunatic who always seemed to be in the wrong place at the wrong time." A pause. "They say you might have saved someone's life."

"They're much too kind." One life had been saved, but one life had been lost, too. Tess didn't know how the Philadelphia cops did math, but she counted it as a wash.

"You telling me everything, Tess?"

"Yeah, sure." She wished, sometimes, that she didn't have quite so many people interested in her well-being, paying attention to her moods. "It's just—I'm tired of dead people."

"Tell me about it." But his voice was more sympathetic than she had any right to expect. Tull had seen hundreds of dead bodies and she wasn't even in the double digits. Yet.

"John Updike, in that book you gave me, he said the dead make space," Tull added. "You know what I think?"

"What?"

"Updike doesn't know dick about what it's like to be a homicide cop in Baltimore."

She laughed, although there had been a time she would have considered such an opinion sacrilegious. Not because it was a smear on Updike, but because it impugned all writers, and writers had been gods to her once. In college, she had read books as if all the secrets of the universe might be revealed in a single line. She had swooned at those moments of communion, when someone so distant from her—someone male, of a different generation and place—had expressed so perfectly what she thought existed in her heart alone. Now she knew writers were no different from anyone else, just humans fumbling with the same questions, albeit with better language skills.

"Hey—" Tull said.

"What?"

"I want a Noël buche, too. Support your local sheriff."

Name and number in hand, she called Tull's contact at Bell Atlantic, a woman named Kelly. It took endless twists and turns through a voice mail system to get to her, but a human eventually came on the line.

"Kelly, this is Janet over at Martin Tull's office. He wanted me to thank you for getting those phone logs out so fast to us."

The young woman sighed. "Not fast enough for some people, I guess."

"Did someone at the police department give you a hard time?"

"No, you guys were great. But the guy from the senator's office gave me fits. He was here first thing yesterday, throwing his weight around. Detective Tull said I could fax the logs, but nothing would do for this guy but to get his photocopies first thing in the morning. He was nice to look at, but he sure didn't have good manners. Not one 'please' or 'thank you' in the mix. I guess being that pretty makes a guy kind of conceited."

Maryland had forty-nine senators. More than one could have a pretty male working in the office, Tess told herself.

"Did you get his name? I'd like to talk to his boss, and remind them that Bell Atlantic is our partner in these ventures, that everyone should be treated with respect."

"His name?" Tess heard a tapping sound, as if the woman was bouncing a pen on her front teeth. "Alan? Aaron? I just remember that he worked for that nice state senator."

"That nice state senator," Tess repeated.

"You know, the one who's on the television now. Dahlgren."

"Adam Moss."

"No, I'm pretty sure it's Dahlgren."

"Adam Moss is the man who was rude to you. Indian, with dark hair and skin. Very handsome."

"Yeah, that's him. Very handsome. And doesn't he just know it."

"Well, we'll remind him not to be so high-handed next time. I'm embarrassed you had to make two copies of the same record, one for the senator and one for the police department. You'd think city and state agencies could coordinate a little better."

"Oh, I'm used to it," Kelly assured her cheerily. "You guys never have your act together. The senator's request came in first, I think that's why his aide got all huffy."

"It came in *first?*"

"Yeah. They called late Thursday. Detective Tull called first thing Friday morning. The requests weren't exactly the same. The detective asked for November fifteenth only, while the senator's office wanted the whole week. They said it was for the ethics probe, and they'll probably need to pull lots more records before it's all over. Just my luck, huh?"

"I wouldn't worry about it if I were you," Tess said. "I think they have everything they want."

She hung up the phone and rested her head on her desk blotter.

She couldn't confront Adam Moss or Dahlgren, not without risking the very things Patrick Monaghan had feared. His job, his livelihood. But she couldn't see how any of this was connected.

Dahlgren had cleaned up the liquor board and thrown out the most corrupt inspectors, only to let Gene Fulton stay. Did Fulton have something on him? Did Nicola DeSanti have more influence than Tess realized? How did someone know what she was going to do before she did it?

If she asked any of these questions, her father would find out she had lied to him. If she went to Tull, she risked losing control of the investigation. Besides, bringing the police department into it wouldn't guarantee her father's job security. Fulton could still figure it out, and he could still take her father down with him. He would do it, too, just for spite.

Punching Whitney's various numbers into her phone, she finally tracked her down at a Mount Washington hairdresser's. Even over the unsteady line of a cell phone, with the roar of several blow dryers in the background, Whitney's voice was clear and silvery as a bell.

"What's up, Tesser?"

"How long will it take them to get that same millimeter of hair cut off that you have cut off every six weeks?"

"They still have to blow me out, but I had a manicure scheduled."

"Can you come see me as soon as you're done? I really need your help, Starsky."

Whitney needed a half beat. "I thought I got to be Hutch."

"You can be whoever you like. It turns out I do need a partner. But not just any partner. A Valley girl with connections and time on her hands. Someone who would make a very credible, very desirable volunteer for Senator Dahlgren's fledgling congressional campaign. You know anyone like that?"

"Why I just might," Whitney drawled. "I might know someone who fits that description to a T."

26

Tess waited in her car outside Dahlgren's district office, a plain storefront in a part of South Baltimore that didn't even pretend to be fashionable. A few yuppies had tried homesteading here, but the rowhouses in this block still leaned heavily toward Formstone and painted screens. The businesses were mundane as well. No chic or funky restaurants, just a shoe repair and a corner liquor store, which was enjoying a pre-Christmas run on Big Game lottery tickets.

Tess was on a side street that afforded an unobstructed view of the district office's front door. Unfortunately, she had to move her car every two hours. Because of Federal Hill's night-time attractions and the proximity of both Camden Yards and Ravens PSINet Stadium, South Baltimore was death on parking. Being in one's car was no protection against the overzealous meter maids who patrolled the area. Twice already, Tess had been forced to drive around the block and find a new spot, just to stay within the law. Surveillance was a cruel mistress; it brooked no lapses. For all she knew, she had lost Adam Moss in one of those quick swings around the block.

Campaign finance laws had made watching Adam Moss more complicated than Tess had realized when she made that first call to Whitney. He worked for the senator, not the unofficial congressional campaign, and the two had to be kept as separate as possible. So while Whitney was in another store-front in an Anne Arundel County strip center, stuffing envelopes and enduring paper cuts, Tess was following Adam Moss through his average day. It was so average as to be mind numbing: Baltimore to Annapolis to Baltimore and back again. All he did was work, as far as she could tell, but she continued to follow him. He was the only lead she had.

He lived in a small rowhouse on Grindall Street, within walking distance of the district office. Most mornings, he stopped there about 7:30 A.M., then left for Annapolis after grabbing coffee at the 7-Eleven on Light. Tess would have thought Adam Moss was a Starbucks kind of guy, or at least a Sam's Bagels kind of guy. Normally, she would have liked some-one better for being a 7-Eleven coffee-and-cruller man, but since Moss might be an accessory to a murder her goodwill toward him was tempered.

Once in Annapolis, Moss was largely inaccessible, closeted in the inner rooms of the senator's office. Dahlgren had ridden the hobby horse of the ethics probe as far as it could go. Senator Hertel was history—he had finally and abruptly agreed to resign just before the vote for explusion, which meant the Democratic Central Committee was hand-picking his replacement. Dahlgren had no official role to play in this process, but his opinion was suddenly valued, and would-be kingmakers came and went, eager for an audience with the rising star. Tess tried to linger in the halls of the senate office building, but strangers were too conspicuous with the General Assembly out of session, and the security guards kept asking what she wanted.

But if she stationed herself outside, Adam Moss could bypass her by using the subterranean passages that linked the buildings in the State House compound. So she ended up spending a lot of time on Lawyers Mall, waiting for him to pop out of any number of doors. She felt as if she were engaged in a large-scale version of the boardwalk game Whak-a-Mole. Whak-a-Moss, actually, and how she longed to. She wanted to grab him by the lapels and demand to know how he had come to have that phone list, and who else might have seen it.

But she couldn't. If Adam Moss realized she was following him, it would get back to Arnie Vasso and, before too long, her father would get another call. Perhaps just a courtesy call this time, an acknowledgment that since he had failed to keep his nosy daughter at bay, Gene Fulton was going to be history, and so was he.

So she waited and watched, grateful for the boring, predictable routine that was her subject's life. Adam Moss was all business. If he went out for lunch, it was always takeout—sushi from Joss Café or the Marvin Mandel sandwich from Chick 'n' Ruth's deli. If the senator had a committee meeting, Moss was there by his side, the first to arrive and the last to leave. The senator cut out early, headed for his campaign office or various fund-raisers, but Adam Moss stayed long after the December sun set. He sometimes cruised through a Burger King drive-in on West Street on his way out of Annapolis, or grabbed dinner-to-go from Matsuri, the sushi restaurant back in his own neighborhood. Adam Moss had a taste for raw things. Then he disappeared into his house and didn't come out until the next morning. Tess knew, because she had spent one cramped and cold night on his block.

Today, he had left Annapolis at three, but he had been here, sequestered in the district office, since arriving in Baltimore. A man and woman had been waiting for him. Constituents, small business owners, judging by their simple, neat clothes, and cheap briefcases. They probably needed a law tweaked in the next session.

Her cell phone rang.

"I'm bored, Tesser."

"Welcome to detective work, Whitney. I hope you're not calling me from headquarters."

"I'm on a pay phone, outside a Royal Farm. I volunteered to make a soda run. You know, we probably shouldn't be talking on a cell phone. It's not a secure line. It can be picked up by shortwave radio."

"Whitney, *you* called me."

"Oh, yeah."

"Have you found out anything?"

"Only that the money is pouring in. Dahlgren himself came in and dialed for dollars for a few hours this afternoon, then took off for some Christmas party. He asked me if I wanted to come with him."

"The happily married senator asked the young blond volunteer to go to a Christmas party with him? That's interesting."

"Actually, it's not. Dahlgren's only passion is money, far as I can tell. He thought I could help shake some loose just by standing there, eating hors d'oeuvres. You know how some men mentally undress you with their eyes? Dahlgren makes me feel as if he's assessing my jewelry. It's my mother he really wants. Not very likely, given his voting record on AIDS programs. Give Mother her due—she still believes it's respectable to be a liberal Democrat."

Tess was only half listening. The lights in the office had gone out, the couple had left, and now Adam Moss was locking the door behind him.

"Gotta go," she told Whitney. "Work hard, and maybe you'll be promoted to answering phones before the week is out."

She followed Adam Moss's car up Light Street. Do cars give any insight into character? Adam Moss, who looked as if he should be behind the wheel of a sports car, drove a Geo, the American-made cousin to Tess's Toyota. The navy blue car was clean, outside and in—Tess had crept up to its windows the night she waited outside his house. There was nothing inside, not even a road map. The radio was a good one, the high-end kind with a detachable face. He had a Club, but almost everyone in South Baltimore did.

He took her past the harbor, onto President Street and the JFX beyond that. He turned off at the Falls Road exit, heading into the heart of Hampden, a working-class neighborhood enjoying a burst of popularity in the city's suddenly, inexplicably hot real estate market. Here, yuppies and rednecks coexisted peacefully. Most of the time.

He parked around the corner from Café Hon, a place where Tess indulged her frequent need for comfort food. She found a parking spot a block up, then sprinted toward the Avenue, as 36th Street was known here. Adam Moss's tall figure was on the south side of the street, heading east, his navy wool coat open despite the chill in the air. She let him stay a block ahead, trying to look as if she were window shopping, then trying not to be distracted by the Avenue's wares. Antiques left her cold, but how she yearned for a painted screen scavenged from one of her East Baltimore neighbors, or one of those old tins from the sausage company that shared her dog's name. It would be even better than a neon sign that said Human Hair. But $75 seemed a bit high just for the honor of owning an Esskay can that boasted its contents were made with pure lard.

Adam Moss was not a window shopper. He walked purposefully, without a single sidelong glance for the people or places he passed. He was almost to Chestnut Street before he turned into a small shop, one of the galleries that had begun springing up in the neighborhood. In Tess's experience, a neighborhood could not pretend to hotness until galleries began to open there. This gallery had no name, not that Tess could see, but it was brightly lit and its front windows had two large, abstract oil paintings on display—angry, red-hued triangles that reminded Tess vaguely of mountain ranges. Or knives.

She crossed to the other side of the street and found a convenient bus stop bench. People still waited for buses, didn't they? Plus, she had the advantage of being in shadow, while the gallery was so bright it was like peering into a diorama. It was empty, except for a striking young woman. Thin, confident enough to wear her hair cut close to the scalp, like a feathery cap—together, she and Adam Moss were almost unbearable in their pulchritude. Yet there was no sexual buzz between them. The kiss Adam gave her was light, almost fatherly. And while they stood very close as they spoke, their body language revealed only matter-of-fact comfort.

They talked for no more than five minutes. Another light kiss, and Adam was gone, heading back down the Avenue. Tess was torn. She had intended to follow him as long as he was out. Yet here was a lead, someone who knew him, and had no idea who she was. What if the girl wasn't there when she came back another day? It would be much harder to track her down outside the gallery, without giving herself away.

Time to become an art lover, her gut told her.

She waited a few minutes, giving Adam time to find his car and leave the neighborhood. She tucked her braid down the back of her coat. Later, if this visit got back to Adam Moss, she could imagine him asking: "Did she wear her hair in a pigtail?" Tess knew people were not naturally observant, because she was still learning how hard it was to get details right. The woman she was about to meet would remember Tess's hair as being collar length, or short. She also would remember Tess's tortoise-shell glasses—she had a pair with clear glass that she carried with her, for moments just like this.

Instead of a bell, the gallery door had a rainstick attached, so it made a soft, whooshing sound when Tess pushed her way in and began browsing.

For all Crow's tutelage, she was still the sort of museum goer given to tiresome pronouncements that she might not know much, but she knew what she liked. The abstract and minimalist work here struck her as worthy of admiration, but it didn't engage her emotionally. Everything—the paintings, sculptures, the jewelry in a small glass case at the front—was cold and metallic, perfect yet mildly cruel looking.

As was the proprietor, close up. *No one that young should look that hard,* Tess thought. Her face was like a well-cut diamond, with sharp cheekbones, pointed chin, and eyebrows waxed into stiletto-thin arches. Amber eyes and a full lush mouth gave the face the flashes of yellow and red that diamonds sometimes have, but added no warmth.

"May I help you?" she asked, in a tone suggesting Tess was beyond anyone's help.

"I'm in this neighborhood all the time, but I never noticed this shop before," Tess said. "Couldn't help wanting to check it out."

"The *gallery* has been open only a month," the woman said.

"Are you the owner?"

The question threw her, but only for a moment. "I'm in charge, I make all the selections."

"I have a friend who owns a gallery in San Antonio. Carries all this wild Day of the Dead stuff. It's creepy, until you get used to it."

"Day of the Dead? Oh, you mean folk art." Her tone was derisive.

"What do you call this place? I didn't see anything outside."

"It doesn't have a name," the woman said. "Names are essentially phony. I won't carry artists who insist on naming their work."

Tess looked around and saw the art was all labeled by numbers. Not sequentially, of course—that would have been too easy. The numbers appeared to have been chosen at random, although Tess supposed the proprietess would insist the #17 canvas could never be, say a #9 or #131.

"Do you have a name?"

"I call myself Jane Doe," the woman said.

It stung, hearing that name, especially when it was used so casually, so carelessly. Jane Doe was Gwen Schiller; Gwen Schiller was Jane Doe.

"Not very original."

"That's the point."

"No, I mean calling yourself Jane Doe as an artistic statement isn't original. Didn't the lead singer of the old punk band X call himself John Doe, way back in the 1980s?"

The woman shrugged ever so slightly. Her thin arms were loaded with bracelets, so the movement made her ring like a wind chime. "Jane Doe is only one of my names. It fit my mood today. Come back tomorrow, and I'll be someone else."

Like Princess Langwidere from *Ozma of Oz*, Tess thought. Born with a detachable head, the princess changed heads daily, according to her whim. Her heads were numbered, not named, as Tess recalled. Sometimes, Langwidere picked a bad head, and she became unbearably peevish.

"You know, I'm in business for myself. So is my aunt, and one of my best friends. Can I give you some advice? This snotty attitude might work in some other cities, but people in Baltimore are not going to buy art from someone who makes them feel stupid. So thaw, okay? Where are you from, anyway, that you have so much 'tude?"

The last question had been the whole point of Tess's little monologue, tucked in so it would seem casual, impromptu. It didn't work.

"Biography doesn't interest me. People are boring. Including me."

"That guy who was just in here didn't look so boring. Boyfriend?"

"Jane Doe" retreated behind the sales counter, a too-precious little desk with spindly legs and a frosted glass top.

"Who are you?" she asked, her voice stripped of its snotty veneer. "Who sent you here?"

"I find names boring," Tess dead-panned.

"I fulfilled my contract," the woman said. "We're not supposed to be hassled, *after*. It's not my fault, what happened."

She had pulled a pair of scissors from the desk, but her hand was shaking so hard that Tess felt more pity than fear.

"I'm not anybody. I'm just a Christmas shopper trying to make conversation. Who do you think I am?"

"Please leave," the woman said. "Once it's over, it's over. That's what they promised."

"I'm not affiliated with any 'they,'" Tess said, trying to make her voice as neutral as possible. "I don't know who you are. I don't know anything about you, or what you're talking about."

"Get out, get out, get out, get out." The woman's voice rose until it was a feral shriek. Shoppers on the Avenue glanced up, startled. Public brawls were not unknown in Hampden, but they were usually confined to side streets, on hot summer nights, when too much beer had been consumed.

Tess left, making a mental note of the number painted on the transom over the gallery's door. Sometimes numbers were more important than names.

Sometimes numbers led to names.

27

Tess had a laptop that had so much RAM coursing through its system, so much power, according to the Crazy Nathan's salesman who had talked her into it, that it might arise from her desk one day and start cleaning her apartment, or prepare a Cordon Bleu meal.

But now, when Tess wanted only to use the Internet to check the city real estate database, her laptop was useless. Not because it wasn't fast, but because the human being on the other end hadn't updated the file for at least three years. She felt a perverse pride in her fellow Baltimoreans for rendering technology so powerless.

The only thing to do was head down to the Clarence M. Mitchell Jr. Courthouse and look up the records in the dusty old plat books. It wouldn't be a complete waste of time. She could chat up her friend Kevin Feeney while she was there, find out if there were any juicy rumors about Dahlgren or Adam Moss, the kind of rumors that never made the pages of the *Beacon-Light*, yet all the reporters traded, like baseball cards.

"Juicy bits?" Feeney's natural expression was a scowl, so he had to work a little harder to give the impression that he was frowning. His careworn face folded itself into a series of creases and furrows. "You mean, like butt buddies?"

"No. You know, not everything is about sex."

"Tell me about it." He sighed at some private memory. "So you're asking if we've ever heard any rumors about Dahlgren we couldn't find a way to squeeze into the paper, one way or another? Not that I recall. Until this ethics thing came along and he hooked up with Meyer Hammersmith, he was a classic backbencher. As for Adam Moss, I know less than nada. Did you Autotrack him?"

Autotrack was a costly computer search, which reporters took for granted, largely because they didn't pay for it. Reporters took it so much for granted that they used it to look up ex-girlfriends and boyfriends, or just to update their Christmas card lists, cheerfully racking up hours of charges. It wasn't something a one-woman private detection agency could afford.

"What a great idea," Tess said. "Can you Autotrack from here?"

"Nope," Feeney said emphatically. "They're not dumb enough to give me access at the courthouse, I have to go into the office. Besides, each of us has his own password. They'd trace it right back to me."

Tess saw no reason to tell him that Dorie had given her the password of one of the paper's lazier reporters to do searches on the *Blight*'s other, less costly databases. "It's not as if you wouldn't have a legitimate reason to look into Adam Moss. Who is this guy? Where did he come from? Maybe he'd make a good profile."

Feeney shook his head. "I'm not risking it. Sorry. They're in a budget crisis this quarter, so they're nickel-and-diming us to death."

"Budget crisis? The paper's so fat with ads I can barely lift it from the doorstep in the morning."

"Yeah, but the new managing editor went on a hiring binge at some job fair. He woke up the next morning, young Ivy League bodies littered around him."

"Whitney said they might hire her back."

Feeney shook his head. "They made her an offer. It's one of those rare times when the lack of institutional knowledge pays off. The M.E. may not know Spiro Agnew was once Baltimore County Executive, but he also doesn't know why Whitney left in the first place. I wish she would come back. The new breed—man, it's total *Village of the Damned* time down there."

"*Village of the Damned?*"

"You know, that movie about those little kids with those big staring eyes? You should be glad you got out of the business when you did."

"Trust me, I am. About Adam Moss—"

"*No*. Besides, you know how many Adam Mosses are going to be in Autotrack?"

"We could get his DOB from DMV." Talking in acronyms, sure sign of bureaucratese. How had she ended up sounding so wonky? "I just want to see if he has a criminal record."

"So ask your buddy down at the police station. Won't he run stuff through the NCIC for you?"

Tess had no ready answer. Yes, under certain circumstances, Tull might help her out. But she was trying to keep Tull at arm's length. She was trying to keep everyone at arm's length, and it was proving increasingly difficult.

"Want to walk down to the document room with me?"

"Darling, I can think of nothing more I'd like to do, but I have a hearing in five minutes. Give my love to our always cheerful civil servants."

Walking through the courthouse corridors, Tess had a moment of paranoia. No building was more public than the courthouse, yet it was full of shadowy corners in which to hide and watch someone. All the time she had been following Adam Moss, she had also been trying to ascertain who was following her. *Someone* had been watching her, paying close attention. She had said at the press conference she had a source in Philadelphia, an unnamed friend who had known Gwen Schiller, but it was only when she ordered the phone logs that Hilde's killer made the connection. But how had Adam Moss known to ask for the phone logs before she even did it? Was her phone bugged? Her office? Tull's office?

For all I know, she thought, flipping through the plat book, *the hands of Hilde's killer have held this book recently, have touched the pages I'm touching now.* She ran her index finger down the column of listings, feeling the shadow of another finger beneath hers. The finger jumped to her spine, a particularly icy finger with a long pointed nail, and she shuddered.

The owner of the property on 36th Street was listed as a corporation, M.H. Hammersmith Properties. Tess didn't have to be a cryptologist to figure out that the man behind the company was one Meyer Hammersmith, campaign chairman for Kenneth Dahlgren, boss of Adam Moss. You also could be as ignorant of the city's history as the *Blight*'s new managing editor and be aware that Meyer Hammersmith owned dozens, possibly hundreds, of properties throughout the city. It was how he had made his millions. He probably owned properties he didn't know he owned, including this modest storefront on 36th Street.

And yet.

Meyer Hammersmith was Ken Dahlgren's finance chairman.

Adam Moss, Dahlgren's aide, had paid a visit to the gallery owned by Hammersmith.

The woman behind the counter, the woman who didn't believe in names, had shown real fear when Tess had come by. But she had been comfortable with Adam, she hadn't been afraid of him.

Tess was on a cul de sac, a big, looping one, but a cul de sac nonetheless, in which every road led back to Ken Dahlgren. Yet there was nothing to connect Dahlgren to Gwen Schiller, or Henry Dembrow, or Devon Whittaker. In fact, there was nothing to connect Dahlgren to anyone. Adam Moss had requested the telephone records. Meyer Hammersmith owned the building. Dahlgren was just the grinning figurehead at the center, the pet that they were grooming to win best of show in a year or two. A former backbencher, as Feeney had said, stunned by his good fortune. He wouldn't ask any questions as long as the money kept rolling in, and rolling in.

She and Whitney had worked out a system: Tess could page her via beeper if she needed her urgently. She did this now, punching in her cell phone number, then going outside and waiting on the courthouse steps for Whitney to find an outside line.

The courthouse steps always felt like the wings to a dozen different dramas. Today there was a wedding party, posing for a photograph, the bride so pregnant that it appeared the baby had achieved legitimacy by mere minutes. Newly broken families, divided into sullen, smoldering camps, tried not to make eye contact as they headed into the building. Lawyers in cheap suits raced by with speeded-up walks that only exposed them for the ambulance chasers they were. Some trial was hot enough to bring out the television vans as well, and the reporters were lining up, ready to go live at noon, even if the trial had yet to recess. Given the choice between gathering information and going live, television reporters always chose the latter. After all, you couldn't have dead air.

Tess's phone rang, and she pulled it out.

"What's up?" Whitney sounded breathless, excited.

"Have you worked your way up to opening the mail yet?"

"Have I? I'm covered with paper cuts. So I started using my Swiss army knife, which seems to make the other volunteers ever so nervous."

Tess had a mental image of Whitney, slicing carelessly through the day's mail.

"Do you see the checks when they come in? Do you have access to the files where campaign contributions are listed?"

"Sure, but can't you get them up at the Election Board?"

"Not the current ones. Besides, I'm looking for certain names, certain addresses. I'm especially curious to see if anyone's bundling—you know, trying to avoid contribution limits by parceling out donations to relatives, or neighbors. I want you to look for donations from Southwest Baltimore, which isn't in the first, or even in the forty-ninth. And I want you to look for anyone who has the last name DeSanti."

"I don't dare take notes," Whitney said, bless her quick, steeltrap mind. She understood instantly what Tess wanted. "At the very least, they'll think I'm another candidate's spy, and they'll can me."

"Just remember as much as you can for now. If I'm right, we'll find a way to come back and get the files."

"He has a big fund-raiser at Martin's West in a few days," Whitney said. "Five hundred dollars a head, and the checks are pouring in. Maybe, if I'm very, very good, I can get them to send me to the bank with the daily deposits. Then I can stop en route and copy down all the names on the checks. Although a lot of it is cash."

"Whatever you're comfortable with," Tess said. "Hey, how well do you know Meyer Hammersmith, anyway?"

"My folks know him. He always seemed like a sweet old man to me, essentially harmless—assuming any real estate billionaire can be essentially harmless. When he comes out to the house, he almost drools, thinking about what he could do with my parents' property. But they're not really friends so much as they're allies, sitting on all these arts boards. My mother was shocked when he signed on with Dahlgren, he's such a philistine. Look, I better get back. I told them I had to go to the drugstore. And when they asked why, I just lifted an eyebrow in that don't-ask-female-trouble kind of way, and the guy let me go. But how long can it take to buy tampons, you know?"

"Whitney—" Tess thought of Hilde, dead simply because she happened to stand between Devon Whittaker and her would-be killer, about Gwen Schiller, about the frightened no-name woman in the no-name gallery. "Be careful."

"Don't worry about me," she assured her airily. "The Swiss army knife isn't the only thing I'm packing, I can tell you that much."

28

It took a mere two days for Whitney to secure the privilege of making the Dahlgren campaign's daily deposits.

"They're talking about making me a paid staffer before too long," she told Tess over the phone on Thursday, almost preening. Only Whitney could go undercover and turn it into a career opportunity.

"I'm not sure it's such a good idea for you to draw a paycheck from these people," Tess said worriedly.

"Oh, I know. I told them I was doing this for love, not money." Her voice lowered, as if she were trying not to be overheard, although she was calling from her snug little cottage. "And there is so much money, Tess. The guy has a real war chest. I know congressional races cost a lot these days, but do you think he might be keeping his options open? Maybe he's really going to run for governor, or U.S. Senate."

"Only if it's an open race. He'd never take on an incumbent. Look, as Deep Throat said to Woodward—"

"Assuming Deep Throat ever existed. I have my doubts."

"Whatever. Follow the money, Whitney. Find patterns, any patterns—in names, in addresses, in fund-raisers. I'm here in my office with Jackie right now, going over Dahlgren's past finance reports, but it's pretty Mickey Mouse stuff. Running for state senate, he was lucky to get $200 from his own father-in-law. It sounds as if he's now raising more in a week than he did for all his other campaigns combined."

She hung up her phone. It was late, almost ten, and she was exhausted. Not so much from working—Whitney was doing more than she was—but from all the lying and deception. If her father was to believe that she had dropped her inquiry into Henry Dembrow's death, then everyone else had to believe it as well.

Even Ruthie Dembrow, who had hot, furious words when Tess told her she was suspending the investigation through the end of the holidays. But it was precisely because of Ruthie's quick temper that Tess had lied to her. She was counting on her to complain to Pat yet again about his unreliable daughter, how she had started the investigation only to drop it for a second time. So Tess was not only working secretly, but for free.

She had enlarged her conspiracy slightly, however, taking in Crow and Jackie. Crow was her sounding board, she needed him at night, when she chanted the litany of what she had failed to accomplish. Besides, he often had good ideas.

Meanwhile Jackie, who had left political fund-raising for more legitimate work years ago, brought an expert eye to Dahlgren's financial documents. She also had been willing to go to the ethics office in Towson and make photocopies. Still paranoid about being followed, Tess didn't want to run the risk of being seen anywhere, doing anything.

The problem was, they weren't getting anywhere. Try as she might, she could not find the final connection that would link Dahlgren to Domenick's or Nicola DeSanti. She sat at her desk with a sketchbook in front of her, trying to make the formula work. Meyer Hammersmith was Kenneth Dahlgren's finance chairman. Adam Moss was Kenneth Dahlgren's aide. Hammersmith owned a building that housed a gallery, a gallery Adam Moss had visited. Adam Moss had requested the phone list. But she could not find a link to the bar, or even to Gene Fulton, who had been a liquor board inspector long before Dahlgren came on the scene.

"I can't link anyone to Hilde's murder except Adam Moss," she said now to Jackie, "and that makes no sense."

"Why not? From what you've said, he sounds cold enough to do whatever his boss asked."

Tess picked at the cartons of Thai food spread before them, looking for something to drag through the leftover peanut sauce. They had been working for almost three hours. It felt like six.

"Political aides don't kill people, except in the movies. Even Gordon Liddy only went as far as burglary and conspiracy, and the bar for political scandal is so much higher now, in the P.L. era."

"P.L.?"

"Post-Lewinsky. The first rule is still deny, deny,

deny. But contrition goes a long way now, if you get caught."

Jackie rubbed her eyes and sighed.

"Well, I just don't see anything unusual, Tess," she said. "Neither here, nor in the photocopies from his ethics file. This guy is so clean he reports the lunches that lobbyists buy him."

"I thought that was the law now."

"Doesn't mean everyone does it."

Tess walked around the desk and bent over Jackie's shoulder. "Does the name Arnie Vasso pop up?"

"Sure, yeah. Lunch here, lunch there. But no more than any other lobbyist. Tell me again, what are we looking for?"

"I don't know," Tess said, falling back on her sofa with an exaggerated sigh. Esskay, unused to sharing her space, gave her a dirty look and stretched out, trying to push Tess away with her rear legs. "Anything, everything. It's like I've got one piece of a jigsaw puzzle, and it's a piece of blue sky, only maybe it's really ocean, or the hem of some girl's dress. But I only have one piece. If I had a few more, I'd find a way to make it fit, I'd pound it in with my fist. One piece doesn't do anything."

"If you found a connection, what would it prove?"

"I don't know. That I'm not crazy."

Jackie smiled. "We already *know* you're crazy. Look, it's late. Help me load my things and the baby in the car, and you get out of here, too. Have a drink, let that sweet young boy of yours make you feel good."

"I'm beyond feeling good these days," Tess said, lifting a sleeping Laylah from her portable crib. As

Tess had told Jackie, she had no generic baby long-ings. But, oh, how she loved this one, with her chubby arms and legs, her puckish face. She hated to think of the day when Laylah would turn on her own reflection, when she would look in the mirror and yearn for the opposite of whatever she saw there. Yet that day came for every female she had ever known. Look at Gwen Schiller, as exquisite as a china figurine, or Devon Whittaker, her cousin Sarah. Men suffered no such self-doubt, even when they should. What Tess wouldn't give to stalk through life with just a little of, say, Adam Moss's arrogance and certainty.

The phone rang, and Jackie and Tess exchanged a glance. Only bad news, wrong numbers, and drunken ex-boyfriends rang at this hour.

"Keyes Inc.," Tess said, remembering to use the firm's proper name for once, using the speaker phone so she could continue to rock Laylah.

"Herman Peters." The young reporter spoke more rapidly than usual, and it took a beat for her to register the name, another beat for irritation to set in.

"I told you, Herman, you'll get your interview when the time is right. Be patient."

"I am patient, but—"

"You call this patient, ringing me at my office this late at night, to nag me about the interview?"

"I'm not calling about the story." He was speaking even faster now, his words tumbling over one another. "I mean, I'm not calling about that story. I'm at the office, working this multialarm fire by phone—we're right on top of deadline, and the call

just went out, so I'm taking feed from another reporter at the scene—and I crisscrossed the address
and I saw the name. It's not an uncommon name in
Baltimore, but I had a hunch, and I called Feeney at
home and he says yeah, they're related, so I thought
I should call you, as a courtesy, really, before you
saw it on the eleven o'clock news—"

"What are you talking about? Who's related?"

"Patrick and Judith Monaghan, over in Ten Hills."

"They're my parents."

"Their house is on fire."

Because she was still holding Laylah, Tess did
not cry out or rush for the door. Denied reflexive
action, she had a moment to think. She wished she
hadn't. Thinking was highly overrated.

"Herman—why all this effort to get a house fire
in on deadline? That's pretty mundane by the *Blight*'s
standards, isn't it?"

Herman Peters asked questions, he was not used
to answering them. She could practically feel him
squirming at the other end of the phone line.

"I'm not . . . It's just that . . ."

Her voice low, in deference to Laylah, she repeated herself. "Why are you working a house fire?"

"Because—because it's a fatality, too. They took a
body out. I'm sorry, Tess, but we heard it on the
scanner. There's a body, they've called in arson, and
they're saying it's a suspected homicide."

29

Tess had just crested the hill at the top of her parents' street when she saw the shower of sparks go up, like the tail end of a low-rent fireworks display.

The roof just went, she thought. *Which means the house is gone.*

Take the roof, she told whatever deity lurked in the night sky, *and I'll believe in you.* Take the house. Take her bedroom, which her mother had turned into a sewing room eight years ago. Take the pine paneled basement, site of all her early forays into vice. Take the sunporch, where she had done her homework in the late afternoon. Take her mother's carefully chosen furnishings, which matched so perfectly they made Tess's teeth hurt. Melt the plastic covers on the living room furniture. Take everything, take whatever you need to be appeased.

But please, don't take my parents. Not yet, not this way.

She saw the body bag first, lying on a gurney, then smelled the sweetish smell she knew from the fires she had covered as a reporter. Funny, she had never asked anyone what that smell was. It was probably insulation, or some other construction material, but Tess had always worried it might be flesh. She knew most people did not actually burn in fires—they died from breathing smoke, they were dead long before flames ever touched them. Still, she had never wanted to know for sure the source of that smell.

A firefighter stopped her, and it was only then she realized she had been running toward the house. Toward the body. "It's my parents' place," she told the rubbery sleeve blocking her path. She kept trying to move toward the body, but the sleeve held her back. Only one body, she saw, only one. Not good enough. She wasn't prepared to make such a choice.

The firefighter forced her to turn away from the house, to face across the street. She thought he wanted to shield her, but he was trying to get her to look at the neighbor's lawn, where Patrick and Judith stood, holding on to one another. Their faces were impassive; they might have been watching someone else's tragedy on the eleven o'clock news. The scene was made only more surreal by the Christmas decorations that surrounded them, an elaborate gingerbread house with grinning gingerbread men who twisted on mechanized bases. Six-foot candy canes, illuminated from within, lined the walkway.

Tess felt as if she had wakened from the worst nightmare of her life and found her parents at the foot of her bed, smiling, reassuring her.

The only difference was that their house continued to burn.

"Mommy," Tess said, running across the street. "Daddy."

They opened their little circle to her, and now they were all three clutching one another. Tess finally understood what it meant to hold on to someone for dear life.

"I never really liked that house," her father said. "All these years, I never really liked it."

They laughed, a little shakily, but they laughed. The smoking shell was a more traumatic sight for her than it was for her parents, even if they were the ones who still lived there. Tess had never known another home. She had gone from there to college, from college to an apartment on the North Side of Baltimore, and then to her little place at the top of Kitty's building. But none of those had been home. In her mind, this white frame Colonial was the only house in the world, the place she thought of when she heard the word *home*. She had known it wouldn't always belong to her family. In fact, she had thought her parents silly to cling to such an oversized place. But she had assumed the house would always be here, that she would have the rest of her life to drive by this spot and measure herself against the girl she had been fifteen years ago, twenty years ago, twenty-five years ago.

She knew too well that people died, but she had thought houses lived forever.

Crow arrived, alerted by Jackie, who had taken Esskay home when Tess went racing into the night. He didn't try to join the circle of family, but stood respectfully apart, quiet and subdued.

"Arson," he said after a while, and it wasn't a question. He pointed with his chin at the investigators who were beginning to examine the scene.

"Where were you?" Tess asked her parents. "How is it that you weren't here when it started?"

"We had an errand, then some dumb Christmas party," her father said. "The woman from your mother's work, who makes that awful eggnog."

"You shouldn't be drinking eggnog anyway," Judith said. "You have to watch your cholesterol. Not to mention what can happen eating raw eggs."

Their house seemed to sigh and settle just then, as if to remind them cholesterol and salmonella were not the only threats to one's longevity.

"Why would someone want to burn down our house?" Judith asked.

"It might not be arson," Patrick said, but he didn't sound convinced. There was, after all, the matter of a body on his front lawn. "The wiring's always been a little off."

The fire captain came over to them.

"If it hadn't been for the wind tonight, we might have been able to save it. As it is, I'm afraid it's a total loss."

"That's okay," Patrick said. "I've got everything I need right here." He hugged Judith and Tess closer to him. "Do you know what happened, though? I mean, the body you found—"

"We think he was an intruder. There's glass inside the house, from where a pane on the kitchen door was broken. The fire appears to have been started there, and that's where we found him when we arrived. The M.E. is going to have to autopsy him. My guess is he slipped on the gasoline he had spread and knocked himself out while trying to get away from the very fire he started."

"An intruder?" Patrick asked. "You mean a burglar?"

"Well, he didn't take anything out of the house, as far as we can tell. We're assuming it's his car we found parked in the alley, although we won't be able to make a positive ID until he's in the medical examiner's office. Car could be stolen, for all we know, but police say they have no report, not yet."

Tess asked, "Did you check the registration?"

"Eugene H. Fulton, address on Erdman. Mean anything to you?"

The name seemed to float above their heads, another piece of charred debris from the fire. Gene Fulton. Her father's colleague. The liquor board inspector with the side gig at Domenick's.

"Why would Gene Fulton want to burn down our house?" Judith asked.

"I don't know," Pat said, looking at Tess. "What do you think, Tess? You got any theories about why Gene Fulton would be holding a grudge against me?"

Her mouth was dry, her throat raw from the smoke and the cold. "I'm not sure."

The case was like a stray cat, she thought to herself. She kept trying to take it farther and farther away from herself and her family, only to come home and find it on the doorstep every night.

"You didn't stop, did you? I asked you to do this one thing for me, I begged you. I told you that you were in over your head, and you still couldn't listen to me."

"No one knew what I was doing," Tess said. "I was careful, I swear."

"Why were you doing anything at all, Tess?" Her father's voice was even, emotionless, and she realized he was as angry as she had ever seen him. "What's really at stake here? The death of some glue-sniffing turd, a spoiled rich girl who ran away from all the help her parents were trying to give her, so she could be a whore in Southwest Baltimore."

"I don't think Gwen Schiller was—"

"A whore," Patrick repeated. "A whore who was killed by a junkie, and then someone killed him in prison, which is what he deserved. So what? Why are their lives worth so much to you, and mine so little? I'm homeless and I'll be jobless before they get through with me. This was a warning, a little bonfire to scare you off, and it got out of control. But just because Gene's dead from his own stupidity doesn't mean it won't get leaked, what I did all those years ago. Did for you, Tess. Only for you."

Judith looked genuinely confused. So he had held her harmless, too, fed her the same bullshit story about the scholarship.

"Daddy, I'm sorry. I never meant for this to come back on you. I thought—"

"You thought you could do whatever you wanted to. You always have. Did I ever give you any grief for the decisions you made? Did I mind that you went off to some overpriced fancy college and majored in English? Did I ever ask you to get a real boyfriend, or even a real job, one where you don't sit in a car all day taking photographs of people cheating on their spouses and insurance companies? Everything I did, I did for you. By the way—" he pulled a rectangular jewelry box from his pocket. "This is what I was doing tonight. This was my errand. We went to see your Uncle Jules, because he gave us a deal on your Christmas present. You don't have to open it, I'll tell you what's inside. It's a watch, a goddamn gold watch because I knew even if you made it fifty years at your crappy little business, there'd be no one to give you anything. Merry fucking Christmas. Ho, ho, ho."

Her father walked away and Judith, after one anguished look back at Tess, followed him. The fire captain interceded, began asking them questions, wanted to know if they needed a place to stay this evening. *Do you have any family?* Oh yes, plenty, Judith replied. Tess just stood where she was. It was bitter cold, she realized. But then it was December, it should be cold. The gingerbread men continued to twist in the wind. The gingerbread house had a gumdrop for a door knob. It was December. It was Christmas. It was cold.

Crow held her, angry not on his behalf, but on hers.

"He shouldn't have said what he did. He'll regret it. You were trying to do the right thing. One day he'll understand that."

"They could have died," she said. "My parents could have been killed because of me."

"Not even your father believes they were trying to kill him. Gene Fulton broke in while they were out. He wasn't going to hurt them."

"Not this time," Tess said. "But what happens

next? Last week it was Hilde. Tonight it was my parents' house. Tomorrow it could be my parents. Or you. Or Jackie and Laylah. Or Whitney." Tess realized she couldn't begin to name all the people she loved, all the people who might be hurt in order to punish her. Such a list should have made her feel warm and happy, rich in relations. Tonight, all it made her feel was vulnerable.

"So what are you going to do, Tess?"

"The only thing I can do. Make a deal."

30

Meyer Hammersmith lived in the only detatched house in his block on Federal Hill. A limestone rectangle, it sat near the top of the hill that gave the neighborhood its name and it was in the Federal style, so its location could be considered doubly apt. The house was not particularly large—it was smaller, in fact, than many of the town houses arrayed in the same block—but because it stood apart, surrounded by an iron fence, it was a source of great status in Federal Hill.

Privacy, Tess thought, pressing the buzzer at the front gate, announcing her name and waiting for the lock to be released. *Meyer Hammersmith is a man who values privacy.*

Adam Moss opened the door. Tess expected him. She had gone through him to arrange this meeting, and he had told her Meyer would insist on this location. Dubious, she had resisted at first. Take it or leave it, Adam said. She took it. She knew she was going to have to take a lot before this was through.

"He's waiting for you in the library," Adam said.

She wouldn't go so far as to say he was nervous, but his manner was a shade less smooth than usual. He reached for her coat, but Tess stepped back, pulling it tighter around her, as if the house were cold. If anything, it was overheated, with the dry, crackly heat found in a run-down nursing home, the kind that ended up getting closed by the state.

"I'll keep it with me," she said. Her gun was in the right pocket, her cell phone in the left. She didn't expect to use either, but she liked having them close.

"As you wish," Adam said, and he led her up a flight of stairs.

"Library" was a misnomer. One wall was filled with books, but the other three were covered with portraits—oil paintings, watercolors, charcoal sketches. No windows, Tess noted, and only one door. Only one way in, and only one way out. She studied the artworks, each hung as a museum might display them, in ornate frames and with indirect lighting. But they were so crowded, the effect was diminished. Why not spread them throughout the house? Tess recognized a Modigliani and a Degas, but she knew the latter only because the girl wore ballet garb. It was a bit unsettling, all these faces staring at her.

Meyer Hammersmith sat in a high-backed chair, one of only two pieces of furniture in the room. The other was a chaise longue, whose red velvet uphol-stery and sinuous lines gave it a decadent feel. Tess could not see herself perched on such a thing under any circumstances, but especially not for this meet-ing. Adam Moss also declined the chaise, standing a few feet to Tess's right, which happened to put him between her and the door.

"Miss Monaghan?" Meyer Hammersmith did not rise, nor offer his hand. This close up, he bore a marked resemblance to a snapping turtle, with his mottled tanned skull, beaky nose, and downturned, rheumy eyes. Even the small hands that poked from the sleeve of his wool jacket were like a turtle's stunted, wrinkled legs. Tess was reminded of an old-fashioned recipe for terrapin, once a prized delicacy in Maryland: *Throw the turtle in the pot for one hour, until all dirt is cleansed from the body. Then remove the toenails and the scales—*

"You are Miss Monaghan?" he repeated.

"Yes."

"Adam said you had a favor to ask of me."

"I've come to you to ask to guarantee my family's safety. My family, my friends, my dog—if you can promise me that they'll be safe, I'll do whatever you want."

Meyer held up a finger, as if to warn her. "You should be more careful. 'Whatever' is quite a lot to promise. After all, who knows what I want?"

Adam Moss shifted his weight from one side to the other, but said nothing.

"I'm ready to do whatever is necessary to protect the people I love," Tess said. She reached into her pocket, made contact with her gun, withdrew her hand, feeling assured. "Or to stop doing it, to be more precise. I don't know what I've done that has put them at risk, or what I've stepped in. But I give you my word I'm stopping. I'll sign something, if that's what you want, give up my investigator's license if I have to. All I ask is that you stop."

"Miss Monaghan, I don't know who you are. I never heard of you before you sought this meeting, although I know your uncle, Donald Weinstein, by reputation."

Something in his tone suggested it wasn't a very good reputation. This hurt, but Tess knew she had to withstand such petty insults.

"Adam knows me." Hammersmith looked at Adam, who gave the smallest of nods. "And you and Adam are the powers behind the throne, right? You're the ones who are orchestrating Dahlgren's congressional run. Toward what end, I can't guess and I no longer care. Just tell me what I have to do, and I'll do it. I'll forget about Gwen Schiller and Henry Dembrow and Domenick's Bar. For what it's worth, I never did figure out how it was connected to Dahlgren, or either of you."

But I must have been close, she wanted to say. *I must have gotten real close if people had to die and houses had to burn.*

In another part of her mind, she also wanted to say: I'm sorry, Gwen. I'm so sorry I have to give you up. But you're dead, I can't save you.

Hammersmith blinked his turtle eyes, blinked them again. "I am Senator Dahlgren's finance chairman. My only concern is to amass a war chest so formidable that other Democrats will think twice before entering the race. Adam is on Dahlgren's legislative staff. He has no official role in the campaign, although he does occasionally help us with opposition research."

"Opposition research? Oh, you mean digging up dirt on potential rivals."

"As you wish," Hammersmith said.

"Do you limit yourself to research, or do you actively create opportunities for blackmail, by sending Nicola DeSanti's girls to local hotels to meet lonely politicos?" She was thinking of Gene Fulton, escorting the pseudo-waitress from Domenick's to Harbor Court Hotel.

If there was any expression to be read on Hammersmith's face, it was boredom. "An interesting idea and I wouldn't be surprised if such things have happened. Nicola has been very active in Democratic politics over the years. But you don't have to fight that dirty, Miss Monaghan, when you have money and a squeaky clean candidate. Backbenchers have their advantages. They're too unimportant to be bribed, or get into trouble. No one has anything on Kenny Dahlgren, because he hasn't done anything. He's never even carried a major piece of legislation."

"Then why did you have my parents' house torched? Why did someone try to kill Devon Whittaker, just because she was the last person to speak to Gwen Schiller?"

Tess did not flatter herself by thinking she was a remarkable judge of character, not with two men this calculating. But it seemed to her there was a subtle difference in their reactions. Adam looked at Hammersmith as if to say, *What she's talking about?*, while Hammersmith merely looked to the side, studying the long, lean face of his Modigliani.

"Surely you're mistaken," Hammersmith said. "This has no connection to us."

"I think it does." Her voice was still hesitant and deferential, but she was feeling stronger. If Hammersmith and Moss had withheld secrets from one another, it gave her leverage. "A week ago, I asked for phone records from a pay phone in Locust Point. Adam Moss requested the same records, even before I did. One of the calls on that log was to Devon Whittaker. I don't know who Adam gave the information to—maybe he used it himself, although I rather doubt it—but Devon's companion was killed and the killer was waiting for Devon when I got there."

Now Hammersmith appeared genuinely confused, while Adam Moss glanced nervously from him to Tess and back again. "I didn't—I mean, yes, I picked up the phone logs. Dahlgren said he had a constituent who needed those records. I didn't ask why."

"Did Dahlgren tell you the constituent's name?"

Adam Moss shook his head. "Part of my job is knowing when not to ask questions. He told me it was a favor for someone from the Stonewall Democratic Club. It's the kind of favor he does all the time and it's not completely kosher, but it's pretty harmless. But I'd never be a party to—I mean, murder. That was never part of the arrangement."

"What was the 'arrangement'?"

The two men were eyeing each other now, each suspicious in his own right. Hammersmith had not known about the phone logs. Adam had not known about the house fire, or the attempt on Devon's life. Yet neither man had asked her: Who is Gwen Schiller? Which meant they knew.

Hammersmith spoke first: "About two years ago, I asked Kenneth Dahlgren to take Adam Moss on as his aide. Dahlgren did this as a personal favor to me. He was resistant at first, for Adam's résumé was—well, let's say it had some gaps. But he has a natural instinct for politics and Dahlgren has been extremely happy with his performance."

"Did you agree to become his finance chairman in exchange for his hiring Adam?"

"No," Hammersmith said. Another surprise for Adam Moss, Tess noted. He looked truly perplexed now, brows drawn tight over his dark eyes. "That was an unrelated negotiation."

"Made about a year ago?"

"Yes, as a matter of fact. I signed on last December, although we didn't announce the fact for several months."

"You took the appointment just after Gwen Schiller was killed."

It was a guess, a feint, nothing more. But Tess knew she had closed the circle. She waited, letting the silence in the room grow, determined not to be the next one to speak. She would stand here for hours, if necessary, until one of them told her what she needed to know.

As it happened, she had to wait only a few seconds. But it seemed much longer.

"We knew her as Beth," Hammersmith said. "Elizabeth March."

"We?"

"I."

"We," Adam Moss corrected. "In fact, I introduced her to Meyer. We were horrified when we realized she must be the girl who was killed in Locust Point, but what could we do? I made an anonymous call, but her name turned out to be fake, as we always suspected."

"How did you know her?"

Another silence. Again, Tess waited it out.

"She lived here, very briefly," Hammersmith said carefully. "As did Adam. And Wendy."

"Wendy? You mean the girl from the gallery." Tess saw another link, a visual one, spread out on the walls around her. Beautiful faces. Beautiful, beautiful faces of all types, male and female, and no two alike. So art was not the only thing Meyer Hammersmith collected.

"How do you know about Wendy?" Adam asked.

"I followed you one night, then checked the property records for the gallery. So you got a job with a state senator and Wendy got her own business. What was going to be Gwen's reward?"

"She did not stay long enough for me to help her," Hammersmith said. Help her? Tess wanted to throw the words back at him, but there was no irony in his voice, no self-awareness.

"You mean she wouldn't sleep with you."

"You misunderstand our arrangement." Meyer Hammersmith actually looked offended. "I'm a mentor. I take in protégés, people who need molding, give them a leg up."

"Gwen Schiller was a billionaire's daughter from the Washington suburbs," Tess said. "She didn't need your 'leg up.'" *Or your scaly little hand up her skirt.*

"I knew her as Beth," Hammersmith repeated,

as if the name made all the difference. "A runaway. If I had known who she was—if Adam or Wendy had known who she was—they never would have brought her to me. They picked her. I knew her as Beth."

Tess looked questioningly at Adam.

"You have to find your own replacement," he muttered, looking at the floor. "Wendy didn't understand Meyer's tastes as well as I did, she was having trouble finding someone new. We were eating in a bar in South Baltimore one night when Beth came in, looking for work. She didn't have an ID, or a Social Security number. I knew Meyer would approve of her, once we got her cleaned up."

"You took her to Domenick's."

"I took her to Domenick's." Adam seemed relieved, as if he had yearned to tell this story to someone, anyone, over the past year. "The DeSantis aren't so picky about things like work permits and they know about Meyer's . . . proclivities. They're always happy to help him out. The strange thing was, Beth was actually happy there, living in an apartment above the bar, waiting tables, being left alone. Me and Wendy, we couldn't wait to get out of there, but Beth—I'm sorry, it's hard for me to think of her by any other name—didn't want to go when her time came."

"You brought her here, to begin her tenure as a 'protégé,' and she ran away."

"I guess so," Adam looked at Meyer. "I assume so. I've never asked too many questions about what happened."

Adam Moss made it a habit of not asking too

many questions, Tess realized. No wonder he was so highly regarded in political circles.

"When the replacement bolts, what happens?" She was thinking of the terrified girl in the gallery, Wendy, her shrill insistence that she had fulfilled the contract.

Adam looked as if he might say something, but Hammersmith cut him off. "Nothing," he said. "Nothing happened. She decided she didn't want the life I was offering her, and she left. Now that I know she was Dick Schiller's daughter, it's all a little clearer to me, I admit. I haven't had a protégé for quite some time."

He had the gall to sound wistful, as if he had been denied something that was his due.

"But only because the waitress from Domenick's wasn't quite right," Tess said, and she knew she had gotten it right this time. Gene Fulton had brought the girl to Meyer, not to some political rival. "You were the tea at Harbor Court, the job that Fulton described as one of the best gigs in the city. I guess Nicola DeSanti knows your 'proclivities,' but can't quite nail down your taste. Pretty isn't good enough. They have to be extraordinary."

"I am interested in young people who want to better themselves, people I can help."

"Yes. You take them in, and you buy their silence by promising them what they most desire. But Gwen didn't get anything from you, so she wasn't bound to keep your secret, was she? You must have been terrified when she ran away. She might have ended up telling someone about your little scout troop."

"I'm sorry she didn't like it here," Meyer said. "But, really, she overreacted. She wasn't my prisoner, she was free to leave any time. I just needed to ensure her discretion. When I asked Nicola to help me out, I expected a very different resolution. I thought she would put Gene on it, as she usually did. Gene was competent, and levelheaded. The boys are so . . . unpredictable."

"The boys?" She wanted to be wrong about this, but knew she wasn't.

"Her grandsons, I believe. No—her grandson and great-grandson. Have you see them? They look amazingly alike. Very unusual faces. Not handsome, but distinctive. Feral, even."

Caught up in trying to describe Pete and Repete, Hammersmith had already forgotten the girl he knew as Beth. But Adam Moss was horrified.

"You knew," he said, stepping around Tess and toward his old mentor. "You knew all this time. They killed Beth, to protect you, and framed the dumb addict. Let me guess what happened next. Gene Fulton carried the tale back to Dahlgren, to get him off his back at the liquor board, and that's how Dahlgren got you for finance chair. Beth was dead, and all anyone could think of was how to turn it to their personal advantage."

"It wasn't my idea," Hammersmith protested. "I didn't want her dead, and I certainly didn't want to work for a troglodyte like Ken Dahlgren. But one does what one has to do. Noblesse oblige, Adam. Didn't I teach you that very concept, over the year I spent transforming you from rough trade to senator's aide?"

"Noblesse oblige," Adam Moss repeated, his voice bitter, his beautiful mouth trembling with emotion. "As I recall, you were born in Pigtown and made your first million as a slumlord. You learned to buy fine things, Meyer, but you never truly appreciated them."

"I bought you," he said matter-of-factly, reaching out to touch Adam's face. The younger man backed away so quickly he almost fell over the chaise longue. "I appreciated you."

Tess pulled her gun from her pocket, and aimed at the center of Meyer Hammersmith's speckled forehead. She heard Whitney's voice in her head: *Heads are too small, aim for the torso.* She could miss, even at this range. But it was so much more satisfactory to point a gun at his face, his unbeautiful face. She squinted her left eye, remembering to adjust for the slight recoil on the Smith & Wesson.

"What are you doing, Miss Monaghan?"

"I came here today because I thought you could protect me, that you must be at the top of this conspiracy, because you're rich and powerful. But you're as much at Nicola DeSanti's mercy as I am. You don't do anything for yourself, whether it's procuring the beautiful young people you desire, or arranging for their silence when they disappoint you."

"You don't understand," he began, licking his lips.

"I understand as much as I can bear."

"What do you presume to do, then?"

"With this?" She looked at the gun in her hand, as if surprised to find it there. "Nothing, actually. I just wanted you to know, for a moment, what Gwen Schiller felt when she saw Nicola DeSanti's progeny coming toward her. Gwen Schiller—not Beth March, or Jane Doe. Gwen Schiller, a seventeen-year-old runaway, whose only crime was wanting one man in the world, her father, to notice her. I wanted you to feel the panic she felt when she saw Pete and Repete. That's when she twisted away from Henry Dembrow, right? He lured her to his house, probably by promising her she could use the phone. He would have been so easy to buy off, all they had to give him was a can of spray paint. And when Gwen died, it was such a joke to the two men who made it happen that they tied a rubber tube around her neck, just for the hell of it. That was for you, wasn't it, Meyer? Your gift, your package, courtesy of the DeSanti family."

"She shouldn't have run," he said. "I'd have let her go, I wouldn't have forced her to stay. I never force anyone, do I, Adam? And I don't hurt them. Tell her, Adam. Tell her how I saved you, tell her everything I did for you."

But Adam Moss was out the door, running.

He was waiting for her just outside the iron gates.

"Were you scared?" Tess asked him.

"Scared that you would kill him, and I wouldn't stop you," he said. "I can't believe Dahlgren knew, all this time, that he set me up like that. I'm an accessory, aren't I?"

They were walking up the hill, toward Tess's car. The city of Baltimore was spread out before them. The top of Federal Hill was possibly the best vantage point from which to view the city. From here, one could take in downtown, Fells Point, the harbor, and Locust Point. The whirligig at the American Visionary Art Museum twisted in the wind. The Domino Sugars sign blazed red in the night. It was a funny thing about that sign. Wherever you went in Baltimore, it seemed to follow you.

"If the police ever come looking for you, tell them what you know and I think you'll be okay. But don't stick your neck out, Adam. Nicola DeSanti is willing to kill to protect her grandson and great-grandson."

"I guess so," he said. "But it's still hard for me to believe. She's a small-timer, content with prostitution rackets and black market cigarettes. You know she's death on drugs, fires her girls if they get caught using. She has her own weird moral compass, however skewed. Dahlgren's the one who scares me. Mr. Law and Order, Mr. Family Man, using a girl's murder for his political gain. I can just see how it went down, how Fulton carried the story of Gwen's death and Meyer's involvement to him, like some dumb, eager bird dog. Love me! Pat me! Don't fire me! It's almost enough to make me feel sorry for Meyer, getting caught up in that."

"Then you're a bigger person than I'll ever be. I can't imagine anyone more loathsome than Meyer Hammersmith."

Adam looked back at Meyer Hammersmith's house. At night, in the streetlights, the limestone glowed white. Another Sugar House, Tess thought. The world was full of Sugar Houses, places that looked so sweet, and left such a bitter taste.

"It's not what you think," he said. "He doesn't want sex. He wants people to think he's having sex. He wants to own things of beauty, things that everyone else wants, and can't have. It was a good deal for me. I didn't even graduate high school. I was a hustler in New York. Meyer was a step up for me. Wendy's from some Virginia backwater where you're lucky to get out without having your cousin's baby. We thought Beth—Gwen—was one of us. More naïve, perhaps, but scrappy. We never would have brought her to him if we hadn't thought she was strong."

"She *was* strong, that was her problem," Tess said. "She was stronger than you. She'd never consent to be someone's slave."

"I wasn't his slave," Adam said, his voice sharp. "More like an indentured servant. It's a contract. You put the time in, you leave set for life. It's not that different from being in on the ground floor of one of those Internet companies, or some start-up like, well, Dick Schiller's. I slept with a lot of men and women before I met Meyer, and all I ever got out of it was spending money and some new clothes. He gave me a new life."

They had stopped beneath a streetlight, where Tess had parked. She was still thinking about Gwen, her death, the details of the autopsy. She felt unfinished somehow. Unfinished—she remembered the fresh tattoo on Gwen's ankle, the line on her leg.

"Show me your ankle," she said to Adam Moss.

"What?"

"You heard me. Show me."

Reluctantly, he propped his loafered foot on the

hood of her car and rolled down his sock. There it was, the same black band that police had found on Gwen's ankle. Only this one went all around the ankle.

"Meyer's mark," she said. "And you think you weren't a slave. They branded slaves, Adam. Holocaust victims, too. You sat there and took it, but Gwen Schiller wouldn't. That's why she ran."

She turned her back on him as she unlocked her car, overwhelmed by the unbidden image of Meyer Hammersmith, leaning over Gwen Schiller with his needle, slowly and deliberately inking a black band around her ankle so she would forever be his. Had she kicked him before she ran, jackknifed her legs into his soft stomach, bruised his chin with her flailing feet? Tess hoped so. She really hoped so.

"Look," Adam said, "we can get them back. We can avenge Beth's—Gwen's—death. I know enough to destroy Dahlgren. There's all sorts of sleazy shit going on with his campaign, stuff that could land Meyer in jail."

"Dahlgren's only a small part of the problem. He can't help me."

"But he's my part."

"Fine, you take care of your part, and I'll take care of mine. Just stay out of my way, Adam. Because when it comes to protecting people I love, Nicola DeSanti has nothing on me."

31

It was Spike who convinced Nicola DeSanti to meet at his tavern, the Point, by persuading her that its West Baltimore location was quieter, less likely to draw scrutiny than Domenick's. She arrived with only Pete and Repete. The terms were no weapons, but Tess doubted the DeSanti clan had honored this request.

After all, she hadn't.

"You know why we're here," Spike said, after everyone had taken their places at a long table in the middle of the bar, the one used for large parties, for birthdays and anniversaries. Sometimes for wakes. "We have to work something out, so everybody's happy, so nobody bothers nobody anymore. I don't see why that should be so hard."

"Who's the little guy behind the bar?" Nicola said, pointing with her chin.

"My assistant," Spike said. "He needs lifts just to get out of bed in the morning, you don't need to worry about him. I'll vouch for him."

This earned Spike a sour look, which he ignored.

Nicola DeSanti settled in with a sigh, fishing a package of cigarettes from her bright red pocketbook, sending Pete to fetch an ashtray from one of the other tables. With her teased brown hair and polyester pantsuit, she might have been settling in for a hot night of bingo at the local parish.

"You know, Spike, I came here because we know the same people, we have mutual friends who'd like everybody to get along, because it's better for them if people aren't feuding," she said. "Baltimore is a small town. But you don't run anything, you don't have any clout. I'm here out of respect to them, not to you."

"Yeah," Spike said. "I also know that all you really wanna do is run your business without anyone coming down on you. Gene Fulton's dead, Nickie, and Kenny Dahlgren's headed to Congress. Pretty soon, Tess's father is gonna be the closest thing you got to any grease on the liquor board."

"Who you kiddin'? He's out of there, too. All that old shit is going to come up the surface, and there's not a thing you or I can do about it. I'm gonna ride it out, and get along without Gene, rest his soul."

Spike nodded, as if to commiserate: Such bad luck to have your politically connected stooge killed while he was trying to burn down an enemy's house.

"Maybe your boys here should have thought about that before they killed him."

"Don't talk shit, Spike. These boys didn't have nothing to do with that. They weren't even there that night."

"Really? Someone was. The investigators found three gasoline canisters. A source tells me they got a print hit this week."

"No way," Pete said. "There aren't any prints on those cans." Repete nodded. "No prints."

"How could you be so sure?" Tess asked. "Unless you wore gloves, of course." The fact was, she and Spike had made up the part about the prints. They weren't even sure Pete and Repete had fingerprints on file, but it had seemed like a safe bet.

The look-alike uncle and nephew rolled their eyes at Nicola, as if they had been caught with their hands in the cookie jar. "He slipped, Gee-gee, honest. We couldn't save him, so we just got outta there."

"People are always slipping around you," Tess said. "You go to fetch Gwen Schiller, to make sure she's not talking to anybody about Meyer Hammersmith, and she falls and cracks her head open. You go to Philadelphia and you kill the woman you find in the apartment, then try to kill Devon Whittaker."

"That was Gene," Pete said quickly. "Gene was running things. We just helped him out sometimes."

"I checked Gene Fulton's schedule and he visited five different bars that day, all over Baltimore," Tess said. "He couldn't have been in Philadelphia."

"But—" Pete began.

Nicola leaned across the table and smacked him, then Repete. It was a short, matter-of-fact slap, just hard enough to get her point across.

"Shut up. You're not supposed to be talking here. I didn't even know why they wanted you here, but now I guess I do." She turned back to Spike. "You want I guarantee these two will be good from now on? I can do that. Right, boys? I can make them be good."

Pete and Repete rubbed their reddening cheeks and nodded ruefully. "No you can't, Mrs. DeSanti," Tess said. "They're out of control. They're responsible for the deaths of at least three people. Gwen's death may well have been an accident, but it seems to have given them a taste for it. Hilde, Gene—people keep dying around them. It's only a matter of time before they do something you won't be able to cover up."

Nicola studied Pete and Repete. Tess could see her innate loyalty warring with her instinctive shrewdness. Shrewdness won.

"What do you want?"

"Gwen Schiller's dead, there's no bringing her back, and no reason to try them for her death. Make them confess to Gene Fulton's murder, and the arson. Even if Fulton did fall, the autopsy shows he died from smoke inhalation. When they left him in the house, they were guilty of manslaughter. Gene was a good employee, Mrs. DeSanti, he did whatever you asked him to do, he gave good value for your dollar. He didn't deserve to die while doing your work."

"I can't let my babies go to prison," she said.

"You should," Tess said. "I wouldn't sleep at night, knowing those monsters were coming and going under my roof. One day, they'll get bored and kill you, too, because they think they know better than you how to run your business. They're already dealing behind your back. And using. Which makes them big security risks for you. Stupid and on drugs is no way to go through life."

The boys shook their heads vehemently, almost

convincing in their outraged innocence. "We never would do such a thing, Gee-gee," said Pete, and Repete lived up to his nickname, parroting his uncle's promises. "We know you don't want anyone around you to get mixed up in that."

"No, Nicola prefers clean scams, like prostitution and video poker," Spike said. "You still do that thing where you let women who are behind on their bills raffle off blow jobs at your bar? I always liked that one."

Nicola glared at Spike. "Who are you to talk? You're a two-bit bookie."

"Never took a bet on a dog race," Spike said placidly. It was an important distinction to him, for reasons Tess couldn't fathom.

"We don't sell drugs, and we don't do them," Pete repeated. "Never, never, never," Repete said.

Tess walked over to the bar, and picked up an envelope of black-and-white photographs. "The quality is a bit off, but I think you'll recognize the two young men on Forest Park Avenue, not even a half mile from here. I guess they thought if they got out of the neighborhood, you wouldn't catch them. As consumers, they prefer crack. When they sell, they tend toward amphetamines. They've been dealing out of your bar for a while now. My guess is that Gene Fulton found out and told them to stop. Maybe that's why he's dead. Maybe that's why he 'slipped.'"

Nicola studied the top photograph in the stack, which showed her "babies" grabbing a few glass vials of crack. Adam Moss had given Tess this idea when he mentioned Nicola's antipathy toward drugs, how she fired girls who used. Tess had remembered the

crazed stink coming off Pete and Repete, and Crow
had been more than happy to verify her hunch, following them for the better part of a day, then chat-
ting up the local Sowebo girls about who hooked
them up. But Tess had been deliberate in choosing
to show Nicola her babies were consumers as well as
dealers. Selling drugs—she might have reconciled
herself to that. But not using, not crack.

"It's what niggers do," she said, her voice flat.
"You're down on the corner with the niggers, buying their drugs. I didn't raise you this way."

"We didn't—" Pete began.

"We were buying it for a friend," Repete said.

"You got no friends," Nicola said. "You never
did. Now I know why. Because you're scum, you
can't be trusted. You did all this, didn't you, just
like this girl said. If you hadn't fucked up the first
time, you realize none of this would have happened? Gene asked you to find a girl, bring her in
to talk. Not kill her. Philadelphia, the same. No one
asked you to kill anybody. You were just supposed
to go up there, see who this girl was that the dead
girl tried to call. Bump into her casual like, get her
story."

Nicola pushed the photos back toward Tess. "I
didn't know nothing about the house fire—I told
Gene to make you stop nosing around, and he said
he had a surefire way. Surefire, get it?"

"Yeah, Gene was the Noel Coward of the city
liquor board," Tess said.

"Well, his death is the one they'll cop to. Not the
dead girl because, like you said, what's the point?
And not Philadelphia, because I don't want my babies

in some Pennsylvania prison, where I can't take care of them. But they'll tell the cops they did Gene."

Tess wasn't finished, not quite. She had one more question to ask, if only to satisfy her own curiosity—and Ruthie's. "Did you arrange for Henry Dembrow to be killed in prison?"

Nicola sighed. "I had to protect my boys. Henry was restless, he was going to start talking about their part in it if we couldn't get him out. They were innocent, to hear them tell it." She looked at them. "To hear them tell it. I believed them then. Now I don't know."

The boys looked incredulous. "You can't make us do this, Gee-gee," said Pete. "She's got no proof."

"You'll do it," Nicola said. "We'll get Arnie Vasso to represent you, and he'll cut a deal. You'll still be young men when you get out. Besides, prison will get you clean."

It was, Tess realized, the same rationalization Ruthie Dembrow had used when she watched Henry go off to Hagerstown.

"You can't make us do anything, you can't make us confess when they got nothin' on us—" Pete began, but Nicola silenced him with a look.

"Go ahead, try to deny everything," Tess said. "Spike's assistant, the guy behind the bar? It's homicide detective Martin Tull, and he had permission from the state's attorney to tape this meeting. The whole place is bugged."

Tull put down the bar rag long enough to show his badge and his 9 mm.

Nicola looked at Spike, disappointment keen in her face. "You lied to me."

"I vouched he was helping me out, and he was. I never seen the place so clean. I wish I could get him to work here full time."

She shook her head. "That ain't right, Spike. That goes against all the rules. Our mutual friends are going to make it very hard for you to do business."

"I'm out of business," Spike said complacently. "I sold this place to Tess's father and aunt this morning. They're gonna do a complete rehab, sell those five-dollar beers that taste like piss, serve finger foods. Ferns and live music on Franklintown Road. Never thought I'd see that day, but they gave me a good price, and I'm ready to retire. You oughta think about doing the same, Nickie. We're old, to be in this game."

Flashing red and blue lights shone through the windows.

"Gentlemen," Tull said to Pete and Repete, "your ride is here. Let's go."

"I *won't*." It was Repete, who so seldom said anything first. "I'm not gonna take the rap for anything, or plead out, or let Arnie Vasso serve me up on a fuckin' platter. We deserve to be rewarded for what we done, not punished. 'Specially me. I'm the one who had to get cozy with the fat chick."

The last two words hung in the air. Tess turned to look at Repete. Even in his fury, he had a smirk for her.

"You're"—she dug for the name—"Paul. Sukey's boyfriend."

"Paul's my given name, but I wasn't her boyfriend. I hung around, got her to tell me all about her boring life, which included what you'd been doing in Locust Point, who you'd been talking to. She couldn't wait to tell me how you were playing with the phones the very day you were there."

"But how did you know about Sukey?" Even as she asked the question, Tess knew the answer, saw herself before the television, bragging about how she had identified Gwen Schiller, dropping the girl's name.

"Yeah, you all but told us how to find her. And you were the one who said you'd been to Philadelphia, so Gene zeroed in on that number when it came up on the phone logs. But man, that was hard work, pretending to be interested in old fatty. Pete here had it easy, compared to what I had to do. He just had to put a bullet in the big foreign lady."

"Shut up," Pete said. "You're making it worse."

"Sukey's only fifteen," Tess said.

"He didn't really do her," Pete said. "He just fooled around a little. Nothing major."

Repete—Paul—shrugged off his uncle's defense.

"I've had younger," he said. "Prettier, for sure. She had big tits, I'll give her that much. But you know what they say—big tits don't count on a fat chick."

Later, Spike and Tull told Tess what happened, as if it were a movie and she had ducked out for popcorn during a crucial scene. But she was there for every minute of it. She simply didn't remember walking around the table and yanking Paul's chair backward, so he landed on his back, hitting his head hard on the wooden floor.

"Hey, you could break someone's spine that way," Pete said. Paul didn't have the breath to object as

Tess grabbed him by the hair and dragged him half-way across the barroom floor.

She had a vague memory of straddling him so his arms were pinned. Leverage, she was thinking, everything is leverage. She could pound his head on the floor, until it cracked as Gwen Schiller's skull had. She could wrap her hands around his throat, squeeze until all the air was out of him, tie a bow around his neck in an imitation of the sick joke he had played on Gwen's body, tying Henry's tube around her neck to ensure the cops fingered him. So many possibilities.

Something hard pressed into her left leg, and she reached into his jacket pocket, extracted the knife he had pressed into her back. She thought of Gwen, of Sukey, of Devon, of monkey-face Sarah, of all the girls who had to live in a world where such men existed. Men who reduced them to their parts, men who used and discarded them, men who failed to love them, when that was all they ever wanted.

"Tess—" it was Tull's voice, gentle but insistent. He put a hand on her shoulder, but he didn't pull her away.

She looked into Paul's face. Fear was there, but something else as well—something evil and ecstatic. It was almost as if he was welcoming her to his world, grinning and nodding, saying "Come on in." Maybe it was simply that he'd rather die than go to prison. Nicola's assurances notwithstanding, he was going to be a very old man before he got out. Tess could kill him now, even with Tull standing there, and there was a certain power in that.

But there was a greater power in letting him live.

She stood up and walked over to the bar, where she put down Repete's knife and poured herself a Rolling Rock from the tap. The officers came through the door, guns drawn, handcuffs ready. Tull told them to leave the old woman alone, it was just the boys who were going to Central lockup.

"How'd the one on the floor get that goose egg on his head?" one officer asked.

"Fell out of his chair," Tull said.

32

On the Friday before Christmas, Tess sat at her desk in the winter twilight, looking at the envelope that had come in that day's mail, an envelope with two tickets to a $1,000-per-person fund-raiser for Sen. Kenneth Dahlgren. There was no return address, and she didn't recognize the handwriting on the unsigned note, which said simply: "Be my guest." Her name had been written on one ticket, while the other bore the name of Herman Peters. She felt a small shiver down her spine. Even now, it was unsettling to be reminded of how closely she had been watched these past few weeks. She pulled Peters's business card from her desk and punched in the beeper number, happy to give him a small jolt at waist level.

Her phone rang almost the moment she placed it back in the cradle.

"Peters here."

"Monaghan here." It was hard not to mimic him. "That big story I promised you is here, just in time for Christmas."

"If you mean the confession in Gene Fulton's murder, I got it on my own, and it wasn't such a big story. It didn't even make metro front. Sorry."

"Come with me to Martin's West tonight, and I'll make sure you get a page-one story, with enough fallout to keep you on page one every day through Christmas."

"Martin's West? What is it, some fund-raiser?"

"What else?"

"When did a fund-raiser ever make news?"

"Make a leap of faith, Herman. And wear a tie. We should look like the paying guests we're not, at least for a little while."

Tess supposed it was possible to spend one's life in Baltimore and never venture into Martin's West, but she didn't know anyone who had managed this feat. All roads eventually led to this glitzy, over-wrought banquet hall on the western edge of the Beltway. If Dante's *Inferno* were updated and relocated to Charm City, it would have to include a new circle of hell—political fund-raisers at Martin's West.

But she was enjoying herself this evening, grabbing hors d'oeuvres from the trays that whizzed by—once she ascertained there was no crabmeat in them. She didn't want to have an allergic reaction and miss all the fun. The food was pretty good, for banquet hall slop, but Dahlgren, a Baptist, had made predictably poor wine selections. All the money in the world, and he cheaped out on the wine, serving Romanian swill. Tess sipped a gin-and-tonic, a relatively foolproof drink.

Herman Peters paced in restless circles around her, disdaining food and drink, keeping in constant touch with the city desk by cell phone and pager.

"There's a homicide in the Eastern district," he said mournfully. "A woman shot her husband because he wouldn't stop changing the channel with the remote. It would be my five hundred thirteenth homicide straight. I hate to miss it."

"You'd hate missing this more," Tess assured him. "By the way, you did make sure Feeney was there to do rewrite, right? This is going to break close to deadline, and you'll need someone who actually knows something about Maryland politics."

"Yeah, yeah, he's there. I just wish you'd tell me more about what's going to happen."

"Go with the flow, Hermannator. Show's starting."

A mediocre jazz band had been playing standards, interspersed with the inevitable Christmas music, on a stage at one end of the hall. They broke after a particularly funereal version of "A Christmas Song," and Whitney came out in the WASP seasonal uniform—long velvet skirt and white silk blouse. At least she didn't have on one of those embroidered Christmas sweaters that so many otherwise sensible women donned this time of year.

"If I could have your attention for a moment, ladies and gentlemen." Between her vowel sounds and golden hair, she had it immediately. "This fund-raiser was to have been a joyful event, celebrating the fact that the campaign has already passed the $1 million mark in contributions. But I'm afraid it has been vershadowed by a tragedy, the apparent death of enator Dahlgren's legislative aide, Adam Moss."

The crowd dutifully murmured in shock, although 'ess sensed they were merely being polite. If any-hing, the party-goers seemed a little annoyed that omeone had the bad taste to cast a pall over what as to have been a festive event.

"State police found Adam's car this morning in andy Point Park, along with a note, indicating he lanned to jump from the Bay Bridge," Whitney ontinued. "A motorist had reported seeing a man valking on the southern span about three A.M., but Adam's body has not yet been found. The senator hought about canceling the fund-raiser, but the etter police found in Adam's car specifically re-uested this event go on as planned."

Herman Peters unsheathed his notebook with ne hand, and began dialing his cell phone with he other. Tess put a hand on the notebook. "Not et," she whispered. "There's more."

Dahlgren walked up on the stage now, his face rranged in a suitably somber expression.

"The fact is," Whitney took two sheets of paper rom one of her skirt's deep pockets, "Adam cared o much about the senator that his note details how Meyer Hammersmith has tainted the campaign by naking illegal contributions. Apparently, Ham-nersmith tried to skirt the federal limits by using lead people and the employees of a Southwest Bal-imore bar owner, Nicola DeSanti, to pour his own money into the campaign."

This earned the gasps and scandalized whispers hat Adam Moss's mere suicide had failed to incite.

Dahlgren stopped and stared at Whitney, forgetting to close his mouth. Tess could imagine her father saying: *Once a backbencher, always a backbencher.* Thinking about her father still stung. They had not spoken since the fire.

"Adam indicates in his letter that Hammersmith's betrayal of the senator may have been the result of a love triangle. It appears the two men had quarreled over someone. Who, it's not clear, but Adam seems to take personal responsibility for the rift. He asks the State Police not to prosecute Dahlgren, whom he describes as a man of integrity"— Whitney squinted at the letter as if reading it for the first time—"the only man I ever . . . Hmm. Well, Adam probably didn't want that part read out loud."

Tess had kept an eye on Hammersmith while Whitney was speaking. He had been backing up steadily along one wall of the banquet hall, until he was at the rear. She watched him slip away now, through the kitchen doors. Herman Peters saw it, too, and started after him, but Tess held his arm.

"The story's here. Don't run after him for a 'no comment.' You can get as much by phone later. I have his number."

Dahlgren, a pale man to begin with, looked ghastly now, his broad forehead sweating, his eyes taking on that Dan-Quayle-in-the-headlights glaze. He tried to nudge Whitney away from the podium, but she didn't yield. He pushed her more overtly. She held her ground, smiling sweetly. In desperation, Dahlgren yanked the mike from the stand and stepped around her, trying to get the crowd's attention back.

"It's Christmas time, a joyful time of year for all us," he said. "And Hanukkah time, too, of course, well as Kwanzaa for many of our friends here tonight. But it's not April Fool's Day, a fact my staffers em to have forgotten. I'm sorry for this ill-advised actical joke. It's not at all funny."

"No, it's not funny," Whitney agreed. She could e heard even without the mike, because everyone the vast room had fallen silent. "You see, Hammersmith made those illegal contributions only ecause you blackmailed him into becoming your nance manager, according to Adam. Murder and xtortion and illegal campaign contributions and rson—it's all here, in great detail. Would you like ne to read the rest of it?"

At this point, Dahlgren bolted from the stage, ooking as if he were going to be sick. Det. Martin ull was waiting for him at the stage's edge.

"Senator, I'm arresting you for withholding evidence about a homicide in the city of Baltimore, a elony crime." A friendly state's attorney had agreed o let Tull take Dahlgren in, knowing the charge vould never stand. The real case against Dahlgren vas in the campaign records, and the only punishnent the state would ever exact was the end of his olitical career. But Tess had been adamant—she vanted a public perp walk for this very public perp. he had even called the television stations she hated o much, and instructed them to wait outside Marin's West. "Good visuals?" the weekend assignnent editors had all chirped. "Superb visuals," she ad promised.

"Now you've got your story," she told Herman

Peters, who wore a rapt expression, like a little b[o]
regarding his first bicycle on Christmas Day. Th[e]
end of his homicide streak was clearly forgotten no[w]

"Do you think she'd give me her copy of the su[i]
cide note?" He was nodding toward Whitney, wh[o]
still held center stage.

"Take mine," Tess said. "I've got a photocop[y]
she gave me when I came in. It's very complet[e]
it explains how everything fits together—
Hammersmith, Dahlgren, the death of Gwe[n]
Schiller. But grab Whitney now if you have an[y]
questions. We're meeting my boyfriend for a la[te]
supper at the Brass Elephant bar."

In the end, Herman Peters never got that commen[t]
from Meyer Hammersmith. No one did. Meye[r]
went home that night, lay down on his chaise longu[e]
and slit his wrists. He didn't leave a note, but th[e]
velvet-lined box of tattoo implements that polic[e]
found next to him told Tess everything she neede[d]
to know. That was Peters's second page-one stor[y]
leading the paper on Monday.

The third one explained how Whitney had infi[l]
trated the campaign at Tess's behest, and how sh[e]
had already been on the trail of the illegal con[-]
tributions when Adam killed himself, distraug[ht]
over Dahlgren's cynical reaction to Gwen Schiller['s]
murder. Then the state police revealed the trun[k]
of Adam Moss's car contained all the documents th[e]
state attorney general and the feds needed to pro[-]
ceed with an inquiry into the Dahlgren campaign['s]
fund-raising. That was page-one story number four[.]

But now it was Christmas Eve, and the Dahlgren saga had petered out. Or maybe it was just on hiatus, while the *Blight* fell back on the old newspaper trick of running feel-good holiday stories. Lord knows, Tess was sick of reading about it.

She sat in her office, reconciling her books for the end of the year, trying to prepare her state taxes before she took a friend to the train station. She was determined to take the last week of the year off, whatever happened. She had earned it. She sorted through receipts, pondered whether she should try to bill Ruthie for the work she had done when she was pretending not to work. Probably not. Ruthie had hung up on her the last time they spoke. She was furious at the deal Tess had cut, letting Nicola DeSanti off the hook for Henry's death in return for giving up her own grandson and great-grandson. Ruthie wanted more. She would always want more, Tess now realized. If Nicola DeSanti went to jail, Ruthie would just focus all her anger and grief on the inmate who had carried out the contract. Henry's death had left her perpetually unfinished and dissatisfied.

Tess also couldn't decide where to file her copy of Adam Moss's suicide note. It didn't seem to belong in her Gwen Schiller file. Adam didn't seem to belong anywhere. She had an image of his body coming to rest on some far shore of the Bay, a ravaged, waterlogged John Doe, impossible to identify. Those were pearls that were his eyes.

But that was not to be his fate, of course, not just yet.

"Who are you, Adam?" she asked the man sitting across from her, waiting patiently for her to finish her accounts.

"The first man," he said. "Why do you think I chose the name Adam?"

"No, who are you, really?"

He shook his head. "That's mine, the only thing I ever really owned, the only thing I'll never give away or sell."

"Where will you go? What will you do?"

"West," he said. "I'll find a campaign. There's a senator who's already thinking about the next presidential race, a governor who wants to be a senator. There's even a Hollywood actor who wants to run for office. I'll find a way. I may have to start as a volunteer, but I'll make staff in a matter of weeks."

"Are you that good?"

"I'm that good. In fact, I'm better at politics than I ever was as trade."

"I doubted you, you know," she said. "Even when you told me what you wanted to do, I didn't think it would work. Never get caught with a dead girl or a live boy. You left Dahlgren with a dead boy, and all the innuendo that goes with it. He'll never recover."

Adam gave her his full, radiant smile. You could rule the world with a smile like that, Tess thought. But all Adam wanted was to advise the people who ruled the world. She couldn't decide if this made him more dangerous, or less.

"I prefer being underestimated," he said. "But then, so do you, right? It's always an advantage."

She handed him an envelope. "Spike got you the

IDs—I don't know how, and I don't want to. You're Joseph Kane now. You have a Maryland driver's license to prove it, and a new Social Security number, courtesy of a little boy named Joseph Kane who died last year and never got to use it." She produced a second envelope. "You also get the petty cash from Domenick's."

"How did you arrange that?"

"Oh, didn't you hear?" Tess said blandly. "There was a horrible mix-up at housing. A demolition permit was issued for a vacant rowhouse one block over, but there was a typo on the work order. Nicola DeSanti showed up for work one morning and her bar was gone."

"You took her bar?"

"She took my parents' house. Look, it's only three thousand dollars. It won't last long."

"You'd be surprised at how long I can live on how little," he said, tucking the money into a thin leather wallet.

"No, I wouldn't. One more thing." This envelope was larger, a little thicker. "Dick Schiller gave me Gwen's remains, to distribute among those who tried to help her. I already gave Sukey her part, we spread them at Fort McHenry earlier today."

"Isn't that illegal?"

"Only if you get caught. I've put aside another portion for Devon Whittaker, when she returns from Guadeloupe. This is yours."

"Thanks, I guess." He folded it in half, and stuck it in a pocket of his topcoat. A new cashmere coat, Tess noticed, one that fit him perfectly.

"You ready to go?"

"I can take a cab, you know."

"Not on Christmas Eve. You'll never get one to come get you over here." He still looked reluctant. "I promise I won't notice which train you board. I won't even get out of the car at the station."

Adam regarded her speculatively. His beauty was still astonishing to her, she could not imagine what it must be like to be at large in the world with that face. To be a woman with such a face, or an about-to-be-woman, as Gwen had been, must have been more terrifying still. Had Meyer Hammersmith thought his "ownership" of these beauties made him beautiful by association?

"I'll let you drop me off," he said at last.

"It seems only fair," Tess said. "Since I'm the one who convinced you to leave your car at Sandy Point Park, and now it's impounded by the State Police."

As she promised, Tess stayed in the car when they arrived at Penn Station. She let Adam Moss get out, watched Joseph Kane disappear into the Christmas Eve crowd.

She then parked her car on St. Paul Street and walked inside, studying the tote board. There was a Northeast Direct to New York in fifteen minutes. But Adam had said he was going west. So he must be on the Chicago train, which left an hour later.

He came out of the newsstand. He was not happy to see her.

"Are you spying on me?"

"Not exactly. But it's Christmas Eve. No one should get on a train on Christmas Eve and not have

omeone to see him off. It's not as if there's someone
vaiting for you."

"You don't know where my journey will end, or
vho might be there for me," he said.

"Well, I also want to give you a Christmas gift,"
ess said. "Wait right here."

She went into the souvenir shop and returned
vith a small bag. "Turn your back," she said. "I have
o make a slight adjustment."

He complied, sighing.

"Okay, I'm done. Turn around."

She handed him a snow globe. The shop had car-
ied a variety of scenes—the Inner Harbor, the city's
kyline. But Tess had chosen the one of the Bay
3ridge, and made a small alteration with a marking
en, inking a large red X toward the bottom.

"Remember, that's where you are."

"Where Adam Moss is."

"Where Adam Moss is," she amended. "How
ou're going to keep from being recognized is be-
ond me. You don't have a forgettable face, you know.
)ne photograph of you and the new candidate—"

"I'm not the kind of operative who ends up in
ohotographs, or yakking on CNBC. I'm from the
ld school. I stay in the background."

The tote board's tiles began turning, and the
Northeast Direct showed "All Aboard" at Gate E.
To Tess's surprise, Adam began walking toward the
stairs.

"I thought you were heading west—"

"I am. But I have someone to see in New York
irst." Mysterious to the end. Adam Moss may
change his name, but he'd never change his ways.

Tess walked with him to the staircase, and down to the tracks, into the icy night air. She wanted to see him get on the train, wanted to know he was safely away. The train swept in, already full of holiday travelers. Intent on getting a seat, Adam pressed forward, not even saying goodbye.

"Hey, Joe—"

He turned at his new name. Good for him.

"Pick a better candidate this time, okay?"

"I couldn't find a worse one, that's for sure."

EPILOGUE

The most surprising thing Tess received for Christmas was an eviction notice.

"I'm so sorry, Tesser," Kitty said, after breaking the news at their holiday dinner. It was a small affair, just her, Tyner, Tess, and Crow. Tess's parents had decided to go away for the holidays, given that it would still be months before their house was rebuilt. "But when I got the permits for the elevator construction, they found out about the apartment on the third floor and reappraised the property. My tax bill has gone up so much that I'm going to have to start charging a fair market rate for the apartment. To justify that, I have to make some improvements. You're welcome to move back in, after the renovations, but I'll understand if you think you can do better."

"It's not your fault," Tess said, suddenly glad that Crow had remembered to put some dope in her Christmas stocking. It more than made up for his failure to find a local beauty supply store willing to part with its "Human Hair" neon sign.

But when Crow saw her rummaging for rolling papers after lunch, he proposed taking a drive instead.

"We can start looking for a new place for you to live," he said. "Check out other neighborhoods. You've got to treat this as an opportunity."

"On Christmas Day?" But there was nothing else to do, except digest turkey and sauerkraut, so she put on her coat, pulled Esskay's new Christmas sweater over the dog's head, and piled into Crow's Volvo.

It quickly became apparent that the drive was much more targeted than Crow had let on. He headed north, into the funky little neighborhood they had found when trying to get to Thirty-fourth Street all those weeks ago. They never did make it to see the lights, she realized, feeling wistful for the holiday season that had passed her by. Next year, she resolved, work was going to be less consuming. There were worse things than divorce work and Dumpster diving.

Crow turned up what appeared to be an alley, although it was marked with a street sign. East Lane. One side was bordered by the long, wide backyards of the large houses one street over, while the other side was a deep slope, with smaller houses and cottages hugging the hillside overlooking a wooded park.

"Stony Run Park," Crow said. "Named for the creek that runs through it."

He stopped at a small dilapidated bungalow, which looked more like someone's abandoned fishing cabin than a real house. Built into the side of the hill, it was virtually a tree house, with decks and screened porches taking up more square footage than the proper living quarters.

"Who lives here?"

"No one anymore. It's for sale," Crow said, taking a key from under an old milk box.

"I don't see a sign," Tess said.

"The real estate agent hasn't listed it yet. He's a friend of Tyner's, said he's going to put it on the market at the beginning of next year."

"So Kitty has been planning to kick me out all along, and you knew it, and Tyner knew it, and you didn't tell me?"

"We thought it would soften the blow if you had a place to land," Crow said, letting her into the empty house. It had the feel of a place where no one had lived for a very long time. She liked that feel. It also had a neon sign that said "Human Hair" hung on the wall. Crow really did pay attention, she realized. He not only listened to her stated wants, he was capable of anticipating her desires as well, desires she had yet to form. She tried to find a downside to this, but failed utterly.

The house was perfect—or could be, with months of work. Walls would have to come down, the kitchen would have to be completely redone, the floors needed sanding and, given the water stains on the peeling wallpaper, a new roof was probably required as well. The window sashes were mushy from dry rot, the doors had swollen with humidity until they scraped the floor, mice droppings were thick in the corners. But all Tess could see was herself, here in the spring, surrounded by trees, living out a Swiss Family Robinson fantasy.

The moment she gave in to the dream, she saw it slipping through her fingers. It hurt, wanting something this much, then realizing she could never have it.

"I can't afford a house in this neighborhood."

"It's surprisingly cheap for Roland Park," Crow said, "because it's so small and in such bad shape."

"No bank would give me a loan."

"They will if you have a cosigner. And when the cosigner's name is Dick Schiller, you'd be surprised at how easy it is to get money. He said he'd give you a personal loan at market rates, if it came to that."

She wasn't ready to give in, not yet. "It needs at least fifty thousand dollars' worth of work. I don't have that much cash, and I couldn't do it myself."

"I could," her father said, stepping out of the rear bedroom. "I'm pretty handy, Tesser, in case you didn't know."

They eyed each other cautiously. Although they had spoken by phone after Dahlgren's debacle, making halfhearted apologies and assuring each other there were no hard feelings, they had not seen each other since the night of the house fire. Her father was always at Spike's place, working, when she stopped by the Catonsville rental that was the Monaghans' temporary home. He was very busy, her mother assured her, and very happy. Tess had tried hard to believe both things were true.

"I thought you were away for the holidays," she said, pushing up her sleeves so he might notice the old watch on her left wrist. She didn't really like it much—it felt prissy and delicate, after so many years of wearing a man's Swiss Army wristwatch. But it told the time, it was reliable. If her father wanted to think a watch could make her more of a girly-girl, he was willing to go along with it.

"We were going to Deep Creek Lake, but Crow told me what he was up to when he stopped by the bar this week."

"Crow was at the bar?"

"He's a partner." Her father smiled at her confusion. "Not a full one, just a little piece. He's going to bring bands in on the weekends. Blues, he says, maybe jazz."

She should have been pleased, but it unnerved Tess a little, this vast conspiracy to make her happy. She wasn't comfortable with anything going on behind her back, good or bad.

"So what do you think, Dad? Is this a good investment for a self-employed businesswoman who can't even get a bank loan on her own?"

"I don't know what kind of investment it is," her father said. "As I told you once, I was never much good at figuring out what makes money. A smart man could probably turn a house fire into an opportunity, but all I know how to do is rebuild it and move back in. For you, though—for you, I think it's a good idea to get out and be on your own. You're a grown-up, Tesser. You're capable of making your own decisions."

"Even if I make the wrong ones, sometimes?"

"Especially when you make the wrong ones."

Esskay circled the room, a little panicky at the

sight of a place with no soft furniture on which to rest. Crow had retreated to the kitchen, where he was opening and closing the cabinets, testing the old-fashioned metal latches, scratching at the decades of paint covering the woodwork. "Pine, I think," he called out. "Maybe maple." Patrick stood with his hands in his pockets, studying the neon sign with the sort of baffled expression he had once reserved for Crow. He didn't understand her, not entirely, Tess realized. He never would. Parents probably never understood their children. That was okay. She didn't understand him, either.

"I would prefer," Pat said, his voice a little stiff, as if he expected resistance, "that I be the cosigner on the loan, if you go through with this. I know I'm not a famous billionaire, but I think my credit's just as good."

"No, you're wrong about that," Tess said, shaking her head.

"What?"

"As far as I'm concerned, it's better. I'd much rather do business with you."

They shook on it. It was a deal, after all, not a time for hugging.

Favors, Arnie Vasso had once said. Your father knows all about favors. He had meant it as an insult, a sly reference to the corners the Monaghans and Weinsteins cut here and there. Now Tess saw it for the simple truth it was: Her father understood favors. How to do them, how to accept them, how to walk away when the price was too steep. It was a lesson she wouldn't mind learning someday.

Maybe this was the place to start.

New York Times bestselling author

LAURA LIPPMAN

BY A SPIDER'S THREAD
978-0-06-050671-1

When his wife and children vanish,
a successful furrier turns to p.i. Tess Monaghan for help.

EVERY SECRET THING
978-0-06-050668-1

Two little girls are about to make a disastrous decision that will
change their lives—and end another's. Seven years later, another child
goes missing in a disturbingly familiar scenario.

THE LAST PLACE
978-0-380-81024-6

A single common thread to five senseless, unsolved murders is
beginning to emerge and leads a disgraced p.i. to the remote corners
of Maryland in search of a psychopath.

IN A STRANGE CITY
978-0-06-207087-6

On the night of the anniversary of Edgar Allan Poe's birthday, a
mysterious caped figure visiting his grave is felled by an assassin's bullet.

THE SUGAR HOUSE
978-0-06-207079-1

A year-old supposedly solved murder case is turning up newer,
fresher corpses and newer, scarier versions of Baltimore's
abandoned Sugar House Factory.

New York Times bestselling author

LAURA LIPPMAN

BALTIMORE BLUES
978-0-06-207064-7

Suspected killer Darryl "Rock" Paxton hires ex-reporter
Tess Monaghan to do some unorthodox snooping to
clear his name.

CHARM CITY
978-0-06-207076-0

In a city where baseball reigns, a business tycoon wants to
change all that by bringing pro basketball back to town—
until he's found asphyxiated in his garage
with his car's engine running.

BUTCHERS HILL
978-0-06-207077-7

A notorious vigilante who shot a boy for vandalizing his car
has just gotten out of prison and wants to make amends.
When Tess agrees to start snooping, the witnesses to
the crime start dying.

IN BIG TROUBLE
978-0-06-207078-4

A new case takes Tess out of her element to a faraway place
where the sun is merciless and rich people's games can have
lethal consequences.

LL3 1111